MORE PRAISE FOR

The Invisible Ones

"This is a murder mystery unpicked at the seams, turned inside out, and stitched together with threads of myth, old griefs, twisted forms of love, and complex family ties into something utterly new and utterly enthralling. Warning: You will not get anything else done till you finish the last page of this book."

—*New York Times* bestselling author Tana French

"In her mesmerizing sophomore outing, Penney wraps a riddle in a mystery inside an enigma that intrigues from the very first page . . . Fast-paced, with characters who will live in full color inside the reader's head, Penney delivers an impressive follow-up to her debut bestseller, *The Tenderness of Wolves*." —*Publishers Weekly* (starred review)

"The story ends with a bone-rattling surprise . . . Another stunner from Penney; highly recommended." —*Library Journal* (starred review)

"This novel pulses with film-noir-esque suspense." —*People*

"Penney gives her plot plenty of twists and saves the best for the end, with a truly unforeseen and unpredictable conclusion."

—*Kirkus Reviews*

continued . . .

"[Penney's] absorbing second novel is sure to mesmerize readers from page one until its shocking, albeit deeply satisfying ending."

—BookPage

"A truly distinctive suspense novel."

—Shelf Awareness

"*The Invisible Ones* is utterly absorbing, a . . . satisfying read that will keep readers guessing to the last page." *—New York Journal of Books*

ALSO BY STEF PENNEY

The Tenderness of Wolves

The Invisible Ones

Stef Penney

Berkley Books
New York

A BERKLEY BOOK
Published by the Penguin Group
Penguin Group (USA) Inc.
375 Hudson Street, New York, New York 10014, USA

Penguin Group (Canada), 90 Eglinton Avenue East, Suite 700, Toronto, Ontario M4P 2Y3, Canada (a division of Pearson Penguin Canada Inc.) • Penguin Books Ltd., 80 Strand, London WC2R 0RL, England • Penguin Group Ireland, 25 St. Stephen's Green, Dublin 2, Ireland (a division of Penguin Books Ltd.) • Penguin Group (Australia), 250 Camberwell Road, Camberwell, Victoria 3124, Australia (a division of Pearson Australia Group Pty. Ltd.) • Penguin Books India Pvt. Ltd., 11 Community Centre, Panchsheel Park, New Delhi—110 017, India • Penguin Group (NZ), 67 Apollo Drive, Rosedale, Auckland 0632, New Zealand (a division of Pearson New Zealand Ltd.) • Penguin Books (South Africa) (Pty.) Ltd., 24 Sturdee Avenue, Rosebank, Johannesburg 2196, South Africa

Penguin Books Ltd., Registered Offices: 80 Strand, London WC2R 0RL, England

PUBLISHING HISTORY
G. P. Putnam's Sons hardcover edition / January 2012
Berkley trade paperback edition / December 2012

Berkley trade paperback ISBN: 978-0-425-25321-2

PRINTED IN THE UNITED STATES OF AMERICA

10   9   8   7   6   5   4   3   2   1

For M

GLOSSARY

chovihano	Gypsy healer or shaman
dukkering	fortune-telling
gavvers	police
gorjio	a non-Romany (n.); non-Romany (adj.)
mokady	unclean, taboo
rai	gentleman
Romanes	language of Romany Gypsies
Romanichal	English Romany Gypsy
totting	scrap collecting
vardo	traditional Gypsy caravan

The Invisible Ones

I.

Civil Twilight

Evening

1.

St. Luke's Hospital

When I woke up, I remembered nothing—apart from one thing. And little enough of that: I remember that I was lying on my back while the woman was straddling me, grinding her hips against mine. I have a feeling it was embarrassingly quick; but then, it had been a while. The thing is, I remember how it felt, but not what anything looked like. When I try to picture her face, I can't. When I try to picture the surroundings, I can't. I can't picture anything at all. I try; I try really hard, because I'm worried.

After some time, one thing comes back to me: the taste of ashes.

As it turns out, the memory loss may be the least of my problems. Technically, I am in a state of "diminished responsibility." That is what the police conclude after paying me a visit in my hospital bed. What I had done was drive my car through a fence and into a tree in a place called Downham Wood, near the border between Hampshire and Surrey. I had no idea where Downham Wood was, nor what I was doing there. I don't remember driving through any fences, into any trees. Why would I—why would anyone—do that?

One of the nurses tells me that the police aren't going to pursue the matter, under the circumstances.

"What circumstances?"

This is what I try to say, but my speech isn't too clear. My tongue feels thick and listless. The nurse seems used to it.

"I'm sure it'll come back to you, Ray."

She picks up the right arm that lies like a lump of meat on the bed beside me, and smooths the sheet before putting it back.

Apparently, what happened was this:

A jogger was beating his regular morning path through the wood, when he saw a car that had run off the road and come to a stop against a tree several yards in. Then he realized there was someone in the car. He ran to the nearest house and called the police. They arrived with an ambulance, a fire engine, and cutting equipment. To their surprise, the person inside the car didn't have a scratch on him. At first they assumed he was drunk, then they decided he must be on drugs. The person in the car—me—was in the driver's seat but could not speak or—apart from a convulsive twitching—move.

It was the first day of August, which went on to develop into a breathless day of milky, inky blue, like August days are supposed to be but so rarely are.

This much was relayed to me by someone I don't remember, as I lay in my hospital bed. Whoever it was told me that for the first twenty-four hours I was unable to speak at all—a paralysis locked my tongue and throat muscles, as well as the rest of me. My pupils were dilated, my pulse raced. I was burning hot. When I tried to talk, I could produce only a gurgling series of unintelligible sounds. In the absence of external injuries, they were waiting for the test results that would tell them whether I had suffered a stroke, or had a brain tumor, or was indeed the casualty of a drug overdose.

I couldn't close my eyes, even for a second.

During that time I don't think I was particularly bothered by what had caused this—confused, delirious, immobile, I was plagued by a nightmarish vision that I couldn't pin down. I wasn't at all sure I wanted to pin it down. It disturbed me because it felt like a memory, but that cannot be the case, because a woman, however mysterious, is not a dog or a cat. A woman does not have claws, or fangs. A woman does not inspire horror. I keep telling myself this. I am not responsible. With any luck, the whole thing was—like that series *Dallas*—all a dream.

Now, someone looms over me, her face dominated by heavy black-rimmed glasses; blond hair scraped back off a high, rounded forehead. She reminds me of a seal. She's holding a clipboard in front of her.

"Well, Ray, how are you feeling? The good news is you haven't had a stroke."

She seems to know who I am. And I know her from somewhere, so perhaps she has been here every day. She's speaking rather loudly. I'm not deaf. I try to say so, but nothing very recognizable comes out.

". . . and there's no sign of a tumor, either. We still don't know what's causing the paralysis. But it's improving, isn't it? You have a bit more control today, don't you? Still nothing in the right arm? No?"

I try to nod and say yes and no.

"The scan shows no indication of brain damage, which is great. We're waiting for the results of the toxicology tests. You seem to have ingested some sort of neurotoxin. It could be an overdose of drugs. Did you take drugs, Ray? Or you might have eaten something poisonous. Like wild mushrooms, perhaps . . . Did you eat any wild mushrooms? Or berries? Anything like that?"

I try to think back, to those slippery, treacherous images. I ate something, but I don't think there were mushrooms in it. And I'm pretty sure drugs weren't involved. Not any I was responsible for, anyway.

"Don't think so."

It comes out sounding more like: "Duh . . . n-sah."

"Have you seen anything strange this morning? Do you remember? Has the dog been back?"

The dog . . . ? Have I talked about her? I'm sure I never called her a dog.

The name on the badge pinned to the front of her white coat appears to begin with a *Z*. Her accent is crisp and loud—East European, of some description. But she and her clipboard sweep off before I can puzzle out the collection of consonants.

I think about brain damage. I have a lot of time to think, lying here—I can't really do anything else. It gets dark and it gets light again. My eyes burn with lack of sleep, but when I close them, that's when I see things, creeping toward me, stealing out of corners, lurking just beyond my field of vision, so on the whole I'm grateful to whatever is keeping me awake. The slightest muscular effort leaves me gasping and exhausted; my right arm is numb and useless.

I can see out of the window to where sunlight hits the leaves of a cherry tree. From that, I deduce I must be on a first floor. But I don't know which hospital I'm in, or how long I've been here. Outside, where the cherry tree is, it's hot, with a heavy, breathless torpor. After all the rain we've had, it must be like the tropics. Inside, it's also hot, so hot that they finally crack and turn off the hospital heating.

My temper has been better. It's like being catapulted into extreme old age—eating mashed food, being washed by strangers and addressed in loud, simple sentences. It's not much fun. On the other hand, there's not a lot of responsibility.

Another now: another face above me. This one I definitely recognize. Soft fair hair that falls over his forehead. Steel-framed spectacles.

"Ray . . . Ray . . . Ray?"

An expensively educated voice. My business partner. I don't know how I came to be here, but I know Hen, and I know he's feeling guilty. I also know that it's not his fault.

I grunt, trying to say hi.

"How are you? You look much better than yesterday. Did you know I was here yesterday? It's okay, you don't have to talk. I just want you to know we're all thinking about you. Everyone sends their love. Charlie made you a card, look . . ."

He holds up a folded piece of yellow paper with a child's drawing on it. It's hard for me to say what it represents.

"This is you in bed. I think that's a thermometer. Look, you're wearing a crown . . ."

I take his word for it. He smiles fondly and props the card on my bedside locker—beside the plastic cup of water and the tissues used to wipe up my drool—where it repeatedly falls over, being really too flimsy to stand up on its own.

Gradually, I find that I can talk again—at first, in slurry, broken phrases. My tongue trips over itself. In this, I have something in common with my ward mate—Mike, a genial homeless drunk who used, he says, to be in the French Foreign Legion. We make a good pair—both of us partially paralyzed, and both prone to screaming in the middle of the night.

He has been telling me about the alcoholism-induced stroke he suffered a few months ago. That's not why he's in the hospital. The stroke led to severe sunburn on his feet because he couldn't feel them burning, but he didn't notice anything was wrong until the sunburn turned gangrenous and started to smell. Now they're talking about chopping bits off him. He's remarkably cheerful about it. We get on pretty well, except when he lets rip in French in the middle of the night. Like last night—I was jolted out of my sleepless trance by a shrill scream, then he shouted, *"Tirez!"* Then he screamed again, the way they do in war films when they're bayoneting a bag of hay in uniform. I wondered whether I should start making my escape—with my legs in their current state, it could take me five minutes to get out the door if he starts acting out his nightmares.

He doesn't want to talk much about his time in the Legion, but he is fascinated when he finds out that I'm a private investigator. He badgers me for stories ("Hey, Ray . . . Ray . . . Are you awake? Ray . . ."). I'm always awake. I tell him a few in a mumbling monotone that improves with practice. I start to worry that he's going to ask me for a job, although, on reflection, he's probably past that point. He asks if the work is ever dangerous.

I pause before saying, "Not usually."

2.

Ray

It begins in May—a month when everyone, even private investigators, should be happy and optimistic. The mistakes of the last year have been wiped clean and everything has started again. Leaves unfurl, eggs hatch, men hope. All is new, green, growing.

But we—that is, Lovell Price Investigations—are broke. The only case we've had in the last fortnight is a marital—that of poor Mr. M. He rang up, and after much hemming and hawing asked to meet me in a café because he was too embarrassed to come to the office. He's a businessman, late forties, with a small company supplying office furniture. He'd never done anything like this before— he said so at least eight times during that first meeting. I tried to reassure him that what he was feeling was normal under the circumstances, but he never stopped fidgeting and looking over his shoulder while we talked. He confessed that just speaking to me made him feel guilty—as though admitting his suspicion to a professional was a corrosive acid, which, once unstoppered, could never be put back. I pointed out that if he felt suspicious, talking to me would not make it any worse, and, of course, he had plenty of reason to suspect his wife of infidelity: abstraction; unusual absences; a new, sexier wardrobe; a propensity to work late . . . I almost didn't need to gather evidence; I could have said, look, yes, your wife is having an affair—just confront her and she'll probably be relieved to admit it. And you'll save yourself a lot of money. I didn't say that. I took the job and spent a couple of evenings tailing the wife, who kept a small shop selling knickknacks on the high street.

The day after I met Mr. M., he rang me—she had just rung to say she would be taking inventory after work. I parked down the street to watch the shop, and followed her when she drove over to Clapham, where she went into a house in a genteel neighborhood popular with families. I couldn't say for certain what went on in the two hours and twenty minutes before she came out, but the next day, the man I photographed her holding hands with in a wine bar was assuredly not the girlfriend she had claimed she was going to meet. I called Mr. M. and told him I had something to discuss with him, and we met in the same café as before. I didn't even need to start talking; knowing what I was going to say, he began to cry. I showed him the photographic evidence, explained where and when the photographs were taken, and watched him weep. I suggested he try to talk calmly to his wife, but Mr. M. kept shaking his head.

"If I show her these, she's going to accuse me of spying on her. And I have. It's such a betrayal of trust."

"But she's cheating on you."

"I feel like a horrible person."

"You're not a horrible person. She's in the wrong. But if you talk to her, there's a good chance you can straighten things out. You have to get to what's behind the affair."

I don't know what I'm talking about, but I felt I had to say something. And I have done this a fair few times.

"Perhaps you're right."

"It's got to be worth a go, hasn't it?"

He wiped his nose and eyes on a dirty-looking handkerchief. His face was a ruin of its former self.

Yesterday, Mr. M. rang to say he had talked to his wife. He didn't show her the pictures at first, and she flatly denied having an affair;

then he brought them out, and she screamed at him with all the vicious rage of the cornered adulterer. Adulterers usually blame their spouses, I've noticed. Now his wife says she wants a divorce. He cried again. What could I say? He didn't blame me, or her, but himself. In the end I told him that it would be better in the long run; if his wife wanted a divorce now, then she had wanted it before he spoke to her. At least I didn't spin out the process to charge him more; and there are some unscrupulous investigators out there who would have. These sorts of cases, which make up the majority of our work, can depress you if you let them.

Today is gray and undistinguished. It's nearly five o'clock in our offices above the stationer's on Kingston Road. I tell Andrea, our administrator, to go home. We've been killing time for hours, anyway. Hen is out somewhere. Through the double-glazed window with its double layer of dirt, I watch a plane emerge from the clouds, uncannily slow in its descent. I have drunk too much coffee, I realize, from the sour taste in my mouth, and am thinking of calling it a day when, just after Andrea leaves, a man walks into the office. Sixtyish, with gray hair slicked back behind his ears, and bunched shoulders and pouchy dark eyes. As soon as I see him I know what he is: there's an air, a look about him that's hard to put into words, but when you know it, you know. Large fists are pushed into his trouser pockets, but when he removes his right hand to hold it out to me I see a roll of crisp new notes—deliberately on show. I guess he's just come off the races after a good day—Sandown Park's less than thirty minutes from here. He doesn't have that nervous, slightly shifty look that people usually have on walking into a detective agency. He looks confident and at ease. He walks into my office as though he owns it.

"Saw your name," he says, after shaking my hand with a crushing grip, unsmiling. "That's why I'm here."

That's not what people usually say, either. They don't usually care who you are or what you're called—Ray Lovell, in my case—they just care that they've found you in the Yellow Pages under "Private Investigators"—confidential, efficient, discreet—and they hope that you can fix things.

We have a form, in duplicate—yellow and white—that Andrea gets people to complete when they come in for the first time. All the usual details, plus the reason why they're here, where they heard about us, how much money they're prepared to spend . . . all that sort of thing. Some people say you shouldn't do this stuff formally, but I've tried it this way and that way, and believe me, it's better to get it down in writing. Some people have no idea how much an investigation costs, and when they find out they run a mile. But with this man, I don't even reach for the drawer. There'll be no point. I'm not saying that because he might be illiterate but for other reasons.

"Lovell," he goes on. "Thought, He's one of us."

He looks at me: a challenge.

"How can I help you, Mr. . . . ?"

"Leon Wood, Mr. Lovell."

Leon Wood is short, slightly overweight in a top-heavy way, with a ruddy, tanned face. People don't say weather-beaten anymore, do they?—but that's what he is. His clothes look expensive, especially the sheepskin coat that must add a good six inches to his shoulders.

"My family come from the West Country; you probably know that."

I incline my head.

"Know some Lovells—Harry Lovell from Basingstoke . . . Jed Lovell, round Newbury . . ."

He watches for my reaction. I have learned not to react—I don't want to give anything away—but the Jed Lovell he's referring to is a cousin of mine—my father's cousin, to be precise, who always disapproved of him, and therefore of us. It occurs to me that he hasn't just seen my name—he's made inquiries; knows exactly who I am and who I'm related to. To whom. Whatever.

"There are a lot of us around. But what brings you here, Mr. Wood?"

"Well, Mr. Lovell, it's a tricky business."

"That's what we do here."

He clears his throat. I have a feeling this could take some time. Gypsies rarely get straight to the point.

"Family business. That's why I've come to you. 'Cos you'll understand. It's my daughter. She's . . . missing."

"If I can stop you there, Mr. Wood—"

"Call me Leon."

"I'm afraid I don't take on missing-persons cases. I can pass you on to my colleague, though—he's very good."

"Mr. Lovell . . . Ray . . . I need someone like you. An outsider can't help. Can you imagine a *gorjio* going in, annoying people, asking questions?"

"Mr. Wood, I was brought up in a house. My mother was a *gorjio*. So I'm a *gorjio*, really. It's just a name."

"No . . ."

He jabs a finger at me and leans forward. If there wasn't a desk between us, I am sure he would take my arm.

"It's never just a name. You're always who you are, even sitting here in your office behind your fancy desk. You're one of us. Where are your family from?"

I am sure he already knows about as much as there is to know. Jed would have told him.

"Kent, Sussex."

"Ah. Yes. Know Lovells from there, too . . ."

He reels off more names.

"Yes, but as I said, my father settled in a house and left off the traveling life. I've never known it. So I don't know that I would be of much help. And missing persons are really not my speciality . . ."

"I don't know what's your speciality or not. But what happened to my daughter happened with us, and a *gorjio* won't have the first clue about how to talk to people. They'd get nowhere. You know that. I can tell by looking at you that you can talk to people. They'll listen to you. They'll talk to you. A *gorjio* won't stand a chance!"

He speaks with such vehemence, I have to stop myself from leaning back in my chair. Flattery, and poverty, are on his side. And maybe there's a touch of curiosity on my part. I've never seen a Gypsy in here before. I can't imagine any circumstances in which someone like him would go outside the family. I idly wonder how many other half-Gypsy private investigators there are in the southeast for him to choose from. Not many, I imagine.

"Have you reported her disappearance to the police?"

Under the circumstances, this might sound like a stupid question, but you have to ask.

Leon Wood just shrugs, which I take for the no it's meant to be.

"To be honest, I'm worried that something's happened to her. Something bad."

"What makes you think that?"

"It's been more than seven years. We've heard nothing. No one's seen her. No one's spoken to her. Not a phone call . . . not a word . . . nothing. Now . . . my dear wife recently passed, and we've been trying to find Rose. She ought to know about her mum, at least. And nothing. Can't find a thing. 'S not natural, is it? I always wondered, I did, but now . . ."

He trails off.

"I'm very sorry to hear about your wife, Mr. Wood, but let me get this straight—did you say that you haven't seen your daughter for over seven years?"

"'Bout that, yeah. Leastways, she got married back then, and I never seen her since. They say she ran off, but . . . now I don't believe it."

"Who says she ran off?"

"Her husband said so, and his father. Said she ran off with a *gor-jio*. But I had my suspicions then, and I have more suspicions now."

"Suspicions of what?"

"Well . . ." Leon Wood glances over his shoulder, in case we're being overheard, and then, despite the fact that we're alone and it's after hours, leans even nearer. "That they done away with her."

He doesn't look as though he's joking.

"You think they—you mean her husband—did away with her, seven years ago?"

Leon Wood glances upward.

"Well, more like six, I suppose. After she had the kid. Six and a half, maybe."

"Right. You're saying that you suspect your daughter was murdered six years ago—and you've never said anything, to anyone, until now?"

Leon Wood spreads his hands, turns his eyes back to me, and shrugs.

I don't often think about my—my what? Race? Culture? Whatever word the sociologists are using these days. The fact that my father was born in a field in Kent as his parents picked hops during the Great War. His parents stayed on the road; traveling and working around the southeast with his brothers. My one remaining uncle is now on a permanent site near the south coast, but only because his health deteriorated and made life on the road too arduous. But after the second war—during which my father met a *gorjio* girl named Dorothy, and when he drove ambulances in Italy, where he was interned and learned to read—after that he deliberately drew back from his family, and we didn't see that much of them. My brother and I grew up in a house; we went to school. We weren't Travelers. Dorothy—our mother—was a brisk Land Girl from Tonbridge who was never going to be seduced by the romance of the road. She was a fanatical believer in universal education—and my father was quite an autodidact, in his dour, humorless way. He even went so far—much too far, for most of our relatives—as to become a postman.

But despite them, we knew things. I (especially me, as the dark one) knew what it meant to be called a dirty gyppo; I know, too, about the long, petty battles over caravan sites, and the evictions and petitions and squabbles over education. I know about the mutual distrust that stopped Leon from going to the police about his daughter—or to any other private investigator. I have some inkling of what made him come to me, and I realize that he must be desperate to do so.

3.

JJ

I suppose my family isn't like most people's. For a start, we're Gypsies or Romanies or whatever. Our name is Janko. Our ancestors came from Eastern Europe, although they've been here for a long time, but my gran married my granddad, who's an English Gypsy, so my mum is half Roma and half Gypsy, and then she went off with my dad, who she says was a *gorjio*. I've never met him, so I don't know. They didn't get married, so my name is Smith, like hers and Gran and Granddad's. JJ Smith. Mum called me after her dad, Jimmy, but I don't like being called Jimmy, and now she calls me JJ. To be honest I'd rather not be called after my granddad, I'd rather be called after someone else—like James Hunt. Or James Brown. But that's not the truth.

We have five trailers on our site. First of all, there's our trailer—that's where Mum and I live. Mum's name is Sandra Smith. She's quite young—she was seventeen when she got into trouble and had me. Her parents were furious and chucked her out, and she had to go and live in Basingstoke, but after a couple of years they relented and let her travel with them again. They had to, really, as she is their only child, which is quite unusual. And I'm their only grandchild. Our trailer is a Lunedale—it's not that big, or that new, but it has oak-veneer walls and has a nice old-fashioned look. It's not flash, but I like it. Because it's just the two of us, I suppose, we're quite good friends. I think she's a pretty good mum, on the whole. Sometimes she drives me mad, of course, and, well, sometimes I drive her mad, too, but generally we get on pretty well.

Mum works as a delivery woman when we stop anywhere for a while. She's good at picking up work wherever we are. She works really hard, and apart from that sort of work, she helps look after my great-uncle, who's in a wheelchair. We all do that—Mum and me, Gran and Granddad, and my uncle. They are the other people we travel with. Gran and Granddad have two trailers between them—both Vickers, and both really flash with chrome trim and cut-glass windows. They live and sleep in the biggest and newest one, and then Gran cooks and does washing up and so on in the other one. And it's their spare room, if they need it. Great-uncle has a Westmorland Star that has been specially adapted for him, although it's the same one that he lived in when Great-aunt Marta was alive. It's got a ramp so that he can wheel himself in and out, and it's also got something that most people would think is a bit disgusting: an internal Elsan. He has to; life would be too difficult otherwise. The nurses said it was either that or live in a bungalow. So it's that.

The last trailer, a Jubilee, is where my uncle and cousin live. My uncle is Great-uncle's son—his name is Ivo, and his son, my cousin, is called Christo, who is six. Ivo's wife is gone—she ran off a long time ago. Gran's name is Kath, which is short for Katarina.

You may have noticed a few foreign-sounding names in our family, although the strangest name is Great-uncle's—his name is Tene, pronounced *Ten-er*. He and Kath are brother and sister. The Jankos came over from the Balkans in the last century, before any of the countries there were fixed or named. Great-uncle just says "the Balkans." He and Gran say we're Machwaya, which are the aristocrats of the Gypsy world, and we can look down our noses at Lees and Ingrams and Woods. Who knows if it's true? No one at my school knows anything about the Balkans. I'm the only one.

Gran and Granddad's number-one trailer is the biggest, nicest one—or at least the flashest—and Ivo's is the smallest and least flash. He has the least money, but that's because Christo is disabled, and Ivo has to look after him. Everyone helps out with money and stuff. That's just the way it is. When I say he's disabled, it's totally different from the way Great-uncle is disabled: it's because he's ill. He's got the family disease. I'm lucky 'cos I haven't got it, even though I'm a boy, and generally only boys get it. The boys don't usually pass it on, as if they have it, they don't live long enough. The only exception to this is Uncle Ivo, who had it when he was younger but got better. No one knows how. He went to Lourdes, and afterward he got better. It was a miracle.

I'm not religious, personally, but I suppose you can't just rule things out. Look at Ivo. Officially we're Catholics, although no one goes to church much, apart from Gran. Mum goes now and again, and so does Granddad. But sometimes, even though people who go to church are supposed to be full of Christian kindness and charity, they've been cursed at in church, and Granddad says that once he was going into a church and someone spat at him. I think that's awful. Gran said that they didn't spit on him, they spat near him, but still, it's pretty rude. I last went to church with Mum and Gran at Easter, just a couple of weeks ago. We were all dressed up and smart as anything, but some of the people recognized us, and there was a bit of muttering and shuffling as people tried not to sit next to us. I saw Helen Davies, a girl from my class, with her family, and she glared at me and whispered to her mum, and then they all stared. Not everyone was like that, but then not everyone knew who we were. I sat there in the pew, getting really tense, just because I was imagining what I would do if someone did spit at me. My fists were clenched and my jaw, too, until it hurt. The hairs on the back of my neck stood on end—I was just waiting for some spit to land on it. I saw myself turning around and giving that filthy *gorjio* a good leathering, even though I'm not really into violence. Granddad was a bare-knuckle boxer when he was younger, so maybe he passed it on.

I didn't hear a word of the sermon because I was so worried that someone was going to spit on my neck. No one did, though.

Anyway, the religion thing is important because that's why I am where I am now—that is, on the ferry going to France. I'm really excited, as I've never been abroad before, even though I'm fourteen. We're taking Christo to Lourdes, to see if he can get cured like Ivo did. "We" is everyone except Mum and Granddad, which seems a bit unfair, but someone has to stay behind and keep an eye on the site. It's a good place, and they need to make sure no one else moves onto it while we're away. Gran is here because she's the one who really wanted us to go. In fact, she pretty much made us go. Great-uncle is here because he's in a wheelchair and gets to do what he wants. I got to come because I do French at school, so I can inter-pret. No one else speaks a word, so I'm vital. I'm glad because I really wanted to come. And then Ivo, and Christo, of course, who is the reason for the whole thing.

I said Christo is ill with the family disease, didn't I? I can't tell you what it's called because no one knows. He's been to see doctors but they can't decide what it is, and because of that, they can't make him better. I don't think doctors are much use if they can't even help a little kid like Christo. He's not in pain mostly, but he's very small for his age, and weak, and he learned to walk only about a year ago—but he gets so tired he can't do it much, so he mostly just lies there. He doesn't talk much, either. That's the illness: it's like he's just so tired, he can't do anything. Often he pants like he can't breathe properly. And he gets infections a lot, so we have to keep him away from other kids, and generally keep things clean around him. If he gets a cold or something, it's really serious. His bones break easily, too—he broke his arm last year, just from hitting his hand on a table. Ivo used to be the same—when he was Christo's age, someone broke his wrist just by shaking his hand. But despite all that, Christo never complains. He's incredibly brave. In a way it's good that he's so small and light, because Uncle Ivo has to carry him everywhere. I carry him, too, sometimes—he barely weighs more than a feather. We get on really, really well. I'd do anything for Christo. He's like my little brother, although technically we're first cousins once removed. Or is it twice? I can never remember. It doesn't really matter.

Anyway, I really hope this works. Ivo doesn't like to talk about what happened to him, but I know that he was ill all through his childhood—although not as ill as Christo. After his trip to Lourdes, he slowly, gradually got better. I suppose you could say it was just a coincidence, but then, maybe it wasn't. And anyway, it can't hurt, can it? I've been trying to make myself believe in God ever since we decided to go on this trip, so that my prayers will make a difference. I'm not sure that I do, but I'm really making an effort; I hope that counts for something. And if God doesn't take pity on Christo, who's so sweet and brave, and has never hurt anyone, then I don't think much of him.

For the first half of the ferry crossing I stared out the window at the Newhaven docks getting smaller and fainter. The crossing to Dieppe takes ages, but it means less driving. This is the first time I've seen England from the outside. It doesn't look that great, to be honest. Flattish and grayish. When the coastline disappears and I've stared at the rather dirty-looking wake in the dark gray sea, I go and stand at the front, looking out for my first-ever glimpse of another country. It starts to rain on me. It's strange: I've never thought that rain falls on the sea as well as the land. Obvious, really. *"Il pleut,"* I tell myself. *"Il pleut sur la mer. Nous allons à Lourdes, pour chercher un miracle."*

It's important to be able to say what you're doing, even if it's only to yourself.

Then Ivo and Christo come and stand beside me. Ivo lights a cigarette without offering me one.

"*Bonjour, mon oncle, bonjour, mon petit cousin,*" I say. Ivo just looks at me. He doesn't say an awful lot, my uncle Ivo. I'm the talker in the family.

"*C'est un jour formidable, n'est-ce pas? Nous sommes debout sur la mer!*"

Christo smiles at me. He's got this brilliant, sweet, happy smile that makes you happy, too. You want to make him smile all the time. Ivo hardly ever smiles. He narrows his eyes and blows smoke toward France, but the wind snatches it away and carries it back to where we came from.

4.

Ray

I have my very own ghost. You might remember the name—Georgia Millington. Went missing on her way to school, age fifteen, in 1978. There was a small hue and cry when she disappeared—after all the goings-on up in Yorkshire, missing girls were news. But then, perhaps missing girls have always been news. They haunt us—those blurry, blown-up photographs in the paper: eager, coy smiles from school photos, or optimistic grins from snaps taken down the pub. Missing girls are always described as pretty, aren't they? Bubbly, popular. Who is going to disagree?

No body turned up in the Georgia case, and weeks after the police wound down the search, her parents—or rather her mother and stepfather—called me in. And after a few weeks, I found her. I found her and brought her back, fuming, uncooperative, and silent. Why was she silent? I still can't work it out. If she had told me about it all, could I have kept my mouth shut and let her disappear? Or did she realize that I was too pleased with myself to listen, having succeeded where the police had failed. It was true, I was pleased with myself: I hadn't been running my own business long; I thought it could be the beginning of bigger and better things—I'd do a few interviews: The Man Who Found Georgia . . . You let your imagination run away with you sometimes, don't you? And then . . . well, you recall what happened next—or at least what happened seven months later. There was a hue and cry then. That was news. I didn't see her again, but I pictured her in my mind. There was nothing pretty or unspoiled or optimistic about that picture.

Since then, I haven't taken on another missing girl. Debt absconders I can deal with. Long-lost relatives, that sort of thing. Maritals—all manner of sordidness, but not young girls.

In fits and starts, then, Leon Wood tells me what happened. In October of 1978 his daughter, Rose, married a boy from another Gypsy family, Ivo Janko. An arranged marriage, although he doesn't put it in so many words. Leon and his family went to the wedding, which took place in West Sussex, then Rose went off with her new family—effectively becoming part of their clan. Leon has not seen her since. This is not quite as unusual as it might sound. I gather that Leon lives on his own private land, but the Jankos are old-style Travelers in the real sense of the word—not house Gypsies, not living semi-settled on a permanent site, but continually moving on, from lay-by to farmer's field to verge, trying to stay one jump ahead of the next police visit and the next eviction.

"Were you happy she married Ivo Janko?"

Leon shrugs.

"They wanted it. Ivo's father, Tene Janko, he wanted it, seeing as we're purebloods."

I get a shock when he says this, a cold, queasy thrill that travels down my spine.

"Purebloods?"

"Come on, Mr. Lovell, you know—pure Romany. That was Tene's big thing, see? You and I know that it's rubbish; there's no such thing anymore, is there? But he had a bee in his bonnet about the pure blood, 'the pure black blood.' You know?"

My father never talked much about his days on the road when he was a boy. There was always the feeling he was . . . not ashamed, but it was over and that was that. A Gypsy was not what he chose to be. When the world looked at him, he wanted it to see a respectable postman, an example of the new world of enlightenment and progress, and that was what he was. When he was asked about his childhood—and when my brother and I were little we were wildly curious—he gave us bare facts but didn't go into detail. He certainly didn't romanticize it, ramble on about freedom and the wind in your hair and the joys of the open road, any of that stuff. He tried to make it sound boring—even the not-going-to-school-all-the-time part, which of course we thought was great. Dad had the autodidact's earnestness about education. After learning to read in the POW camp, he seized every opportunity that came his way, subscribed to *Reader's Digest*, and would look things up in a vast serial encyclopaedia called *The Book of Knowledge*, which had been published in the 1920s. Mum said that when he was younger, he used to read an entry a night, committing it to memory. Later, he became a devotee of television documentaries, although he increasingly disagreed with them, suspicious of any findings that departed from the Book.

As a result he had some pretty funny ideas about things, but he wasn't interested in any pure black blood. I remember Tata—my grandfather—referring to it. He was angry and, I belatedly realized, hurt, when Dad married out. He refused to speak to him and Mum for years—until my brother and I were both walking. Then, as children often do, we softened him. I knew I was his favorite because, as was made abundantly clear to me, I took after Dad and, by extension, him.

"You're a real Romany *chavi*," he would say to me—a real Gypsy boy. Unlike, by implication, my little brother, who took after Mum—tall, rosy-cheeked, with far-seeing gray eyes, Mum and Tom were built to stride over a grouse moor, although, born into the struggling lower-middle classes, that was never going to happen. Tom, aware of the favoritism, hated going to Tata's. I loved it.

Once Tata took me on his knee—I was probably seven—and said, "You have the pure black blood, Raymond, despite everything. You're my father come back to life. Sometimes that happens. You have the pure blood in you."

Presumably we were alone at the time. I remember the deadly serious look on his face, and his fervent eyes; I remember my discomfort, even though I had no idea what he meant.

"So he was wrong," I say to Leon. "Your family aren't pure Romany?"

"Who is? But he seemed to think we were, and Rosie was willing enough. He was a good-looking boy, Ivo."

"I've never heard the name Janko—are they English?"

"Yeah. Sort of. Tene claimed they're Machwaya or something— that his father or grandfather came from Hungary or some bloody place—but I don't know. They're related to the Sussex Lees in some way. Cousins or some such. So maybe it's all rubbish about Hungary."

"And how did you know them?"

He shrugs.

"You'd see them about. Knew people who knew them. You know how it is."

"So . . . after the wedding, you didn't meet up with them at the fairs . . . they didn't come to visit?"

Leon stares down at his hands. Perhaps he is after all a little upset about the daughter he mislaid a handful of years ago.

"The Jankos . . . kind of kept themselves to themselves. Used to go off on their own. Private like. Didn't mix much."

His mouth clamps shut.

"But still, your daughter . . . You'd want to see her, and your wife, presumably?"

"When you travel . . . I wasn't surprised she didn't come back.

She was a Janko after the wedding. Not a Wood anymore. But now . . . there's certain things—I'm sure something bad happened to her. I'm sure of it."

"You mean you think the Jankos harmed her in some way?"

"I suppose, yeah."

"Why?"

"I don't trust them. There was always something not quite right . . . It's hard to say exactly."

"Perhaps you could try."

"Like . . . Tene's wife died, and no one knew what of. She was there and then she wasn't there. And Tene had a sister what run away and left them. I think he had a brother what died, too . . . Unlucky. But too unlucky—you know what I mean?"

"I'm not sure I do."

"Well, maybe it wasn't all bad luck. People used to talk . . . All that bad luck . . . Well."

He shakes his head and hisses through his teeth.

"That didn't bother you when Rose got married?"

Leon presses his lips together, as if I am trying his patience.

"It was what she wanted. And to be honest, she wouldn't have had many chances, you know, what with . . ." He waves his hand at shoulder level and pushes a photo toward me. "Not many boys would've had that."

The young girl in the picture looks entirely normal, except for a port-wine birthmark on her neck. The size and darkness of it are slightly alarming, until you realize what it is.

"Anyhow, the Jankos used to go off on their own and wouldn't be seen nor heard for ages. So, next we heard, she'd gone. Run off—and they didn't know where."

"So that could be what happened."

"I feel sure she's gone. I feel it in my bones. I just know it."

"Right . . ."

Leon clasps his hands and bangs them down on the desk in front of him.

"To tell you the truth, Ray—and I say this to you as you're one of us—I had a dream recently . . ."

I have a sudden thought that someone is trying to put me out of business, or at least make me look ridiculous.

"In my dream she was dead. She came to me and told me that Ivo and Tene done her in. Now I'm not a great one for dreams or *dukkering* or none of that; I'm not that way inclined, but this was different. I just know it."

I stare down at my notepad, irritated. I can't imagine a more hopeless case. On the other hand, it could mean a lot of boring but lucrative work. One can't be too fussy in this life.

Leon is staring at me.

"I know what you're thinking. You're thinking I'm a crazy old man . . . dreams and whatnot, huh? 'S been a long time, I know that. But she's not here, my daughter. And no one knows where she is, or if she is anywhere at all. So what happened to her?"

The phone rings. It makes me jump. Andrea must have forgotten to put the answerphone on. I pick it up and put it down again. Too bad if it's another case. More likely to be the landlord.

"Do you know how to get in touch with the Jankos?"

"They won't tell you nothing. They say she ran off seven years ago, or six it was, with some boy."

"We still need to start there, with where she was last seen. Then work forward."

"They had a bob or two, the Jankos. Tene liked to move on. He was one for the old ways, you know, determined."

"When did you last see the family?"

Leon fidgets in his chair.

"I haven't really seen them since then. No."

"Since . . . the wedding."

He shakes his head.

"Ray . . . Mr. Lovell . . . you know as well as I do that if I went to the police with this, they'd laugh in my face. They'd think, here's some cracked old gyppo—put him in a home. Who cares about his poxy daughter, anyway? One less gyppo—good riddance, that's what they'd think."

My eyes are drawn to the bulging notes peeping out of his pocket, and he notices. They, at least, look real enough.

"You can look at all the official stuff, can't you? All them computer things. You know about all that."

He looks happy, knowing that he's snared me, despite myself. He looks confidently at the Amstrad on my desk as though it's a crystal ball, as though I can switch it on and see anything I want. And I agree to look into it. I give him the usual qualifications about missing-persons cases—long, expensive, often thankless. And he reminds me about Georgia Millington. So he does read the papers. Or someone reads them to him. And before he leaves, he takes one of the rolls of tens out of his pocket and leaves it on my desk, where it uncurls slowly, like a creature awakening after hibernation.

When I'm alone again, I flick through the notes—I've seen plenty of fakes, and these are real. Then I sit there rattling my pencil against the desk. Strange, isn't it, how you can think of yourself as one thing for ninety-five percent of your waking life, and then an encounter with something or someone jerks you into remembering you're something else, that other five percent that's always been there, but slumbering, keeping its head down. I'm subtly different from the person I was before he came in. The office is subtly different, too. Leon has left a trace of himself, changing my office from the way it normally is. I really must cut down on caffeine, I think; it's making me paranoid. Then, after a minute, I register that difference as a tangible thing: a faint, lingering aroma. Cigarettes? Cigars? Something like that, but not that. I'm relieved; for a moment there, I thought I was going crazy. Then I get it—it's wood smoke.

I look at my watch. It's long after six, on a gray, drizzly May evening in the suburbs. Another plane roars overhead, on its way somewhere nicer.

I have to get going. Not that I'm going somewhere nice. I've got work to do. You might say it's a labor of love.

5.

JJ

It takes ages to get to Lourdes. We have to keep stopping to make food, or to take Christo out for fresh air, or to make Great-uncle more comfortable. Gran drives the Land Rover pulling her trailer, and Ivo drives the van pulling Great-uncle's. There was a massive row when Gran wanted to take the number-one trailer—basically to show off to any French Travelers we might meet, but Granddad put his foot down. He calls this one "the kitchen," and as far as he's concerned, it's nothing to do with him. So Gran had to put up with taking number two, although it's flash enough to impress anyone, I would think. We haven't seen any French Travelers, anyway, not yet.

We pull into the service stations—they're called "airs" here in France for some reason—to use the toilets and so on, and no one gives us any hassle. French service stations are much nicer than English ones. They have free ice machines and microwaves you can just use—you don't have to pay or anything—and proper coffee dispensers that give you really great strong black coffee. I love coffee. Mum keeps moaning at me that I'm too young to drink so much coffee, but I can't stop, I love it so much. I reckon I'm addicted. I don't think coffee's so bad, though. It's not like heroin or fags. Uncle Ivo's smoked a pack a day since he was ten, he says, and Great-uncle never said anything about it.

We're in the middle of France now. There's still a long way to go, as Lourdes is right down at the bottom. Gran pulls into an air surrounded by some skinny little trees, and I carry Christo out into the sunshine.

"Look, Christo, a lake—*un lac. Regard!*"

It's beautiful here—there really is a lake, with ducks and geese bobbing up and down, the water shivering in the slight breeze, which makes the leaves of the trees flutter like millions of tiny pale green flags. They make a lovely, gentle noise. It's clean, too—no rubbish anywhere. Over the past day and a half, I've decided that I love France; I wish we could live here forever and didn't have to go home.

Ivo gets out of the van and fires up a fag. He looks fed up, which is quite a common expression on his face. He comes over and offers me a fag, but I shake my head, as Gran will be out in a minute and then she'll shout at me. She smokes like a chimney herself and couldn't care less, but Mum made her promise not to let me smoke.

"How're you, my love?"

Ivo strokes Christo's hair, and Chris gives him his sweetest smile. My uncle's often moody, but he really loves Christo—anyone can see it. I think he's mainly unhappy about all the doctors who couldn't help his son, and I can't blame him.

I pass Christo over—he's so light it's like handing over a bag of shopping—and Ivo wanders off along the shore of the little lake, fag still in mouth.

I realize the lake is man-made, and quite recently: there are still scar marks in the earth at the water's edge, and the bushes are surrounded by bare soil. But you can tell that very quickly, the plants will cover the bare earth and it will settle down and look like it's always been here, with the ducks and the sunlight. The obvious care that these French people took makes me happy. It's just for the people who are passing through for a few minutes; no one lives here. Maybe they'll stop for half an hour. But still they bothered to make it beautiful.

"JJ!"

Gran yells from behind me.

"Tene needs you."

This always happens. When I'm looking at something lovely and feeling happy, my family comes along to annoy me. They seem to get more annoying as I get older, I've noticed.

"I know you heard me."

I turn away from the lake and go to lower Great-uncle's chair down the trailer steps. The ramp is too heavy to get in and out all the time, so we left it behind. This is the bargain that I struck so I could come—as well as speaking French, I also help get Great-uncle to the toilet, because even though he's got the Elsan, he won't use it unless he absolutely has to. So Ivo and I take turns doing this. The speaking French part is fun, though a challenge; the toilet part is not a bit fun.

"Watch out!"

Great-uncle swears as I bang the chair on the side of the door. He's really heavy—not fat, but he was a big man, and though he's a lot thinner than he used to be, he still weighs a lot in his chair.

"Hell's bells, kid, what are you doing?"

I can't answer, as I need all my breath for lowering the chair down the steps without dropping it. It feels like the veins in my face are going to burst. Also, I'm sure it was Ivo's turn.

"Sorry . . ."

"Right, let's go and visit my aunt."

That's how Great-uncle asks to go to the toilet. I've never heard him say the word "toilet"—it isn't nice.

Inside the service station there is French pop music and the smell of real coffee. I must say, French pop is pretty awful compared to English pop, which is the best in the world, but then, maybe that's just the stuff they play in service stations. When I live here I expect I'll find out about the good stuff that they keep to themselves.

We head for the gents', where Great-uncle, as usual, asks me to wait outside. It's to preserve his modesty, and mine, I suppose, but honestly, I'd rather go in than hang around outside the men's lavs looking like a gaylord. I'm not allowed to walk away, either, as he's been known to shout for me when he gets into difficulties. I try to look as though I'm not remotely interested in anyone else going into the gents', but they always stare at me. Maybe it's because I've got long hair. Yesterday, a man came up and asked me for the time. I told him, in my best French, that I didn't have a watch (*"Je suis désolé, monsieur, mais je n'ai pas une montre"*), but he just smiled at me and jerked his head toward the door. I stared back, confused. Then he made a filthy gesture. Suddenly I realized what he meant, and I ran like the clappers. Great-uncle was really cross—he'd managed to drop his pipe, and it rolled behind the toilet where he couldn't reach it. He kept yelling until some man and his wife came and found us. They said my grandfather needed me. They looked scared—people often do around wheelchairs. Great-uncle wouldn't speak to me for the rest of the day. But how was I to know?

I don't want to give the impression that I don't love Great-uncle. I do. He's interesting to talk to and can be really funny. We like the same TV programs—old black-and-white Western serials and police shows. He knows lots of bloodthirsty Gypsy stories, and used to tell me them when I was younger. He doesn't do it anymore, because I'm too old—and maybe because I used to ask tons of questions that annoyed him—like "But why did the king's son get a golden feather? He didn't use it!" and "How could the second brother be so stupid? He sees his brother die, and then he does the same thing!"

He also lets me listen to his records—Sammy Davis Jr., Johnny Cash, lots of old American stuff. He likes country and western, as it's about people having a really bad time, which makes you feel better when you listen to it. Take Johnny Cash: a lot of his songs seem to be about how he's killed someone, and now he's in prison, having a bad time but deserving it. I like those ones. Last year in art, we had to do still-life painting. Most people did fruit and stuff, but I did murder weapons. The teacher wanted to talk to Mum after that.

But they weren't bloody or anything, it was more Agatha Christie–type things—candlesticks, a rope, poison bottles . . . (they didn't have a gun in the art cupboard, which was a shame, as I'd have liked one). And, I mean, painting it isn't the same as doing it, is it? In the same way that singing about killing people isn't at all the same thing as killing them. Johnny Cash has never actually killed anyone, as far as I know, and no one wants to talk to his mum. People can be so literal.

Great-uncle has a lot to put up with, of course. He wasn't always in a wheelchair. He was in a car crash a few years ago and broke his back. He was driving his car by himself and drove off the road and the car went into a wall. It was amazing that he survived at all. Ever since then, he hasn't been able to walk, and that—if you've ever tried it—makes living in a trailer really difficult. They wanted to make him go and live in a house after the accident, saying he needed a bungalow without steps and you can't have a trailer without steps, so what else could he do? Great-uncle just said he would rather die than live in a house—he wasn't a house Gypsy and never would be. He said he had his family around him and they would manage. Although, actually, he didn't have his family around him then: it was just him and Ivo and Christo at the time, but when Gran and Granddad and Mum found out what had happened to him, they saw that they would have to help Great-uncle, and Christo, too, so we all came back together and have been together ever since.

That was six years ago, more or less. In fact, a lot of stuff happened around then. With our family, things tend to happen together—it's like we're accident-prone or something. Great-uncle had his car crash and went to the hospital for ages, and at about the same time, Ivo's wife, Rose, ran off because they found out that Christo, who was only a baby, had the family disease. So they were all pretty bad things. Even though I was only seven, I was really sorry. Especially about Rose running off like that. I met her only once, at the wedding, but she was nice.

When I say I met her once, it was actually a few times over several days, which was how long the wedding lasted. It was one long extended party with lots of eating and drinking, as far as I remember. I remember playing hide-and-seek with her in a pub. And I remember the funny mark on her throat; she was always putting her hand over it to hide it, which just made you notice it more. I told her that her throat was dirty and she should wash it, and she told me it wouldn't come off. I stared, and she let me touch it. It was soft, like the rest of her skin, not scary at all.

I didn't care about the birthmark. I thought she was lovely, not like someone who would run off and leave their baby because he was ill. But then, what did I know? I was just a kid.

6.

Ray

Sometimes you can know too much. Of all people, I know this to be true. Ignorance is bliss. Knowledge is power. Which would you prefer? I have seen countless people walk in through our door, having, like Mr. M., chosen option B. They end up miserable, and paying me to make them so. Because they have to know. I once asked another client—a likable man—if, having found out his wife was unfaithful, he wouldn't rather go back to living in ignorance, and he paused a long time before answering.

"No, because there was something I didn't know. She knew, and I didn't. And that was stealing my life. All the time she lied to me, I didn't have the choice about whether to stay with her or not. She had the choice and I didn't. That's what I can't bear. The years I lost."

"But it's only now you look back, knowing that she was cheating on you, that you are, retrospectively, miserable. You weren't miserable at the time. That time wasn't lost—or stolen. When you didn't know, you were happy."

"I thought I was."

"If you think you're happy, then you are. Isn't that the best we can hope for?"

He smiled a difficult smile. I think he really cared about her but was divorcing her nonetheless. I shrugged. I don't tell people what to do; I'm just the man they pay to sift through their rubbish. They wouldn't listen to me, anyway.

Anyway: stakeout.

It's better than rubbish-sifting, which usually isn't as fruitful as it's made out to be. To be honest, there's a certain excitement about a stakeout—at least for five minutes, when you park across the street, camera on the passenger seat, Dictaphone, thermos, sandwiches, spare roll of film . . . It's the same as the door to our office. I insisted on a half-glass door when we were fitting out our premises. Why? So we could have our names on it, like Philip Marlowe in *The Big Sleep*. Every private detective I've ever known talks about how there is no glamour in the job. They're all liars. There's plenty of tedium, of course, plenty to depress you: uncertainty, insecurity, meeting a lot of people who are not at all happy to see you. But every time I walk through that door, run my eye over the somber gold letters and think, That's my name, there it is, just for a second: a thrill of pleasure. Isn't that the same thing as glamour?

Same with stakeouts. You've all seen the movies. Well, so have we. Anything could happen, at any time. Usually doesn't, granted, but you never know. Although there isn't any glamour this time, but that's because this particular party is one I've seen before; I've already got evidence, bags of it; this evening is just by way of backup. Nail in the coffin of guilt.

For fifty minutes nothing happens, unless you count my eating a ham sandwich and drinking a cup of tea. I'm watching a house on a street of identical houses on the edge of Twickenham. There's a light on upstairs, but it could be on a timer, so I don't read too much into that. At 7:28 a car parks down the street, and a man—fortyish, slightly overweight, foolish face—gets out, walks up to the house, and lets himself in with a key. There could be a flicker of movement inside the hall, but I can't be sure.

He has a key.

At 8:09 the door opens again and the man comes back out, having changed his jacket for something warmer. So he has clothes at this address. Now he is accompanied by a woman of a similar age, flamboyantly dressed, good-looking, slim, Chinese. They walk toward his car, side by side but without touching, seemingly without exchanging a word. As they turn out of the gate and onto the street, the woman flicks her head in my direction, but I can't tell whether she's registered my car or if it means anything to her. Ruler-straight dark hair swings across her face as she does so—like the swift strokes of a brush. I take a couple of photographs. They're not very good ones, profile at best, and the light is pretty poor, so there won't be much detail. Not that it matters.

I know exactly who they are.

In the morning, Hen eyes me warily from his desk. He's had a row with his wife, Madeleine—that's clear. He also has a sleep-deprived, haggard look about him—apparently Charlie, the youngest, was up all night with some unidentified childhood ailment.

"All right now, is he?"

"I expect he'll live."

The pencil between his teeth waggles up and down—a cigarette substitute.

"Madeleine wants me to invite you for dinner. Tomorrow."

"Tomorrow? Oh, I don't know that—"

"She won't take no for an answer."

"What if I have a prior engagement?"

"Do you?"

"I might have. I might have a life. Why does she assume I spend my evenings drinking myself into solitary despair?"

"Because she's met you. No . . . You know, she just wants you to . . . keep meeting people."

I look at him.

"I don't think she's invited anyone, actually. Come on—just dinner. It'll be . . . fun."

The order of the day is simple. We have only one active case on file—Rose Janko, née Wood. Her father was finally persuaded to come up with some concrete facts and a couple of photographs. The first one Leon gave me—the one that shows her birthmark—was taken a couple of years before the wedding. She's sitting with her mother in a stand at the races. She has a demure, self-contained air about her but is smiling slightly. Her hair is mousy, straight, and long; she has strongly marked eyebrows and a heavy, rather round jaw. Her head is turned slightly away from the camera, and you can clearly see the dark stain on her neck. It looks a bit like a hand, if you half close your eyes: as though someone is reaching around her throat from behind. I wonder if Ivo saw it before the wedding, if any of his family did.

The second photograph is from the wedding itself. In it, the newlyweds pose in front of a glossy cream trailer, holding hands but standing apart. A dog is a moving blur behind them. Chrome trim winks in the sunlight, and both have their eyes slightly narrowed against the glare. Rose has had her hair done—permed, lightened, and arranged into blond flicks that frame her face. The high neck of her wedding dress hides the birthmark. She smiles nervously. Her new husband, Ivo Janko, wears a black suit; he is blade thin, with longish, slicked-back dark hair, high cheekbones, and large dark eyes. He's very good-looking, and looks as though he knows it. He does not smile—his expression appears arrogant, even hostile. He seems to be leaning away from her, his body tense, his chin lifted. Studying his face in the photograph—looking for clues—I decide that his expression is due less to arrogance than to nervousness. They are both very young, after all, and are marrying a person they hardly know. Who would look at ease?

Other facts are few and far between; Leon seemed to struggle to remember his daughter with any clarity. When I asked him what she was like as a person, he said that she was "quiet" and "a good girl." But the girl at the races doesn't look like a pushover. Rose was the third child, and the third girl. I imagine her status in the family, with her mousy hair and strange, sinister birthmark, was lowly. Perhaps that was why she ended up marrying the son of a family who seem to exist—from what I have gathered—on the fringes of Gypsy society. Both, in their different ways, ill-favored.

Apparently, she and Ivo had a son within the year, and then— according to Leon—the next he heard was that there was something wrong with the child, and that Rose had run away with a *gorjio*, who was never named. Leon was angry that his daughter had deserted her husband and child. The duty of a Gypsy wife lies with her husband and his family—providing him with children and seeing to his domestic comfort. She obeys and puts up with whatever is dished out—including blows. To run away from her marriage— especially with a non-Gypsy—is to put herself beyond the pale. At the end of the day, Rose should have stayed, because her place was by her husband's side.

Harsh rules. My dad never explained it, but he didn't have to. He drove a deep rift between himself and his father when he married Mum. My grandfather never put it into words, either. But my brother and I understood that for him—for Tata—Dad had made himself unclean by choosing her. And even after he relented, and let her into his house and she could sit at his table, she wasn't allowed near the sink, couldn't wash up, and he had a special set of cutlery and crockery that he brought out only for us when we came over. He said it was the "good" china for guests, while he used the every-day stuff, even when we were there, but I am sure it was a special set reserved for "others." He wouldn't put a fork she had touched into his mouth. It just wasn't done. Dad and he had a lot of arguments, but we were still young when his dad died, and I could never ask him about it. Tata was always nice to us boys, but then children can't be unclean. We were innocent and in a state of Gypsy grace; dirty, yes, but not unclean—not *mokady*.

We don't have a lot to go on. First we run the obvious searches: DVLC, electoral rolls, utilities, land registry. The name Rose Wood or Rose Janko doesn't appear anywhere. I would have been surprised if it had. Even now, few Gypsies have passports or appear on electoral rolls. And if Rose has changed her name, we're not going to find a thing there, anyway. With a missing person, there is a set of procedures to follow. You check the official records—dull, time-consuming work. You run "hookers" in the papers—small ads asking for the missing person to get in touch to find out something to their advantage, or to collect an inheritance. When you don't know what area someone lives in, that's a very big net to catch a small fish—and not everyone reads the small ads—but still, you never know. And, of course, you talk to the people who knew them, starting with immediate family and widening out in ever-increasing circles—school friends, work colleagues, acquaintances, hairdressers, doctors, dentists, local shopkeepers, paperboy . . . Only with Rose, there doesn't seem to be a set of increasing circles; there is just one. No school friends, because she barely went to school; no colleagues, because she never worked. There is only family, and that so long ago: a small, tight, closed world from which a good girl does not stray.

At 7:30 the next evening I trudge up the drive to Hen's house. Thanks to Madeleine's money, they live in a vast detached house in a leafy neighborhood. Even though it's much closer to central London than I am, I feel like I've come to the country. When I ring the doorbell, Madeleine answers and pecks me on the cheek. I've always had the feeling that Hen's aristocratic wife doesn't really like me. One look from those pale blue eyes, and I feel like I should be coming in through the tradesmen's entrance.

"Ray . . . How lovely to see you. It's been too long."

I hold a bottle of wine up in front of me. It's probably the wrong kind, but this is one thing, over the years, I have stopped worrying about.

"Oh, lovely. Thank you. We promised Charlie you'd read him a story. Would you mind?"

I don't mind. Charlie is their youngest child and my godson. I can't imagine how Hen managed to talk Madeleine into that one; perhaps he has a file of incriminating photographs stashed in a vault.

Charlie is in the kitchen, hanging on to Hen's leg and dragging his security blanket, which he sucks, wrapped around one thumb. He has his father's floppy pale hair and diffident approach to life. I put the bottle of wine in the fridge. Blu-tacked to the fridge door is a typed list of the skills that Charlie needs to work on to bring him up to scratch. I read it with interest: "Speech—do not give him anything until he has named it properly. He must eat only without his blanket—do not give in! Hand-eye coordination—throwing and catching soft apple or blue ball. Numbers—get him to repeat them every day . . ." The list is laminated. Charlie peers at me with watery green eyes, a tinge of resentment in them: he knows I get to walk away from the list at the end of the evening, but he's in it for life. He drags me upstairs to read a story—about a big wolf who scares people without meaning to. But Charlie is more interested in telling me that there was a big storm, and it made him wet his bed.

"When was that, Charlie?"

"When I was young."

Charlie is four years old. I think his development is frighteningly advanced.

The evening is tolerable, for dinner at their house. There is a nasty moment when Madeleine springs on me that she's invited a friend of hers along—allegedly at the last minute. Vanessa is recently divorced—purely a coincidence, of course. Hen raises his eyebrows to signal that it's none of his doing, but would I please go along with it? Actually, Vanessa is surprisingly okay: not too many expectations, not overly bitter. A handsome streaked blonde, solid but shapely, a legal secretary. We eat lasagna and drink red wine (mine was the wrong color), followed by a lonely salad, and a bitter coffee-flavored trifle with a foreign name—all made by Madeleine, who needs to prove she can do everything. The two older girls—both in their teens—are "studying with friends," apparently, although I half hope they are doing something much more reprehensible.

Actually, the conversation is reasonable, the atmosphere surprisingly unstrained. Vanessa laughs at my jokes and appears genuinely interested in our work. I suspect Madeleine of exaggerating the exciting nature of our setup—to make Hen look good, of course, but I am her husband's boss. Of course, she will have added—as a spice—that I am half Gypsy. A little bit of rough.

For a while, I'm grateful to be sitting at a table, having a meal and talking—like people do when they don't go to pubs anymore. It's normal. I suppose it's nice. Vanessa's nice. She deserves someone better than me. I ponder this—for Madeleine to line her up with me, she must be a rather low-status friend. I stop pondering when Vanessa comes home with me afterward. She's fun, a good sport, but half my mind is occupied with wondering if she's going to tell Madeleine, and then feeling sorry in anticipation for Hen. Madeleine will complain to Hen about my rascally behavior, and he'll be the one—not me—to get it in the neck. The other half of my mind is somewhere else, too. Not that Vanessa seems to notice my distraction.

She leaves in the morning with a smile and a wave, and there is none of that tremulous, brittle fishing around about calling or phone numbers or seeing each other again. Sensible woman. Low expectations: the key to happiness.

7.

JJ

We're only ninety-eight miles from Lourdes! So hurray. Hurray even though it's my job to cook tonight. I'm doing Joe Gray, which is stew made with a tin of soup—any soup—potatoes, onions, carrots, and bacon. It's traditional, and one of my favorites. I discovered that bacon's called *lardon* in French, which makes me laugh. I make a joke about it putting the lard on; I think it's rather good, personally, but only Christo laughs—and that's because I'm clowning around, not because he gets it—and Gran just smiles a bit. No one else laughs. Uncle Ivo and Great-uncle have had some sort of major falling-out, but I don't know what it's about. Ivo took Great-uncle off for a walk earlier, and they came back not speaking. In fact, Ivo came back without Great-uncle at all, and I had to go and find him. It was just starting to rain. Luckily, he wasn't very far away.

Now they're both sulking for England. Ivo smokes and stares out the window. This despite Gran's having asked him four times to put it out or go outside. Great-uncle is staring into space and smoking his pipe. He's allowed to smoke indoors, since he's in a wheelchair and there has to be some compensation. But it smells horrible. I can hardly breathe. He breaks the tense silence with a sigh like a gust of wind.

"You break my heart, you do, kid."

This to Ivo, who ignores him, other than by sucking his teeth in an insulting way.

"Ivo, for Pete's sake . . . We're about to eat."

That's five. See, I can keep count, assess everyone's bad moods, and cook at the same time.

"Open the window."

"You could think of your son!"

This is absolutely guaranteed to wind Ivo up. He pretty much does think about Christo all the time.

"Jesus Christ, Kath—"

And this is guaranteed to wind Gran up.

"So help me . . . we're going to bloody Lourdes! Sometimes I really wonder about you."

She says this in a really low voice, although we're all crammed around the table, so it would be hard for anyone to miss it. Ivo looks daggers at her. Great-uncle taps out his pipe.

"Come on, now. JJ is about to dish up. Smells delicious, kid."

"Here it comes, here it comes. Bacon bacon bacon bacon. Come on get your lard on. Come on get your lard on! Get your lard on while it's hot . . ."

I can keep this sort of thing up for hours. Just switch my brain off and let my tongue go on automatic. It's a good way of annoying everyone so much that they stop having a go at one another. Gran, who appreciates this, even if no one else does, smiles in encouragement.

"Thank you, my darling. Doesn't that smell good. It smells different from at home, doesn't it?"

Ivo finally puts his fag out.

I slosh the Joe Gray onto everyone's plate, and they're off, eating like starving dingoes. Ivo, though, eats only a few mouthfuls, then pushes his plate away and gets up. He goes out of the trailer even though it's still raining. He leaves a sort of hollow vacuum behind him—it sucks your good mood into it. Sometimes, I swear, I don't know what gets into him. I know everyone gets depressed from time to time, but with him it's different.

I've been thinking about luck as we drive south, and France gets warmer and hillier and covered with trees. I wonder if it's true that some people are born lucky and some unlucky. I reckon it is. Apart from the obvious thing of some people being born rich and others poor—and I know you can argue about money not being necessarily a good thing—there are people who seem to suffer more than is fair. Take Great-uncle, for instance. He had two brothers who both died of the family disease. He was the only boy of his generation to survive—like Lon Chaney Jr. in *Hawkeye and the Last of the Mohicans*, which we used to watch together. Then he married and had two sons who died as babies—Mum says it's because Great-aunt Marta was also his first cousin, so they probably both had the disease in some way. Then he had a daughter and a son—the son was Uncle Ivo and the daughter was my aunt Christina. At first they thought Ivo was all right, but then he began to get ill. Then Great-aunt Marta died of cancer. Ivo was only fourteen when she died—the same age as me—so that was awful, too. Then, two years later, they came to Lourdes and Ivo had his miracle and got better. But at the same time, my auntie Christina—who was only seventeen at the time—was killed in a road accident. It was almost like she had to die so that Ivo could live, or something. I think that's an awful lot of deaths for one family—I mean, I really don't think that's normal. Unless you're in Africa, maybe. And as if that wasn't enough, after Ivo's wife ran off and left Ivo with Christo, Great-uncle had his own car accident and lost the use of his legs. Still, despite his luck, which has got to be unusually bad, Great-uncle is pretty cheerful. Ivo, though, who has also had lots of bad luck (although he never knew his brothers, who died before he was born, so presumably he doesn't miss them), is not cheerful. Gran says that he and his sister were very close—they were what she calls Irish twins, which means they were born less than a year apart—and he was never the same after she died. Although I imagine that having your mother die, and then a miracle cure, would also change you. Maybe he feels guilty about being the one to survive. Whatever the reason, he's not an easy person to live with. He's got a terrible temper. I sometimes think of that when Great-uncle curses Rose for running off. Uncle Ivo's said some nasty things to me, even when I was little and it wasn't really fair. I used to get upset by him, but I don't mind so much now. Mum once said that it must cut him up to see me—who was basically a mistake—healthy, when his own son and the only heir to the Janko name is so ill.

Later that night, I'm lying in the drop-down bed in Gran's trailer. She sleeps at the end, on the big bed, and there's a vinyl curtain that draws across between us. There's only the two of us in this big trailer, while the other three are in Great-uncle's smaller one. I suppose they're used to being together. But I can't sleep. After dinner, as I was taking Christo to put him to bed, Great-uncle said something to Gran about children, and the curse, and before the door shut, I heard her shush him and tell him not to be so stupid. But you do wonder, when so much bad stuff has happened. I found Ivo sitting in the other trailer, smoking and staring into space, although he pulled himself together when he saw me and Christo.

"All right, then?" I said.

"Yeah."

"You not hungry?"

"No."

"You looking forward to tomorrow?"

He shrugged. I can't understand why he isn't more excited about Lourdes. After all, he is living proof that it can work. He just smiled at Christo.

"You know, we've got to be careful. They bathe you in holy water."

"Yeah . . . So?"

"We have to be careful he doesn't catch cold. They wet your hair and everything. We've got to make sure he's dry and warm immediately after. Bring some towels or something."

"Yeah, okay."

Ivo was kneeling on the carpet, getting bedding out of the drawer.

"Is that why you were in a mood? Because you're worried?" I knew this was pushing it a bit. "He's going to be fine. Look at you."

"Yeah, well . . ."

The rain has stopped and a bright moon is shining on the window nearest me—it lights up the edge of the curtains, and a sickle of moonlight lies across my chest like a claw. And then one of Great-uncle's gruesome stories swims into my mind—one of the saddest, most awful stories—called "The Illness Demons." It says there are nine demons who cause all the diseases in the world—colds, stom-achaches, eczema, everything. I can't remember what all the demons are called, but I remember the one called Melalo, because he scared me the most. Melalo was the oldest child of the demon king and the fairy queen; he is a two-headed bird with sharp claws who tears out your heart and puts madness and violence in its place. Melalo is what causes people to murder and rape. I've broken into a sweat. I shift the curtain so that the claw shape becomes more of a blob. There's another demon called Minceskro, who causes diseases of the blood, like the one Christo's got. Maybe we should all be praying to her. Maybe I could pray to her, secretly.

I wonder whether—like the last time—one person has to die in order for someone else to get better. I don't think that would be very Christian—although I know an eye for an eye is in the Old Testament. But Lourdes isn't Old Testament, is it? It's Mary, who's definitely, I think, New Testament. And I don't think Mary would demand a life for a life.

But if she did, say . . . I wonder, who would it be?

Would it be Great-uncle? Would it be me? Would I be prepared to die for Christo?

I don't want to answer this question.

8.

Ray

According to Leon, the person who knew Rose best was her sister Kizzy. Kizzy Wood is now Kizzy Wilson, and lives with her family on a council-run site near Ipswich. We spoke briefly on the phone. She said she hasn't seen or heard from her sister since the wedding, so there wasn't much point in my coming. I said it was no trouble. She said, "Well, if you must."

I haven't been on a council site in years. This one is large—there are more than twenty trailers. Regular, neatly lined-up plots with hard standing. Tubs of flowers outside. A large amenities block. I am watched by curious faces as I tap on her door. It is opened by a small woman who looks older than her twenty-eight years. Her hair is pulled tightly back into a ponytail, revealing premature worry lines etched into her forehead. I search her face for any resemblance to Rose but find little: Kizzy Wilson is sandy-colored, almost shockingly freckled, with pointed, delicate cheekbones and a sharp chin. The only feature they seem to share is the mouth: full, even, symmetrical lips; very white teeth. She looks like she would have a good smile, but right now she is not smiling. I introduce myself.

"Well, come in, then. I was expecting you a bit earlier."

The door is near the back of the trailer, next to the kitchen, where steel bowls sit on an immaculate countertop. There's a gas stove, a fridge, but no sink—that hasn't changed since my grandfather's day. The walls are lined with shiny cream-colored Formica, there's a wood-burning stove—unlit—under a mantelpiece, and mirrors, chased with floral patterns, hang on every wall. On the U-shaped seating at the back, surrounded by flounced ivory curtains, sits another woman—and at the sight of her, my heart jumps briefly into my mouth.

"My other sister," says Kizzy Wilson. "Margaret."

Margaret Wood—or Mullins, as she turns out to be now—does look like Rose. Thick, straight, mousy hair and a round jaw. Dark, straight eyebrows. But—obviously, now I know—older than Rose would be, heavier. And without the birthmark.

"Kizzy said you were coming. I live here, too. I'm the eldest."

She doesn't extend her hand.

Kizzy ushers me toward the seats, and I lower myself onto slippery cream vinyl, planting my feet on the floor so I don't slide off.

"You've a lovely trailer, Mrs. Wilson."

"Thanks." Kizzy tips milk and water into mugs and brings them over, tea bags floating like drowned mice.

"I'll have to go and pick up the boys soon," she says, with a nod toward a loudly ticking cuckoo clock. "I don't have long."

"Of course. This shouldn't take long. I really just want to get an impression of what sort of person Rose was—and anything you remember about the wedding . . . or afterward."

I direct my comments to both sisters. They've positioned themselves on either side of me, so I have to turn my head like a spectator at a tennis match. Kizzy speaks into her mug of tea.

"I said on the phone, I didn't hear from her at all after the wedding. That was the last time I saw her, and the last time I spoke to her. People who travel . . . you don't see them that regular, you know."

"And you?" I turn to Margaret.

"Same. We were all at the wedding." She shrugs, mouth down-turned, as though it's a matter of little concern. "And then . . . nothing."

"You didn't think it was strange, not hearing from her?"

"No. Not at first. She was married, wasn't she?" Margaret looks at me, a hint of defiance in her eyes.

"And later, when did you first know that something was . . . not right?"

The sisters exchange a glance. Kizzy speaks.

"Grapevine. Someone had heard that Rose had upped and left. No idea who with."

"But she'd gone off with someone?"

"Yeah. That was what they said."

"And you had no idea that things were going badly before that?"

It's like pulling teeth, getting them to talk. They feel that I'm accusing them of not caring about their sister. They insist that it is not unusual not to see family for long periods, that they were busy wives, busy with husbands, with children. They heard nothing. They knew nothing about Rose's marriage. They didn't try to find out.

"Could you tell me what sort of person she was when you knew her? You were close, weren't you—growing up?" I smile at Kizzy.

"Suppose. She was my little sister. I used to look after her."

"In what way . . . ?"

She shrugs.

"In every way. Walk to school with her. Play together . . . You know."

"Did she have any other friends—at school or . . . otherwise?"

Kizzy shakes her head.

"Rose was quiet. Really quiet. Shy, you know? She wouldn't speak to someone she didn't know. She used to follow me round, like my shadow. I would've known if she had other friends, and . . ."

She shrugs, and then her shoulders droop again.

They exchange looks again.

I address Margaret. "You two seem to have stayed close."

Margaret glares at me.

"We married cousins. Steve and Bobby work together."

"Oh, I see. The Jankos weren't close to your family?"

"No."

"What did you think of Ivo Janko?"

Margaret snorts but doesn't answer.

"You didn't like him?"

Kizzy frowns, deepening the creases in her forehead.

"How well did you know him before the wedding—or any of the family?"

"We didn't, really. No one knew them well. They were sort of private—different."

She looks at her sister, for help.

Margaret says, "Kizzy means they weren't well liked."

"It was funny. Ivo really made a play for Rose—didn't he, Marg? And lots of girls hung round him. Girls who didn't care about the family. Rose seemed like the last girl he would ever . . ."

She looks down, as if she feels disloyal. Margaret takes over.

"Too pretty by half. You shouldn't marry a man who's prettier than you, was my feeling."

"They didn't seem like an obvious couple, then?"

Margaret shakes her head and tuts.

"Rose was so quiet. She should've chosen someone . . . sweet. Ivo wasn't sweet. He didn't care about anyone but himself."

She looks at her sister.

Kizzy looks miserable now, clutching her mug of tea. She chews her plump lower lip and speaks so quietly I have to lean forward to catch the words.

"I couldn't believe it when they told me she'd run off—and I hadn't heard a thing. I thought, where else would she go? Who else did she know? I kept waiting for her to turn up. But she didn't. I was fed up. I thought she'd come to me if she wanted, but she didn't want. I had two kids by then—what was I supposed to do?"

She looks at me again, the emotion animating her face, making her look younger, prettier. I feel a stab of pity.

"What do you think happened?"

"I dunno, do I? I wouldn't be surprised if he treated her bad, but . . . I'm surprised she had the guts to go."

She says the last sentence with a break in her voice, looking out the window.

"I've got to go and get the boys."

"Kizzy, have you ever wondered if Rose was dead?"

Kizzy looks around, her mouth opening. She looks genuinely shocked.

"What? No! That's a terrible thing to say! I'm sure she's alive. She just had to . . . Maybe she went abroad . . . I don't know."

Margaret draws herself away from me in distaste.

"That's a wicked thing to say."

"Your father thinks she's dead. After your mother died, he thought she would have heard . . . got in touch."

Margaret mutters a curse under her breath.

"Dad . . . Jesus."

Kizzy rolls her eyes and gets up. Her eyes gleam with unshed tears.

"I've got to go. They'll be standing around in the cold. She's not dead."

On the Formica wall there are framed portraits of two stiffly smiling little boys with haircuts that make them look like miniature squaddies. One of them has the heavy jaw that is such a feature of Rose's photographs. Her nephews.

Margaret stands up, too.

"I'm afraid there's nothing else we can tell you, mister. I hope you find her, though, and I hope Ivo Janko gets what he deserves."

Kizzy Wilson picks up a leather jacket, and we file outside. I thank them for their help. Her sister stands like a stocky sentinel in the doorway of the trailer—in case I try to sneak back in? A few yards away, Kizzy pauses for a moment.

"If I think of anything, I'll ring you."

"Thanks. Anything at all, even if it seems stupid."

She hunches her shoulders against the thin rain.

"We should've done this ages ago. Isn't it too late?"

"No. No, it's . . ." I search for some words of comfort. "I'll do my best."

She nods, unhappy. Clearly I do not inspire her with much confidence. She turns without another word and trudges, head down, to her car.

9.

JJ

At last we're at Lourdes. Everyone is tense, wondering what's going to happen. We arrived last night, having got lost three times driving down little roads among green hills. Down here in the South of France, every single road is signposted to a place called Pau. So every time we thought we were on the road to Lourdes, we ended up heading for Pau instead. It was a bit funny, really, heading for a cartoon punch in the face. I thought so, anyway, but I didn't say anything, as Gran was getting cross. It was so late when we finally found Lourdes that it was dark, and we drove about looking for a place to pull on, blind as bats. There aren't any streetlights outside the town, so we pulled onto a dark field that seemed quiet and where we thought we wouldn't bother anyone.

This morning, we were woken up at six o'clock by a giant groaning, roaring noise. I leaped out of my bunk and looked out the window—and it turned out we had pulled onto a bit of land right next to a factory, and all the machinery was starting up for the day. We all got up really quickly, and sure enough, in a few minutes a man came over from the factory to shout at us. I'm not sure what he said, but we kept saying "Lourdes" and pointing to Christo and Great-uncle's wheelchair, and eventually he calmed down and went away.

Lourdes is kind of a weird place. The shrine seems quite separate from the town proper. For a while we drove around, not sure where to go; then I realized that we had to follow the signs to "Sanctuaires" to get to the grotto, where it all happens. There are lots of churches, and there are a lot of people. Lots of coach trips and people in uniforms. Most of the people are old. Some of them really old. I watch this one coach spewing out its load of passengers, and it takes ages. The ones who aren't in wheelchairs can hardly walk, and cling on for dear life as they clamber down the coach steps. They've all had plenty of life. Between them, there must be a couple thousand years in that one coach alone. Literally. Christo's had only six years, and all of them with the disease. I think he deserves a miracle more than any of them. I hope God takes note of this.

We park in a coach park and set off for the grotto first, as that's where Mary apparently appeared to Saint Bernadette many years ago. Ivo carries Christo, and I push Great-uncle. It's funny. Now that I'm here, I'm quite excited. I really feel that something might happen, even though I've been secretly doubtful up until now. I mean, Bernadette was this girl who had special needs—a retard, in other words. And she was my age. I can't imagine anyone appearing to any of the girls I know at school. Most of them are incredibly stupid or really tedious, or both. Helen Davies, for example, who is supposed to be such a devout Catholic, would love it if something appeared to her, as she could be even more high and mighty than usual. But she's totally prejudiced against Gypsies. Then I wonder what Saint Bernadette thought of Gypsies. Great-uncle is always saying how in all parts of Europe people have persecuted us, usually much worse than they have in Britain, so actually we're quite lucky. Like, during the Holocaust, Gypsies were gassed like Jews. But if you were only a quarter Jewish, you counted as not Jewish and were allowed to live. But if you were only one-sixteenth Gypsy, then you were still a Gypsy and they would gas you. That's how much they hated Gypsies. And in Romania, for centuries and centuries

Gypsies were actually slaves, bought and sold like cattle. They don't teach you that in school. But Great-uncle tells me. He knows a lot about it. So maybe Bernadette was prejudiced against Gypsies, too. Maybe no one's ever asked. I did wonder at first whether we shouldn't go and ask for a miracle from Saint Sara—who is the patron saint of Gypsies, after all. Her shrine's not that far from here—and we could all go to the seaside at the same time. But no one listens to me.

There's a railing along the side of the road, next to a cliff, and Bernadette's grotto is up above our heads. You can't actually climb up to it because of the railings. People wander past, quite casually, as if it's no big deal. I wonder if they all really believe in how holy it all is—they don't look that bothered, most of them. There's a big candelabra thing at the bottom, also behind the railings. It's pretty. I prefer it to the statue of Mary that's in the grotto—which is rather plasticky, in my opinion. I shut my eyes, though, like Gran, and try to pray. She has her eyes shut, and her lips are moving silently. When I open my eyes, Christo is gazing up at the statue with a look of total calm. I wonder what he's thinking. At this point, Great-uncle suddenly swings his chair around and starts pushing himself off as if he's in a hurry. He doesn't say anything to any of us. I start to go after him, but Ivo puts his hand on my arm.

"Leave him," he says. Gran opens her eyes and looks furious.

After we've looked and prayed, Ivo takes Christo off to the bath-houses. This is where the afflicted are bathed in the holy water—presumably where the miracles take place, if they're going to. Before we got here, I was a bit worried about whether I would manage to explain things to people here, but there are lots of helpers here of different nationalities—in fact, most of the young people you see seem to be helpers rather than supplicants. That's what we are—supplicants. Ivo has found one who speaks English, although he's actually a French-Canadian called Balthazar (cool name!), and he goes to the bathhouses with them. Ivo doesn't look him in the eye, as though he's embarrassed about the whole thing. I wish he'd make a bit more of an effort. I ask Ivo if he wants me to go with them, but he says no. He has a towel around his shoulders, although it's really warm and sunny, so I don't think he needs to worry about Christo getting cold. I'm sure Lourdes will have thought of that, anyway. Maybe they have hair dryers.

Then Gran and I are left behind. Gran joins the queue to touch the walls of the grotto and look at the spring. She wants me to stay with her.

"I don't want you wandering off by yourself. What if something happened to you?"

"Like what?"

"We're abroad. Anything could happen!"

I point out that we are in a place of pilgrimage that's full of unhealthy religious people. Christians aren't going to do anything bad to me, are they? And I can speak French, unlike her. She can't think of a reply to that, so I promise to come back—she's obviously going to be stuck in her queue for ages—and she sulkily lights a fag.

Balthazar told us where we could get holy water to take home with us—you help yourself to it, which is very Christian of them, so good for Lourdes. You can buy little plastic bottles to fill, which have a picture of Mary on them and the word "Lourdes," but I realize that actually you can use anything you want. So I go all the way back to the trailers and get a couple of plastic jerry cans.

I join the queue at the tap. Most people have got little bottles—mainly official Mary ones, although some people are filling Coke bottles and water bottles as well. Some of them look at the jerry cans and mutter, but I don't know what they're saying, so I don't care. When it's my turn I hold the jerry cans under the tap and fill them up, ignoring the muttering that's going on behind me. Honestly, it's just a tap coming out of the ground, like a standpipe on a site. I don't know what makes it so holy—it's supposed to come from the spring under the grotto, but it could come from the river—how can you tell? And lots of people have splashed it around, so

I don't think it can be that precious. All in all, I reckon that, a) it's fine to fill the jerry cans, and anyway, b) Christo's illness is quite severe, so he probably needs more than most people.

The downside is that afterward I am staggering along with two full jerry cans of water. I take them back to the trailers and leave them, along with a big note saying it's holy water and not to be used for washing up (exclamation mark!). I draw a little picture of Mary with a halo underneath, just to be on the safe side, although everyone in my family, except Christo, can read, at least a bit. Belt and braces, as Gran always says, twice. Belt and braces!

I go back to the grotto to find Gran, who is waiting on a bench by the river. There's no sign of the others. She's worrying about Great-uncle, but I'm so hungry I can't worry about anything until I've eaten, so we walk off to find lunch. Eventually we find a place— it's almost in the town itself, where we can get a bit of lunch for a prix fixe (even Gran understands this) of only fifteen francs, which is cheap. It's delicious—an omelette and a pile of thin, crispy chips, which they serve with mayonnaise on the side. Weird but nice. Gran eats it, which surprises me, as normally she won't touch *gorjio* food. She's in such a good mood that I bring up the idea of living in France. She smiles in a tired sort of way, like she does when I'm talking amusing nonsense. I don't think she realizes that I actually mean it.

Later that evening, after Great-uncle reappears—he found a bar and talked to a French Gypsy—and Ivo and Christo have come back from the bathhouse, we all go back to the grotto. After dark, it's much nicer—the candles on the candleholder are all lit, and a soft light shines on the statue of Mary, so that it no longer looks plasticky but could almost be a real person—or a vision, like the one that appeared to Bernadette at night, all those years ago. All around us, around the town, there are lights on the steep wooded hills, and on the highest one, far above us, a huge lighted cross. It's a warm, mild, beautiful night. There are insect noises in the trees, and millions of stars—far more, and brighter, than I've ever seen at home.

A priest gives some sort of service. His voice is beautiful—he sort of sings the words, rather than talking. Gran keeps annoying me by asking me what he's saying, but I don't know. I catch maybe one word in ten, but I like not being able to understand what he says—it makes my mind wander to new places, freed from its usual boring habits. I look up at the lighted cross and the stars, and the statue and the candles. All the people around us are murmuring answers to the priest. Then some music starts up from somewhere—soft, soothing music, with a woman singing. I want this to work so much, I don't dare look at Christo anymore. It actually makes me cry. Gran puts her arm around my shoulders. She's crying, too.

At that moment, I really believe it. I believe it all.

Eventually, we have to leave the grotto to get something to eat. Gran pushes Great-uncle up ahead, and Ivo carries Christo, who has fallen asleep in his arms. He must be really tired after all that holy stuff. Ivo gives me a cigarette. He seems much calmer now.

"Was it good—the baths?" I ask. I can't really picture what must have taken place in there.

"Yeah. It was good."

"It's good it's so warm, isn't it? I'm sure Christo is fine."

"Yeah."

"Was it the same as when you came before?"

"Yeah, pretty much. They have more helpers now."

He stares off into the dark night.

"Could you tell at the time—when you were there, I mean—that you were being cured?"

"Not at the time. It was just water. Just like any water. Quite cold."

"That's what I thought," I say. I'm relieved, though. I had always wondered if he knew right away that he was cured.

"Balthazar wanted me to go back and talk to the priest about what happened to me."

"Yeah? Maybe that would be good."

I'm a bit doubtful of this. Maybe they feel they own you, if you've had a miracle. And I know from his voice that he won't, not in a million thousand years.

"What did you get up to, kid?"

"We had omelettes and chips. It was great. Oh, and . . ."

I can't believe I forgot until now.

"I got four gallons of holy water!"

Ivo smiles at that. Then he laughs—a happy laugh, not a mean one. He actually laughs. I haven't heard that for a long time.

10.

Ray

"Mrs. Hearne? My name's Ray Lovell. I'm trying to get in touch with your brother and your nephew."

"My brother?"

"Tene Janko. And Ivo."

There is a silence.

"Is this a joke?"

"No, not at all. Mrs. Hearne . . ."

"It's Janko. Miss Janko."

"I beg your pardon. I've been told you might be able to help with your family's whereabouts."

"I'll have to call you back. What's your number?"

I give her the number of the office. Luella Janko is a suspicious woman. She calls back about ten minutes later, having presumably looked us up in the phone book. Andrea puts her through.

"Why do you want to speak to them?"

"It's about Rose Wood. Rose Janko. I'm trying to track her down."

"You're trying to find Rose? That was years ago."

"Yes."

Another longish pause ensues. I'm not altogether surprised at this caginess; Gypsies have plenty of reasons to be suspicious of people asking questions about their families. Finally she agrees to meet me, in a café in the center of town. It's probably another stalling tactic, so that she can do some asking around.

"How will I know you?" I ask.

"I'll come up and introduce myself," she says tartly. "What do you look like?"

"Dark hair, brown eyes, five-ten, forty."

I wait for a second.

"I'm a Gypsy."

There is a pause at the other end, and then she says, "Right. I'll know you."

I get to the café in Reigate town center fifteen minutes early but can't spot anyone who might be her. I order a coffee, which comes in a tall glass—weak and nasty, like a hot milkshake—and sit in the corner, from where I can keep an eye on the door. Back to the wall, eye on all exits. Something I didn't need to be taught by my first employer, since I had learned it from Doc Holliday at the age of seven. I have the pictures of Rose with me. There's something indefinably old-fashioned about them, even though they are less than ten years old. Partly the seventies clothes and hairstyles but also the color of the prints, as though they were taken on out-of-date film, rendered all the more distant and other by chemical attrition.

I'm looking at the wedding picture when a woman arrives at my table.

"Mr. Lovell."

It's not a question.

"Hello, Miss Janko. Sit down . . . I'm sorry about the other day. There was a bit of confusion over which name you like to use."

"Since Mr. Hearne buggered off, I'm not particularly attached to that one."

Luella Janko. The first thing is, she's younger than I expect. Tene must be pushing sixty; his son Ivo late twenties. Luella must be at the other end of a large family; she looks about my age. All I know about her is that she divorced her Traveler husband, settled in a house, and never sees her family. She is the closest I have got to the Jankos. Physically, she's small and slight. Her jet-black hair is probably dyed; she wears a little too much makeup, giving her powdery-white skin, and shiny red lipstick. There's an element of mask to the makeup—almost like a geisha, a front. Her clothes are anonymous but smart: sensible gray trouser suit and one of those giant, slouchy handbags that could cover every eventuality of weather and circumstance. She looks pretty well *gorji*fied, like me.

"So you're looking for Rose?" she says, when I bring her coffee over. She's already looking at the photographs.

"Can you tell me anything about her?"

"Like what? I only met her once. At the wedding."

"Right. That was the last time you saw her?"

"The first and the last."

"Do you know where she is now?"

"No."

"What do you understand about what happened?"

"She ran off—with another man, apparently."

"Who told you that?"

"My brother and sister."

"Would the brother be Tene Janko?"

"I only have one."

"And the sister?"

"Kath. Kath Smith."

"When was this?"

She sighs but appears to be thinking about it.

"About a year after the wedding, I think. Maybe a bit more . . . I didn't ask a lot of questions."

"Why not?"

"Why would I?"

She glances at me briefly, then stares out the window. She has light hazel eyes and spidery, mascaraed lashes that emphasize the faint lines around them. Her voice is light and brittle, verging on snappy—though that could be the circumstances.

"I'd have thought it's normal to ask questions if a relative's marriage breaks up."

"Depends on the family, I should think. We're not close. Although, I suppose, I wasn't that surprised."

"What—that she left?"

Luella Janko smiles slightly and looks me in the face for the first time. Assessing me.

"Look, Mr. . . . Lovell—that's why Leon Wood hired you, I suppose, because you're one of us? There's not much I can tell you. I think they'd only met a couple of times before the wedding. She seemed very quiet, very mousy."

She pauses for a bit, her eyes downcast.

"I don't think Ivo would be easy to live with. And Tene can be a bugger, too."

"But she had a child."

"Yeah, another man to run around after. You know what it's like for Gypsy girls, Mr. Lovell. She'd have been a skivvy."

"Could you tell me where I can find your nephew?"

"No. I can only tell you where you might find him."

"Well, that would be a start."

I write down what she tells me; it's vague but better than nothing.

"Why don't you see your family more often, Miss Janko—if you don't mind me asking?"

"I do mind. It's got nothing to do with Rose. Actually, I . . . We're just different. Me and Tene. I don't want to live in the past. What's the point?"

Her tone is matter-of-fact.

"And what is the past, in this instance?"

Her lips tighten.

"Let's just say that they don't approve of me living in a house. I've gone over to the other side, to hear them talk."

She shrugs—her movements, like her voice, are abrupt, almost jerky.

"Could Ivo have harmed Rose, do you think?"

Her eyes widen. She turns a withering look on me and smiles—a pitying smile at my foolishness.

"My family didn't do away with her, if that's what you're thinking. To think Tene or Ivo could have done something to her . . . you're really barking up the wrong tree."

She shakes her head and seems genuinely amused, biting at her lip so that she wears off some of the redness.

"I just wondered. I have to consider every eventuality."

" 'Every eventuality.' "

She rolls the words around on her tongue and smiles, like I'm a complete idiot: a little boy playing detective.

"I'm sure there's plenty about my family that would make her want to run away. Go and ask them. I don't know where Rose is. If I knew, I'd tell you."

As she's getting up to go, Luella Janko pauses, shunting her sack onto one shoulder. It's now got my business card in it, lost in the depths, just in case she remembers anything. I'm not holding my breath.

"Wait a minute . . ."

She turns around, impatient.

"Did you like Rose?"

She looks genuinely surprised, as though it's never occurred to her before.

"Like her? I only met her once. Like I said, she was quiet, didn't talk much, a bit of a mouse—didn't make a big impression, you know?"

Luella Janko walks out, smacking the swing door aside with a vicious gesture. She's wearing high-heeled shoes—the sort that make that lovely, crisp, ticking noise—which I see are as red and shiny as her lipstick.

Rose Wood didn't seem to make a big impression on anyone, not even on her own father. I feel a wave of frustration with them all—at least those I've met so far; a sheltered nineteen-year-old girl disappears and nobody lifts a finger, not even to dial 999.

Suddenly I am absolutely determined to find her, because no one else really seems bothered.

When I get home, there's a message from Hen. He's been talking to a police contact in missing persons. There's no sign of Rose there, meaning that no one has ever reported her missing. Put another way, no one ever wanted her back. I know that women—especially young women—have low status in Gypsy families, and daughters-in-law lowest of all, but still . . . Despite what Luella Janko said, Rose might be dead. Even if there was no crime, people still die.

The way it works with investigations—any sort of investigation—is that once you have some information, you form a working hypothesis. You gather more information, and see if it fits your hypothesis. If it doesn't, you have to reform your hypothesis accordingly. But information on its own is not really much use to you. Information is hearsay, anecdote, opinion. It's what people tell you, and people have any number of reasons to lie. You have to turn that information into facts—by checking and cross-checking, by using all the sources at your disposal. When you have one or two corroborating pieces of information and it all seems to add up, then you can start talking about facts. But even facts aren't any good—not if you're going to court. You have to turn the facts into evidence—by which I mean attested documents, photographs, film, forensics, confession, and—as a last resort—expert witnesses. That's how I learned to operate as an investigator. There isn't room for speculation or feeling. Tangible, rational, explicable: that's how you have to think.

The danger is that you get stuck on one hypothesis. You have to be flexible. Admit that you can make mistakes. And sometimes you can be right and still get it wrong. Like with Georgia Millington.

The answerphone also contains, to my surprise, a message from Vanessa. Asking in a very casual, roundabout way if I would fancy going to see a film one night. I suppose Madeleine gave her my number. It makes me sigh, even though there was nothing wrong with her or with that night. In fact, maybe I do want to see a film sometime. Why not? I'm a single man, footloose and fancy-free. I can do whatever I want. I write down her number on a piece of paper, which I then hide in the general mess by the phone. Then I erase the message. No message: no evidence that she ever called.

If I pour myself a stiff vodka and tonic after this, and if I sit drinking it as the light drains out of the living room, allowing the darkness to steal up and wrap around me like a blanket, it's not because I'm thinking about the woman who is still, technically, my wife. To be rational, I'm not thinking at all. To prove how very rational I am, I decide to ring Vanessa tomorrow. If I have decided that, it doesn't matter what I do or think tonight, because tomorrow I'll behave normally.

Alcohol's great, isn't it? Without it, I think I would have killed myself. Hen would agree with me about alcohol, even though he's been on the wagon for years.

When we first met, Hen was a stockbroker. I hated him on sight. He was everything I wasn't—privileged, well educated, confident (on the surface, at least), with that penetrating drawl that carries across ballrooms and heather-covered hillsides. And there was me—mongrel Gypsy boy, who had dragged himself to a polytechnic and a diploma in business studies. I was on a job—looking into some anomalies at a small City firm. I had a knack for figures, so Eddie generally passed that sort of thing on to me, even after I stopped working for him. My investigation swiftly narrowed to one point—Henry Hamilton-Price, and I realized what the problem was; he was covering up a drink problem and struggling to maintain his posh wife and two young daughters. He had "borrowed" some of the firm's money, and inevitably, the thing started to unravel. There hadn't been the need for much direct surveillance, so I was surprised when, on one of my undercover visits to the firm's premises, Hen cornered me in the vice chair's office.

"I know who you are," he hissed. "You work for a firm of private detectives. And I know what you're doing."

"I am not at liberty to discuss my activities," I intoned. I've always enjoyed saying that.

"Please . . ."

That's when I realized he wasn't threatening me. He was begging me.

I wasn't accustomed to being implored by someone so obviously my social better. It was intoxicating. He said that he would shortly be able to pay the money back, that if he lost his job his wife would leave him and take the children. Then after a minute gazing intensely into my face—I don't think I had said a word—he stopped and drew himself up, as if forcing his back to straighten.

"I'm sorry. You must, of course, do whatever you think is right."

He turned abruptly on his heel and walked out, leaving me stunned. He was absolutely convincing. I didn't doubt his anguish for a second. I shopped him anyway. Of course, he was fired, but the firm refrained from pressing charges, which was more than decent of them. And to everyone's surprise, especially his, Madeleine stood by him. I have to give her that much credit.

I tracked him down a week later, because I couldn't work out how he had rumbled me, and offered him a job. He was deeply touched that anyone would trust him again, knowing what he had done, and for my part I was touched that he was completely unsnobbish.

He has never made me feel that he was better than me; in fact, he has always given the impression that he admires me—my independence, my professional skill, and, in the old days, my marriage to Jen. He used to think—he said—that we were the perfect couple.

So did I.

They say booze kills you, but it doesn't; otherwise, we'd all be dead. It's sadness that kills you, if that sadness is so heavy and overpowering that you simply cannot bear to be sober, or even conscious.

I thought, when she left me, that my sadness could not be any greater, that the pain could not be any more acute, and that I couldn't survive it. But I was wrong, because here I am: drinking, admittedly, but not an alcoholic. I know the difference. When things get bad, and even after two years, they still get bad, I can drink until it doesn't hurt so much.

The first thing I ever knew about Jen was that she had a heart murmur. I was eight and walking down the street after school, and a girl I had seen around the neighborhood—I knew her parents kept a Chinese chippy nearby—came up to me. She had no trace of shyness.

"I've got a secret in my heart," she announced.

"A what?"

"A secret."

She put her hand over her solar plexus.

"That's not where your heart is. Your heart's here."

I tapped my left collarbone.

"Mine's here," she insisted. "It's got a secret."

I pondered this for a minute.

"Why are you telling me?"

"The doctor said it might kill me."

She didn't seem upset. Rather, proud at being singled out. "Probably not, though."

"Oh."

I was flummoxed.

"Did he say it was a secret?"

"He said . . ."

She frowned with concentration.

"Maybe not," she conceded. "But it's very, very quiet. You can only hear it when he puts a snake over it."

She had truly black eyes and shiny black hair cut in an astonishingly square geometric fringe. I was fascinated by it; I had never seen hair so straight and glossy, like doll hair.

"Well, bye."

She ran off down a side street.

Her parents had arrived in this country from Shanghai, having fled the revolution. Jen was their youngest child. Of course, she hadn't understood the word "murmur," and when her mother explained it, she described it as the way of speaking when you tell a secret. After this chance meeting I saw her around from time to time, but we never spoke. We went to different schools and moved in different circles. It wasn't until years later, after we had both left home and returned only for dutiful parental visits, that we ran into each other—almost on the same street corner as that previous meeting. She still had the wonderful hair, although now scraped up into a spiky knot with wisps sticking out in all directions, and vivid purple eye shadow winged out from her slanting eyes—very unusual in those hippie days. She looked fantastic. I couldn't remember her name.

"It's Jen!"

She semi-pouted, as if offended. I really didn't want to offend her.

"I remember your heart murmur, though. You called it a secret in your heart."

Her eyes widened with amazement, and she burst out laughing.

"Well, you're the Gypsy boy."

I nodded. We were both smiling.

"My parents wouldn't let me do games for years. I got really fat for a while."

"But you're all right now?"

"I wasn't that bad!"

"I mean . . . your heart. Is your heart all right now?"

"I think so. The murmur went quiet. Actually, I'm pretty tough."

She wasn't lying about that.

That was the beginning, although we didn't go out for another couple years. She had a boyfriend—someone who'd been at art school, too. Someone more exciting and bohemian than me. And I had a girlfriend, although I can't remember which one of a series of medium-term relationships I was in at the time. But we ended up together, because that's what you do when you meet the one person who makes everything make sense, who knows what you're thinking before you say it, whose sentences you can finish and they don't even mind.

No, that's all wrong. That sounds much too insipid. I fell in love with Jen because she was the missing piece of me, and I was the missing piece of her. There was nothing to weigh up—of course we would move in together; of course, one day, we would go out and get married, without telling anyone, imagining the eye rolling and the disapproval (more from her family than mine)—so we sneaked into a register office, giggling like schoolkids. There was never any doubt. We lived in a republic of two, speaking our own language and making up our own rules. What else is there to say? Talking about happiness is boring.

Perhaps it was too perfect. Perhaps we were too self-contained, too comfortable. I don't know, I really don't. God knows I've thought about it often enough—how can the person you trust more than you trust yourself betray you? And I had no idea. Ironic, I know: the private detective, who uncovers adulterers every week, had no idea that his own wife was cheating on him.

The dark is nearly complete in my sitting room. It's the time of day the French, so I'm told, call *entre le chien et le loup*—between dog and wolf. First the sun sets, then, as dusk deepens, when the sky reaches a certain shade of dark blue that is not yet black, the dog retreats, and the wolf is waiting in the wings, or padding toward us around the corner. The shape in the shadows could be friend or foe. I wonder how long it lasts, the moment that belongs to neither. I stare out the window, in order to find out, at the tree that fills most of the view. It's an ash tree, barely in leaf even now, that cuts the sky into badly fitting jigsaw pieces. The pieces slowly lose their color. Is it now that the wolf appears? When the distinction between twig and sky is starting to blur?

Is it . . . now?

Did I miss it?

When I saw her the other night, I had to put my head between my knees until the feeling that I was turning inside out had passed. I don't even know why I went—back to the house we bought together and used to share.

I'm supposed to be moving on, as people keep saying. But I'm a creature of habit. I got into the habit of loving her. And anyway, when you move on, where are you supposed to go?

11.

JJ

I'm determined to go and live in France when I'm old enough. I wonder if I could persuade Mum to come and live here as well. Of course, I'll have to learn proper French—it turns out, whenever I try to ask for something, that I can't speak it nearly as well as I thought. I really wonder if our French teacher has ever been to France—when she speaks it, it sounds completely different from when the French speak it. Someone should tell her.

The day before we arrive back in boring old England, it's Gran's birthday. She's fifty-eight. In some ways, that sounds ancient, but I suppose it isn't, really, not compared to all those extremely old people staggering around Lourdes. I bought her a present when we were there. I couldn't think what to get for her before we left, so I risked having to buy something out there, which could have gone horribly wrong. But there turned out to be loads of gift shops in Lourdes. Unsurprisingly, there are lots of places selling religious stuff: endless statues of Mary and the grotto and Saint Bernadette (Bernadette is always smaller and cheaper than Mary). In this one shop, Gran picked up a sponge bag with the grotto on the front. It said on it "Get 'Holy' Clean!" And inside there was a sponge and bubble bath and some soap and stuff, all with jokey titles like "Cleanliness is next

to Godliness" and "You Filthy Sinner!" Gran laughed and laughed.
It was like they were saying, "Even though we're Christians, we still
have a sense of humor!" So I went back and bought it for her later. I
also got an enamel bracelet to give to Mum, and a bag of mints made
with holy water (for when your breath smells like Satan?).

When Gran opens her present—I got them to wrap it in nice
paper in the shop, after a lot of miming—she frowns first, and then
smiles and hugs me. I don't know whether she really likes it. She
seemed to love it in the shop, but now I'm not sure. But no one else
has got her a present at all, other than Christo, and that's because I
bought one for her from him, too—it's a little mirror, the kind
women keep in their handbags, with an enamel back covered with
blue flowers. It's really pretty. When she opens that, she smiles
straightaway, and leans over to kiss Christo. He grins delightedly.
Obviously, she knows Christo didn't buy it. Maybe she thinks Ivo
did, although she should know better. Great-uncle keeps saying,
"Girl, you don't look a day over twenty-one," which makes her laugh
(it's not true), but she's pleased. Even Ivo smiles and wishes her a
happy birthday. Everyone is in a reasonably good mood, for once.

I have this feeling, though, that we're all kind of holding our
breath. We have to be on our best behavior, as we're waiting for a
miracle, and we'd better not do anything that might put it off. I
keep glancing at Christo, to see if anything's changed about him.
I'm sure everyone else is doing the same. I know it's been only a few
days since he was washed in holy water, but still, you can't help
wondering. Some miracles are supposed to happen straightaway:
people getting up out of their wheelchairs and walking, blind people suddenly being able to see—that sort of thing. But so far I can't
see any change at all. We have to give it time, I suppose. Either that
or it's all a load of stupid crap, and I really don't want to think that.

But the farther we drive away from Lourdes, the more ridiculous
it all begins to seem. The plastic statues that are made in Taiwan

(I checked); the crowds of old, slow, sick people; the helpers with their eager eyes and friendly smiles. The Coke bottles full of holy tap water. I don't know. Of course we give Christo holy water to drink every day, and he seems to like it. I wonder if he realizes what's behind it all—he hasn't spoken recently. I don't know what he thinks; maybe he believes it—because he is six and we tell him that the holy water is going to make him better, and we're grown-ups, so we must be right. But we don't say anything to one another about miracles and stuff. In a weird way, it seems like a play we're putting on for a six-year-old's benefit. A play with a cast of not-very-good but desperate actors.

Apart from Gran's birthday, one other big thing happens on the way home. Ivo and Great-uncle make us drive to a village called Saint Jean-sur-Something. It's a bit out of our way, and we have to turn onto some pretty small roads to get there. It's about halfway up—somewhere in the middle of France but hillier than the way we came down. Wild country—bleak, not warm and leafy like farther south. Gran and me follow as they drive out of this little village and then stop. She's fed up, because it's taking longer this way and she's had enough of being abroad. It's not beautiful, like so many of the places we've come through, and I can't see why anyone would stop here. She sighs and lights a fag.

"Could have been past Paris by now."

I get out and go over to Great-uncle's trailer. Ivo lifts Christo out of the front of the van.

"Will you take him for a bit? You go with JJ, okay?"

I settle Christo on my hip.

"Why have we stopped here?"

Ivo gives me a look that makes me wander off without asking anything else.

"Shall we go and sit on the grass over there? Come on."

Ivo goes back into the trailer where his dad is and shuts the door.

Maybe they're having another row—they've been doing that a lot recently. Gran comes over as we're strolling along the verge. It's been raining, and it's wet and there's nowhere nice to sit.

"What're they doing now?" she asks me.

"Dunno."

"Bloody hell. I just want to get home, don't you? See your mum?"

"Yeah."

I do miss Mum, but in other ways I wish we weren't going home, which means going back to ordinary boring life, and school, and being hassled about next year's exams.

"I think it would be great to live in France."

I didn't really mean to say it, but it comes out in a rush.

Gran takes the fag out of her mouth and stares at me like I've just said wouldn't it be great to have two heads.

"Live here? And do what?"

"People do. Come and live here. You have to learn French, that's all."

"Oh, yeah?"

She smirks and looks at me in that annoying way that grown-ups have—like there are so many things you don't know, they can't even be bothered to start.

"What's wrong with that?"

Gran shrugs, still smirking.

"I could. I know what you're thinking. And you're wrong."

"Oh, you know what I'm thinking? Do you?"

I'm on thin ice here, but something makes me keep going.

"Yeah."

She pokes her finger in front of my face.

"You have no idea what I'm thinking, young man."

"You're thinking that people like us don't move to France. You're thinking, There's stupid JJ off again with his head in the clouds. He'll learn. When he goes totting with his granddad he'll get all that *gorjio* nonsense knocked out of him."

My cheeks are hot with daring as I say this. Gran's face goes hard.

"Don't you dare disrespect your granddad. Who do you think pays for your precious education? Granddad and his lorry—that's who."

"School's free, actually."

"Free? You should be working at your age, not sitting around on your arse. You should be helping your mother. Be a man. But no— you're like your father . . . a useless *gorjio*!"

I really think Gran's going to hit me for a moment. I've actually forgotten that I'm still holding Christo in my arms and we're arguing over his head, ridiculous as that sounds.

Gran must be furious—she hardly ever uses curse words, although whenever she's cross with me she brings up my useless *gorjio* dad. This is really unfair, as a) I can't help who my dad was, and b) I don't even know his name—I don't know anything about him, so what can I say in response?

Just then Christo holds up his finger and pokes me in the chin. It's his way of saying, "Stop shouting, you two."

"I'm sorry, Christo. We're being silly. Aren't we?"

Gran says, "Yeah, Christo. I'm sorry. All this driving's making me tired. I want to go home."

Glaring at me, still: "I think we all need to go home."

Ivo gets out of the trailer and lights a fag. He walks over to us.

Gran says to him, "Let's get going, for God's sake. My grandson's driving me up the frigging wall."

"Sorry, Auntie Kath. Dad and I wanted to have a chat. You see, the reason why we stopped here is because . . ."

He looks back along the road.

"This is where Christina died. On this road."

"Oh," I say.

"God, Ivo," says Gran, crossing herself. "You should've said."

Ivo shrugs.

"We could go and visit her grave, if you like," Gran says.

Ivo looks at my right ear.

"No," he says. "She was . . . cremated. You know."

"Oh," I say again.

I look up and down the road, thinking we should pick some flowers and leave them here. But there don't seem to be any—just a lot of grass. You can't leave a bunch of grass for someone who's died.

Ivo reaches out to take Christo, who leans his head on Ivo's shoulder. Gran and Ivo walk up and down the roadside, talking in low voices, ignoring me. Of course Gran remembers Christina. I don't—I was only two when she died, and I hadn't even met her, as that was when Mum was still in disgrace in Basingstoke.

Rooting around in the grass, I find some tiny little flowers, and the more I look, the more I find. I get quite carried away and sort of forget why I'm picking them, even. Eventually I've got quite a respectable bunch, with some ferny leaves and things. It looks really nice. I wonder about this person I never met. I don't know whether she liked flowers, but who doesn't? I walk back to the others. They're climbing back into the vehicles, and when I get there, there's no one to look at my bunch.

Gran shouts from the Land Rover: "JJ! Come on. What're you doing grubbing about?"

The engine starts up with a threatening roar.

"See you around, then!"

I lay the flowers on the verge, saying, "This is for you, Christina, from your nephew, JJ." And then I get in.

12.

St. Luke's Hospital

The visions return now and again, just when I think I'm free of them. They attack without warning, and leave just as suddenly. I see things that I know aren't there. Mostly—and I don't know what I have done to deserve this—the visions are horrific, terrifying. Not at all like the effects of acid, which were, as far as I remember, wondrous, stupid, and extremely funny. Although this time, before the dog-woman arrived, there was something wonderful about the curtains at the window. Blazing, extraordinary. That's not a good description, but the words don't exist to describe these things.

She's a stranger but with something familiar about her. Bad familiarity—like when you see a middle-aged man in the street and realize that the last time you saw him you were both at school, and that your face must be as changed as his. The creature is riding me, like before, and yet I'm nagged by the fear that she doesn't want this, that I have in some way forced her. There is an atmosphere of . . . unwillingness, I suppose. The unwillingness may even be mine, but I am powerless to stop myself. Then, in the—for want of a better word—dream, she begins to devour me. She has long teeth. She has claws and too many heads. It is no longer a woman at all but a creature of horror. But I am paralyzed and mute, helpless to save myself. The thing reaches into my chest—the pain is abominable—and tears something out of me. It is my shame, the part of me I most despise, the thing I can't live without.

Why am I thinking, "Rose"?

It's a relief when Dr. Zybnieska marches in with her clipboard and sits on my bedside chair. She looks unusually pleased with herself.

"Well, Ray, how are we this morning?"

The volume of her voice is always a shock. I try not to flinch.

"All right," I murmur. My voice sounds okay this morning, to my ears.

"Good. Any more nightmares last night?"

I shake my head firmly.

She leans over and picks up my left hand and examines it. She scribbles something on her clipboard. Looks at the chart over my bed.

"And the right hand? Still nothing?"

I lift my head and glance at it. I can't lift it, so it's the only way of checking it's still there.

She produces a metal instrument and presses it into the flesh of my wrist. I can't feel a thing. She makes a note.

"Okay. We finally have some test results."

She looks excited. Like someone about to deliver a punch line.

"The toxicology results show diverse traces of tropane alkaloids in your system!"

I say nothing, as I don't know what to say.

"We have found traces of what looks like scopolamine, hyoscyamine . . . also ergotamine. Very interesting. That would certainly explain the hallucinations you've been having."

Hallucinations. Thank God. Thank you, God. Not real. There was never anything, nor anyone, there. I try to tell myself this, but . . .

"You know what they are?"

"No."

"Alkaloids that come from poisonous plants. More to the point, they are psychotropic in effect. Were you experimenting? Tripping? Maybe an accidental overdose?"

I shake my head as vigorously as I can manage. In my long-gone experimental days, no bad trip came close to these horrors.

"You would have to have ingested two or three different toxic plant species to show these results. Do you know how that happened? Do you grow your own vegetables? Pick mushrooms in the woods?"

I shake my head, thinking, She should see the contents of my fridge. Like Dad, who, having experienced hedgerow food as a child, embraced processed food with evangelical fervor, I know that natural is not always better.

She makes a note.

"Strange. Ergotamine . . . Do you know what that is?"

"No."

"Its more common name is ergot."

This doesn't mean a whole lot more to me. She seems enlivened by the whole thing. From my point of view, I don't see that it's that exciting.

"Ergot is a fungus that grows on cereals. Where fungicides are not used, it can still occur, especially in wet summers—like now. But there probably hasn't been a case of ergot poisoning in this country since the Middle Ages!"

She leans back, beaming.

"So you are a very rare case."

"Thank you."

"LSD is a man-made derivative. Perhaps some people still use ergot to get high. Is that what you did?"

"No."

"No idea how you could have ingested it?"

"No."

I say no, but, of course, I have begun to form an idea.

"Will it go . . . Will I recover?"

"There is every reason to hope so. The picture is quite complex . . . The paralysis is unusual, although there are documented cases of ergot poisoning causing paralysis and hallucination. Some people think that cases of bewitchment in the Middle Ages were due to eating bread contaminated with ergot. Perhaps every case. You're very lucky. All of these compounds can be fatal."

"Will I remember what happened?"

"We'll have to wait and see. But with scopolamine poisoning, memory loss is often permanent."

"Is that a fungus, too?"

"No. It comes from plants of the datura family. Deadly nightshade and henbane. Any part of the plant is poisonous, but it has a bitter taste, so it's not so easy to eat by accident. It's a deliriant, but highly toxic, easy to overdose."

She's watching me, I suppose, to see if I start to look shamefaced. The last thing I remember is being in the trailer. Beer. Food. A peace offering. Smiling. Talking. It was all . . . normal.

I shake my head, meaning, I don't know, perhaps. Then something does swim into my mind.

"Isn't ergot poisoning the same thing as Saint Anthony's fire?"

"That's a kind of ergotism, yes. Lucky for you, you didn't ingest enough for that. Saint Anthony's fire is the gangrenous form of ergotism. The capillaries constrict, your extremities shrivel up and drop off—but it's almost always fatal, anyway. You've got a little desquamation, but that's all."

I must look puzzled, because she picks up my left hand again and turns it around to show me the skin on the forearm, flaking off as though I've had too much sun.

"There—not enough blood getting to the skin. Not serious, in your case. You only ate enough to cause the convulsive form: muscle spasms, weakness, hallucinations . . ."

"So . . ." I don't really know how to put this. "If you took these things deliberately, what would you hope to happen?"

"I'm not an expert on this kind of thing, but I suppose you would expect to get high, to have hallucinations. But you'd be taking a huge risk."

"Could you use it to poison someone? To kill them?"

She looks troubled.

"I would think if you wanted to be sure of killing someone, you would give them a higher dose. You have had a very low dose. Scopolamine is used to make people forget. Where I come from, they used to give it during childbirth. It was called 'twilight sleep.' Women forgot the pain."

"So I won't remember?"

"Perhaps not."

She looks at me with a calculating face, assessing something. Perhaps she's about to tell me something else, but she doesn't.

I have to think about this. Put the pieces together. There is a gap in my memory, but there are things I do remember. I know them without a doubt. And perhaps—I'm not saying more than that, just perhaps—my being here, in this state, is another piece of evidence. Because that's the only way it makes sense.

I wonder when Hen is coming back to see me. Did he say? I'm sure I need to talk to him. Wasn't there something I needed to tell him? Something about Rose . . . Something important but just out of sight, like a distant shore hidden by fog.

Then I remember it. And though Hen doesn't know yet (how could I not have told him?), it doesn't seem that important now, to tell the truth. It's no match for the overwhelming desire to sleep.

It was all such a long time ago. After all, it's not as though by finding her, I've saved her.

I'm far, far too late for that.

13.

Ray

It turns out to be off a slip road of the A32, not too far from Bishop's Waltham in Hampshire. The road drops down behind a cutting, and there's a half-hidden turning between overgrown hedges that leads toward a scrubby piece of woodland. A belt of evergreens planted as a windbreak ensures that passersby will simply pass by. You have to drive through a narrow, angled opening to discover the paddock where the Jankos live. If I hadn't been told the trailers were there, I would never have spotted them. I know this is farming land, privately rented; rather different from the council site where I met Kizzy Wilson. Here, the trailers—I count five—are arranged in a loose circle, tow bars outward. The large windows face one another, but small trees grow between them here and there—only the central space is clear, and there are signs of a fire. Other vehicles—a late-model BMW and a Land Rover—are parked behind the trailers. There must be other vehicles elsewhere, judging by large, deep wheel ruts in the mud. There's a pile of bin bags next to where I have driven in, but otherwise it's fairly tidy. There's no sign of anyone. Not even dogs. But a small generator hums, and a smudge of smoke comes from the chimney pipe of one of the trailers.

I get out of the car, shut the door, and wait for something to happen.

A door opens in the largest trailer, bright with chrome and glossy paint, and a small, stout woman comes out. She is in her late fifties, with dyed black teased hair fluffed around her face and heavy tan makeup. She wears a brown-and-cream trouser suit and holds a cigarette in her hand.

"This is private land. No trespassers."

"Hello. My name's Ray Lovell. I'm looking for Ivo and Tene Janko. I was told they might be here."

She looks me up and down for a moment or two.

"Yeah? Who told you that?"

"Tene's sister, Luella."

"Lulu? Christ! You've seen Lulu?"

"Er, yes."

"What did you say your name was?"

"Ray Lovell. Are you Mrs. Smith?"

Her mouth twitches—she obviously doesn't want to answer.

"What's this about?"

"Well, it's about . . . I'm trying to track down Rose Wood—Ivo's wife."

"Bloody hell. She's not here, so you've wasted your time."

"I know it was a long time ago. I'd just like to talk to them. I'm a private investigator. I'm talking to everyone who knew her."

She seems to think about it for a minute: a minute in which she scrutinizes me carefully. She has doubtless registered my Gypsy name, but even without that, she could tell by looking at me. I think of what Leon said—how he was right: a *gorjio* wouldn't stand a chance.

At last she says, "Hang on," and goes to another of the trailers—the one farthest from the entrance. I look around at the others as I wait. The woman—who I assume is Kath Smith—came out of the most expensive trailer, and the largest. The one she has just gone into is older; a 1960s Westmorland Star about twenty feet long. The other two are smaller, and modest by comparison. I wonder if anyone else is watching me—there are usually plenty of people in a Gypsy site, lots of children and dogs—although I've seen no sign of either here. I'm curious, but I don't want to poke around too obviously. It would be rude, so I wait by my car until she reappears and tells me to come in.

Inside, I feel as though I'm stepping into another era.

The trailer is dim, the windows obscured by short net curtains, and there's a faint odor of tar. The kitchen area is bleak, but the stove is lit, making it warm and stuffy. At the back, right in the middle of the bay window, an elderly man sits behind a fold-down table. He seems large for the space, or perhaps it's the ornaments that make it feel crowded—the top cupboards are full of china and cut glass, and almost every inch of the wood-veneered walls is hidden by photographs, plates, and pictures.

"Please . . . don't mind if I don't get up—not so spry as I used to be."

Tene Janko has thick dark gray hair springing off his forehead and curling over his collar. Dark brown eyes, a pleasantly weathered face, and a heavy mustache. Deep lines around his eyes give him a look of good humor. He looks like a romantic painting of a Gypsy elder; a handsome, old Romany *rai* on the cover of a children's book. I didn't think anyone looked like that anymore.

From where he sits, he extends his hand to me and shakes firmly.

"Pleasure to meet you, Mr. Janko . . . Thank you."

I ease myself onto the seat he indicates.

"Kath, let's have some tea."

He speaks without looking at her. She goes to the kitchen through the keyhole arch, and puts on a kettle.

"Perhaps Mr. Lovell fancies a nip."

"Oh, no, I'm fine with—"

"Well, I do."

Kath glares at her brother, bangs down the tea caddy, and goes out of the trailer.

Tene looks at me, elbows on the table.

"It's a lovely trailer you've got here, Mr. Janko."

"Thank you. I've kept it the way my wife had it, when she was alive."

"Oh . . . I'm sorry to hear that . . ."

"So you're a private detective. Never met one of those before."

"You haven't missed much."

"Feel like I'm in the movies . . ."

"Well . . . it's not that exciting, Mr. Janko."

"Call me Tene."

"That's an unusual name."

"An old family name. But you are a Romanichal, so not familiar with such names."

"Well, my father settled. My mother was a *gorjio*."

"But you're still a Lovell."

"Yes."

"I thought all private eyes were ex-policemen, but something tells me you're not. Nor ex-army, either."

"No. I went to work for a private investigator after I left college. And liked it."

"College? You've done well. Your daddy must be very proud of you."

"He's passed away now. But he was, yes."

"He was a postman, wasn't he? Bart Lovell."

I feel a mild shock, and pause to breathe slowly.

"That's right. Did you ever meet him?"

Tene shakes his shaggy head.

"He wasn't a one for the fairs, was he? Wouldn't go to Epsom or Stowe, nothing like that."

"No, well, he was a postman, as you said. He didn't have much time for holidays."

Tene nods.

"As for us, we've always kept on the road."

"That must be hard, these days."

He shrugs.

"So where is your family from? I don't know the name Janko."

"My granddaddy came over with the Kalderash in the last century. From the Balkans, what was still the Ottoman Empire then. But he forgot to go home. Got married to a Romanichal girl name of Talaitha Lee. And they said her mammy was a Lovell. So you see, we must be related."

He smiles broadly. I take this as an indication that I am to listen to him with a large helping of salt.

"Could be."

I smile, but I fear deep black blood cannot be far away.

"Girl's father hire you, did he?"

"I'm afraid I can't disclose my client."

He actually winks at me then, nodding. Like an actor in a silent film, all his gestures seem larger than necessary.

"Why now, 's what I'm wondering. She's been gone a long time."

"I'm sorry I can't be more open about that. I'm just talking to everyone who knew Rose—which you did. And Ivo, of course."

I wait for a bit, to see what comes up next.

"'Twas very sad, all that. Her leaving. We were all very sad. Terrible."

"Do you know where she is now?"

"I don't. And if you told me she was standing outside this minute, I'd have nothing to say to her."

"Could you tell me what happened?"

"Certainly. I don't know what her daddy told you, but this is the truth—and who else would know? She ran off with a *gorjio* and left my son and my dear grandson, and we've never seen her since. Not hide nor hair."

"When did this happen?"

"Six years ago . . . more or less."

"It would help a lot if you could tell me what you remember about that."

Tene shakes his head, wagging his shock of gray hair. There's something leonine about him, almost regal. He stares out the window; painters would go wild for that profile.

"A very sad thing. What mother could go off and leave her child like that?"

"That's what I'm trying to find out."

Tene looks at me and grins.

"We should have hired you six years ago!"

"Did you ever try and find her?"

He shrugs.

"She ran off with another man. You can't force people, can you?"

At that moment, Kath returns with a bottle and a tray. Richly painted and gilded china, a cut-glass bowl full of sugar lumps, and plates piled with Jaffa cakes. She puts the tray on the table in front of Tene and pours tea into shell-thin cups. She plonks the brandy in front of her brother and goes out again.

"And, of course, my grandson is afflicted. Afflicted from the day he was born."

"I'm sorry to hear it. Your sister Luella said something of the sort. What's wrong with him?"

"One of those . . . blood things."

"I don't understand—one of those blood things?"

"A disease in the blood. He was born with it. There are others in the family who have suffered. There is no cure."

He waves his hand, as if it's too painful to talk about. He unscrews the brandy and pours a small glass for each of us.

"They come up with new cures all the time . . . thanks . . . so maybe, there will be."

Tene nods, looking at the table. His face is tragic.

"It must be hard for all of you."

"Yes. But we must follow our Lord's example, mustn't we? Bear our burdens without complaining. Not run away from them."

"Is that what Rose did?"

"Some people don't have the strength."

"Can you remember the order of events? Exactly when she left? How old was the baby?"

He shakes his head with a deep, theatrical sigh.

"It would be a great help. For example, where were you pitched at the time? Was it near here?"

"I think it was maybe . . . It was winter. It was cold. It was a good stopping place, the Black Patch—before they sold it off. Yeah, that was it, up by Seviton."

I nod, not knowing the exact place, but there used to be hundreds of stopping places on common ground, or private land owned by a tolerant farmer. Now, over the last twenty or thirty years, most have been swallowed up by developers building new houses. Or councils have got too nervy to let people stop, what with the locals on their backs all the time.

"When is your grandson's birthday?"

"Twenty-fifth October. He was just a few months old when she went. Five months, four . . . something like that."

"Was it evident by then, his illness?"

"Yes. Oh, yes. He nearly died. We had to take him to hospital."

"And how long after that did she leave?"

"A couple of months . . . Maybe less? It's hard to remember."

I note this down.

"Had anything happened just before she ran off? Had she rowed with her husband?"

"That wouldn't be for me to say. All I know is one morning she wasn't there. Just went, leaving Christo, leaving all of us."

"Christo's your grandson? Did she take a lot of clothes? Personal possessions?"

"Well, I'm sure she took clothes. She wouldn't'a gone bare, would she?"

He bursts out laughing, as though simply referring to a woman's nakedness is a shocking indiscretion.

"If someone takes a lot of possessions—clothes, money, personal items—they've usually planned it well in advance."

"She took most of everything she had . . . Yes, she planned it, all right."

I flex my writing hand to ease out the cramp.

"Can you remember the names of her friends? Acquaintances?"

Tene shrugs again.

"I can't honestly remember. She used to borrow the car and go off now and again, but I don't know where she went. Never met anyone, I don't think."

"Rose was a proper Romany, wasn't she? A full-blooded Romany."

"Yeah."

"I believe she was a shy girl. She didn't have a lot of friends, according to her family . . . I'm just wondering, where would she have got to know a *gorjio*?"

"I don't know, Mr. Lovell. But she did go off, after we found out about Christo; it was then. She couldn't really cope. She must have met someone then."

"But you thought it was a *gorjio*, not a Gypsy, isn't that right? That's what . . . your sister said. What made you think that?"

Tene leans suddenly toward me, his hand bunches on the table; it's the first sign of aggression he's shown. "If it was a Gypsy, we'd have known about it. We'd have heard. You know that. But there was nothing—so . . ."

He leans back and drains his glass in a final sort of way.

"You're being very helpful, Mr. Janko, but I'd really like to talk to Ivo. Is he here?"

Tene shakes his head.

"He was broken when she left. All alone with that tiny baby. His dear mother had passed on by then, God bless her. What was he to do?"

"What did he do?"

Tene looks fierce again, the lion stretching out his claws.

"What a man does: he's father and mother to the child. Bringing him up all on his own."

"He hasn't married again?"

Tene shakes his head.

"It's hard for him. With a sick child. Ivo does everything for him. Christo is his life."

I nod sympathetically.

"They live here with you?"

"It was terrible for him. There's nothing he can tell you. He was asleep with the baby when she left. He kept waiting for her to come back. Not knowing—that's the worst. If she'd've left a note saying she wasn't coming back—that would have been better. He wouldn't have had to wait for months . . . years. Nearly drove him crackers. If you go and stir it all up again—I don't want him going crackers. He's the only parent that poor boy's got."

"I understand. But he is still her husband. Don't you think it's strange that even her own family haven't heard from her since?"

Tene blows air out of his nostrils in an impatient snort.

"If I'd have done something like that, I'd be ashamed to show my face, too."

"What if something had happened, and she couldn't come back?"

Tene looks at me, astonished.

"Couldn't come back?"

"It's possible, isn't it?"

"Like . . . kidnapped, you mean?"

"Not that, especially. Something may have happened to her afterward. Finding out what did happen . . . could give everyone some peace."

Tene snorts again.

"My old dad used to say, 'Let sleeping dogs lie.' And I've always found that to be advice worth taking."

I smile inadvertently. It's not a cliché you often hear as a private investigator, although I feel like saying it to clients sometimes—on average once or twice a week. I never do, though.

"My dad used to say that, too."

"Well, then. I'm asking you not to bother my son. It won't help you, and it will hurt him."

"I appreciate what you've said, but I can't promise not to talk to him."

Tene glares at me and then seems to make up his mind about something.

"I understand, Mr. Lovell. You're just making a living like the next man."

As I'm getting my card out of my pocket, I stand up and knock my knee against the table. Tene reaches out a hand to steady it, lifting the lace tablecloth as he does so. And I realize, with a shock, that his seat is a wheelchair.

"I'm so sorry . . ."

A checked blanket is tucked over withered legs, out of proportion to the rest of his body. I'm embarrassed. And I can't believe I didn't notice before.

"Whoops-a-daisy." Tene is unconcerned.

"If you think of anything else, Mr. Janko—if you remember something that might be relevant—anything at all . . . You never know what can have a bearing . . ."

Kath Smith is outside, to watch me clear off.

"Got what you wanted, then?"

"Yes, thank you for everything. I don't suppose you can tell me anything about when Rose left? You don't know who she went with?"

"We weren't there. It was just Tene and Ivo and her. We heard later on."

"Do you know where I could find Ivo?"

"Last we heard, he was up in the Fens somewhere."

"He travels?"

"Yeah."

"Whereabouts?"

A pause.

"Wisbech way. I think." She takes out a packet of cigarettes and lights one. "Last we heard."

"Okay. Thanks."

I smile breezily.

"Nice to have met you, Mrs. Smith."

As I pick my way through the worst of the mud to my car, I think there is a whisper of movement from one of the trailers— perhaps a flicker of a curtain. I wonder if Ivo Janko isn't in the end trailer. If he isn't, I'll eat my investigator's license for breakfast. But I don't want to antagonize them. Not yet. And after six years, I don't suppose another day or two is going to make a great deal of difference to Rose Janko, wherever she is now.

14.

J J

After class today, our form teacher, Mr. Stewart, held me back until everyone else had gone.

"Well, JJ," he started. Never a good sign. "End of term soon."

"Mm."

"And we still haven't decided about your exam subjects, have we?"

"Erm, no."

"Your mum didn't reply to the letter we sent out."

"Oh."

That's not surprising, as we don't live where they think we do.

As if he suspected something of the sort, he gave me an envelope.

"Here's another copy. We'd like her to come in so we can all sit down and talk about your future."

I nodded. It sounds so serious when they say things like that.

"Will you make sure she gets it this time? There's nothing to worry about. You could have a very promising future, you know."

"Okay."

He smiled. I think he was really trying to be nice. Mr. Stewart's all right, unlike some of the teachers, even if he loses his temper sometimes. He can't stand it when people muck about; he really shouts. Sometimes he throws chalk.

After school, Granddad picks me up in the lorry. He's been out totting. I'm glad everyone else has gone, because nobody else gets picked up from school in a lorry. It's not that I mind, really—it's just that some people take the piss, and I can't really be bothered with that. Granddad's all right. He doesn't go on about how I should be working at my age. Although he doesn't say so, I think he agrees with Mum about school. It's fine not being able to read and stuff if you work with your family—tarmacking, say, or scrap dealing. But you have to stick together for that to work; there has to be lots of you—lots of children, or brothers marrying sisters (not their own sisters, obviously), and our family isn't very good at that, on account of the disease. Even without the disease, look at Uncle Ivo and Mum: they haven't managed to stick together with anyone. So they don't think there's much hope for me. If you're on your own, it's better to have an education. Anyway, I like school, in some ways. I like reading; I always have. This makes me a bit strange in my family; Mum will read only if it's a form, or the paper if there's a good murder. Great-uncle can barely read at all, but he knows more than anyone I know.

Last year, when I first came to the school, we were on the council site. Some of Granddad's relatives had gone on the road, and they let us sublet. You're not supposed to, but still. It wasn't that nice. The other people weren't friendly, apart from the girls who used to hang around Ivo. But most of them were young and stupid. By the time a girl's Ivo's age—he's twenty-eight—she's been married for years, unless there's something wrong with her. And hardly anyone gets divorced. You don't want to marry someone who's been married before, or marry someone who's a lot older than you. It's just not done. When they told us we had to leave because we were illegal, we weren't that sorry.

This is a good site, the one we're on now. It's private, and there aren't any neighbors to kick up a fuss. Granddad can bring scrap back, and there's even a stream of clean water. Great-uncle and

Gran love it—it's like the old days, apparently. Ivo likes it, too; he is a very private person, and he didn't like the girls pestering him all the time, and cooing over Christo, just because he's so cute.

Mum's still out when we get back, so I have tea with Gran and Granddad. Granddad puts the telly on, and we eat bread and butter and watch an ancient American cop show. I think I get on best with Granddad when we're watching telly. Gran is in a bit of a mood, but neither of us asks her why, which is sort of deliberate, to see how annoyed she'll get. She gets her own back by waiting until the most exciting bit in the cop show to tell us.

"A private detective came snooping round today."

"Kath, shush. We're watching," says Granddad.

I say, "What?"

"He came round asking all these questions about Rose."

"Rose?"

Now she has Granddad's attention.

"Can you believe it? After all this time, her family want to find her."

"Well, they won't find her here."

"I know, but Tene's decided he doesn't want him talking to Ivo. We said he was in the Fens. Wisbech. So don't either of you say any different, if he comes back."

Granddad shrugs, turns back to *Dragnet*, and turns up the volume to let us know it's over, as far as he's concerned.

I stare at Gran, wondering if she's made all this up. It seems incredible—far too exciting to happen to us.

"What did he look like?"

"What did he look like?"

"Yeah. The private eye."

"Well, he's a Gypsy."

"Really? Is he coming back?"

A Gypsy private detective—I've never heard of such a thing.

"What are you so excited about?"

"I'm not excited."

Later, I go back home to find Mum and Ivo and Christo about to have supper. We quite often eat together, what with Mum working and Christo to take care of. Mum and Ivo are talking in low voices when I come in, and Christo's watching telly. He cheers when he sees me. I stick out my hand, and he twines his fingers into mine: it's our thing.

"Here's trouble," says Ivo. He used to say this when I was little, but it sounds a bit weird now that I'm fourteen. It reminds me that it's been a while since he's said it.

"You heard about this private detective?"

"Tchah." Ivo rolls his eyes.

"It's daft, them coming round now. What do they think they're going to find out?"

This is Mum. From this I gather they've been talking about it, too.

"You're supposed to be in Wisbech."

Ivo grins at me.

"Yeah, well . . . could be, I suppose."

"Great-uncle tell you he's a Gypsy?"

"Yeah. Half, anyway."

"I've never heard of a Gypsy private detective. Have you?"

"No. Fancy it, do you?"

"Dunno."

Mum smiles. I'm glad she's not too tired tonight. Sometimes when she's been driving around doing deliveries all day, she's so tired she can hardly speak. She just collapses on the settee and falls asleep after supper. She usually cheers up when Ivo and Christo are around, though. She and Ivo are good friends.

There is one thing, though, that I'm not glad about. None of us are. Christo hasn't been very well. It's been four weeks since we got back from Lourdes, and he hasn't got any better. In fact, I think he's got worse. He talks less, and seems weaker. He does almost nothing but lie around on the settee at Ivo's or ours, looking at everything with eyes that seem too big for his face. He's so small and thin—about half the size of other six-year-olds. And sometimes he doesn't even look at things. He just lies there, and you can hear his breathing, as though he's panting, even though he's not moving at all. Sometimes I want to scream. Why can't anyone do something?

How long does it take God to cure a six-year-old? I asked Ivo how long afterward before he started getting better, and he said he couldn't really remember, but he thought it was so gradual you couldn't really notice—which wasn't very helpful.

I think we have to face the fact that there isn't going to be any miracle, not this time. In fact, let's face it, folks, it was all a big, fucking, stupid waste of time. And now what?

15.

Ray

The scrap of paper with Luella's number on it is buried in the pile by the phone, where it's been for some days. I know it's there, but I sit by the phone for a couple long minutes before picking it up and dialing.

To my surprise it's picked up almost immediately. Her voice sounds more relaxed than it did before, less defensive.

"Hi. It's Ray Lovell."

A pause.

"Oh."

The defensiveness returns, along with reinforcements.

"I'm sorry to disturb you again, but I wondered if I could ask you some more questions?"

"I've got to go out. What is it?"

"Well, maybe we could meet? Whenever's convenient. I can come to you if you like."

"Did you see my brother?"

"Yes."

I don't say anything else. Perhaps she has some vestige of curiosity about him.

"I've got to go through Wimbledon. There's a pub on the

Broadway, the Green Man. Near the theater. I could meet you there at nine. For half an hour. That's all."

"Thank you very much, Miss Janko. I appreciate your taking the time. I'll see you there."

To be honest, I don't know what she can tell me. I'm not even sure what I'm going to ask. Possibly, I'd be better off spying on the encampment down in Hampshire, although that sort of surveillance is extremely difficult, with no buildings or vehicles around to camouflage you. It would mean hopping about in the bushes with a long lens like an idiot. Tomorrow is always a better day to be an idiot.

This time she's waiting for me; I'm on time, but she's early, sitting at a corner table, smoking a cigarette. She's dressed more casually, in jeans and a long baggy sweater that makes her look even smaller. Still the heels and lipstick, though; I have a feeling she doesn't leave home without them.

"Thanks for meeting me, Miss Janko. Let me get you something."

"Just a tea, please. And call me Lulu. I keep thinking you're talking to someone else."

"Lulu. Gotcha."

I get a tea, and a half for myself. No overdoing it tonight.

"So how was my brother?"

"I didn't realize he was in a wheelchair."

She shrugs and sips her tea.

"Must make living on the road very difficult."

"He's got family to run around after him."

"Still . . ."

"Did you find out anything about Rose?"

"Not really. I wanted to see Ivo, but Tene doesn't want me talking to him. Said it would be upsetting. Where does Ivo travel?"

"With Tene, or always used to."

"They said he was in the Fens."

She shrugs again; the sharpness of the gesture—though nothing else about her—reminds me of Tene.

"Maybe he is."

"You don't know?"

"I told you, we don't have much to do with each other. I haven't seen them for . . . about three years."

"You spoke to Tene, though?"

"Yeah. He is my brother."

"Of course. I met your sister, too. And I . . . I got the impression that Ivo was there. Why should she and Tene hide him?"

Lulu frowns at me.

"You think they're lying?"

"I think they're protecting him. But why?"

"Like he said, I suppose he's still upset about it. And if he doesn't know anything . . ."

"People usually know more than they think they do."

"Is that why you're asking me where my nephew is? Even though I told you I don't know?"

I smile in acknowledgment. "I suppose so. And you have a phone."

She tuts, smiles, and looks at the ceiling.

Are we flirting? I ask myself.

"Rose buggered off a long time ago. She didn't want anything to do with them. Why should they want anything to do with her? Or with anyone who wants to ask about her?"

I sip my half and find it almost empty. Her tea is still steaming.

"So, er, why don't you see your family?"

Lulu sighs.

"You liked him, didn't you?"

"Tene? I . . . He's quite a charismatic figure."

I suppose she's right. I did like him.

"Yeah. Charismatic."

She makes it sound like a dirty word.

"You don't go round shouting that you're a Gypsy, do you? Nor do I. But Tene does. Does this big act. Only it's not even an act. When he thinks about anything, it's Gypsy first, everything else second."

She shakes her head, not meeting my eyes now.

"It's not the beginning and end of everything to me. You can't live like that anymore, can you? Going on about the old days and the 'pure black blood.' Like there ever was any."

That phrase again.

"Is that something Tene cares about?"

"Yeah. Not just blood. The culture, you know—the life. Not being forced to settle in a house and just . . . disappear."

"Like I have."

"And me. I'm the traitor."

"Traitor? That's a strong word."

She shrugs again. She isn't going to rise to my prodding.

"There wasn't going to be anything for me in that life. A girl's a slave. What have you got to look forward to? Get married, get beaten up. Not again, thanks. I've got my little house and my job, and it hasn't been easy with the amount of school I got."

"Were you close to your brother, as children?"

"God, no. He's seventeen years older, so he was more like an uncle. When I was born, he'd already moved out on his own."

"Any other brothers and sisters? Apart from Kath."

"Another sister."

"Ah."

"I expect you'll want her number, too."

"That would be very helpful."

"I doubt it. Sibby lives in Ireland. You're welcome to give it a try."

"I wanted to find out a bit about Christo's illness. It seems that that might have frightened Rose off. Your brother didn't say what it was, but he said there was no cure."

"That's right."

Her face tightens. If she was flirting before, she isn't now.

"He said others in the family had suffered."

She drinks her tea.

"Yeah."

"Sorry, I, em . . ."

She lights another cigarette, frowning at her recalcitrant lighter. She smokes too much, I think, or maybe just smokes during difficult conversations. She speaks quickly.

"We had two other brothers. Istvan died when he was a baby, and Matty . . . He wasn't so bad, he made it to thirty."

"God, I'm sorry. Is that why Tene . . ."

"No. No, he was in a road accident. Tene's fine—in that way. But he and Marta had two sons before Ivo. Stevie . . . again, was only a baby. Milo was six."

I can't think of anything to say to this.

"They just took Christo to Lourdes. I suppose anything's worth a try. It worked for Ivo."

"Ivo was ill, too?"

"Yeah, when he was young. But he got better."

"I thought you said there isn't a cure."

She shrugs. I like it when she shrugs, I decide.

"I dunno. Maybe Lourdes is the cure. Maybe he had something else. Not the same."

"Is it just . . . boys?"

She looks up at me; her eyes are pained. I wish I wasn't making her look like that.

"Yeah. Seems to be."

"I'm so sorry."

She puts herself together again. As if she's held together with poppers: *snap, snap, snap.*

I wonder about her marriage. Did she have any children?

She looks down, checks her watch.

"I have to go to work."

"Okay. What sort of work do you do?"

"Go-go dancer."

"Oh, great."

A brief, sarcastic smile.

"I'm a carer."

"Oh, great."

"I like it."

"You work in a home?"

"Private."

"Well . . . thanks for meeting me, and . . . talking to me."

"Good luck."

"Can I ring you again?"

It doesn't come out quite how I meant it to.

"In case something else comes up."

She shrugs. Her shoulders make me think of wings—she is unfurling them, taking off.

"Can't stop you."

She taps out of the bar, and I listen to the receding tick of her heels on the pavement, like time ebbing away.

It's appalling, if what she says is true. I think it is true. It makes me think of something . . . the Russian Tsars—didn't they have a disease that affected only the boys, and therefore the Tsar's succession? Something to do with Queen Victoria, too, I think, but can't remember what. My dad would have known. And if he didn't, he would have looked it up. But my brother, Tom, got *The Book of Knowledge*. Jen said it smelled, and wouldn't have it in the house.

16.

JJ

One of the worst things about living in a trailer is that you can't ask people back to yours. I've noticed this at school, with girls, especially: they'll be talking and stuff at the end of classes, or walking to the bus stop, and one of them might say casually, "Come back to my house. We can study/have tea/listen to the Pet Shop Boys LP." Easy. No big deal. Then they get on the bus and go and have a lovely time.

I never walk to the bus stop, because our site isn't anywhere near a bus stop, so there's not much point. Usually Mum picks me up, often in the van that she's driving—which might be a florist's van, or a van for delivering bread. Once, embarrassingly, she picked me up in a refrigerator truck with "Best Sausages" on the side in huge letters. Danny Sinclair and Ben Goldman—who else?—saw, and I was called Sausages for about a year afterward. Other times she picks me up in Granddad's car, which is cool, as it's a BM. Very occasionally Gran or Granddad come and get me—and that will be at whatever time suits them, so I've spent endless hours hanging around on street corners, looking suspicious, probably. Mum usually shouts at them later, but it doesn't make them any quicker. Whenever she has a complaint against them they remind her that she's lucky they took her—and me—back at all. I'm used to waiting.

Only once did I try inviting anyone back to our trailers. It was

Stella Barclay, shortly after I started going to this school, when she seemed to be my friend. I don't know whether Stella is still my friend or not. She is one of the nicest people at my school, and we've had some really good conversations. She likes the same sort of music as I do—she introduced me to The Smiths, who I love, and not just because my name is Smith. But now she's become friends with a girl called Katie Williams, and when they're together she doesn't really talk to me. It's like she doesn't notice me anymore. So I don't push myself onto her.

Anyway, this was last year. I'd told her that I lived in a trailer—this is when we were on the council site—and she seemed interested in it. So I asked Mum if I could invite a friend back for tea. She looked a bit wary but said of course I could, as long as I gave her some warning, so she could make it tidy and get something nice in to eat. So I asked Stella if she would like to, and she said yes. Then I asked Mum, and she said okay, what about tomorrow, and I told Stella, but that day she had a judo class, so I went back and forth until we had set a date—it was all quite complicated, mainly because of judo and clarinet and dance lessons. I don't have any extra lessons. Then, on that day, Mum came to pick us up—on time, after I had stressed the importance of this to her about twenty-five times. In fact, she was early. She was very nice and friendly to Stella, and she had made an effort and put on a dress—the blue-and-gray one, which looks very nice on her. She seemed to know that it was important to me that she look like a nice mum, and I was really glad she did. Stella and she seemed to get on all right, but then we got to the site, and that's when I realized that it was all a horrible, horrible mistake and I should never, ever have suggested it.

Stella looked around at the other trailers with a mixture of fear and fascination. I know that she'd never seen a Gypsy site before, and maybe she'd heard stories about how awful and dirty Gypsies were, or something. I suppose it did seem a bit weird, with all the trailers lined up on their concrete pads, and loads of cars, and piles of bin bags in a big heap rather than in a dustbin. There were lots of dogs running about. But it wasn't dirty. Granddad came out of their trailer and stared at Stella in a rather unfriendly way, and even when I introduced them, and he said hello, she looked like she was scared of him.

We went into our trailer, which Mum had made look quite cheerful and nice. Everything was—as usual—clean and sparkling, and Mum made tea and bread and cheese. She'd bought some Mr. Kipling French Fancies, too.

Stella was really interested in the trailer. She looked at the kitchen, and exclaimed that there was no sink, and Mum told her how we wash things in different bowls and throw the dirty water outside. Because washing water is *mokady*, which is more than dirty. I mean, you wouldn't wash your clothes, and then things that you put in your mouth—like forks—in the same bowl, because that's disgusting. Isn't it? Stella nodded and said, "Yes, I see."

Obviously we couldn't go into my room, because I don't have one, so we sat on the settee at the end, with the stove lit, and Mum asked Stella boring, grown-up questions like what her favorite school subject was and how long her family had been living around here. For the first time ever, I felt really uncomfortable in our trailer: fidgety, like cheesy bugs were crawling all over me and there was nothing I could do about it. I began to feel that I could hardly breathe, and I thought I was going to explode. When Mum said she would go over to Gran's and leave us for a bit, I thought I would die, even though all the time I had been secretly longing for her to shut up and go. There was a silence after she'd gone out. Stella kicked her heels against the bench seat.

"Do you really live here, both of you?"

Her voice was incredulous. Not mean or anything, just like she really couldn't understand how we did it.

"Yeah."

"Where's your bed?"

"This is it," I said, indicating the bench we were sitting on.

"But don't you get any privacy?"

I thought about this.

"Not much. I can pull this curtain here . . ."

I demonstrated, but it seemed to confine us both into such a small, airless space that I panicked and pulled it back immediately.

"I don't think I could stand it. Not being able to go into my own room and shut the door. I mean, your mum's really nice and everything, but not to be able to listen to music on your own, you know . . . What if you get into a bad mood?"

"It's okay, really. I don't think about it."

"Oh."

She smiled.

But I knew that from then on, I would think about it. I wouldn't be able to stop thinking about it.

We had more tea and French Fancies, and talked about The Smiths, who were our joint favorite band, like we often did at school, but there was something in our conversation that hadn't been there before, something hot and sour, that made me feel as if my hands had suddenly swelled up to twice their usual size. Like I was a freak.

And then something really bad happened. She said, "Um . . . where's the bathroom?"

"Um, it's outside."

"Outside?"

Stella looked horrified. Like I'd said it was on Mars. Or there wasn't one. It honestly hadn't occurred to me before—that having an outside bathroom is bad. I mean, why would you want your toilet in with you—you want it as far away as possible, don't you? I mean, yuck.

"Yeah, it's just . . . We've got a key. It's our own bathroom . . ."

We went outside, and I took her to the bathroom. Which was a cubicle in the toilet block. It would have been nicer if it had been ours, but we were only subletting, so we couldn't do much about it.

Unfortunately, when we got there, Great-uncle was already in there. We had to wait, then he came out, in his wheelchair, and looked a bit fed up that we were waiting, and this strange *gorjio* girl was seeing him come out of a lavatory. She looked a bit startled when I introduced them, but she said hello. It was all really awful.

Stella went in there, and then she came out and was rather quiet. We went back inside and talked some more, but I wanted to die. I don't think it was Stella's fault. It wasn't as if she turned her nose up at our old Lunedale, or treated it like it wasn't good enough or anything. I just remember thinking, I can never, ever, do this again. I must not let anyone I like see where I live.

And I did like her. I really liked her. She was the best friend I've ever had at school, or anywhere.

After what felt like about a year, Mum drove her home, and we dropped her off at her house. It was in the residential area north of the town center, where nice, detached houses sit between front and back gardens, with extra space at the sides for garages and bikes and things. I'd never seen her house before, and it made me realize what a shock our trailer must have been to her—who was used to having her own room, probably with matching furniture, and a little sister and a dog and a tortoise, and a father who was a physics teacher and a mother who worked part-time in a clothes shop. It was all so *gorjio* and nice, and so unlike the Jankos, with their dead boys and their sublet toilet and their wheelchairs and their terrible, fatal luck.

I waved good-bye as Mum turned the car around, and she waved back from her doorstep. I felt as though she was going back to another country and I would never see her again—not in the same way as before. Mum said, "She seems like a nice girl," and I said, *"Mmm."*

And that was all we ever said about it.

In the school library, I read this book called *Down the Lane: A Threatened Way of Life*. I wondered what other people thought about us. This book was written by a *gorjio* for other *gorjios*, and even though it was aimed at schoolkids, it seemed stupid and simple. It talked about bender tents and wagons, and wooden flowers and horses and mending knives. It said that Gypsies have dark skin and hair, and "particularly bright eyes." What does that mean? How can some eyes be brighter than other eyes? By being wetter?

I suppose some of the things it said were true. Some Gypsy men used to make wooden flowers, but it all seems long ago and not much to do with me or my family, or anyone I know. The book said that we're in touch with nature and know how to make old herbal remedies and stuff like that. Well, I don't know. Great-uncle's wife knew all about herbs and plants, apparently, but she's dead now. You get the impression that Gypsies are supposed to be wild and free. But there was nothing about O levels in there, for example. Apparently, Gypsies don't do exams. They don't become doctors.

When I saw Stella again at school it was different. Nothing big, initially—we still talked and sat beside each other for a couple of lessons, but there was something missing—that secret thing that made it seem like we were two of a kind, however different we might be on the surface. Gradually, we talked less and less, and then she became best friends with supersnob Katie Williams, whose father is on the council, and moved to sit beside her, usually, and now we hardly speak, except to say hi, sometimes.

Gorjio. I know more what Great-uncle means now, when he says that we're different. Not better or worse, just different. Like me and Stella—we might both have dark hair and speak English, and both like The Smiths, and both hate geography lessons. But we're like trains on tracks that run more or less parallel but will never meet. I can't go on her tracks, and she can't go on mine.

17.

Ray

The next day the heavens open. Gutters fill and overflow. The ground, saturated from spring, can't soak it up. It has nowhere to go. Headlines obsess about the weather. Everyone talks about it. How the rain might be radioactive, might kill us.

I look up Seviton. It's in Sussex, on the Downs, an unremarkable village too far from a station for commuters, too nondescript for weekenders. But it has a pub—the White Hart—the sign a modern interpretation attached to a mock-Tudor building. Inside, the usual gaggle of fruit machines and stale reek of fags. A couple of locals stand at the bar, although they're preretirement age and it's not yet half past eleven. I order a tonic water and ask around for the where-abouts of the Black Patch. No one seems to know what I'm talking about. I mention it might be a place where Gypsies once stopped, and one of the men drinking alone wrinkles his forehead.

"There was a place, off Egypt Lane. There's an old chalk pit where Gypsies used to stop, but they closed it down a couple of years ago. It was always a mess, rubbish everywhere . . ."

He gives me directions. The name is a whopping clue. You find a few names like this all over southern England—Egypt Wood, Egypt Meadow—and it means that the place was once an encampment for the people of Little Egypt. When the first band of exotic, dark-skinned Travelers arrived in England five hundred years ago, the leader called himself the King of Little Egypt. They weren't from Egypt, but no one knew any better, so the name stuck: Egyptians . . . Gypsies. They claimed they had been ordered to wander for seven years as a penance, and were allowed to beg for alms. They carried a letter from the Pope saying so. Or perhaps it was from the Holy Roman Emperor. Anyway, they didn't go back to wherever they'd come from when the seven years' penance was up. We're still here.

Egypt Lane is a narrow road leading out of the village. There are soggy fields on either side, but nowhere that you could pull off and stop. After a few minutes' drive into a wet wood, I find a turning toward the hillside, and am stopped by a newish barbed-wire fence and a sign that says "No Entry. No Fires. No Overnight Camping." Code for "No Gypsies."

I get my wellies out of the boot, climb over the fence, and struggle through a healthy growth of brambles. It's dark, what with the overhanging trees and the bulk of the Downs looming to the south, but I can see it is an old chalk pit—a big bite out of the hillside, revealing a whitish cliff streaked with green matter. It feels likely, but I know it's the right place when I find the rusting hulk of a pickup, stranded, wheelless and gaunt, surrounded by head-high nettles and meadowsweet.

What the owner of the land thinks he can do with this place is beyond me. But then, that probably wasn't the point. The point would have been to get the Travelers to go somewhere else—anywhere else—even if it was just over the parish boundary. Often, land that used to be commons—places Gypsies were allowed to use like anyone else—was reclassified as parks or residential areas, specifically to prevent them from stopping there. Fields were plowed up to make them impassable to motors. Concrete fences were built. At Kizzy Wilson's, a prefab concrete wall surrounded the whole site so that you couldn't see in—or the inhabitants out. Despite the open entrance, it gave it the flavor of a prison.

My dad used to tell stories of the *gavvers*—the police—coming with tractors to drag trailers away by force. Sometimes they didn't even give people a chance to pack up their things, so all their china and glass got broken. No point complaining. No such thing as compensation for Gypsies. And before you ask, it still happens.

I try to get a feel of what it was like as a stopping place—small, secluded—something the Jankos seem to like. I try to picture Tene's Westmorland Star here—and another trailer with the elusive Ivo and the even more elusive Rose. Where would she have gone to meet the *gorjio* boyfriend? Seviton? The White Hart? I can't see a shy Gypsy girl going into a pub on her own. Or did that never happen? Did something happen to her here, under the concealing trees? The sheltering cliff?

Back in the White Hart, drying off in front of the electric coal fire and warming up with a single Bell's, I get to chatting with the oldest man I can see. He remembers with some nostalgia Egypt Lane being a stopping place, but not that it was ever called the Black Patch. I ask if there are any council sites around here instead, and he just laughs. Then he stares at me.

"Why're you so interested in Gypsies, anyway?"

"I'm looking for a girl who went missing round here. A Gypsy girl."

I show the pub patrons the picture of Rose at the races. Heads shake. My friend shrugs, not particularly interested.

"I doubt anyone in the village would see the sort that stopped there. They came and went all the time. How would you know if one had gone missing? You've got to have somewhere to go missing from, haven't you? How would you know?"

He falls about, finding himself very witty.

"She had a family. She went missing from them."

It's true what Leon said; it feels like two different worlds, Gypsy and *gorjio* living side by side but not face-to-face. A lot of people don't realize there are still Gypsies living on the road in this country, until some tabloid headline kicks up a fuss about dirty sites or con men with dodgy tarmac. They like to think that Gypsies are something from the past, like flagons of mead and horses delivering your weekly coal. Picturesque, maybe, but essentially gone.

"They weren't real Gypsies there, anyway—more like pikeys—scroungers, you know."

"Real Gypsies? I'm not sure I know the difference."

"Haven't been real Gypsies as long as I've been here. Proper Romanies, I mean. And I've been here all my life. There's no such thing."

I don't know how many times I've heard this stuff about real Gypsies. Everyone loves real Gypsies. No one agrees who they are, but they're fairly sure there aren't any left. The people they're trying to get off their common land are . . . something else. Most of the time, I try to remain neutral. After all, I'm here on a job. But I don't think I'm going to find out any more today.

"My father was a Gypsy. A real Gypsy. And he worked all his life."

I smile and stand up, putting my glass on the counter. As I walk away, I think I hear him mutter "Gypsy cunt" in a low voice, but I couldn't swear to it in court.

It occurs to me only as I drive out of Seviton that I have been an idiot. No one recognized the name Black Patch because Egypt Lane isn't called the Black Patch, and never was. Names last, even when the places themselves have changed beyond recognition. Take a walk around the City of London.

In that case, why did Tene say the Black Patch was at Seviton? Inconsistencies matter. Work your fingers into a little crack and you can pull the whole thing apart. Either Tene made a mistake or he was trying to throw me off the scent. A slip of the tongue, or a lie. Either way, it's the first interesting thing to happen with this case.

. . .

I was right. A couple days later I find the real Black Patch. I phoned Lulu Janko again. She sounded weary when I announced my name, so I just asked about the Black Patch. Surprised, she said, "Oh, that's just outside . . . God, Watley, was it? Near Ely. Yeah, we used to stop there. I think it was sold off some time ago."

Then she made her "I've got to get to work" excuse again—this time at half past three in the afternoon—and I found myself wondering about her mysterious private-care job.

Hen came up to my desk this morning, thus announcing his awkwardness; his desk is only twelve feet away, and my hearing is fine.

"So . . . the other night, at ours. It was nice, wasn't it?"

"Yes."

"I just wondered . . . you know. She's nice, Vanessa, isn't she? We thought . . ."

"Please, don't start this. Okay?"

"Don't look at me like that!"

"I'm not looking at you like anything."

"So . . . what did you think?"

"You can tell your wife that I thought she was very nice, but . . . she's not my type."

Hen is too much of a gentleman to point out that I slept with her, but he knew. I could tell.

He nudged the wastepaper bin with his loafer.

"We worry about you."

"I'm touched by your concern."

"It's been more than two years."

"I know how long it's been."

I looked down at my notebook, picked up my coffee cup, and drank from it, cold though it was. He didn't move.

"Is there something else?"

Hen nodded, determinedly not meeting my eye.

"It's time you stopped spying on your ex-wife."

I froze, the cup of coffee in midair.

I have been so discreet. Where did I slip up? I couldn't be angry with him. He's supposed to notice things.

"She's not my ex-wife."

"For God's sake, Ray . . ."

I told myself to calm down. There is no sense at all in which Jen and I are still man and wife, other than on paper, and she has been asking me to sign the divorce papers for several months. Or rather, her lawyer has. I don't know why I haven't, really.

"You're right. And I have . . . stopped."

It has been more than a week since the last time. Am I finally getting bored with it? Is that how it happens?

"Well . . . good."

"Did she see me?"

Hen looks severe.

"So you'll tell Madeleine to leave me alone?"

"As long as you behave."

"Actually, I think I might have met someone."

"Really? Who?"

"I don't know if there's anything in it . . ."

"Is it Vanessa?"

"I just told you . . . No! It's no one you know. So I'll thank you to . . . go back to your desk and . . . do whatever it is that you do here."

I waved my hand, mock dismissive.

Hen grinned and sat on my desk.

"So what was she like?"

"Who?"

"Oh, come on . . . You did the dirty deed!"

Public-school boys. They never grow up.

.   .   .

This time I'm in Fen country. All the way around the M25, then out toward Ely, Stowmarket—that strange, flat land punctured by cathedrals and air bases. They entertain themselves around these parts by thinking up bizarre names for their villages—I drive through or past Bruisingford, Shangles, Soberton. I find the village Lulu mentioned, home in on the pub—real Victorian as opposed to fake Jacobean—and ask around. This time it's easy. I am pointed toward an elderly gentleman who's knowledgeable about local history. He tells me the origin of the name Black Patch: the former common land on the edge of the village was the paupers' burial ground for victims of the Black Death, although he scrupulously points out that this is, as far as he knows, unsubstantiated. When I sound him out about missing girls, though, he has nothing to add. Recent history—less than a hundred years old—seems not to interest him.

Burial ground or not, the Black Patch is now a dump. Close to a new supermarket, acres of earth have been churned into a vast, muddy moonscape—big enough to double the village population. A hoarding on the roadside announces the imminent arrival of "Alder View—An Exclusive Development of New Riverside Homes," with an unlikely picture that bears no relation to the craterous mess in front of me. I can't see a river, either—until I realize that the line of willows and alders beyond the site must conceal a watercourse. A couple diggers have halted with their jaws in the air, acid-yellow against the gray earth. A lone hard-hatted man smokes by a Porta-kabin. I wade through the mud toward him.

"Excuse me, this site is private."

"Sorry. I just want to know if this is the place called the Black Patch."

He grins.

"No, it's Alder View now. But yeah, that's what it used to be called. Not so appealing to the yuppies, though, is it?"

The builder, Rob, says work on Alder View is going slow because of the wetness of the ground. It's crazy, in his opinion; they're building houses on the floodplain. Lots of agricultural work around here: soft fruit and market gardens—and in the old days, if it flooded, the Gypsies would just move on. I ask him if the digging has turned up any evidence of plague victims, but he shrugs: not to his knowledge. Shards of pottery, and the odd fragment of bone, probably animal: most likely rubbish. I explain why I'm here: because it is, possibly, where a young woman went missing six years ago. I stress that I am not looking for a body but for a living person. Just in case he hears anything. My new friend—by now—is so excited that he promises to ask around. I give him my card.

There's only one problem with this lead. According to Rob, the Black Patch was sold off nearly ten years ago—long before Rose went missing. Was it still used as a stopping place—illegally—while mired in a complicated, glacial planning process?

Rob thinks not.

I find myself hoping he's wrong.

18.

JJ

Last night was the worst night of my life. We were woken up by a bang on the trailer door at about two o'clock. It was Ivo, and he sounded scared. Christo couldn't breathe. Mum and I threw some clothes on and ran over, and though I was only hovering in the doorway behind them, I could tell it was bad. His breathing wasn't just short and shallow, like it is sometimes, but rasping and rattling. It was horrible.

Mum said, "We've got to take him to hospital."

Ivo went as white as a sheet. He hates hospitals. I mean, no one likes them, obviously, but he really hates them. Like he's got a phobia or something. I suppose he had enough bad experiences when he was a little boy and ill—and they didn't help. He nodded, though, as no one could really argue. We were all scared. Gran woke up at the noise we were making—no one was trying to keep that quiet—and agreed that he should go to the hospital. Everyone was being very practical and helpful, like they are in emergencies, offering scarves and blankets and Vicks rub. You have to keep your mind busy, I think, on little details, so that you don't think about the worst that could happen—as though Vicks rub could stop that.

So we ended up all going to the hospital—that is, Mum, Ivo, Christo, and me. Mum tried to make me go back to bed, but there was no way I could have slept, and anyway, it was Saturday night. I thought Christo would probably like me there, too, if he could have said anything. Anyway, we drove down to the nearest hospital—there's one in town, so it took only about fifteen minutes—and rushed into the casualty department. Ivo carried Christo up to the front desk, and after a brief conversation, they took them off to a room, ahead of all these other people who had been waiting for ages. There were blokes sitting there with blood on their faces, people lying across chairs—they could have been dead. I mean, it was packed. I don't know if casualty departments are always that busy, but maybe they are: one nurse—the nice one, as opposed to the snobbish one behind the desk—said "usual Saturday night" as she rushed past.

Me and Mum sat with the waiting people—lots of them were drunk, I realized (obvious, really, it being Saturday night)—while Ivo and Christo were off with a doctor somewhere. Some of the people were muttering and swearing—or groaning. I thought the groaner was probably exaggerating a bit, since if he had been in a really bad way, they would have taken him off to look at him, instead of leaving him there for hours, which is what they did. Another man kept yelling out, shouting and calling the nurses really rude names. They ignored him, and I decided that he probably wasn't right in the head and didn't know what he was saying. The nice nurse walked past once and said, "We'll see you when we see you, Dennis," which made it sound like she knew him. Maybe he goes there every Saturday. Once I looked around and he was staring straight at me. His eyes were awful: one of them was red where it should have been white, and there was dried blood coming out of his nose. He was like something out of a horror film: *The Tramp from Hell*. I turned back, pretending I hadn't even noticed him or his horrible eye, or the pee smell coming off him, scared that he'd start shouting at me or worse.

I got some coffee from the drinks machine to keep us going. It wasn't very nice—too hot, and really bitter, even when you put lots of sugar in it. I wanted to get some crisps or something as well, being starved, as usual, but we didn't have any more change. I moaned at Mum when she refused to change a five-pound note—it was all she had left. I sulked for a bit, and then realized I was being selfish and should be thinking about Christo, who might be really ill, not myself, who was basically fine, if hungry. The hours crawled past like doddery old millipedes. Despite being starved, I ended up falling asleep, and woke up to find Ivo and Mum whispering together.

They seemed to be arguing. According to Ivo, the doctors wanted to keep Christo in the hospital while they worked out what was wrong with him. I thought this was a good idea, but Ivo seemed angry about it. He kept saying, "They just want to stick their noses in." Mum got quite cross then, arguing that the hospital was the best place for him. I agreed with Mum but thought I'd better not say anything. Ivo was particularly cross because they'd asked him to fill in some forms—lots of stuff, like where we lived—so he'd lied and made up a house address, so they wouldn't know we were Gypsies. But they asked all sorts of tricky questions, like who your regular doctor is, and we don't have one, so there was a bit of trouble about that.

It ended up with Mum and me driving home at about six a.m., as the sun was rising, leaving Ivo and Christo behind. And I slept late this morning. In fact, it was after twelve o'clock, so actually, it was afternoon. I had thought I might take Christo fishing today, and the weather is perfect for it—damp and mild. But as it is, I can't concentrate on reading or music or anything, because we're just waiting to find out what's happened.

Ivo finally comes back at about five, and Christo is with him. We all rush out of Gran's trailer, where we've been sitting around, twiddling our thumbs.

"How is he?"

"Shouldn't he still be in there?"

"He's all right, aren't you? Eh?"

Ivo kisses the top of his head. Christo is asleep, but his breathing does sound better than it did last night.

"They've given him some antibiotics. Said he might as well be at home."

Ivo shrugs. He looks absolutely exhausted, all dark around the eyes.

"You'll have to make sure he's kept warm. Ivo, why don't you have a kip in number two and I'll put Christo to bed?"

"That's a good idea. You look done in."

Mum touches his arm gently. She looks worried.

"I'm fine."

"Come on, Ivo, go and have a lie down."

Gran holds her hands out for Christo. Ivo steps back.

"I will. We're both going to lie down. In our trailer. I can look after him. All right?"

"We're just trying to help—"

"I don't need help."

He turns and walks off to his trailer.

Gran says, "What's got into him?"

"Mum, he's tired. He hasn't had any sleep."

"I know! We're offering to help him. There's no need to be rude!"

She shouts this last bit so that Ivo can hear on the other side of the paddock; he just bangs his door shut.

"No bloody manners, that boy. He's never had any manners since—and he was such a lovely kid."

"He's got a lot to put up with, Mum."

"Don't know why you're always standing up for him."

They glare at each other like a pair of cats.

Since Ivo doesn't want us, we give up. I can't help thinking that Christo would have been better off staying in the hospital for a while. Who knows—maybe they could find out how to really cure him. Scientists are working all the time on stuff like that. They might have come up with something new since he was a baby.

When Mum and I go back to our trailer for another cup of tea, she looks a bit worried, so I ask her: doesn't she think Christo would be better off in the hospital, for the moment?

She sighs and shakes her head.

"I'm sure they wouldn't have let him go if they thought he needed to be in hospital, love."

"Yeah, I know, but . . ."

But I don't know, so I don't say anything else. Then a horrible thought occurs to me. I suddenly wonder if maybe Ivo took Christo out of the hospital even though the doctors had wanted to keep him there. Maybe they're not allowed to stop you if you're a parent. Maybe they didn't even see—there are so few of them, and they're so busy. It seems a pretty awful thing to think about Ivo, so I keep quiet. But for some reason I can't help thinking it.

It's funny; when I was younger, I really looked up to Ivo. Despite his temper and his funny moods, he seemed to be a grown-up I would want to be like. Maybe you need someone in your family or nearby that you can do that with: "When I grow up, I want to be like them." I don't have a dad, so who was I going to look up to? Not Granddad, with his bulging eyes and raw, red skin that looks sunburned, even in winter, and his paunch—it's hard to believe I'm related to him at all, to look at us. He's all right, but he doesn't do much, either, other than what Gran tells him to, and when he's had a couple drinks he's liable to tell stories about when he was a boxer and knocked out the teeth of someone called Long Pete, or Black Billy, or something like that. I don't even know if they're true. Gran's always moaning about how useless he is. And I wouldn't want to be like Great-uncle, the unluckiest man around, although I do like talking to him when he's in a good mood. But you can't want to be like someone who's in a wheelchair and who you have to wheel to the lavs when you go on holiday, can you? So that left Uncle Ivo.

When he—and Great-uncle and Christo—came to live with us, I was seven. All I'd known up till then was first Mum and then Gran and Granddad. I'd barely even been to school at that point. I suppose you could call it a sheltered upbringing. Or if not sheltered, from things like evictions and police harassment, then . . . small. Underpopulated, as my geography teacher would say. Great-uncle and Ivo certainly livened things up. And Ivo was cool. He was—and is—not tall but skinny, and pretty good-looking, I suppose. He's got dark hair and dark eyes, and really smooth skin, and a way of looking at people that seems really confident, like he knows he's better than them, no matter who they are. If we walk down the street, girls always turn and look at him. Otherwise, people tend to be a little bit scared of him. But when you see him with Christo, you know that he's got a really good heart. And when he smiles at you, you feel like he's given you a special present. It makes you feel great. So I looked up to Ivo. Sometimes people who didn't know us thought I was his son, because we do look alike—same hair, same eyes. I'm not being vain when I say this—we really do. I used to be pleased when people made this assumption, and secretly imagined that, maybe, he really was my dad. After all, Mum wouldn't talk about the *gorjio* who supposedly was my dad—I've never even seen a picture. I don't even know his name, for Chrissake. That's how little she's told me. So I thought maybe that was why Uncle Ivo and I had a sort of special bond and why I got on so well with Christo—that is, until I got a bit older and thought about it, and realized how silly that was. Ivo was only fifteen when I was born (and he wasn't very well, either).

Since coming back from France, I've asked Mum about my dad again. She said, "When you're older, sweetheart. You've got enough to be getting on with, what with your exams and that."

Sometimes I wonder if this *gorjio* ever existed.

Anyway: Ivo. Since I've been more worried about Christo, I'm not sure what to think about Ivo. In fact, I think I'm angry with him. I know he loves Christo, but I think he could be doing more to find a cure. Going to Lourdes was all very well, but it doesn't seem to have helped at all. The level of holy water in the remaining jerry can is slowly going down—still with my note on it—but Christo is lying in bed with a respiratory infection. Not talking, not walking. And Ivo won't let him stay in the hospital, where, maybe, they could find out more about what's wrong with him. What harm could it do? Just because he doesn't like hospitals doesn't mean it mightn't be good for Christo. I can't help feeling that he's being selfish.

I can't remember why I felt so hopeful in France. When I think about myself in Lourdes just a few weeks ago, I can't believe I was that optimistic. It's like I'm looking back at a totally different, much younger, more naive, much stupider person.

19.

Ray

Hen greets me at work with a smile and a clap on the shoulder—he knows it's my birthday, and though I suspect that, left to his own devices, he would happily ignore it, goaded by Madeleine, he asks if I have plans.

"Yes," I say.

"Which are . . . ?" he says.

"No one you know," I say.

"*Oh-o-oh . . .*" He draws the vowel out to ridiculous lengths. "The mystery woman?"

"Maybe."

"*Hm.* It was just that if you didn't, you would be very welcome to come to our house."

"Thanks. But I really do have plans."

He looks at me. Apparently satisfied, he insists on taking me out to lunch.

We review the Rose Wood case, although there's not much to say. I talked to Leon about the Black Patch and Egypt Lane, and though he recognized both names, he had little to add, and nothing concrete about dates. He didn't know for certain that Rose had ever been there. In fact, we know next to nothing: neither where she went missing, nor exactly when, nor who her friends were, if indeed she had any. We have found no record that anyone has seen her since that winter six years past. None of her sisters ever received so much as a postcard, according to them. She appears on no official records. She has pulled off a remarkably successful disappearing act.

"She's dead," Hen says at the end of it. "Got to be."

He's confirming what I have started to believe. But there are no positive signs of a death, either. I wonder for a second whether, in fact, she ever existed at all. I sigh in frustration.

"Everyone I've spoken to . . . they're all so bloody vague."

Hen twirls his coffee cup and raises an eyebrow. He grins.

"Maybe she's at the bottom of a lake."

A childhood friend of Hen's mother's dumped his wife's body in a reservoir several years ago. He claimed she ran off with one of several lovers, and apparently no one had been suspicious. The body was found only when they dragged the reservoir to look for someone else. She had been garroted with her own tights. As a result, Hen and I are quite fond of lakes. No lakes are indicated in this case, but that's not to say it didn't happen. And, of course, if wives are murdered, they are usually murdered by their husbands. Ivo Janko again. Saintly, caring, long-suffering Ivo.

It's at that point that the phone rings. Andrea puts the call through to me.

"Been thinking," he says, "you should meet Ivo, maybe, after all."

It's Tene Janko. He has got someone to drive him to a phone box. He has thought about this.

"Yes. Good. Where is he?"

None of my inquiries have turned up his whereabouts. I was beginning to think him as elusive as his former wife.

"He'll be with us. Tomorrow. If you want to come over."

"Same place?"

"Same place."

"I'll be there at about . . . eleven?"

I put the phone down.

"Why's he phoning me now?"

"Because he knows you're getting suspicious?"

"They're getting their stories straight."

"You want me to come?"

I shake my head.

"Softly, softly."

I wonder about Lulu Janko—has she been talking to her brother again?

It might have been during lunch that the mad, bad idea came into my head. Hen's gentle pokes about my mystery date this evening—of course, I have none—and the wine I drank joined forces in a decidedly unhealthy way. My father used to say—or anyway, said at least once, in a rare moment when he wasn't shouting at the television—"Find out what you're good at, and do it."

All right, I thought, over the half bottle of burgundy (Hen drank water) and the carpetbagger's steak he insisted on standing me as a birthday present. All right, I will.

So here I am, hours later, doing what I'm good at outside a house in Richmond. It's a large house, with elegant proportions over four stories and a wrought-iron balcony spanning the first floor. Floor-to-ceiling windows are swagged with heavy curtains. The front garden is a discreet jungle of evergreens.

Initially, I sat in my car with a telephoto lens, but the drive is too long and curving, the shrubbery too thick for the envious gaze of oiks like me to penetrate. So I wait until dusk, then slip into the shadowy driveway and melt into the darkness of the bushes—great, overgrown, welcoming rhododendrons and camellias. The dark indigo is seeping out of the sky, and I'm a dark denim shadow in the shadows. Between dog and wolf. Which am I?

All the lights seem to be on on the ground floor. Upstairs—most of the house—is in darkness. I have to work my way through thick jungle to the back of the house, to where a pair of tall, uncurtained windows spill light across an unkempt lawn and more of the funereal bushes. Despite its size, it feels like a garden that no one ever goes into or thinks about. Well, I reason with myself, it belongs to someone old and infirm. Someone who both needs a private carer and can afford to pay for it.

I followed Lulu Janko from her house. Waited until she left and drove over here, following her tinny little beige Fiat with its handily broken brake light. She parked on the quiet street among the Volvos and Audis and Range Rovers and let herself into the house with her own key. I didn't see another thing until I sneaked into the back garden. Then this is what I see:

Lulu pushes a wheelchair in through the door and parks it near the fireplace. From the warm and mobile light, there seems to be a fire going, even though it's not cold. Inside, it must be boiling. The first surprise is that the man in the wheelchair is quite young. Probably younger than me, and undeniably handsome—he has longish dark hair brushed back off a thin, fine-featured, aquiline face. Aristocratic-looking is what comes to mind, although it could be the surroundings that make me think that. His mouth opens and shuts like hers as they talk. From her body language, they seem comfortable with each other, like they've known each other for a long time, which may indeed be the case.

I inch forward through the damp shrubbery so that I can see more of the room. Lulu looks intently toward the window for a moment that makes my heart skip a beat, even though I know I'm completely hidden in the rhododendron thicket. They seem to be discussing whether to draw the curtains or not. After a moment's hesitation, she doesn't. Then she goes out, leaving him staring into the fireplace.

Why do I hate this man? He deserves my pity. Although his mouth moves and his head turns from side to side, nothing else does: he is paralyzed from the neck down. He's helpless.

Lulu comes back in with a tray, which she puts down on a small table. She picks up a kind of baby's feeding cup and offers it to the wheelchair man. Did she help her brother Tene when he was first in his wheelchair—is that how she got into this line of work?

Then the door opens and a well-groomed, impressive-looking elderly woman looks in. She's instantly recognizable as the wheelchair man's mother—they have the same face, down to the thin, pointed nose and arching eyebrows. They speak for a minute—everyone smiling and laughing away—and then she goes out. They all seem as happy as anything—I can't see why. For a moment I am not concentrating as I try to figure out the elderly woman's movements. I think I hear the front door close—that makes sense—the paid help is here, so Mummy gets to go out for a well-earned break—sherry, bridge, governing the local school, that sort of thing. I hold my breath in case she decides to come into the garden, but, of course, she doesn't.

Lulu holds the feeding cup for her charge. She's smiling—they keep breaking off to say something. I can see only half of his face, as Lulu is between us. Suddenly he jerks his head away from the cup and a trickle of brown liquid runs down his chin. He smiles, obviously embarrassed, and she leans forward to wipe it away. But instead of scuffling for a cloth—for, in fact, the cloth that lies on the tray by her side, as you might expect, she does it with her finger. Just her finger. He smiles again. What expression is on her face, I am unable to say.

Then she lifts the cup to his lips again and tips it up for him to drink. Somehow, annoyingly, the same thing happens again. I find myself holding my breath, anxious for her, thinking, How clumsy: this time he's going to be impatient with her—angry, even. The trickle of liquid runs down his chin and down his neck, heading toward his shirt collar. He seems to be staring at her, but she doesn't rush to wipe it off. It's very odd. Then I'm not even sure what I see; she seems to lean toward him and—it looks like, although I can't be absolutely sure of this—it looks like she licks the trickle of liquid off his neck and chin. It happens so quickly, I think I must have imagined it. Because how could that be the case?

The next moment she is back in her chair and all seems normal. Then I see why—the sitting-room door opens again, and the elderly woman pops her head around it. She seems to be laughing—perhaps she has forgotten something. Lulu and wheelchair man laugh, too. Happy people, these three. Hilarious. The mother goes out once more. This time Lulu gets up and goes out through the door, too, leaving him alone. I stare at him—who is this guy? What the hell kind of sick setup is this? Does he have some sort of hold over her that means he can force her to do these things? Demeaning her. Lulu comes back into the room and closes the door, a smile on her face. Saying something. Then she moves the tray and feeding cup and cloth and all onto the table by the door, and moves his chair a little nearer to the fire. She bends down to put on the wheelchair brake, and almost in the same movement, swings her leg over to sit on his lap, facing him. He moves his head back as far as it will go. I stare at the knobs of spine that are visible through her T-shirt, at her red high-heeled shoes: they are the same ones—the ones she wore when she met me. I see the scuff marks on the soles, the glint of nails where she's had them reheeled. She must really like those shoes. She wriggles herself a little closer to his body—he can do nothing other than sit there, of course—and bends her head to kiss him.

As far as I can tell—from my experience of this sort of thing—he kisses her back. There is nothing wrong with his head, after all.

I find I am breathing hard, mashing a handful of leaves to a slippery, sharp-smelling pulp. I feel sick. Hot. Ashamed. This wasn't what I came for. This wasn't supposed to be like this.

What was it supposed to be like, Ray?

When two people are sitting in the same wheelchair, everyone else should leave. And so I do.

I don't wait to find out when she leaves the house in Richmond.

I drive away with a petulant squeal of tires. The squealing says, I don't give a fuck. I don't know why I came. I'm not interested. I'm just trying to fool myself into thinking I'm getting over Jen. I even go and pick someone who looks a little like her, for Christ's sake. Stupid. I wasn't even thinking. Stupid.

Back at home, I sit in the front room in the dark, rocking in my chair, vodka and tonic in my hand, clinging to the edge of the abyss, staring through the ash leaves at the railway tracks that run along and over the main road. Toylike trains bundle slowly over the bridge, hypnotizing me: brakes hissing and clanking, wheels rattling over the points, the train windows like frames of a film running sideways, snapshots of humans being carried home to their loved and loving ones, not caring that I'm out there in the dark as they rattle past.

Maybe some of them are going home to dark houses where no one waits. Some of those people doing the crossword or staring sightlessly at the night might also be imperceptibly desperate; bored faces concealing a tangle of hopeless wreckage. After all, what could be more common than a failed marriage? What could be more mundane?

Is ten years the most you can ever hope for?

Happy birthday, Ray.

20.

JJ

I've got to go and see the headmaster. Mr. Stewart didn't say what it was about, but I've got a fair idea. All the teachers have been banging on about O levels recently, and I had this feeling I'd be hauled in before too long.

Mr. McDonagh—our headmaster—isn't too bad. He looks up and smiles at me when I slip in through the door.

"Well, James, come in. Sit down."

It always feels weird when anyone calls me James. I wonder who the hell they're talking to.

"It has been brought to my attention that your attendance has been rather patchy this year."

Oh.

"James, have you had any problems at home recently?"

"No."

"It's just that you've always done so well with coming to school."

. . . for a Gypsy, he doesn't say, but I know that's what he's thinking.

"So I wondered if anything has changed with your circumstances?"

I shrug. I don't want Mum to get into trouble. She probably already is in trouble.

"No. It's just . . . sometimes, when Mum's working . . . I can't get a lift in. It's miles to the bus stop."

That sounded all wrong. Like I'm blaming her, and it's not her fault.

"Right. Where are you living now?"

The question I always dread. I think he thinks we're on the council site near the new supermarket. As far as I can remember. Somewhere that has its own bus stop. But we haven't been there for months and months.

"Backs Lane." I mumble the lie eventually. But McDonagh doesn't look suspicious or even very interested.

"It's not that I want to pry, James. You have a very reasonable chance of getting some qualifications, and I don't want anything to take that chance away from you. I want to help."

How is he going to help me? By giving me a lift to school every morning? Don't think so.

"I'll make sure I get a lift," I say, which sounds a bit stupid.

"Yes? Because we can arrange help with that sort of thing, you know, if there's a . . . problem."

"Thanks. It's okay."

"And what about homework? Do you have somewhere quiet where you can study?"

I nod vigorously.

"Because you know you're always welcome to stay behind after classes and work in the library if you need some peace and quiet."

"No, it's fine . . . It's . . ."

Since it's just Mum and me, quiet is not a problem. Much better where we are now than on the council site, where you look out the window and you're practically in the bedroom of the trailer next door. And you can hear everything that goes on. I mean everything.

"If there's anything else you need, you know you can always come to me, or one of your teachers. We have high hopes for you, James."

He smiles in a sincere but slightly sickly way. I hope this is nearly over.

"Thanks, Mr. McDonagh," I mumble.

"So do you think you can improve on your attendance?"

"Yeah."

"You have a lot of promise, you know. Mrs. Casanada has spoken very highly of your English. If all goes well, we could be talking A levels."

He says "A levels" like it's the punch line to a really good joke. *Ta-dah.*

I nod like an idiot, not knowing what else to say.

"Well, all right. Thank you for coming to see me, James."

He always says thank you, like he didn't just order you to come and see him. (Does this make him a nicer person? I don't know.) I say thank you, too. We have a big reputation for good manners in our school. It's the main reason Mum was so pleased I got in.

Somehow it's already half past four, and the last lesson finished some time ago. It's raining. It seems to have rained nonstop since the beginning of spring, and now it's June. The papers keep going on about how it's a record or something. Gran is supposed to come and get me today, but there's no sign of any of our cars. I sit on the wall outside the school gate. There's a tiny bit of shelter from the trees on the edge of the playing field, so I try to get under that, but it doesn't make much difference—the wind seems to blow the rain under the leaves and straight at me. I close my eyes and pretend that it's not raining, and when that doesn't work, I try to imagine the rain is warm, like the showers at the swimming pool, which keep running as long as you keep hitting the button. Brilliant. When I live in France I'll have one of those showers. And it'll always be warmer than this, anyway. Even though it's June, the rain is bloody cold. My hair is wet, and water keeps running down my neck, which is not a nice feeling. Then I remember what some people at school have been talking about: that rain is killer rain. That it's full of poison because of that explosion in Russia, and it will give you cancer. If that's true, it's probably too late for me already. It doesn't seem any different from normal rain, though. It tastes the same—of nothing. I start to imagine getting cancer and dying. Would Stella come to my funeral? Would she cry?

I must have sort of drifted off, because when I open my eyes, there's a black Range Rover in front of me. The only person I've ever seen get into one of these cars is Katie Williams, but the windows of this one are tinted, so I can't see who's inside. Then the driver's window slides down with a slightly creaky electric hum. A woman with a nice face and an expensive-looking streaked hairdo looks out with a smile.

"Have you been stranded?"

Shocked that someone I don't know is talking to me, I shake my head vigorously. Then the shiny head of Katie Williams leans forward from the backseat.

"We'll give you a lift, JJ. Get in."

Katie Williams, who hates me—at least, I've always assumed so. Astonishing. It must be a joke. She must have something horrible in store, and everyone will laugh. It will be "Sausages" all over again.

"I'm waiting for my gran. She'll be here soon. It's all right. Thanks."

"Oh, but you've been out here for ages! When I came to pick Katie up from her oboe lesson I saw you out here—that must have been twenty minutes ago."

Mrs. Williams looks kind and concerned. She makes me feel like a small kid again and in need of looking after. I quite like it.

"She's just a bit late. I'm sure she'll be here soon."

"You're absolutely soaked! You'll catch your death of cold."

"I'm all right. Really. Not cold at all."

"Your teeth are chattering. We can't leave you here . . ."

There is muttering inside the car.

"Katie says you live just off the Eastwick Road. It's not far out of our way. And if your grandmother's been delayed . . . There may be a problem with her car or something . . . I'll explain it. Don't worry . . ."

The door is open, and somehow, although I keep saying that I'm all right, I seem to be getting into the back of the Range Rover, impelled by the power of money, or something. The seats are made of soft, squeaky leather, and I'm worried about ruining them. Once inside, I feel a hundred times wetter than I was outside. Katie, dry and sleek and smelling of strawberry lip gloss, stares straight ahead and chews gum and doesn't look at me. How does she know where I live? Did Stella tell her? What did she say? The very thought of what she might have said makes me feel sick and hot all over. But also, the thought that she talked about me at all is strangely thrilling.

Classical music plays softly on the car radio—a load of people are singing in a way that makes me think of an army marching with very measured steps, pausing between each one.

"You done your Jane Austen?"

Katie speaks without looking at me—I feel this rather than know it, because I am not looking at her, either.

"Um. No. Not yet."

"JJ's really good at English," Katie announces suddenly, to my total and complete surprise.

Mrs. Williams speaks half over her shoulder.

"I wish you'd give Katie a few tips."

I sort of smile, as the idea is so bizarre it's funny.

"Why don't you come back to our place? We can look at it together. You can get dry . . . and we'll give you a lift back afterward—please, Mum?"

She leans forward, smiling in a toadying way at her mother's ear. I'm so stunned I can't speak. Katie Williams, strawberry-scented supersnob, asking me back to her house? What?

Mrs. Williams glances over her shoulder at me.

"Well . . . maybe that's a good idea. You look so bedraggled."

"Um . . . Mum will be waiting."

"You can ring your parents and tell them where you are. We're only a minute away."

"I . . ."

I don't want to say that I can't ring Mum because we don't have a phone. Katie must know this. Or maybe she doesn't realize—maybe she can't imagine anyone not having a phone. I don't know what to say, so I don't say anything, and this is taken for agreement, because a minute later the Range Rover glides down a long drive to a house that makes Stella's house look like a garden shed (and our trailer like a dog kennel). It's a mansion. I can't imagine how many rooms there must be. Loads. It's practically as big as the school.

Maybe Katie Williams is all right, really. We have mugs of tea, and cake—a really nice fruitcake that's delicious and probably good for you as well. Probably made in the gigantic kitchen, which has a breakfast bar—which is literally a bar where you have your breakfast—as well as a big long dining table—presumably for lunch and tea, as there's also a separate dining room where about twenty people can sit down at once. In a little room off the hall where the phone lives, I pretend to phone Mum. I mumble a bit at the *brr*, though no one's listening, anyway. I can't believe the phone has its own room. Katie doesn't have any brothers or sisters, so there are just three people living in this enormous house. Ten rooms each, I reckon. I don't think I could stand to live here, personally. It would give me the creeps.

Now we're sitting in Katie's study (!) with our books out and more mugs of tea. I feel like something's going to happen, but I'm not sure what it's going to be, or if I'm going to like it. She has a proper desk and a chair on wheels like in an office, and there's a set-tee, and posters on the walls—some are copies of real paintings: there's a ballet dancer, and a horse on its hind legs. There's a poster of Tears for Fears, and another one of Madonna. And it's not even her bedroom.

"How's Stella?"

I have to break the silence somehow. Stella's been off school for nearly a week with the flu.

"I don't know."

I'm surprised. Aren't girl best friends supposed to ring up and gossip to each other every day?

Katie studies her fingernails, which have sparkly pink varnish on them, chipping off. Then she says, "You like her, don't you?"

"Who . . . Stella?"

"Yeah. You were always hanging out together, last year."

"Yeah, well. That was last year."

Before you stole her away from me, I think. Although, to be fair, it wasn't Katie but the visit to the trailer that spoiled everything.

"So do you still fancy her?"

"God! I didn't fancy her! We were just mates. You know . . ."

This bursts out before I can stop it. I feel bad as soon as I say it, because I did—do—fancy Stella, quite a lot. Although I've sort of given up on her over the last few months.

"She likes Andrew Hoyte now."

"Oh. Yeah. I know."

Andrew Hoyte is old news. Most of the girls like him—he's tall and blond, and looks about twenty. I think he's got premature-aging disease. I say this, and Katie giggles.

It's astonishing. It's almost as though we're friends. Encouraged by this, I start to talk about some of the other arseholes at school. Katie falls about at almost everything I say. She seems to agree with me. Amazing.

"Do you like The Smiths?"

She's crawling toward a cassette player on the floor before I can even answer, and puts on the new album—the one I haven't got yet.

"What's your favorite song?"

How does she know I like them, unless Stella told her?

"Um, 'Hand in Glove.'"

"Yeah? I'd have thought it would be 'The Boy with the Thorn in His Side.'"

Actually, my real favorite is "Please, Please, Please, Let Me Get What I Want," but I'm not going to say all that in front of her. She might think it was some sort of awful clumsy pass.

"Why?" I say.

Katie is staring at me. Her eyes seem almost feverish and strangely brilliant, as though she's about to cry.

"Because you are the boy with the thorn in his side, aren't you?"

I try to laugh. I don't know what she means. What has Stella been saying about me? Katie smiles a rather strange smile. I feel like she's really saying something else, but I don't know what it is. Like she's speaking German, which she takes and I don't.

Why would I have a thorn in my side?

I shrug, which probably makes me look stupid, but it's the best I can do right now.

"So you don't care that Stella likes Andrew?"

I shrug again. I seem to have a shrugging disease.

"No."

Katie picks up her Jane Austen and slides closer to me on the little settee. She had said when we came in, very airily, "That's where I do my thinking." Like thinking is a specialized activity that you have to do in a special place, like a swimming pool. She wriggles around a lot and tosses her hair every few seconds. Gradually she seems to get closer, until her thigh is touching my thigh, but she doesn't even seem to notice. Yet how can she not notice? I try to slide away from her, but very casually, so it looks accidental. But she only wriggles some more and ends up touching me again. Maybe she's one of those people who is very casual about touching other people—and it is a small settee. She's opened the book and is pointing at some passage or other. We're sort of sharing the book, so maybe it's normal to be sitting so close together.

"This is the bit we're supposed to start with, isn't it?"

"Um . . ."

I can't remember what we're talking about, or anything about the book at all, at the moment. She bends forward so that her hair falls out from behind her ear and hangs like a shiny curtain between us, and then she flicks it back. It must be deliberate; the hair flicks right in my face, but she doesn't apologize. She has pretty hair—honey-colored, flat, and quite long. A piece of it brushes my lips, and all of a sudden, I have a tremendous erection. Panicking, I lean forward so she won't notice, and pretend to be studying *Sense and Sensibility*, but of course I don't read a single word.

I'm not even sure what happens for the next minute or so; I'm just clutching the book while trying to think about horrible, disgusting things, like the pencils-and-feet smell of the boys' cloakroom, but then (how? why?) the book isn't in my hands anymore. From being beside me, Katie is sort of kneeling and pushing her mouth against mine. Her lips are hot and soft and lightly sticky, and then her tongue is in my mouth, wrestling with my tongue, tasting of tea and fruitcake. I don't know if I respond, because every molecule of sensation is in my mouth, tasting her hot, wet tongue. I don't know what my hands are doing, or any other part of me.

Eventually (after a second, ten minutes?) Katie pulls back. It turns out that her hands were on my shoulders, and mine were lying moronically by my sides. She looks at me through half-closed eyes, panting slightly. A strand of hair crosses her face at a diagonal, glued to her lip with our spit. Her lips look redder than they did before. It's all I can do not to lunge at her again.

"Did you ever do that with Stella?"

"No."

Surely she knows that—or maybe Stella didn't tell her everything. Maybe she's seeing if I'd lie and say we'd gone all the way, although the most we ever did was talk.

I try to kiss her again, but she leans back, her hand pressing lightly on my chest.

"You won't tell anyone about this?"

"No. Will you?"

"No."

"Not even Stella?"

"Why, do you want me to?"

"No. But you're best friends, aren't you?"

She shrugs in a very offhand way. If I was Stella, I'd be really insulted. However, I'm not.

"I don't tell her everything. What I do is no one else's business."

"Right."

Just as I think she's going to remove her hand from my chest and we can get back to snogging, that strange half smile appears on her face again.

"Do you want to see my horse?"

For a moment I think she's joking—or that "horse" actually means something else—but it turns out it doesn't. She really does have a horse—her own horse, for God's sake, out in a stable behind the house. The stable has electric lights, running water, and a heater. It's got narrow yellow bricks on the wall, and bluish bricks on the floor. It's a palace. I don't know much about horses, although Katie seems to think I should. But I can see it's a beautiful animal—apparently, it's a purebred something or other called Subadar ("which means 'captain' in Hindustani," she says) and "He has the champagne gene," whatever that means. He has a really intelligent expression in his big dark eyes. Katie led me outside by the hand, although once in the stable she let go. I wonder if she's going to kiss me again—I don't think of trying to kiss her again, because she's posh and I'm not, and what if she screamed? But anyway, instead, she flings her arms around the horse's neck and kisses and caresses it in such an abandoned way that I feel instantly jealous. She croons endearments, rubbing her lips against the silky golden-brown neck—"Feel his nose, how soft it is"—and I obediently pat the horse while looking at Katie and feeling myself getting hard again, which is ridiculous as well as embarrassing.

I'm nowhere near stupid enough to think that suddenly Katie Williams is my girlfriend, because only complete spazzes think things like that. In fact, I would bet that tomorrow in school she'll ignore me, the same as always. But right now, we're here, stroking her horse's beautiful chestnut coat, and there's something strange but great going on, as though a magnetic current is buzzing through the horse's body, shooting from my hand to her hand and back again, traveling right through me with a shiver of delicious excitement. It means I can't take my hand off the horse's neck, and neither can she. It binds us. The horse looks at us, detached but understanding. Maybe it'll never happen again, but I want to remember it. Remember this.

I'm just thinking with wonder how her horse lives in a nicer place than I do—which seems fair enough: it's such a prince of horses— when I remember what time it is—or must be. It's nearly dark. Mum doesn't know where I am. She'll be worried. A sense of dread builds inside me. What if this isn't great at all? How could it be? It's wrong. It was never meant to happen. This is Katie Williams, for God's sake . . . The police are probably on their way right now!

"I'd better go. My mum . . . I said I'd be back soon."

I can't meet her eyes. Even the horse turns its head and looks at me like I've done something wrong and stupid.

"Okay, then."

Katie lifts her hand off Subadar's neck, breaking the circuit. The magnetic current is switched off, and I feel exhausted all of a sudden. Her tone of voice implies that I've missed out on one of life's great opportunities.

The leader of the local council grudgingly gives me a lift—in a different car: a blue saloon. At least I'm dry by this time. Katie waves briefly and disappears upstairs, leaving us to it. I don't take my eyes off her, but there is no meaningful eye contact between us. No heavy-lidded look to savor, no promises or squeezes of the hand. I wonder if Mr. Williams is going to drive me off into the woods and kill me.

"So you live on the Eastwick Road?" he says shortly. Mrs. Williams must have told him I'm a Gypsy. My heart's in my mouth as I wait for what's coming next. (She started it! I didn't move a muscle—not voluntarily, anyway . . .) But it doesn't come. He asks me about living on a private site and a council site—I suppose he's got a professional interest. I manage to say a few words, but I can't tell him what it's really like. I don't think he actually wants to hear that.

"So what made you move out?"

"Um . . . There was no room. It was someone else's pitch. We just sublet it for a bit."

"Oh. People aren't supposed to sublet, you know."

We all know that, but why shouldn't you go off for the summer, if you've got a trailer with wheels on it? *Gorjios* go on holiday and no one moves into their house; why shouldn't we? But if you leave your pitch empty, the council puts someone else on it, so you have to make private arrangements or you lose it. I told a couple people at school that we'd been to France (although not that we'd been to Lourdes asking for a miracle) and they looked at me like "But you're Gypsies—what are you doing going on holiday? You're supposed to be poor." So I stopped talking about it.

"Where shall I drop you?"

We're driving along the A32 now. It's not far to our site. But I know, more than anything else in the world, that I don't want Mr. Williams to see where I live. If he sees that, I'll never be allowed back in that house; I'll never be allowed near Katie's beautiful stable, or the settee where she does her thinking—or anything else of hers—ever again.

"Um, you can just drop me at the next corner. It's really close."

Luckily, it's not raining anymore.

"Sure? Okay."

He doesn't press me. He wants to get back to his armchair in front of the telly after a hard day telling people they can't sublet their sites. He pulls the car over to the verge, and I get out.

"Thanks very much, Mr. Williams . . . and thank Katie and er . . . for . . . the lift and everything."

He drives off almost before I've finished speaking. Can't wait to get out of there. I hang around until the car is out of sight, so he doesn't know that I don't walk down the side road but set off in the other direction, until I can see a light from one of our dear old trailers, winking dimly through the trees.

I walk up to our trailer. I'm not particularly trying to be quiet or anything, but Mum hasn't drawn the curtains, so that's when I see the weirdest thing of all in the whole of this pretty weird day. To be honest, I don't even want to think about it.

21.

Ray

He's instantly recognizable from the wedding picture. The longish dark hair, the watchful eyes, the attitude. His delicate good looks have hardened only slightly: the cheeks have become a little more hollow, the eyes a little more bruised. Slight and wiry, he is dressed in a rather old-fashioned way for a young man—one that proclaims his identity: a long-sleeved shirt, a heavy waistcoat buttoned up to the neck—even in June—and a handkerchief knotted around his throat.

When Kath shows me into his trailer (the Jubilee that I recognize from my first visit, as suspected), Ivo is sitting at the table with a small child on his lap, feeding him from a bowl of sodden Weetabix. He doesn't get up but nods toward the seat at the end.

"Dad says you want to know all about Rose."

I stare—though I try not to—at the child. I know he is six years old, but this child is tiny, a fledgling bird, smaller than my godson, Charlie. I would have guessed three, or four at the most. And I would have guessed that it was a girl, had I not known otherwise. Christo Janko looks like his father, with almost black, longish hair, and huge dark eyes in a heart-shaped face. A beautiful child but palpably odd: the head too large for the fragile body and slender neck, the limbs denim-covered sticks.

I smile at him.

"Hello, Christo."

The boy stares at me but doesn't respond.

I glance at Ivo.

"Does he understand?"

"Course he does, don't you? He just don't talk much."

Christo grins at his father.

"Didn't they tell you about him?"

"Yes. Well, not what the matter is, but . . . yes."

"It's the family curse."

"What is it?"

"They don't know, do they? We've been to the doctors and all that, but they can't say. I had it, too, when I was young, but I got better. So we hope, don't we?"

Ivo has a strange, compelling voice—light and rather young-sounding, yet hoarse, as though he's getting over a cold. The sort of voice that makes you lean forward to catch every word.

"You recovered from it? That's, er . . . great. I believe a few of your relatives died from the disease."

Ivo looks down.

"Yeah. I was lucky."

"You don't know why you recovered?"

He shakes his head. He doesn't seem to want to talk about it.

"If we did . . ."

I look at him and the boy. Wondering, if a mysterious and deadly disease can recede, can it also return? What marks has it left on Ivo? He appears normal enough, though slight, and unusually boyish. But if he used to be like Christo, that would explain it.

"Anyway, that was what frightened her off, I reckon. Rose. When we realized that he was afflicted, she couldn't take it. Didn't want anything more to do with us. I don't know that I could blame her— who would want to have more kids, when you don't know . . ."

As I ask him to recall the events of six years ago when Rose left, he avoids my eyes, talking to his son—asking him if he's had enough to eat, if he wants a drink. He never seems to get an answer, but there must be some wordless communication between them that I cannot read, because he reacts as though Christo has spoken to him. I can't tell if he understands what is going on; he pays no attention to the conversation, focusing on items on the table or the figurine of some action hero he holds. I suppose Ivo is used to this, but the overall impression I get is that Ivo is hiding behind him. Christo and his mystery illness is his barricade against the world. The world and the questions of impertinent private detectives.

Ivo is now wiping some invisible dribble off Christo's chin.

"You say Rose left in the middle of the night. Didn't that strike you as odd?"

"No."

"Your father said that the Black Patch was quite a long way from any stations. Thetford is the nearest, isn't it?"

Ivo looks up. Is that a sharp look? A moment later he's shifting position, lifting Christo's legs and resettling them.

"It was the Black Patch near Seviton."

"Oh, right."

"Why d'you say Thetford? We haven't stopped up there for years and years."

"I'm sure your father mentioned it. Just by Watley . . . near Thetford."

"Nah. Watley . . . It were fenced off—I dunno—ten years ago? And we wouldn't have gone there in winter. It always flooded."

"And the stopping place at Seviton . . . that was an old chalk pit?"

Ivo glances up again.

"Yeah. You know it?"

"I've been there. And that was known as the Black Patch, too?"

"That's what we called it."

He looks like he's genuinely thinking about it. There's no tension there now, that I can see.

"My father gave up on the road. Doesn't get any easier."

Ivo just grunts in response.

"So—at Seviton—how do you think she got away?"

"She must have got someone to give her a lift. That's what we thought. She'd been going into Seviton a bit. Used to take Dad's car and go off for hours. Must have met someone."

"Did you ever see her with anyone? Hear her mention a name—anything like that?"

Ivo shakes his head slowly. "I had no idea. But . . . I was thinking about Christo all the time. I didn't maybe pay her too much attention." He looks down at the boy again, and his face softens.

"What did she take?"

"Pretty much everything."

"What about money?"

"I suppose she had money, yeah."

"She didn't take money from you?"

He shrugs.

"There weren't much to take. She took her jewelry and stuff, just, like, bangles and earrings, you know."

"Do you have anything of hers left, now?"

Ivo shakes his head.

"What she didn't take, I got rid of."

"What did she leave?"

He looks at me like I'm an idiot. Shrugs.

"Some clothes."

"And what did you do with her things?"

"Like I said, got rid of them."

"You didn't think she'd come back?"

"I wouldn't have taken her back. Not after she left. I was that angry."

He looks down at his son, who smiles up at him—a smile of eerie sweetness. Ivo smiles, too—properly, for the first time—and kisses the top of his head.

"Just you and me, kid, innit? Didn't know what she was missing."

There's a sadness about his smile as he looks up and catches my eye for a brief moment.

"And this was . . . in November?"

"Yeah. I think so. I can't remember exactly."

"So Christo was just a few weeks old?"

"Yeah. Or . . . might have been a bit later."

I jot this down in my notebook. Tene had said that Rose had left when Christo was a few months old—implying that it was after Christmas. But people do forget.

"She had sisters, you know. Have you spoken to them? They'll likely know."

"Yes. They've not heard a thing."

Ivo raises his eyebrows and shrugs again.

"I knew she wasn't happy. After he came along. Sometimes she would say these really strange things. Like, sometimes, she would . . . Listen, let's go outside for a bit."

Ivo jams an old man's cap on his head, pulling the brim down over his eyes and, still carrying his son, leads the way to the Lunedale, where a young teenage boy opens the door. Clearly another Janko. This boy takes Christo in his arms and carries him inside.

"Who's that?" I ask in a conversational way, as we stroll off and Ivo lights a cigarette.

"JJ. My nephew."

"Oh. You have a brother . . . or sister?"

I think back to what Lulu told me. Didn't all the boys die, apart from Ivo? A sister, then.

"Well, he's my cousin's boy. Sandra. So he's, er, what—my cousin as well. Once removed, or something. I dunno . . ."

Without Christo, he seems nervous. He sucks hard on his cigarette. Seen in broad daylight, his skin is remarkably smooth, almost waxen. I think of the illness again. Is this one of its marks?

"You have any sisters?"

A pause.

"I did. But she died."

"Oh. I'm sorry. Was she ill, too?"

"No. Car crash."

"Oh. Was that when your father was injured?"

"No. Long before. I was sixteen. She was seventeen." Ivo glares at me through his cigarette smoke. There's a truculence showing through his reserve. He's losing patience.

"What were you going to say, indoors—about Rose—the things she said?"

He squints off into the distance, cigarette balanced lightly on his lip so that the smoke curls into his eyes. He doesn't blink, just narrows those long eyelids. Long, sweeping eyelashes. Then he pulls the cigarette out with a jerky movement. Flicks it too hard, so that the lit end flips into some dandelions. Not so cool.

"She started to act like Christo didn't exist. Like she'd never had him. I didn't know what to do. I was afraid that . . . she might hurt him or something. I wouldn't leave him alone with her. When she went . . . it was sort of . . . a relief."

Ivo seems to be focusing on a tractor that's crawling up a lane toward the horizon. There's a white estate car right behind it, impatient to pass.

"Would you say she was depressed?"

"Dunno. She didn't seem happy."

"Some women suffer from postnatal depression. The symptoms can be quite severe. And if the baby wasn't well . . . that wouldn't help."

"No one ever said. But she wasn't happy. She didn't seem right in the head."

"Did she see a doctor?"

"No."

His tone implies, Why would she have done that?

"Did you . . . talk to anyone else about her?"

He shakes his head.

"Not even your father?"

"I didn't want him worrying. Besides, she was my wife. It was my family. My business."

He relights the broken cigarette and sucks it, hollowing out his smooth cheeks even further.

"Did you love her?"

He stops fidgeting. The only thing that moves is the cigarette smoke.

"Mr. Janko . . . ?"

Suddenly a vision of Lulu flashes into my head. Lulu straddling the inert body of her—what?—lover? Client?

Ivo hasn't answered. He seems to be struggling with the idea.

"We were married, you know . . ."

"Was it a happy marriage, I mean, to begin with?"

"I didn't do away with her. That's what you're thinking, isn't it?"

There's nothing aggressive in his tone—his voice is as soft as ever, and he's still watching the tractor inching along the lane in the distance.

"I would never have hurt her. She left us. I think she couldn't take it. Had a . . . breakdown or whatever you call it. I think she wanted to wipe Christo and me out of her mind—like it never happened. Start again. That's what I think."

He flicks the spent cigarette into the hedgerow and turns to walk back toward the trailers. I am dismissed.

I follow him back to the trailer where he collects his son from the young cousin. The boy dawdles on the step, peering at me through curtains of dark hair.

"You're the detective."

"Yeah. I'm Ray. Ray Lovell."

I hold my hand out. Slowly he takes it and shakes.

"JJ."

"Hi. Could I have a word?"

I'm trying to remember how to talk to teenagers. Unfortunately, I never knew.

22.

JJ

I don't think Mr. Lovell can be a very successful private detective—his car is quite old and dirty. He seems all right, though. Some people make you feel uncomfortable, and some don't. He doesn't. He makes you feel at ease. I asked him about being a private detective, and he said he'd tell me one day. It was funny—I don't think he was just putting me off.

About a minute after he drives away, Ivo flings open the door to the trailer.

"Jesus! Can't you knock?" I say.

"What did he want?"

"What?"

"The snooper. What did he want to talk to you about?"

"You know . . . same as he asked you. What I remembered about Rose."

"What's he asking you for?"

"I dunno."

"What did you tell him?"

"What I remember. About the wedding. That's all. Why?"

"Why's he asking you? You were a snotty little kid!"

"I don't know, do I? I suppose he's asking everyone."

"I don't like the way he keeps nosing around. Like he's suspicious. Like he thinks I did something to her."

"I don't think he seemed like that. He seemed all right."

"He's not going to think you did away with her, is he?"

I sigh. I hate it when people burst into the trailer without knocking. It's the least they can do when you don't have your own room, in my opinion.

"I don't think . . . that he thinks anyone did away with her." But this has never occurred to me before. I look at my uncle with fresh eyes. Could a relative of mine have murdered his wife? My uncle Ivo? No, of course not. Ivo seems to relax.

"Sorry, kid, it's just . . . on top of all the worry about Chris, that's all."

"Actually . . . Mr. Lovell asked about him, too."

"About Chris? Fucking hell. Christo's nothing to do with him! Fucking nerve."

"He said you should get a second opinion. Take him up to London and see a specialist."

"Yeah? What sort of specialist?"

"A children's specialist. I don't know. Maybe we should."

"Oh, you're an expert now and all, are you? Going to pay for it, are you?"

"No."

I'm really fed up with him; otherwise, I wouldn't say what I say next.

"But there's not going to be some stupid miracle, is there? Why are we all pretending? It's all crap, isn't it?"

Ivo doesn't disagree. He doesn't agree. He doesn't say anything at all. He looks sad.

"Because when you—"

He grabs my hair then, right at the neck, so it hurts, and puts his face right next to mine, and shouts, so that I see the nicotine stains on his teeth, so I can smell his stinking faggy breath.

"Christ, JJ! Can't you ever shut up?"

His eyes look wild, like a stranger's, a madman's. I'm too shocked to speak. My uncle Ivo hasn't shouted at me for years. He doesn't ever lose it. Not really. Even when he's really angry, it's a quiet, sulky sort of anger. He lets go of me then, and grabs his own hair between his fists. His mouth screws up like he's trying to keep something in. For a freaky minute I think he's actually going to cry, or something, but he swallows it.

"Sorry, JJ. Sorry. You're right. We should. We'll do that. Yeah? A specialist."

"I'll come with you, if you like."

"Yeah. Okay. We'll do that. You and me."

He says this in a way that means we're not going to talk about this anymore. He takes out his fags and pokes one in his mouth.

"Want one?" He holds out the pack of JPS. I shake my head, even though Mum's out at work and wouldn't ever know.

Ever since the other night, when I came back from Katie's, I've felt kind of twitchy with Ivo. I've been trying not to think about it, but it's hard not to. Trying not to think about what I saw, but it keeps going through my mind, jostling for space with Katie's hair and her red lips, and the beautiful chestnut horse in the stable that was more beautiful than their house. You know what I mean—like sometimes you can't get all the pieces in your head to lie down and stop moving for long enough to look at them? What I saw was . . . I don't even know. I was walking up to the trailer, and the curtains weren't drawn, although the lace curtains were, of course, so I could see in because the lights were on, but not totally clearly . . . and Mum and Uncle Ivo were inside. That was quite unusual in itself—without Christo or me or someone around, I mean. But the weird thing was—it looked like they were . . . not kissing. No. Not kissing, but she—Mum—had her hands on his face, in a way that you don't touch people normally. In a way you don't touch your cousin. Normally. But it was just for a second, and then he pulled away from her and went to the door and went out. And she put her hands on the kitchen counter and leaned there, with her head down, with her shoulders hunched, looking really sad.

I froze in the shadows outside, not knowing what to do. Ivo stopped a few yards from the door, and I held my breath, hoping he hadn't seen me. He sighed and lit a cigarette. I just stood like a statue, waiting for him to go home, or to see me, or something, and at long last, he went into Great-uncle's trailer. I breathed a sigh of relief. But I wasn't relieved. I didn't know what to do. I still don't.

I think about how I used to pretend that Ivo was really my father, when I was too young to know what that meant. And I think about how Great-uncle did marry his first cousin, and that's why all their sons apart from Ivo died of the family disease. Then I wonder if I'm going to get the family disease, too. And, come to think of it, his father, my great-grandfather, who was called Milos Janko, married his first cousin, too . . . So, so . . . if that was all okay, why didn't Mum marry Ivo? Because he was ill? Because he was younger than her? Does she love him now?

Where was I? Katie. I don't want to think about them at all. I want to think about Katie. About tea-flavored kisses and silky hair sweeping across my mouth. It had exactly the same cool, soft feeling as when you take a brand-new brush in art class—one of the expensive ones that are made of squirrel hair (from their coat fur, not their tail fur)—and brush it against your lips when no one's looking, because you can't not. What would have happened if I hadn't said I had to go home? On the blue-brick stable floor . . .

Just as I'm getting into this fantasy, I see Mum and Ivo again—it is, apparently, seared onto the insides of my eyelids. It was the expression on her face that scared me so much. Could I really tell from outside? What if I've got the whole thing wrong?

Normally, when I have the trailer to myself for a bit—even without the help of Katie Williams—I celebrate by having a wank, but at the moment, I'm too depressed.

23.

Ray

When I came home from Richmond the other night, it was a struggle to stop myself from picking up the phone and calling Jen. I fought the urge by reminding myself what would happen if I did speak to her. She would sound distant and bemused. Relieved that she didn't have to deal with me anymore. Hatred, screaming, abuse I could take: it would feed me, it would mean she still felt something. It's the detachment that crucifies.

When she first told me she was having an affair, she said she didn't love him. She did care about him, because, she said, she wasn't a callous person. Even in my state of shock, I saw red.

"Yes, you are," I shouted. "You are callous. You've done this to me! How could you do this to me? To us?"

Jen sighed, a bone-deep, weary sigh. There was a glimmer of tears in her eyes. For her, my tough, loud girl, that was something.

"Oh, Ray . . . You have such high expectations. Of how perfect it all has to be. You want to be everything to me. I can't stand it. And I'm not perfect!"

I couldn't believe she said that. Complaining because I wanted to be everything to her. What was so wrong with that? I didn't say— because I couldn't trust myself to speak—that she had always been everything to me.

I paced up and down the sitting room. It was still barely ten o'clock. My hands were shaking. When she'd told me, my hands shook all the time, as though I had contracted Parkinson's. My hands never shook like that when I became an orphan. Someone told me that the death of the second parent is the worst, because that's when you realize that there's no one standing between you and the grave. When my father died, following my mother to the cemetery plot just outside Hastings, with a view of the English Channel, I did cry for him. I mourned him—acutely, at times. But only in short bursts. Suddenly, from the depths of grief, I would find myself dialing for a pizza, starving, obsessing about pepperoni. I do find it strange that adultery, which is by no definition a tragedy, is so much more painful than death.

What did I say? Of course I called. I called anyway, despite everything. The phone rang and rang. But she either wasn't there or was wise enough not to answer. At length I put the phone down and scrabbled through the papers on the table. I found the piece with Vanessa's number on it and dialed, trying to sharpen my memory of her face. I realized, with a pang of guilt, that I couldn't quite remember what she looked like.

More than two weeks had passed since the night we spent together, so I wasn't surprised to get a guarded response.

"It's been a while."

"I know. I'm sorry. I've, um . . ." I discarded the idea of saying "I've been busy." It would have been insulting. "I wasn't sure what I wanted. I don't know if Madeleine explained, but I'm getting divorced, and . . . I'm not very good at moving on. Isn't that what they call it?"

"So why are you calling?"

"Well, I . . . I wondered if you still wanted to get together sometime—for a . . . film, or something? You know . . ."

There was a pause. I pictured her weighing her options. I suppose she was thinking that most men she might meet—at our time of life, I mean—would be, to some degree, damaged goods.

"I don't know. Can I think about it?"

"Yes. Of course."

"Okay, then. Well . . . Bye."

I put the phone down, a bit startled. It had the result of taking my mind off things, at least.

The next evening, when she phoned back, I felt my spirits lift. I had decided that she wasn't going to ring, to punish me—which was no more than I deserved—so I was all the more pleased to hear her voice. Then she told me she had thought it over, and although she liked me, she didn't want to get involved with someone so unreliable. She said she was too old for that. She said she was sorry, which was kind but unnecessary. I said I was sorry, too, and I understood. We were both sorry and understanding. When I put the phone down I felt a hundred years old.

Today, on the other hand, Lulu sounds cheerful, if anything, even pleased. I ask her to meet me again, to "clear up some points." She doesn't ask what they are, or why I can't clear them up over the phone.

We meet in the same café as before. It's busier this time, being a Saturday. Lulu walks in a minute after I do, wearing jeans, and under them—I can't help noticing—a pair of black, shiny, viciously high-heeled boots. She seems more relaxed, as if a weight has been lifted off her mind. Even her hair looks softer, less aggressively black.

"How is your investigation going?"

"Not very well, I'm afraid. Working day today?" I really didn't mean to say that, but somehow it fell out.

"No."

"I hope I'm not interrupting your day off."

"You are. But it's okay. I wanted to do some shopping, anyway."

Lulu scrabbles in her shoulder bag, and at length fishes out a packet of Silk Cut and a plastic lighter. She has to click the lighter a dozen times before it lights.

"I suppose being a private carer can be pretty long hours?"

"Can be. Yeah. But David—the guy I look after—his family's very supportive. He lives with his mother. She still does a lot for him."

"Oh—he's not old, then?"

I sound casually surprised, I think.

"No. He's disabled. It's terrible, really. When he was twenty, he had a tumor on his spine. They operated, but they damaged his spinal cord. Not once but twice—can you imagine? He's pretty much paralyzed from the neck down."

"Poor guy."

She nods.

"Really makes you count your blessings. He's so cheerful, though. Most of the time."

She smiles fondly. I just bet he is.

Lulu crosses her legs and stares at one of the glossy boots flashing as she wiggles it up and down. I wonder what else she does with wheelchair guy. I've heard about people like that—they like to be in control, to have someone else absolutely in their power. Is that why she does it?

"So how did you get into that line of work?"

"When you've got no qualifications, you don't have a lot of choice. And when you're a woman—and not as young as you used to be—it's either that or cleaning." She doesn't sound bitter about it, just stating a matter of fact.

"It sounds like a decent job."

"It is. I used to work in an old people's home. This is . . . better."

She smiles. I can't think of a suitable reply. We sip tea.

"No sign of Rose yet?"

"No. But I met your nephew—and his son."

"Oh. And?"

"He doesn't seem to remember much about his wife's disappearance. Or he didn't want to tell me."

She doesn't rise to this.

"There were a couple of things which I don't quite understand."

"Oh? Like what?"

"Tene said that Rose went missing while they were stopped at the Black Patch near Seviton."

"That's when you asked me about it."

"And you said the Black Patch was near Watley, which it is."

"So he made a mistake."

"The site at Seviton isn't called the Black Patch. It's called Egypt Lane. No one calls it the Black Patch."

She shrugs.

"But Ivo insisted it was near Seviton, and that it was the Black Patch."

She looks confused and wary.

"So what?"

"Maybe nothing . . . but you didn't know Seviton as the Black Patch?"

Lulu looks unhappy now.

"Not that I remember . . . but I haven't been there for twenty years. I didn't know where they were. I only know what I heard—and that was later."

"When?"

"God, probably when Tene had his accident. Yeah. It was. That was the first time I'd seen them since the wedding."

"His accident. When did it happen?"

"What has this got to do with Rose? It was after she'd gone."

"I know it may seem irrelevant. Not very much does seem

relevant at the moment. I've looked for a few missing persons, and . . . it's odd that there is no trail at all. I'm looking for anything."

She sighs, and stares at a corner of the ceiling for a moment, lips pursed, tapping out a rhythm with her foot.

"I got a phone call from Kath, saying that Tene had been in a car crash. He was in hospital."

"Where was this?"

"Cambridge. So I went up there. He'd broken his back. And at first they thought he might have brain damage."

"How did the accident happen?"

"He was driving at night. Lost control and went into a wall."

"Was he alone?"

"Yeah."

"Was it icy? Was the weather particularly bad?"

"No. I don't think so. No, just dark. They thought he'd fallen asleep."

"Where was he going?"

"I don't know."

"So who did you see in the hospital?"

"Kath, Jimmy, Ivo, and Christo, of course."

"They were together at the time?"

"No, just Tene and Ivo. Kath and Jimmy came when they realized what had happened."

"And who told you about Rose?"

"I asked where she was, and Kath told me she'd run off with a *gorjio*."

She shakes her head.

"It was a disaster. Tene's the head of the family. The only Janko man of his generation to survive. We didn't know if he was going to live. Then . . . it's almost impossible to live on the road if you're disabled. They threatened him with a care home—it would have killed him. It fell to the family to take him on, and that wasn't easy. Kath and Jimmy and Sandra and Ivo all agreed they would stick together, so that he could stay on the road with them."

"That was very good of them. Especially Ivo—with a sick baby to care for—quite an undertaking."

"They didn't know he was ill then. God, if we'd known that—maybe they wouldn't have agreed."

My note-taking hand slows to a halt.

"Then Rose didn't know he was ill, either."

"No, I suppose not."

I think about this for a moment.

"Did you speak to Ivo about Rose, too?"

"Oh, I think I remember saying I was sorry about it."

"And?"

"And nothing. He seemed dazed by the whole thing—the shock of Tene, and having a small baby to look after. Knackered, probably."

She hesitates.

"He was never talkative. He was a sweet kid, you know. But with all that happened—his mother and sister dying . . . he sort of shut down."

"When did they die? And . . . what of?"

Lulu sighs again.

"Marta had lung cancer. His mother. She died when he was about fourteen. And Christina"—she exhales a stream of smoke—"died in a car crash in France. They'd been to Lourdes, of all places, for Ivo. It was Marta's dying wish to take him there. To ask for a miracle."

She gives a bitter little laugh. I make noises of sympathy.

"She was only seventeen."

Her eyes slip out of focus, dwelling on something that isn't on the table in front of her.

"I bet you're thinking, How likely is it that one family can have had so much bad luck?"

I shake my head.

"No. I'm just sorry."

"We couldn't believe it. I mean . . ." Lulu lights another cigarette. "You don't smoke, do you? Have you heard of *prikaza*?"

"*Prikaza*? No . . . ?"

"It's from my grandfather's side. Things don't happen by chance.
Illness isn't bad luck. *Prikaza* is punishment for breaking the laws of
mokady."

"Does your family believe that?"

Lulu smiles and shakes her head slightly.

"Makes you wonder, though. One of the main reasons for *prikaza* was mixing too much with the *gorjio*."

"Did your family do that a lot?"

"Hardly. It's the tradition in our family to marry a first cousin.
Maybe we did something even worse. Did you know that scarlet is
really *mokady*? Like, if you wear scarlet, or paint your wagon scarlet,
you get *prikaza*."

I think of her red high-heeled shoes, and the last time I saw
them. Mustn't think about that. Must not. But I have a feeling she's
thinking about them, too.

"So Ivo's reaction to Rose leaving . . . ?"

"Just no reaction, really."

"Did you ever wonder . . . if Rose was in the car with Tene?"

She stares at me as though I'm stark raving mad.

"No! Of course not! What a weird thing to think. She was long
gone. Long gone! Honestly . . ."

"Sorry, I have to ask. It's a coincidence, though, these two things
happening at about the same time."

Lulu shakes her head in disbelief.

"Tene broke his back . . ."

I take a moment to catch up on my notes, then to ease my writing hand, which is starting to cramp. Lulu smokes with intent, as if
she's trying to burn the cigarette down as fast as possible. It's the one
thing about her that reminds me of her nephew. Lulu regards what
little is left of her cigarette, having showed it who's boss.

"Are you good at this?"

"What?"

"This private-detective stuff. Are you a good private detective?"

"I'm not doing very well at the moment."

I say this to try to make her smile, and she does, to my delight.

She seems sincere, even in her confusions. But the information remains as slippery as ever. Times, places . . . the order in which things happened—all these shift and twist and slide out of reach just as I think I've got hold of something. No one remembers clearly. No one saw anything. No one was there.

Way back, when I was looking for Georgia Millington, I was at the same stage. I had nothing. No clues, no leads, no idea. I worked tirelessly. Going over the same facts, the same witnesses, talking to people again and again. And then there was the turning point: as so often happens, someone slipped up. In this case, it was a school friend of Georgia's who gave two conflicting accounts of the last time she'd seen her. Her name was Jakki Painter. They called themselves Jak and George. She'd known where Georgia was all along.

In that case, I wish I'd failed. I wish the turning point had never come. But you don't know what people are capable of, do you? Until they do it.

"So what are you going to do now?"

Lulu leans back in her seat, swinging one leg. I wish I could erase the image of her in that room in Richmond.

"I thought I'd ask you to dinner."

It comes like a bolt from the blue, even to me. And the worst thing is, I'm not sure if I'm asking because I want to have dinner with her (although perhaps I do) or because I want to see if she'll squirm.

She looks astonished. But a muscle at the corner of her mouth retracts.

"Is that allowed?"

About as allowed as screwing a vegetable, says a little voice in my head.

"Well, I'm divorced . . . single."

"I mean as a private eye—and me in a . . . case, or whatever you call it."

"I don't suspect you of anything."

"Oh, um . . ."

Twice in two days. Women struck dumb by an invitation from Ray Lovell.

"I don't know if that would be a good idea."

"I'm sorry. You're seeing someone . . . I should have asked."

"Well, it's . . . Sorry. I don't think I should. Sorry."

She seems genuinely embarrassed. She neither confirmed nor denied that she was involved with someone. So what does that say?

At this point, I suppose, it's academic.

24.

JJ

I asked Mr. Lovell if he tails people. He smiled and said sometimes, but said it was boring. And he does surveillance, too. Like on the telly. He said he doesn't carry a gun, though, so he's not like Crockett and Tubbs from *Miami Vice*—more like *Shoestring*. I've been thinking—and I've got too many things to think about, not counting my O levels—but when I think about this I feel a bit less stupid and helpless. I think I could find out some things, about my dad, maybe. Mr. Lovell explained how you move from information to facts to evidence: that's the investigators' procedure. He said he sometimes has to go through people's rubbish bins to find evidence (I'm still not entirely sure how evidence and facts are different, but apparently they are). He said people are very careless about what they throw away. I said, "Like what?" and he said, "Well, like credit card receipts," which apparently show everyone what you've bought. I didn't say I've never seen a credit card. And also things like pill packets, so you know if there's something wrong with them. This made me feel uncomfortable—I mean, that stuff is supposed to be private, but he said that's part of the job, and if people are doing something wrong, it's fair enough.

If I'm clever, maybe I could find out about Ivo and Mum. Only

I don't think there's anything in our rubbish—or in our whole trailer—that I don't already know about. It's so small. I mean, we're quite good at being private from each other when we need to be, but that's not very often. Mum's never been that touchy about her stuff. I used to play with her jewelry when I was younger, go through her box and take out all her earrings and bracelets and lay them all out on the floor, things like that. Since then I've been through her things a couple of times. I'm not proud of it, but I don't think she ever knew. I never found anything other than what you'd expect to find in a woman's things. I thought maybe she'd have a picture of my dad, or something else of his, some clue, but I never found anything. I can't follow Mum or Ivo when they go off in their cars. I can only ask questions while not making it too obvious what I'm asking about. I've tried that. So far, nothing.

So today, when I come back from school, I say I'm going fishing. I take my rod and go fishing for a bit, but nothing's biting. I don't catch anything except a wet bum from sitting on damp grass. After it gets dark, finally, I walk back, sticking close to the trees so no one will see me.

I can't hear the radio from Great-uncle's, which probably means that Gran and Granddad have taken him to the pub. Maybe everyone's gone. The lights are out in Ivo's trailer. I creep and stop, creep and stop, until I'm right under Ivo's trailer window. The curtains are shut, and try as I might, I can't see through the cracks. Then I hear a voice, but it doesn't sound like Ivo talking, so maybe the telly's on—something weird. Someone's moaning. Maybe it's a thriller.

Then I have a sensation like someone has dropped an ice cube down the back of my shirt. Because the telly isn't on. The weird noise is coming from a person. It sounds like someone's moaning and speaking at the same time. I listen to catch the words, but I can't. It doesn't even sound like English, to be honest. Maybe it's Romanes, but I know only a few words. It's the weirdest sound I've ever heard. I start to worry—what if it's Christo and he's ill again? It doesn't sound like Christo, but . . . Or what if Ivo's ill? Maybe something's happened to him and Christo can't help.

Then another thought hits me, like a fist in the gut. What if it's Mum in there with Ivo, when everyone else is down at the pub. What if they're . . .

I walk away for a few steps, not really realizing what I'm doing, and then walk up to the trailer like I've just got there. I deliberately walk on the stones, kicking things, making lots of noise, coughing . . . you name it. I walk right up to the door and bang on it. The moaning stops, but no one says anything. I knock again.

"Ivo? Are you there?"

Silence.

"Ivo?"

More silence. Then a scuffling noise.

"Ivo?"

"Not now, kid."

"Are you all right?"

There's a silence, then the door opens a tiny bit. Ivo peers out.

"Course. Just a bit tired, that's all. Christo's asleep."

"Oh, it's just that I heard something . . . I thought . . . Is he all right?"

"Yeah. He's fine."

He obviously wants me to go away, but I don't move. Ivo sort of shrugs, opens the door, and gestures for me to come inside.

"Since you're here."

I go in. Mum isn't there. The trailer looks strange, but I can't think why. Then I get it—the only light is coming from some candles on the table.

"Has the genny run out?"

"No."

Then he realizes why I've asked.

"Oh . . . those. Nah. Just . . . Look."

Christo is lying on the bed, eyes open. It gives me a chill, seeing him there, with just the candlelight, and the strange noises I heard. I feel a hand grab my throat—that's what it's like, anyway—and I start toward him, convinced for that split second that he's dead . . . but he turns his head and looks at me with his big brown eyes. He smiles.

Part of me wants to run away, to think of an excuse to go, but how can I leave Christo there?

"What's going on?"

Ivo looks at me across the candles. It's weird; the trailer seems bigger when you can't see much of it, and his face looks strange, sort of smooth and pale, like he's made of wax. His eyes are like twin black mirrors with the candle flames reflected in them.

"You know when we went to Lourdes . . . we were hoping Chris would get better. We were hoping for a miracle. And it hasn't happened, has it? You were right."

I shrug as though it's never occurred to me before.

"Maybe it just hasn't happened yet. Maybe it takes time . . . like with you."

"He's got worse, if anything."

He looks at Christo, lying there all good and quiet. Patient. Never asking for anything. Never moaning. Ivo looks different when he looks at Christo. Softer. I wish I could disagree with him, but I can't.

"I've been trying to tell myself he's not, but he is. I can't stand it. Seeing him suffer. I know it hurts . . . and it's all my fault. I made him like this."

His voice changes and goes hoarse. He makes an impatient gesture with his hand. With a terrible shock, I realize that he's crying. Ivo. With a thrill of something like terror, I see a bead of water slide down his cheek.

"It's not your fault. We can't help it."

"I should never have—"

"There's nothing you could do. It's not your fault!"

This is terrible. I want to put my hand out and touch him—on the sleeve or something. I've never seen him so upset. But this is Ivo we're talking about, so I don't.

"So . . ."

He looks down and sniffs loudly.

"So, this is . . . It might sound crazy, but it's no crazier than expecting a miracle, right? We're Gypsies. This is our curse. So maybe we should give him a Gypsy cure. Have you ever heard Kath or Tene talk about the *chovihano*?"

"No."

"The *chovihano* is a medicine man. A healer. Like a shaman—do you know what that is?"

I say, "Shamans live in the Arctic. They can turn into bears and stuff. And fly."

"Yeah . . . kind of. A *chovihano* is a Gypsy shaman. Someone who can cast out illness."

Visions of boiling herbs dance before my eyes. Dissected toads, and plants with names like mugwort and asphodel. I stare at the table, where a bowl of dark liquid throws back a reflection of the moving candle flames. This is worse than I'd imagined. I hardly know where to look—certainly not at Ivo.

"Because in the old ways . . . illness is never just illness. It's *prikaza*. Like . . . like a punishment."

"But why would Christo get punished? He's never done anything!"

"The whole family is punished, in the blood."

"For what?"

Ivo shakes his head. "I don't know. We've had this curse for generations."

"Come on, Ivo . . ."

"Is it any crazier than going to Lourdes?"

"It worked for you, didn't it?"

There is a silence for a long moment.

"What happened to me isn't going to happen to him."

His voice is small and strange. When I dare to look at Ivo, there are tears running down his cheeks.

Christo coughs.

"So that's what I'm doing. Trying to cast out the illness."

"You're a . . . *chovihano?*"

Ivo sort of smiles, as if he is at least a bit aware of the weirdness of the whole thing.

"My mum was—did you know that? She knew all about herbs. Healing. She taught me a bit. There are recipes and things. Written down. There's nothing dangerous in there."

He gestures toward the bowl of dark liquid. There is also a container of salt on the table, and, I realize, there's salt everywhere, like he's been pouring it all over the place.

"What's in there?"

"Plants. Stewed up."

"Oh."

"I reckon if anyone qualifies to be one, I do."

I don't know what Ivo means by this, and I really don't want to ask.

I suddenly feel terribly sorry for Ivo. He must feel so helpless. We all do—but it must be so much worse for him, as Christo's dad.

"Mr. Lovell said he knows a children's doctor. Up in London. A specialist."

"Yeah?"

"Maybe we should talk to him about that. If everybody chipped in, I expect we could afford it."

"Yeah. Maybe."

"It's worth a try, isn't it? For Chris?"

"Okay. Yeah."

"Okay, then . . . Well . . ."

I smile, wanting to cheer him up. Wanting him to be normal and put the electric light on. It's strange—I feel like I'm older than him. "See you later."

"Yeah."

"Are you coming over for tea?"

"Yeah. We'll be over in a bit."

I look at Christo. He looks at me calmly. He doesn't seem distressed.

"All right, Christo?"

He grunts at me, which means hi. Just like normal.

I go out with relief, wondering if he's going to start groaning and throwing salt again. I suppose it doesn't matter much. Maybe it is okay. It's just hocus-pocus. Candles and funny smells and a bit of moaning.

I mean, what harm can it do?

25.

Ray

We take an afternoon to drive up to Cambridge. It's the hospital where Tene was treated, and Hen knows one of the pediatricians there—they were at school together. Gavin is Irish, not as posh as Hen, a scholarship boy. He always looks exhausted. I like him.

"So it's feasible that a woman who'd had a baby two or three months previously, say, could just run off and leave everything."

We're sitting in the hospital canteen, discussing postnatal depression. Gavin can't even take enough time off to leave the building. He shovels congealed pasta bake into his mouth as we talk.

"You don't have to be psychotic to do that. There could be all sorts of reasons."

"Her husband said that before she left, she pretended—maybe really believed—that the baby didn't exist."

Gavin shrugs.

"I can believe that. There can be all sorts of manifestations. Mental illness is a slippery bugger. Literally anything you can think of is possible."

"Suicide?"

"Anything is possible. Glad I could help you!" He grins at us. "I'll send you my bill."

He's joking. And that's not the real reason we came. I've described

Christo's symptoms as best I can. Gavin listened intently, total concentration on his face. When I've gone as far as I can, he looks up.

"What do you think, Gavin?"

"I've no buggering idea."

When I meet people like Gavin, I wish I were an expert in something. Even when you don't know the answer, you inspire respect.

"I'd love to have a crack at him, though. You say the father recovered?"

He scrapes his plate clean.

"Can't believe I eat this stuff. Do you think you could get them both up to London—come to the clinic?" Gavin does his consulting on Harley Street. He's very eminent, by all accounts.

"I was hoping you'd say that. Ray will do his best."

"Thanks, Gavin. While we're here, could you do us another favor?"

Despite his reluctance—something to do with the Hippocratic oath, I believe; I stopped listening at that point—we get to see some office bod who looks up the records. I sense that if I was here on my own, I wouldn't get anywhere, but Hen's public-school accent and charm is a skeleton key in many instances—this is one of them.

We stress that we don't want to know any private medical details, just when he was there, and, Gavin having vouched for us, we get the information that a fifty-five-year-old man called Tene Janko (it seems unlikely that there are many others) was admitted to the spinal injuries department six and a half years ago, on December 18, 1979, having suffered a broken back in a car accident. He was in the hospital for eighteen weeks, and then discharged himself, against advice. There are no records of outpatient treatment.

Hen says, later, "Maybe she did commit suicide."

We've ended up in an old-fashioned tea shop in the town center.

"So where's the body?"

"Maybe she jumped down a disused mineshaft. Or a well. She could have walked into the sea."

All of these things are possible, and yet . . .

"Ivo's aunt, Lulu Janko, said that Rose had already gone when Tene had his accident, and they didn't know about Christo's illness then. 'Long gone' was the phrase she used. But Ivo and Tene both say Rose left after she found out the child was ill—that his illness was the reason for her going."

Hen shrugs.

"They're blaming her for leaving—less embarrassing than . . . admitting that you beat your wife, for example."

"So you agree that they're lying? You agree with me?"

Hen smiles. "Looks like it."

26.

JJ

I've been thinking a lot, ever since seeing Mum and Uncle Ivo together in our trailer. It makes me feel sick. Not that that was a wrong thing for either of them to be doing—I don't even know what that was, for sure. But it's as though someone has pulled the carpet out from under my feet; I'm trying to keep my balance but don't know if I can. And since that night with Ivo doing his witch-doctor stuff, I'm even more off balance. It hasn't had any effect that I can see, other than weirding me out: Christo seems just the same as before.

One thing that's happened, which I think is a good thing, is that Mr. Lovell came back to see us and suggested that Ivo take Christo up to London to see a specialist in children's diseases. I didn't even have to bring it up. Apparently, he knows a doctor who will do it for nothing. There was a big family meeting about that—or rather, there was a family meeting for everyone except me, because, although I have to clean up and do my own washing and generally be responsible—"Now that you're fourteen, you're not a kid any-more"—when it comes to decisions like this, it seems that I'm not an adult, either.

I pointed this out to Mum, and she said, "Well you aren't an adult yet, are you? You can't drive, and you still go to school. Anyway, you should be glad you're not an adult; there are things you don't know, and you should be glad you don't know them." And I said, "What are you talking about? Maybe I do already know them," and she said, "No, you don't know about this, I know you don't." And I said, "You don't know what I know," and she said, "Yes, I do."

After that, I got even more worried, trying to think of what could be so awful that I've never heard of it (but she has). I mean, I already know about lots of awful things, like the Holocaust and war and rape and torture—how can it be worse than those?

Then I wondered if she was talking about Rose. Something must have happened for her to vanish so completely. Why would she not want to come back and visit Christo? Even if she and Ivo fell out and couldn't stand each other, Christo is still her son, and she would want to see him, I should think.

Then I remember that my father didn't want to see me.

Mum says it's different for men. It just is. I wonder why I never put the two things together before: Rose and my father. Rose had a baby with a Janko and disappeared. My father had a baby with a Janko . . . and disappeared. For a wild moment I must admit that I thought something crazy—that Ivo was my father, and that Mum was Christo's mother—before I remembered, with relief, that I had met Rose. She really existed. And I would have noticed if Mum had had another baby, wouldn't I? I may have been seven, but I wasn't a total idiot.

Even without exams to worry about, my head is exploding.

My investigations start with Gran. Mum was living with them— although in her own trailer—when she got pregnant.

"Can I ask you something?"

Gran looks at me from the kitchen of trailer number two.

"You just did."

"Did you ever meet my dad?"

Gran puts down the carrot she is peeling.

"Have you been talking to your mum again?"

"She won't tell me anything."

"Well, it's up to her."

"No, it isn't. I have a right to know where I come from!"

"Oh, you have a right, do you? The only right you have is to do what your mum tells you."

"It's not fair."

"Life's not fair."

"Did you meet him?"

"No, I didn't. We never knew him, not even his name. God knows we tried to get San to tell us, but she was that scared Dad would go and break his legs, she never did. She was right, too."

Gran snaps her mouth shut, looking grim and angry.

"He ruined your mum, that *gorjio*. Is that someone you want to talk to?"

"Didn't say I wanted to talk to him . . . I just want to know. It's like . . ."

I don't know what to say. Like I only half exist?

I poke my finger behind a button that's coming loose on the upholstery. When I look up again, Gran has gone back to her carrots.

I don't feel like asking Ivo just yet—I think I should get everyone else's version first. So next I try Great-uncle. Unsurprisingly, he's not much help.

"You know what they say, 'It's a wise child that knows his own father.' "

"What?"

Great-uncle twinkles his eyes at me.

"My kid, you should count yourself lucky. You're the son of the Gypsies, and every one of us looks out for you, you know that."

Sometimes he drives me up the wall. This is one of those times.

"You always say family matters more than anything. 'Family first. Family first!' But I don't know who half my family are. Half my DNA comes from somewhere else—and I don't know anything about it! You don't know what that's like! It's . . . horrible!"

"Be careful what you wish for, my kid; you might get it. And then you might wish you hadn't have got it."

He looks more serious now.

"JJ, you'll have to ask your mother. When the time is right, she'll tell you."

"She won't know when the time is right."

He wags his finger at me now.

"Don't you be disrespecting your mother. Your mother knows more than you will ever know."

"'S not surprising if no one tells me anything."

Great-uncle throws his head back and laughs, but there's an element of "watch it" in the laugh.

"Oh, no one ever tells you anything, do they? You're going to that fine school, getting your *gorjio* education. You'll know it all one day."

"That's not what I mean. I mean . . . things about us."

"What things about us? What don't you know?"

I shrug.

"Lots of things. Like what happened to Rose."

"Oh, Rose, is it? You been talking to that detective fellow again?"

"No. So? I remember her. She was nice. She played with me. I was sorry she went."

"So were we all. And you know as much as I do about that one."

"But you were there! You must remember something about who she went off with, or why . . . or what had happened just before . . ."

Great-uncle frowns at me, drawing his great furry eyebrows together in that way that he has, so that his eyes seem to peer out from under a bush.

"People can just go. Like your dad. He just went. And maybe they don't want to have anything to do with the people they leave behind. And maybe you're better off when they leave—have you thought of that?"

"Was Ivo better off when Rose left? Was Christo?"

I expect him to get angry. But he doesn't. He looks . . . sad.

"I don't know, kid. She wasn't . . . right in the head."

I stare at Great-uncle, openmouthed. I've never heard anyone say this before.

"What do you mean 'not right' . . . Is that why . . . Christo?"

"We don't know. Maybe that's one of the things we'll find out from this doctor fellow."

"So . . . she didn't go off with someone else?"

"I don't know. She may have. We God-honestly don't know. JJ, when people don't tell you things, it may not be to hide things—it may be we don't know ourselves. Only God knows everything. And listen . . ." He leans as far forward as he can go in his chair, and sticks his finger in my face. "Don't go bothering Ivo about this. He's got enough to worry about. I want you to promise me. Promise!"

"Yeah. All right. I won't."

"Promise?"

"Promise."

"Swear on your mother's—"

"Yes!"

Not very helpful. This is a fairly short example. You can talk to Great-uncle for hours and hours and come away with absolutely nothing. It's an amazing talent of his. Practically a superpower.

27.

Ray

Persuading Ivo was easier than expected. I drove down and found him talking to his cousin Sandra. They are chalk and cheese: where Ivo is dark and sullen, Sandra is blond, slightly plump, and friendly. I warm to her. It was probably down to her that they agreed to Christo's consultation. Ivo said they would have to think about it, but it was only a day later that Sandra rang the office to say they would love it if my friend would see Christo. That was the word she used: "love."

A week later: I offer to collect Ivo and Christo from the site and drive them up to London, but Ivo insists on taking his van. I worry about them being late for the appointment—or not turning up at all—but when I arrive at the café where we arranged to meet, around the corner from the clinic, I find Ivo and Christo ensconced in a corner, several cigarette butts in the ashtray. Christo smiles at me when I walk in. I smile back.

Ivo is visibly nervous, pulling hard on another cigarette, his eyes constantly darting to mine, then sliding away.

"What's he going to do, this doctor?"

"I imagine he'll just ask questions, to start with. Maybe do some blood tests. This is just a preliminary meeting, and he might refer Christo to someone else if he thinks they'll be more suitable."

"Someone else? Like who?"

"I don't know. Another specialist. It depends on what he finds."

Ivo nods determinedly but seems to be quelling his nerves only with an effort. Christo, sitting on the seat and leaning against him, doesn't seem either nervous or unhappy—but it's hard to tell.

"Gavin's a good man. Very straight. He really does want to help. And he's a top guy in children's medicine; we're really fortunate."

Ivo looks down at his cigarette, clenched almost flat between narrow fingers. A slight tremor there. His mouth moves as if he's about to say something, but he doesn't.

"There's nothing to worry about. It's just a chat."

"He's going to want to know stuff?"

"Well, stuff about the disease, yes. He'll need to get a picture of what's happened in the family, I imagine."

As usual, he doesn't look me in the eyes.

"And . . . it's not going to cost us anything?"

"No, absolutely not. Don't worry about that."

I smile in a way that's meant to be reassuring, although Ivo doesn't look at me, so doesn't see.

Ivo carries Christo to the clinic. Once we're through the heavy glass doors to the lobby, which swish closed behind us with a sucking sound, all outside noise is cut off as if with a scalpel. Footsteps are muffled by a thick, dense carpet. It even muffles voices. The hush that—in London—only money can buy. I go up to the receptionist— a perfectly made-up middle-aged woman with a shining helmet of hair—and explain who we are. Ivo stands in the middle of the carpet, looking uneasy and out of place.

I find myself wishing he'd made a bit of an effort with his appearance—instead of which, his greasy cap is pulled down over his eyes, and he wears the same buttoned-up waistcoat and maroon handkerchief . . . In fact, I have yet to see him without them. While we wait, in a room full of cream-colored armchairs and beige carpet—even I glance down to see if I've left footprints—I try to engage Ivo in conversation. But he either is too nervous or is incapable of small talk. He responds with grunts or mumbled monosyllables, fussing with Christo's hair, combing it with yellowed fingers. He smells of cigarettes and fear. His fingernails are bitten to the quick, cuticles rimed with black. Despite my frustration, I feel a stirring of sympathy for this difficult young man. He's had a lot to put up with in his short life. Something my dad used to say comes to mind: that the Gypsies are genuinely hard done by, but, by God, they don't half make it hard for people to sympathize.

The receptionist tells us that Gavin is free. I offer to come in with them.

"No. It's all right . . . thanks."

I read a *National Geographic* article about a doomed attempt on Annapurna. The silence in the waiting room is so absolute, it makes me wonder if the world has been wiped out in a stealthy nuclear attack. A clock ticks. After half an hour the receptionist puts her head around the door. She looks put out.

"Is your friend here?"

"No. Why?"

She gives a tight little smile.

"We don't seem to be able to find him."

"He's probably having a cigarette outside."

"We've looked. He doesn't seem to be anywhere in the vicinity."

I stare at her.

"And the boy?"

"Oh, his son's still here, in with Dr. Sullivan. Perhaps you could . . . ?"

I hunt for Ivo on the block, around the corners, then on the neighboring blocks, the nearest place you can buy cigarettes, in the café where we met . . . I can't imagine where else he might have gone. Or why. When I come back to the clinic, the receptionist, and then Gavin, have searched the entire building, including the cellar.

There's absolutely no sign of him.

28.

J J

Mum has always been really cagey on the subject of my dad. She said since he went off and left her before I was even born, good riddance to bad rubbish. Which is basically what she says again, this time, over dinner.

"I just want to know who he is," I say. "I don't even know his name. You know . . . I have the right to know where I got half my DNA."

"The right?"

She glares at me over our plates of stew. Then she sighs.

"I know he's your father, sweetheart. But he broke my heart. I don't want him to break yours as well."

I can tell she's considering giving in, so I say nothing.

"You'd have to find him first, before he could break your heart. And I wouldn't know where to start, to tell you the truth."

"I'm not saying I want to find him," I mumble. It's an alarming thought. Knowing about someone is one thing. Seeing them in real life is quite another. "If you had a photograph or something . . ."

"Well, that's easy. I don't have any photographs, so I can't show you one. You don't look like him; you're a Janko through and through."

My heart skips a beat. What does she mean by this?

"Just tell me his name, Mum. Please."

She sighs again, and stares at her plate for ages. My heart is thumping. My mouth is dry. I wonder if it's too late to back out. What if she says something terrible, and once I know it, I can't ever unknow it?

"I suppose we had to have this conversation at some point. But you know . . . I just don't want you to get hurt."

"Why would knowing his name hurt me? Is he in prison or something?"

"No, no, of course not! Well, as far as I know . . . You know, if you're adopted, they give you the information when you're eighteen."

"But I'm not adopted, am I."

"JJ, he was a . . . well . . . You deserve better. You deserve the best father in the world, sweetheart, but I can't give you that."

"I'm not saying I want to find him, Mum. Just his name. I'm fourteen. I have a right to know that."

Mum looks at me without speaking for a good thirty seconds. I time it by the yellow clock.

"All right, JJ . . . His name was Carl. Carl Atkins. I met him at a disco. We went out for a few weeks. He was a *gorjio*, a plasterer's mate. I hadn't had a boyfriend, so I didn't know anything about anything." She studies her plate, as though it might tell her what she should have known at the time. She looks at it for a long time without saying anything else.

"Did you . . . love him?"

She smiles sadly.

"I thought he was the bee's knees."

"Did he . . . Did he think you were the bee's knees?"

She almost laughs, as though I've said something funny.

"Well . . . he said he did. Said he was going to marry me."

She shrugs, in a way that's painful to watch. As if what's on her shoulders is unbearably heavy.

"I was a fool."

"Why?"

Another sigh.

"Old story: young girl, innocent. Flash geezer, bit older, gets her into trouble . . . Then she finds out he's already married."

She gives a horrible fake smile.

"He was married?"

"Yeah."

"How could he?"

"Oh, sweetie . . . Men can."

"But how . . . I mean, where was his wife?"

"Back home. 'Cause he was on a job, no one knew him. Knew anything about him."

My father is an arsehole. This is something I have to come to terms with. What if I am like him? I feel sick, I can't eat anymore.

"And you didn't know?"

"Of course I didn't know! Good heavens, JJ. I wouldn't have had anything to do with him if I'd known!"

"Couldn't you tell?"

"No. You can't 'tell.' "

"So then . . . what did you like about him?"

I try to tell myself I don't care what he was like, as he obviously didn't care two hoots about me, or Mum, either, but I'm seized with the need to know, a horrible, whiny need I can't control.

"Well . . . he was funny. Made people laugh. And generous. He'd always pay for a round. He earned decent wages, and he wasn't mean with them. He had dark curly hair, and he wore gold earrings. Had blue eyes. Had a rose tattooed on his arm. I used to joke that he wanted to be a Gypsy. He was handsome . . . Maybe you do take after him in that way . . ."

She leans forward and takes my hand. I take my hand away, cross my arms so she can't get at me.

"I thought I didn't look like him. I thought I was a Janko through and through."

"You are. But there's something . . ."

She studies my face, trying to smile, but it looks like it's harder and harder work. She leans forward again, puts her hand on my arm.

"Pet, this is why I didn't want to tell you. It was bound to upset you. Better forget about him. You have your family here. We all love you. You're too good for him!"

I hug my arms to myself. I'm trying not to be angry, I really am.

"Did he ever . . . see me?"

It's not what I mean to ask, but it's what I say. She hesitates.

"No. It happens, JJ. It's horrible, but some people are like that, and the best thing is to . . . walk away from them, try and forget about it. You should be glad you don't know a man like that. Now, that's enough, all right? I've told you what you asked. I've got washing up to do."

She gets up, scrapes the food off the plates into a bag, takes them over to the kitchen, and starts clattering around. I am left sitting at the table, feeling dirtier than I've ever felt in my life.

Fathers, even if they're absent from birth—even if they're dead, for Chrissakes—are supposed to leave something behind for their kids. A locket with a picture in it, or a rare book. A box that contains a special, wonderful secret. In stories, that's what they do.

But in real life, you get nothing. I knew this, of course. This isn't some fairy tale. I wasn't expecting to discover I was a prince, or be given a million pounds. I don't know what makes me so furious all of a sudden.

Because I think she's lying.

And I am furious. Boiling. Something unleashes inside me; a dam breaks; like I'm a volcano about to explode, red-hot lava rises behind my eyes, building up to an eruption.

"You could have kept up with him. For my sake. You must have known I'd want to know about him sooner or later."

Mum's got her back to me, clashing plates and things in the washing-up bowl, so I don't know exactly how she reacts. She speaks without looking around.

"I had my dignity. I wasn't going to go chasing around after him, when he was married."

"You had me! His son! If you'd cared about me you could have done it. At least . . . found out where he was. Like Mr. Lovell. That's what he does. He finds people. Even when they don't want to be found!"

I'm shouting. Mum drops the saucepan she's holding into the bowl with a slap that sends soapy water slopping onto the floor.

"Well, he hasn't found Rose, has he?"

There's a thick silence. She's reveling in her triumph, I can tell. She turns around now.

"JJ, if you want to hire a private detective when you're eighteen to find this man, that's up to you. I'm sorry things happened the way they did. I'm sorry I couldn't give you a good father. I'm sorry things aren't different . . ."

"You mean you're sorry you had me!"

"No, of course not . . . JJ, that's enough!"

Looking at Mum, I feel as though I'm looking at someone I don't know. I don't recognize the woman with frizzy blond hair and reddened hands—an ugly, frightening stranger who's standing in my trailer.

I speak very coolly.

"You talk about dignity. What were you doing with Uncle Ivo the other night, when I came back? I saw you."

Stranger-Mum seems to shrink back against the counter. Her lips move, but no sound comes out. And then a harsh red flush flares over her cheeks; she looks so guilty, and so ashamed, that I don't need to hear anything else.

"You don't know what you're talking about."

I give a sort of nervous, stupid laugh. I've no idea what it means, other than that, right now, I hate her. I hate her, and I despise myself.

"Take that disgusting smirk off your face. You don't know anything."

"Don't I?"

"No."

"Don't need to say it. Saw it with my own eyes."

Her eyes seem to have got larger still. She's very, very angry, too. I wonder whether she's going to admit it and say something like "Don't you understand, Ivo's your real father."

I wait. Nothing would surprise me.

She doesn't say that; instead, everything goes very slow, like in an action film when something explodes. Everything is crystal clear: I can see every molecule of her reddened face in amazing microscopic mega-vision. I see it coming, but I can't do anything about it, because I've gone very slow as well.

Mum hits me, a proper hard slap on the face with a wet, soapy hand, right on the cheekbone. It doesn't hurt much, but it's shocking. She hasn't hit me for about five years. It makes me twice as angry as I was before. From red-hot to white-hot. And it makes me glad, because now I'm allowed to be as bad as I like.

I smile, feeling water and soap suds slide down my cheek, run under my shirt collar.

"What would have happened if I hadn't come home just then?"

Whack.

Backhand. This time I feel the ring on her middle finger connect with my ear. Blood whistles and roars in my head like the crashing surf in *Big Wednesday*.

"No wonder you weren't worrying about where I was."

Whack.

She's losing control, just brushed my cheek, fingertips, with no power in it. She looks like she's about to cry, her cheeks all mottled red and white, her eyes screwed up and glittering.

"Get out! Get out!"

She yells it in a funny deep voice, all hoarse, and, feeling bad and glad and volcanic and terrible, I crash against the table so hard that it sends glasses sliding onto the floor—Good!—and go.

It's raining. I don't care. How could she throw me out when it's raining? She shouldn't be allowed to be my mother. All the other trailers have their curtains drawn, so very little light comes out. Mum is probably thinking that I'll go to Gran's for a cup of tea, or Great-uncle's, but I won't. That would be too easy for her. I'm going to go, like she said.

But first I break into Ivo's trailer. He's in London with Christo, seeing the doctor. I break the window in the door with a stone. I don't hear a sound. I don't feel a thing. I kind of hope I cut my hand doing it, but I don't. I could pour with blood and not feel pain right now; nothing can stop me. Inside, I close the door, draw the curtains, and turn the place over.

I am ruthless. Thorough. Mr. Lovell would be proud of me.

Why? I don't really know. I don't know what I'm looking for. I have no more than the haziest idea—something that might give me a clue to the disappearance of Rose? Something that might prove Ivo is my father? I have no real conviction that he did anything to Rose. I have no more than the vaguest hunch about the other thing. But I want to punish him. For carrying out a crazy exorcism and making me know about it. For being in my trailer with Mum. For making her touch his face like that, and then lean over the counter, crying.

For making me hate her.

I've never broken into someone's place before. Never stolen anything. It isn't really me; it's the volcano that does it. (I am the volcano.) Am I bad, because I do a bad thing? If I find something that proves a crime, does that cancel out the bad and make me good? In the end it doesn't seem to matter. I do find something, but it isn't evidence of a crime. Women's private things—a bit disgusting—but why? Is it left over from Rose? Why wouldn't he throw them out? Or . . . is it something to do with Mum? It's not proof of anything, really.

And then, at the back of a cupboard in the kitchen, behind some cleaning stuff and old cloths, I find a tightly tied poly bag. It looks like rubbish. We never keep rubbish inside the trailer—you put it outside, where it won't smell. But I think of what Mr. Lovell said— that you can find secrets in people's rubbish—and this bag is pushed right to the back of the cleaning cupboard, where no one would want to look. I undo it, careful not to tear the plastic, and then . . . I find myself pressed against the opposite wall in revulsion. The women's things aren't left over from Rose, for here is one—used. A dark, dry stain. The metallic smell hit me before I jumped back. It's so *mokady* it's untrue. It makes me *mokady*, too . . . Did I touch it? This is something a man should never see or hear about. It has the power to make him unclean. I'm shaking. But still, I have to put it back in the bag, and tie it up, and push it back in the cupboard.

It's not proof of a crime, of anything really wrong. It's proof that they're lying to me. What else could it be? Not a crime. But breaking into Ivo's trailer that night is the worst thing I have ever done. It is the thing I most regret.

29.

Ray

By now it's after six, and everyone else has gone home. We hang around for another hour, in case Ivo decides to return, but there is no sign of him. Gavin's secretary calls local casualty departments, but no one answering Ivo's description has been admitted. I don't know where he parked his van, and Christo makes no response that I can understand when I ask him, so in the end I have to phone Lulu. She is, after all, a blood relative, and she has a phone. And she's the nearest. Luckily, she's also in.

"You're where?" I've just explained the situation, rather succinctly, I think. "You're with Christo? In Harley Street?"

"Yes. And Ivo's disappeared. A family member needs to be with him. He's got to go to hospital. Great Ormond Street. You know—the children's hospital."

A silence.

"I'm supposed to be going to work in twenty minutes."

"I'm really sorry. I just didn't know who else to ring. I'm not a relative, so . . . someone needs to be here, you know, to give consent. You need to sign something."

I think I hear a sigh of capitulation at the other end of the phone.

"And you're sure Ivo's not coming back? He must do!"

"He's been gone over three hours."

"I'm going to kill him."

"So you'll come?"

Gavin is a star. He hangs on until Lulu arrives, which takes more than an hour; then he explains what he thinks should happen. I keep thinking that surely Ivo will walk back into the clinic with some reasonable-sounding, contrite explanation. But he doesn't. Finally, Gavin ushers us out and hails a taxi. He rolls his eyes comically when I say I owe him one. I can't think what I could do for him. Spy on his wife for nothing, perhaps.

I fetch my car and drive back to find Lulu and Christo waiting on the pavement. Christo seems calm, despite the turmoil around him. Lulu is tense. For the first time, she isn't wearing heels. I checked as soon as she arrived: plimsolls, sensible shoes for saving people's bacon. We're very polite. Neither of us mentions our last meeting. Now we're back on a professional footing. And yet she and this strange, pitiable boy are in my car, accepting my help. I am of some use to her, after all. In some ways, it's more intimate than any dinner could be.

I explain how we have come to be here in the first place, how Ivo excused himself to go to the bathroom and never came back. Gavin had just asked him to provide a blood sample.

"I suppose we should thank you for doing this for him."

She doesn't sound grateful. I shake my head.

"Do you know if he had a needle phobia? That's what Gavin thought it might be."

She shrugs.

"I don't know."

"Have you any idea where he might have gone?"

"Maybe he's gone home."

"Can we get in touch with Tene?"

"Not directly. Might be quickest to drive down there. God . . . How could he leave Christo there on his own? This family, I swear . . ."

She's sitting on the backseat with Christo leaning against her. Her arm is around him. Rain slicks the streets as we head for the children's hospital, blurring lights into smears of color on the windows. I watch the two of them in the rearview mirror. Lulu looks out the window. Her lipstick looks darker in this light; it makes her seem different, unfamiliar. Christo is looking back at me in the mirror—pool-dark eyes wide, his face shining like a pearl. Lulu said she hasn't seen him for nearly three years, so can he really remember her? He would have been barely four years old. Perhaps he would be this tranquil with anyone. Perhaps, in his mind, Ivo is still with him. Perhaps he knows exactly where his father is.

"I just hope you get to find out what's wrong with him. That would be something, wouldn't it? Then maybe they can help him."

Lulu smiles absently but doesn't reply. With a foolish jolt I remember that, whatever the illness is, she too may harbor it, slumbering in her veins. What did she say before—that it affected only the men of the family? Does that mean it's one of those things that can be carried by women, like a poisonous gift? The ability to give life and take it away in a single transaction.

From the shadowy safety of my driver's seat, I steal glances at her. Blue-white cheek. Dark, slanting fringe. One eye flickering with reflected lights. I see the ghost of a dark vein that goes down the side of her neck, before disappearing under the collar of her blouse.

The blood beneath her skin.

A couple hours later, I'm driving down the motorway, following a red river of taillights heading southwest. A soothing flow of bright red corpuscles streaming down a nether vein of the night. I don't think she really expected me to offer, which is why I did, earning a smile, first of disbelief, then of genuine, astonished gratitude—my prize for the night. I imagine her relating this to a friend (but not a disabled male friend): "I don't know where we would have been without Ray.

He even drove down to Hampshire in the middle of the night to find Ivo. Can you imagine? I'd have been lost without him . . ."

Of course, she probably doesn't call me Ray.

The rain comes on again, harder than before, then harder still, and the wind gets up, scudding and punching against the car as I near Bishop's Waltham. The streaming tarmac shimmers like blood under the brake lights.

Why, tonight, do I keep thinking about blood?

30.

J J

Like the climax of a film, it's throwing it down when I leave. I don't care. In fact, at first, I'm so hot that it's a relief to feel cool water pelting my skin and hair. I'm not wearing a coat. If I had been, I'd probably have taken it off so that I could be even more righteously wronged and they would be even more sorry. Although, by the time I've crouch-run past the trailers, keeping close to the trees, it's dark, anyway; the only light comes from the swooping headlamps of passing cars, and they don't care that I'm there, if they see me at all—I'm not thinking of anything. Other than that I'm getting out of here and as far away from them and their dirty secrets as I can. Is this what Mum was talking about—that thing I can't possibly know? I see her stranger-face, red-eyed, hot, shamed, and I hate myself for what I said. But she told me to get out. She said that.

I jog along the verge of the main road, but there are too many cars around, dazzling me with their headlamps. One car blares its horn exactly as it goes past—they probably think it's funny—and I nearly have a heart attack. So I head off down the little narrow road called Swains Lane, which is pretty unused this time of night. There's a fair old wind stirring the tops of the beeches that arch over the lane and make it into a tunnel, and rain splatters down between them. Under the trees there's a churning sound everywhere, a roaring, as though the countryside is being stirred by a giant hand. It hides me; it drowns my gasping breaths that are almost sobs. I have to slow to a walk now and again just to get my breath back, but as soon as I have it and my heart has stopped trying to burst out through my ribs, I have to run on.

About halfway down Swains Lane a funny thing happens. I see a parked car at the end of the lane, where it joins the bigger road that leads back toward the industrial estate. There are no lights on inside the car, and there's no one in it, and yet there are no buildings in sight. I can't think who would have left their car there on a night like this. Just for the hell of it, as I go past, I put my hand on the door handle and press the trigger. And it opens.

After looking around to check that there's no one coming, I sit inside for a minute out of the rain and imagine I'm a totally different person who knows totally different things. Who doesn't know what I know. Who hasn't got old trainers with holes in, that squelch. Maybe I'm a twenty-five-year-old man with a wife, and I'm about to go home to her. Maybe I've been to the races today and won thousands of pounds. I haven't yet planned what I'm going to do with all the money; that is a pleasure I have to look forward to, along with telling her about my win. The money's on the seat beside me, a roll of notes snug inside a red rubber band—I've seen them, passed from bookie to pocket. How happy she will be. My wife who looks like Katie Williams, with honey-colored hair.

It would be nice to stay in the car—maybe curl up on the backseat, hide under a dry checked blanket, and go to sleep. Maybe wake up hundreds of miles away. Far away, with a new name. But there is no blanket.

I open the glove box. There's nothing inside but a map, a notebook with some figures in it that don't seem to mean anything, and a tin of those bullet-hard travel sweets: the sort that have a disk of paper on top of them and are meant to stop you from getting carsick when you're on a long journey. Suddenly I'm starving, so I cram a handful of the floury sweets into my mouth and put the tin in my pocket. Icing sugar dusts my fingers; water floods my mouth with lemony black-currant sweetness. There's a windscreen scraper in the door compartment, and I take that as well, just for the hell of it.

Then there's a strange noise outside. I whip around, heart jammed in my throat, pumping painfully, pins and needles in my feet and hands. I get out of the car and run off, convinced that someone has seen me and will yell at me or is leveling their gun sight on me from the shadows.

But no one runs toward me out of the woods. No one yells. No one shoots. No one is watching.

No one cares.

It doesn't occur to me to be scared out here. I'm much more scared of going home and looking into Mum's eyes—or seeing him—than I am of this. But still, I don't want to take the shortcut through the woods; I don't think I could find the path in such darkness. Instead, I stick to the road, walking fast but not too fast, and that's how I come across two more cars that have been left in dark, deserted places.

For some reason that I can't fathom, I have decided by now that it's necessary to break into the cars, as a test, and take something—a talisman—from each one. By now I'm kind of imagining that I'm in a fairy tale, where the hero has to have three apparently everyday but really magical objects that, when he is in the greatest danger, will come to his aid and save his life.

I am the hero, I hope, but don't we all?

I approach the second car not believing there will be no one inside it—probably some sad old snogging couple who won't give a toss about me—but there isn't. Again: no one. This door is locked, though. So using my new bad-person skills, I break the quarterlight with a rock, neat as anything. This time all I find is a pair of driving gloves: those ones that old men wear with the leather palms and the string backs with holes in. They've been well worn; even in the glove compartment they are rounded, molded around the ghosts of the driver's hands. They're soft and greasy, almost worn away at the finger ends, and much too big for me, but still. And as I walk away—no running this time—I feel my chest swell with the power of Getting Away with It. No one sees me. No one hears me. I don't even have to hurry.

Because no one cares.

It dawns on me then: this is the secret they have been keeping from me. All the things that you are supposed to do and not do— why bother? Because no one really gives a toss.

Look at my dad.

I have no idea how long I've been out in the rain when I come to the third car. I'm as wet as if I'd jumped in a river; even my underpants are soaked. I'm so cold I can barely feel my hands. I could be made of marble, a moving statue. I raise my marble fist and punch in the side window. It needs a couple of goes before it breaks, but I don't feel anything. I unlock the door and sit inside. Water drips down my fringe and into my eyes. I can't feel my ears at all. In the glove compartment I find a porno mag and a flat bottle of whiskey. I think about taking the magazine, but, considering where I'm going, it doesn't feel right. And maybe the whiskey is too useful, too magical; I should find something else. On the floor there's another windscreen scraper, but that's it. I decide to swap this scraper with the one from the first car. This seems incredibly funny—I wonder when they'll notice that!

There's nothing else to take, so I open the bottle of whiskey and take a swallow. I don't taste anything other than a metallic bitterness that seems to have been in my mouth forever, but after a second or two I feel its fiery trail scorch its way down my throat. It's brilliant—the heat and cold. Lava and ice. I take another swallow, and a second later I retch as it hits my stomach. I lean back in the seat, panting, the insides of my cheeks running with water, until the urge to puke passes off.

So here I am, soaked, dripping, frozen, sitting in the driver's seat of a Ford Sierra that belongs to God knows who. I'm overwhelmed with tiredness. I don't know how much farther I have to go. My earlier certainty has been washed away. Suddenly I start laughing silently, sort of shaking uncontrollably. The whole thing is pretty funny, when you think about it, pretty bloody absurd. Is it incest if you do it with your cousin? People at school make jokes about farmers being as thick as pig shit because their parents are related. But maybe that's not true—and maybe Mum and Ivo is more recent than that, anyway . . . Maybe . . . Maybe not. I take another gulp of whiskey. This time it doesn't burn so much, and I don't feel sick anymore. There's a nugget of warmth deep inside me, and the hard knot inside my chest is slipping, dissolving. The fourth mouthful I barely feel at all.

Rain hammers on the roof of the car—a comforting, monotonous drumroll. It's been raining since forever. I lean back in my seat, look up at the sky, at the raindrops hurtling through space toward me—it's like being on the Starship *Enterprise*, zooming through endless spiraling galaxies, going nowhere.

I break off the shard of broken glass that's still poking out of the car window, and stare at it. It's shaped a bit like the mountain on a Toblerone packet, only thinner.

A glass dagger. A true magical object, winking in the dark.

Sometimes you know exactly what to do.

I roll up my left sleeve and press the point of the dagger against my skin. Under it runs the Janko blood—the pure black blood. At least half of me—and maybe all of me. Janko through and through. Diseased, incestuous, cursed. I press harder, watching the dent grow under the point.

Harder—then pull sharply downward.

There is a strange mewing sound.

I open my mouth wide and watch my own darkness well out of me.

31.

Ray

Slowed by the storm, I don't arrive at the site until close on mid-night. All the trailer lights are blazing away; the rain falls diago-nally, the wind whipping the trees into an ecstasy of self-flagellation. Before I've even pulled up, Sandra Smith runs toward my car—her blond hair turning flat and dark between her trailer door and mine. Her face is shiny white in my headlights, a mask of fear.

"Where is he? You haven't found him?"

She's staring into the backseat. She seems almost hysterical. I can't see why.

"I don't know where he is, but he's got his van . . ."

"What?"

Then Kath and Jimmy are beside her. Jimmy leans in.

"Where's Ivo?"

"That's what I'm trying to find out. He hasn't come back here?"

Kath pulls the younger woman away from my car. I strain my ears to hear her.

"It's the detective. He's not here about JJ. Come on . . ."

"Mr. Smith, what's going on? Has something happened?"

Jimmy jerks his head to one side, meaning Get out.

"Her boy's run off. She's out of her mind with worry."

"Oh, God, I'm sorry . . . Well, Ivo's run off, too. He left Christo at the doctor's. I called your sister-in-law—she's with him now, in the hospital."

"Who?"

"Lulu . . . Luella."

"What'd you get her for?"

"Well . . . she's the only family member I know with a phone."

Jimmy stares at me, as though he can't compute all this information, then starts to lead me to Tene's trailer.

I wonder if there is a hole somewhere, in the fabric of England, and Jankos are falling through it, one by one.

Now we're waiting for Ivo to come back. I daren't go back to London and face Lulu without information of some sort. Tene has been the soul of courtesy, insisting he sit up with me, pouring glasses of whiskey, claiming he won't sleep until "the boys" return. But he seems confident that they will, and confident, too, that his sister, no matter how estranged, will take care of Christo.

An hour ticks by. Then another. We have run out of things to say. Tene smokes his pipe. The rain hammers on the roof. I can't imagine how anyone could sleep with such a racket; it's like being inside a drum. At length Tene asks me if I know any Gypsy stories. I shake my head. If my dad knew any, he kept them to himself. He wanted his sons to be postmen, like him; vacuum cleaner salesmen, like my brother.

"There's one I've been thinking of, my dad used to tell us. Do you want to hear it?"

"Sure."

Tene clears his throat. His voice drops a couple tones. He looks down, and when he looks up, his face is changed, lit up. Of course, he would be a born storyteller.

"Once, the land far away was ruled by a queen and a king. The queen of the fairies was very beautiful and lived on a mountaintop in a castle made of crystal, and under the mountain lived the king of the demons, who was as evil as the queen was good.

"The king saw the queen's beautiful face and fell in love with her. He asked for her hand, but she refused. In his anger, the king declared war on the fairies and began to annihilate them. To save her people, the queen agreed to marry him, but she found her husband so disgusting that he had to drug her before he could lay a finger on her. So they had nine children, but they were the most terrible children the world has ever seen, for they caused all the diseases of mankind.

"Their firstborn was Melalo, a two-headed bird who claws his way into men's hearts and makes them mad and violent; the fourth was a daughter, Tcaridyi, a worm who causes fever; and the eighth was Minceskro, who causes illnesses of the blood. But worst of all was the ninth child, Poreskoro, who was neither male nor female but both, and who spreads the plague. Even the king of the demons was frightened by this child, so he let the queen go at last, and she went into hiding under the mountain, where she sheds her tears, and there she remains to this day.

"And at the end of a story, my dear dad used to say, 'Now, ask me no more to tell you lies!'"

Tene leans back with a husky laugh. The air is hazy with smoke from his pipe. He doesn't seem to feel the cold, but that might be because he's swaddled in several layers of mismatched jumpers. I'm freezing: saturated with damp, wind-driven, three a.m. cold.

Tene tries to refill my glass, but I put my hand over it. I still have to drive home, at some stage.

"You see why I thought of it. Minceskro . . . I can't remember the names of all of them. My dad could, but . . . it's shocking how you forget. My sisters aren't interested. And the young ones—they don't care about the old stories. They only care about pop music and football, *gorjio* rubbish like that . . ."

The sound of a car engine penetrates the fug. I jump up, as fast as my creaking limbs can propel me, and go to the door. Tene's face changes—anxiety floods his eyes. He says something like "Go easy on him."

It's Ivo's van. My fury gets me as far as halfway to the driver's door. Kath, Jimmy, and Sandra are already there, surrounding him. They look furious, too. Jimmy takes his arm and mutters something in a low voice. Ivo looks up once, in my direction, his face haunted. He looks defeated and very young.

"What the hell happened to you?"

As soon as I've said it, I realize I've blundered. The others turn their faces toward me, shielding Ivo. But he pushes past them. His eyes are hollowed out, exhausted.

"Is Christo . . . ? Is he okay?"

His voice is even hoarser than usual, a shadow of a whisper.

"Okay? I don't know if that's the word for it. Gavin gave you his valuable time for nothing—you can't mess around with people like that. Why should he help you again?"

He makes no reply, just stares at me, pleading.

"Lulu's taken him to hospital for more tests. Yeah, he's okay. Probably wondering what happened to you, though. Probably terrified."

A spasm of anguish crosses his face.

"I . . . couldn't. I'm sorry. I had to—"

Kath seizes his arm and pulls him roughly toward their trailer.

"Mr. Lovell!"

He turns around; in between the three of them, he looks like a prisoner being dragged away.

"Thank you for what you did for him. It was really nice."

Then he's hustled inside and the door slams, leaving me alone.

"Please don't be too hard on him."

Tene is at his door, struggling with his chair. I feel a stab of sympathy for him. He is the head of the family in name only; he cannot control them, or even keep up with them—all he can do is apologize.

"We'll straighten him out. We'll sort it out, don't you worry. Don't go yet . . . Not yet."

Inside, he offers me more whiskey, trying to smooth things over, atone for the mess his relations are making of their lives. And, consequently, of mine.

"You have to realize, he has grieved so much. I had two brothers, you know. Matty and Istvan. They both died. Istvan when he was a kid, so Ivo didn't know him, but he knew Matty; he lived till he was thirty."

Tene wouldn't imagine Lulu would have told me some of this. I'm not supposed to already know.

"What did they die of?"

"They both had it. The disease. Istvan was worse than Christo, you see. Didn't have the strength to grow up. Matty was ill, too, but it wasn't so bad. He just kept getting infections: pneumonia and so on. He was great. A lovely man."

"I'm sorry."

"Then Ivo lost his brothers. Milo and Steven. They died when they were little."

I nod.

"But we had Christina, and then Ivo. And we thought—Marta and me—we thought, at last, our luck had changed. But Ivo got ill when he was four or five. They were like twins, those two. And then my wife passed—cancer. Two years after that, Christina died."

"I'm so sorry."

I whisper it. Too much repetition, and the words begin to sound like an insult.

He doesn't volunteer anything more. His grief is suddenly present, immediate, in the trailer, as though it happened only yesterday.

"I . . . I really am sorry."

I feel I have to say it again, but after so many condolences the platitude sticks in my mouth. So many losses—I can't even begin to imagine what his life has been like. Or any of their lives, come to that.

There is a black-and-white photograph on the wall, in a silver frame. It shows a young dark-haired woman, dressed in the fashion of the early sixties. A solemn, middle-European face, wide cheekbones. She is sitting in front of a photographer's backdrop—a satin curtain—and two children are pressed up against her. The woman is Tene's wife, Marta, and the children are Ivo and Christina. The survivors—at that point, anyway. Ivo is smaller than his sister—of course, he's the younger—and desperately thin, but with a sweet, happy smile. He must be about six—the same age Christo is now. Christina has her arm around him: a fierce older sister, glaring at the camera with her chin tilted up. They are very alike.

Presumably they knew then that Ivo was suffering. They didn't know how long he would have.

It's dawn by the time I get home. The message light on my answerphone is blinking, and although I'm too tired to care, I automatically hit the button. I don't recognize the man's voice.

"Ray? Mr. Lovell? I'm sorry to ring you at home, but since it's the weekend . . . I wanted to tell you that . . . Sorry, it's Rob here. Rob Anderson from Alder View. I think you should come up here again. All the work's been stopped. They've found something on the site. They've found human remains."

II.
The Trick
of Forgetting

32.

St. Luke's Hospital

For some reason, my right hand stays numb and inert even after the rest of me comes back to life. Naturally, I'm right-handed. I can pick up the right hand with the left, squeeze it, bend the fingers, pinch the skin, but I feel nothing. It's like handling a glove full of sand.

One of the nurses comes daily and pricks me with a needle. It fascinates me to watch her pushing the metal tip under my skin, while the expected pain doesn't materialize.

"What if it stays like this? Can't you do something?"

The nurse is young and cheerful. She has rosy cheeks that she ineffectually tries to tone down with greenish powder, and a small gold cross around her neck that swings out of her cleavage and dangles over my bed like a benediction. Even without the cross, you can tell that she's swaddled in the love of Jesus.

"We'll organize some physiotherapy for you. But there's no physical damage, so the nerves should recover on their own. You've got every hope."

She smiles at me. She's so young—about twenty-four—so confident, sweet, and pleasant. I bet she wanted to be a nurse from the age of five.

I have every hope. That sounds so nice. I wish it were true.

I am getting better; I can tell. Over the past few days—I don't

know how many it is—I have been recovering speech and movement. But I still can't remember how I came to be here. And I can't
atone for the mistakes I have made. Being a victim doesn't exonerate
you. After the Georgia debacle, people said to me it wasn't my fault;
I couldn't have foreseen what would happen. But they were wrong.
I had met her killer. I looked into her killer's eyes. I should have
known.

Sometime later—I must have finally dozed. I open my eyes to see
someone sitting beside my bed on one of the leakproof plastic chairs.
(They don't even trust visitors to be continent.) At first, it's only
because the broken sunlight coming through the cherry tree makes
a different pattern. A pattern splashed with red. Lulu Janko. With
her red shoes and red lipstick, her red, bitten nails. And, today, a
thin crimson scarf wound around her neck like a slash of blood. It
takes me a second to remember why I should be surprised that she's
here; my sluggish brain, fogged by the sedatives they give to help me
sleep, creaks into action, and I am duly ashamed. But she is here.
I'm not sure whether to be happy about this or worried. I think that,
on the whole, I am happy.

"Are you awake? Ray? Hello, Ray."

She looks a little irritated.

"Hello."

My voice comes out reasonably clearly.

"You look much better today."

"You came before?"

I try to think back—I can't picture her in the hospital room at all.

"Yes. You weren't awake, though. Not very . . . with it. I didn't
stay long."

God. What sort of state was I in? But she has come—twice! Take
that, wheelchair man.

"That must have been a pretty sight."

"Yeah."

She smiles.

"What brings you here?"

The smile goes. I didn't mean to sound aggressive.

"Would you rather I went?"

"No. I didn't mean that. I'm really glad you came. I know the last time we met . . . Well, I'm sorry—about it all. Wouldn't be surprised if you never wanted to set eyes on me again."

Shouldn't have said "really glad." Just glad. Or touched. Or . . . indifferent: something less than the truth.

"Doesn't matter. So you're feeling better?"

"Much better."

"That's a relief."

"So are you on your way somewhere?"

She shakes her head.

"I just wanted to see how you were."

"Oh."

I can't think of anything to say. I am full of questions, just not appropriate ones.

"Erm . . . How is Christo?"

There's something nagging away at the edge of my conscious mind. Something to do with her.

"He's doing well. He's still in hospital, but . . . they're really looking after him."

The more I think of it, the more I don't understand why she's here, why she's being nice to me at all.

As though she's reading my mind, she says, "I phoned your office. I spoke to your boss. He told me you were in hospital and . . . so here I am."

"My boss? I don't have a boss."

"Oh . . . well, the man there. He sounded . . ."

"Posh voice?"

Caught out, she actually blushes. She isn't the first person to assume Hen is the boss.

"Did he tell you what happened?"

"He said that you'd been taken ill and crashed your car. And that you were in quite a bad way."

She shifts in her chair.

"Yeah. I was poisoned."

Her eyes widen.

"Poisoned? What do you mean? Food poisoning?"

"I went to see Tene and Ivo. I think they gave me something to eat. And . . . here I am."

"Oh, God."

She leans forward, her forehead creasing. She looks horrified.

"What did you eat? Was it shellfish?"

"I don't know. I don't remember. But I wondered if . . . they were okay. They might have got ill, too."

"Oh . . . God, I don't know."

She takes a deep breath and lets it out in a short, sharp sigh.

"I'm so sorry, Ray, that's awful."

She called me Ray. She can't be too angry with me.

"According to them here, it was plants."

"Plants?"

"Yeah. Poisonous plants. I think . . . henbane was one . . . and ergot."

She doesn't look at me anymore. The crease in her forehead deepens. Finally, she says, "Do you . . . have any idea how it could have happened?"

"Well . . . I suppose it must have got into the food, somehow."

I am speaking to the top of her head. For the first time, I notice a little stripe of gray at the roots of her parting. She must have been too distracted to see to it. Distracted . . . by what? For some reason, this fact squeezes my heart with an almost physical pain.

"You should check on them. It wouldn't do to be ill like this and not be in hospital. Especially Tene."

She nods, fiddles with the handbag on her lap, although "handbag" is a misnomer. You could get a cocker spaniel in there.

She looks at me, finally. I'm not sure, but there could be tears in her eyes.

"I'm so sorry about this, Ray. I . . . They do collect stuff to eat sometimes, like mushrooms, berries, and things, you know—I suppose it's easy to make a mistake . . ."

"Yeah."

I shut my eyes for a minute. After the harsh sunlight, searing patterns scribble themselves on the insides of my eyelids—they resemble monsters with long teeth and filthy claws.

Lulu seems uncomfortable, uncertain. A couple times she almost stammered. It strikes me that this is the first time she doesn't have a default position that puts me automatically in the wrong: defiance, suspicion, outrage.

"I'm really sorry about all this. My family drive me mad, but they aren't bad people. They wouldn't hurt you deliberately. Ivo . . . I know he doesn't always seem very . . . polite, you know, but he loves that boy with all his heart. He's really grateful for all you've done for him, with the specialist and so on."

I don't know what to say. I don't think I accused him to her face.

Then I think, if she hasn't seen them, how does she know he's grateful?

She jerks her head toward the door of my room.

"They say you're going to be fine. I hope you get better very soon."

"Thanks. You should tell Ivo, though . . . in case he doesn't know. It's dangerous."

"Yeah, yeah. I will."

I am still bothered by the feeling that there's something important I need to remember. Something involving her.

I just can't for the life of me think what it is.

Lulu avoids my eyes and stares into the middle distance, chewing at her lipsticked mouth, wearing off the harshness of the red, leaving it blurred and sore-looking. A strand of dark hair has slipped out of her barrette and falls in a long wave down the side of her face—it forms a reverse curve: the elongated *S*, the most beautiful of lines, according to Chinese aesthetes: the line of a woman's hip and waist when she's lying on her side . . .

Oh, my girl, you don't know. You don't know what you do to me.

"You know, I found something," I say, recklessly, because now I'm afraid she's about to go; I can feel her attention slipping off elsewhere, tugging at the leash. I want it back. "I was about to tell Tene, but I didn't get a chance . . ."

I try to move my right hand but can't. Still dead meat.

"About Rose . . . About . . ."

A look of anxiety comes over her face, and she leans in to me. And suddenly, with a jolt like a thousand electric shocks, I'm aware of her hand on mine. My numb right hand, lying on the cover with its plastic bracelet like a dead snared rabbit. With as much feeling. She's holding my hand. Well, not holding but definitely touching— I can just see it out of the corner of my eye. Typical. She touches me when I'm paralyzed—or, perhaps, because. And I think: of course, that's the way she likes them. I can't feel a thing. Not a thing. Although I imagine that I can.

I imagine everything.

"What is it?"

I realize I can't remember if I told her before. Or was there something else?

"You told me about the . . . bones they found. Is that it?"

I open my mouth to speak. The human remains . . . Yes. And there was something else, I'm sure, but the thought is breaking up even as it forms in my head. Maybe if I whisper, she'll lean down

toward me, her ear an inch from my lips. Maybe I will catch a whiff
of her cigarettes-and-perfume smell.

At the same time she seems to become aware of my eyes on our
hands, and though I try not to react, she moves her hand away, and
it dives into her vast handbag and starts to scrabble in the murky
depths. For what? The answer? It comes out again, empty.

"You look tired. I shouldn't keep you any longer." (No! No! You
should!) "I have to go, anyway. Got to be at work soon."

It's like a slap in the face. Go. Work. Him.

The illusion of intimacy evaporates like scent.

"Work. Of course."

She gets up, glances at me suspiciously, although I didn't say it in
any way at all. But then she stands by the bed for a long moment,
about to speak.

"Ray . . . uh, I hope you feel better soon. I'll see you. Okay?"

She walks out, her shoes busily ticking off the seconds down the
linoleum corridor. I listen to the sound fade, and time returns to its
normal hospital crawl.

In the slow hours that follow her visit, I have the time to think
about things. Like, what was she going to say at the end, before she
changed her mind? Like, why did she come and see me, twice? To
check that I wasn't dying, so she can report to the family that they
don't need to skip the country?

To assuage her own guilt?

And what on earth does she keep in that vast sack of hers that she
needs to drag around with her all day? Her purse, her cigarettes, a
selection of red lipsticks . . . a year's supply of hostility . . . an econ-
omy pack of disapproval . . .

The secret, inexplicable blueprint of all my desire and delight?

How did it end up there?

33.

JJ

The pain wakes me. I come to, having no idea where I am. I'm curled up, surrounded by something prickly. A strange smell. Something hard juts into my hip. My right fist is throbbing, and, when I try, I don't seem to be able to straighten my fingers.

I shift, and there's a rustling all around me. It's very quiet. Then, from somewhere nearish but outside, I hear a car engine—a smooth, expensive car engine—start up and drive off, and I remember where I am. A soft thudding comes from much nearer, which means the horse is walking around in his stall. An explosion of air from horse nostrils. It's a good sound. I was right to come here, I think. It's going to be all right.

I had to break in to the stable last night: the door was locked, which surprised me—it hadn't occurred to me that people would lock a horse in for the night, but luckily one window was open, so I slithered through, scraping a load of skin off my hip bones on the windowsill in the process. The horse was moving around but didn't seem alarmed at my appearance. He didn't start making a lot of noise, anyway. I spoke to him in a low voice, reminding him who I was. I could just see the gleam of his eyes in the dark. He seemed mildly curious, that's all.

I didn't want to put the light on in case someone saw it, but

I remembered that the stable was divided into three loose boxes and a small extra bit at the end for tack. There are wooden walls in between that don't go all the way up to the ceiling. The end box is where Subadar lives; the middle one is empty, apart from a couple bales of hay and odds and ends, and the one at the other end is where they keep the straw for his bed, and tools, and his food and stuff. There's a big stack of straw bales—I remembered that you couldn't see the top when I was here before, but that was a couple weeks ago, and there is less now. Still, I climbed up and made a sort of hollow where I couldn't be seen from the door, and fluffed lots of straw around myself, so I'd be pretty hard to spot even if you were standing right next to me. The only bad moment was when I slid down to fetch one of Subadar's stripy horse blankets. I reckoned he wouldn't mind. I managed to knock over a metal bucket in the dark, and it made a horrendously loud clanking and ringing noise as it rolled around on the brick floor. I froze, sweat springing in my armpits, waiting for lights to come on everywhere and police sirens to start, but nothing happened. I suppose Subadar kicks buckets quite often. I climbed up onto my straw platform and lay down, pulling the blanket over my head, trying not to giggle with nervous horror because I had kicked the bucket.

I'm superstitious, I suppose. I told myself it was just a coincidence. People—farmers and so on, especially—must kick buckets all the time, and they don't die. Not right away, anyway. To calm myself down I drank some more of the whiskey and ate a few more sweets—I'm rationing them, of course—and then I don't remember anything else.

The longer I'm awake, the more I remember about what happened last night, and the more I realize what a mess I'm in. My right hand is purple and swollen from where I punched in the window of the last car. My knuckles are bruised, and there's dried blood on them.

My hip bones are red raw where I slithered over the windowsill, and there's a long, sore scrape down my side—I have no idea where that came from. The worst thing, though, is my left arm. I remember digging the glass dagger into the skin above my wrist, but in a strangely detached way—it's as though I'm thinking about someone else doing it, a crazy person that I'm watching for some reason. I wasn't trying to kill myself, or anything stupid like that; it wasn't that at all. I just knew I had to do it, like lancing a boil or something. Letting out the poison. It was horribly fascinating. Hard to do, despite the whiskey. I had to force my right hand as though someone else was pulling my arm away.

I had to grit my teeth.

But the rush when I saw the blood well up and run down my arm—it was amazing.

I remember all this now with great clarity, although, in daylight, it seems like a pretty dumb thing to do. I kind of wish I hadn't done it, to be honest. I don't think the cut itself is too bad—I mean, it's not that deep, and it's not bleeding anymore, but it hurts quite a lot, and it makes me feel sick to look at the inside of myself exposed to the air like that, so I pull my sleeve down to cover it up. It throbs with a hot sort of pain. I can't cover that up.

I eat two more of the sweets—an orange one and one of the not-very-nice green ones. What are they supposed to taste of, anyway? There are only four left, and three of them are green. I'm incredibly thirsty, and I have to go to the toilet quite badly. Luckily, I have my watch on, so I know that by now Katie will have been taken to school, and there's probably no one here. Or maybe just Mrs. Williams. Very slowly and cautiously, I peer over the top of my nest, then slide down the straw stack. The stable is so luxurious there's even a tap in here, so I put my head under it and drink and drink, and then try to wash off some of the blood. Subadar looks around mildly. Now I see he's tied up to a ring on the wall, probably to stop him from eating all the hay at once. He's got some food in his rack, so it seems likely that someone has been in this morning and didn't notice anything odd. I feel a warm rush. Was it Katie? Was she near me while I slept?

Halfway through an endless pee—I do it in the gutter that runs along the stalls, reckoning that as the horse does it there, it must be all right—I remember that it's Saturday. Why did I think Katie would be at school? She could come in at any minute. Luckily, she doesn't—I don't think I could have stopped peeing, no matter what. After, I shoot back up to my hiding place and lie down. I don't feel too great. I feel kind of sick, and my head hurts, probably from the whiskey, and my various scrapes and cuts ache with different degrees of sharpness and heat. Soon I'll be very hungry. And then—but only then—I'll have to think about what to do.

When I wake up again I know, without having to look at my watch, that it's afternoon. Where is everybody? Does she leave the horse on his own in here all day? Surely she'll come and take him for a ride. I'm starving hungry and eat the rest of the sweets, even the green ones. I can't see any point in saving any. But putting something in my mouth just makes me hungrier. My headache has gone, but the cut on my left arm is itching like mad. When I pull up my sleeve to have a look, the skin has gone red and swollen, and it's hot—I can feel the heat coming off it when I hold it up to my lips. The raw flesh is disgusting—wet and crusty at the same time. I know this is not good—it'll have to be disinfected. Stitched, probably. And my right hand is completely stiff, bent into a swollen claw shape, so it's not very easy to do things with it. I wonder if I can hold out for another night.

The thing is . . . here's the thing. The thing is, me and Katie, we're not boyfriend and girlfriend. In fact, I've barely spoken to her in the last two weeks. Since that afternoon in her study, which I've thought about at least a thousand times a day, we've gone back to our previous habit of basically ignoring each other's existence. This is the way I expected it would be at school, so it was no surprise, and I didn't mind too much. She lifted her eyebrows at me on the second day, and I smiled before I could stop myself, and she turned away with a toss of her hair, quick as a flash. I felt I'd failed some kind of test, and I cursed myself for being so uncool. Stella has been talking to me more, though, which made me wonder if Katie had told her anything. On the whole, I don't think so. She didn't say anything that made me suspect that she knew what had happened; she was just her normal, friendly self, like before she came to our trailer and it all went wrong.

Somehow, though, I've had the feeling that Katie was thinking about me, too. I had a feeling that I would see her outside of school again—and not like this, by breaking into her stable—properly, I mean. Because she wanted to. Despite that, I'm very aware that it's a big risk to jump out at her, which is why I was planning to leave it for another day. But I'm getting worried about my arm. And, I tell myself, it won't make any difference to her whether I've been here for one day or two.

Sometime afterward, the door opens and she walks in. I can't see her—I don't dare raise my head, but I can hear footsteps, and I reckon they sound like hers. Then I hear her talking to Subadar in that cooing, babyish voice she uses to him. My heart is thumping a mile a minute. I feel dizzy. I raise my head until I can see the glint of her honey-colored head, and take a deep breath.

"Hey . . . Katie!"

I try to make it a whisper that will travel just to her. And it does. She freezes. I can feel her fear from here.

"Katie . . . over here."

Her head snaps around, her eyes wide and suspicious.

"Stella?"

She looks cross. Why on earth does she think it would be Stella?

"Katie, it's JJ . . ."

"Yeah! I'm just coming . . ."

Stella is outside, that's why. She walks in through the door; I bury my head in the straw, but it's too late. Katie can see the voice didn't come from outside, that it wasn't Stella.

I sit up, furiously brushing straw out of my hair, in time to see the looks going from one girl to the other, and then from both to me—hard, sharp, suspicious.

"It's just me. Sorry if I scared you."

"Fuck!" says Katie. She sounds scared. "Christ on a bike, JJ."

Stella says, "What on earth are you doing here?"

She looks furious—but she's looking at Katie, not at me.

I swing my legs over the side of the stack and slide down. As soon as I do, I feel really dizzy, and my legs don't feel like they're going to hold me up. With a muzzy feeling that things could go either way, I decide to go with the flow, and sort of collapse in a heap at the bottom. My eyes close, and my head comes to a stop at an awkward angle against something hard and painful—the same bloody bucket that tripped me up last night.

I think, Okay, I'll just wait and see what happens now.

For a long moment, no one moves or speaks.

I imagine them looking at each other in horror.

"God, do you think he's dead?" says Katie.

"I think he's just fainted," says Stella.

Someone moves toward me.

"What's he doing here?" Stella is quite near to me. I can hear the sharp edge in her voice.

"I don't know! I didn't know he was here!"

"Really? But he's been here before?"

"Well . . . once! Ages ago . . ."

"We should get your mother."

"Oh, she's in a foul mood. She'll think it's my fault."

"You really didn't know about this?"

"No! God, look at his hand . . ."

"Oh, gross . . . JJ?" Stella kneels in the straw beside me. She prods my shoulder gently.

"JJ, are you all right?"

How long do faints last? They never say in those old books, just talk about smelling salts bringing people around. I have a feeling it's not very long, though. Plus, they might call her parents at any minute.

I make my eyelids flicker a bit, then open my eyes. I think about groaning, too, but am not sure I can pull it off.

"JJ?"

"Yeah?"

Stella looks relieved but still cross. Katie crouches down beside her and smiles. She doesn't look pissed off now.

"God . . . What's happened?"

"Katie . . . I'm sorry about this. Being here. Didn't know where else I could go."

"It's all right."

I don't think they're going to call anyone. They're both on my side now; I can feel it. Amazing. All I did was fall over.

"What happened to your hand?"

I raise my hand to be the center of attention: it's purple, bloated, and horrible-looking.

"I was in a fight . . . I had to get away. He threatened to kill me."

Sharp intakes of breath.

"Who?"

I feel a bit bad about this, but, shutting my eyes as if I can't bear to think about it, I say, "My uncle. He . . ."

With an effort, I use my injured hand to pull back the sleeve on my left arm. Both girls gasp in horror.

"Oh my God! He did that?"

"JJ, you should call the police!"

I shake my head. There are limits, even with Ivo, that I am not prepared to cross. "No, no, I can't. Everyone would get into trouble. My mum, my great-uncle . . . They'd get evicted."

"That looks infected. It's all red. You have to . . . get it seen to."

Katie sounds worried. I don't think I've ever heard her sound worried before. It's kind of nice.

I move my head off the bucket, and both of them hover over me, sort of helping without touching, as I sit upright against the straw.

"I'm really sorry about turning up here, but I didn't know what to do. I had to get away, and then I ended up near here—it was the middle of the night . . . I just wanted somewhere to sleep, and think."

"You should have woken me up."

Katie looks soft now, her lips parted. Stella glances at her.

"We have to get something for that cut. You should really go to hospital. You need stitches."

I touch my bad hand to my forehead, which brings an entirely unfeigned gasp of pain.

"I don't want to do anything that'll get my family into trouble. You mustn't call the police or anything, please. Will you promise?"

I look them both in the eyes. Both of them nod. Stella more reluctantly than Katie.

"If I can just get some antiseptic . . . and something to eat. I'll be able to work something out."

I have no idea what I could work out. But I figure that if I sound like I know what I'm doing, they're less likely to go and get the council leader. I don't think he would be too sympathetic, somehow.

"You can't hide in here forever, though. Her parents are bound to suspect something."

"I know. I know. Just for a day or two."

"Does your mum know about this . . . fight?"

Stella is frowning, thinking things through.

I hesitate for a moment. What to say about Mum? I can't even imagine speaking to her at the moment. What would I say?

I nod. Stella looks shocked.

Katie is, by contrast, businesslike.

"Of course you can stay here. I'll bring you food and stuff. That's easy. Then we can think about what to do. You can't go back home. Not at the moment, anyway."

Katie looks pleased. I think she's decided to enjoy this. It's a game, a secret she can keep from her parents.

"Okay. I'll go and get some stuff from the bathroom. And then . . . I'll say we're going to take our tea with us when we take Subadar out. We can get stuff from the kitchen."

She grins, excited.

Stella still looks unsure. She chews her lip.

"Thanks, Katie. I really appreciate this. I don't know what I'd do otherwise."

Katie stands up, her eyes gleaming with plans.

"Stella, come on . . ."

"Okay." Stella still looks grave.

"Can you get back up there by yourself?"

"Yeah, I think so."

"We won't be long."

I feel light-headed with relief. I'm overwhelmed with love for them both. They are angels.

Katie goes back over to Subadar for a moment, as if to reestablish her alibi, then the girls go out, chatting, sounding as natural as though they are walking down the school corridor, and I am some-where else, miles away.

As soon as I lie down in my little hollow, I start shaking. I haven't eaten for nearly twenty-four hours, on top of everything else that has happened. For a minute I think I'm going to be sick, but instead, for some reason, I start crying. Why now, I don't know. Tears run sideways out of the corners of my eyes into the straw. I must be a bad person. I have done so many bad things—breaking in to some-body's home, smashing and stealing and lying. But aren't other people worse than me?

I want to see Mum, and I can't bear the thought of her, all at the same time. I hope she's feeling sorry about throwing me out last night, and about saying what she did. I am sorry about the things I said to her, although it seems to me that they're all true. And Ivo must have come back by now. They're going to realize that it was me who broke into his trailer. Maybe he will even realize that I went through everything. That I saw what he keeps in his cupboard. So what? I don't care. I'm never going to see him again. I just need to get a message to Mum at some point, to let her know that I'm all right. Eventually.

One thing at a time, I tell myself. One thing at a time. All I have to do now is stop crying before Katie and Stella come back and catch me.

34.

Ray

The building site at the Black Patch has become a crime scene. I spot the fluttering yellow tape strung across the entrance as I drive up. That's the first thing you see from the road; the second is the pall of sullen brown water creeping across the site from the watercourse under the alders.

There's a little green tent on the southern edge of the site. The water hasn't reached it. Not yet.

It's not a promising situation. I have to persuade someone in charge that I have something they need. I've brought copies of the photographs of Rose; it's the only bargaining chip I have.

Police figures clad in cheap macs crawl around the tent like ants. The mud sucks at my boots as I wade toward them.

I track down the inspector in charge, a man with hooded brown eyes and brown shadows under them, smoker's skin, and slightly too-long hair that—he might think—makes him look like an aging Turkish film star. His name is Detective Inspector Considine.

"Ray Lovell."

I show him my license.

"When did this happen?"

He glares at me with bored superiority, an expression that plainly says he doesn't have to tell me anything.

"What are you doing here, exactly?"

I've already explained myself to two underlings, but it's part of the game, so I go over it again.

"I've been hired to investigate a disappearance. A nineteen-year-old girl who went missing around here about six years ago."

I hand over the photocopied flyer that features our two photographs of Rose—the race-day one and the wedding snap. He glances briefly at them, not betraying too much interest.

"These don't even look like the same person," he says, his voice dismissive.

"They were taken two years apart. This is the most recent."

I tap the wedding picture. Actually, I now notice that he has a point. Somehow, the photocopying process has exaggerated the differences wrought by those two years: the carefree girl with her solid jaw and secret smile; and the bride, tentative, uncertain—almost as though she was already beginning to disappear.

"It is the same girl. Her name is Rose Wood. Rose Janko when she married."

"Janko? What sort of a name is that?"

"A Gypsy name. Eastern European origin. English family."

He grunts. Not in the pejorative way a lot of people would. He's actually a little more interested. I wonder whether he has Gypsy blood himself, but that's not something you ask a policeman on first meeting.

"About six years? Can't you be more specific?"

"The reports are inconsistent. January or February 1980. She definitely disappeared in winter."

"Well, okay, thanks for that."

He's not dismissing it.

"So what happened?"

I take out a packet of cigarettes and offer him one. He accepts, so I take one, too, to keep him company, and produce my lighter. We're just two buddies standing out here in a muddy field, smoking in the rain.

He's weighing up how little he can get away with telling me.

"Digger turned up some bits of bone. Someone saw them and called us in."

"And this is the first time, at this site? I mean, I've heard it was an old burial pit for plague victims—they must have got all sorts here."

"Oh, that. No, it's the first time. I think the plague pit is just a rumor spread by the locals. Or maybe they're below the level of the foundations."

"So these bones weren't that deep?"

I'm trying to sound casual, but an excitement grips my insides.

Considine smiles, man to man, detective to detective.

"Look, I'll tell you what I know, and then you'll piss off, right? And it's not worth much."

I nod.

"Sure."

"It's about four feet down. Digger went right through it, chewed it up—it'll be a nightmare to piece back together, even if we find all the bits. I mean, we're talking jackstraws down there."

"Age and sex?"

"Don't go together."

I ha-ha, politely.

"Can't tell anything like that yet. They've got bits of rib and arm and vertebrae. Won't know till they get it in the lab, and you'd think those bastards were on an hourly rate, pace they move."

He shrugs.

"I'm just telling you because you brought these."

He flaps the photos and a fat drop of rain hits Rose's photocopied face with a splat. I fight the urge to snatch the pictures back.

"Appreciate it."

"So don't go blabbing to all and sundry. I'm sure I don't need to tell you that."

Although he has just told me that.

"Of course. When do you think you'll have some more information on the body?"

DI Considine shrugs. He sucks the dregs from the fag and flicks it into a puddle.

"We'll let you know."

He says it grudgingly.

"We would really appreciate it. The family are anxious to know of any . . . news, you understand."

Considine heads back to the tent, and then turns around, I'm sure, so he can have the last word.

"The river's supposed to rise again, so we'll probably have to pack up this lot. Then it's anybody's guess. Don't hold your breath."

Dismissed, I walk over toward the river, up to the edge of the creeping floodwater. The builders would have had to stop work, anyway, even without the discovery. From here you can see the original course of the river winding through the trees and scrub, even though it has overflowed its banks. The water looks brown and somehow viscous, thick like oil, holding things in suspension: things it has taken from the earth, secrets. A crisp packet is borne along on invisible currents, chased by a carrier bag. Wands of hazel and alder pierce the surface. Anything could be hidden under there. Turning around at the edge of the water, I look back across the waste that used to be the Black Patch.

I imagine there were more trees before the bulldozers moved in, ringing the site, perhaps, possibly along the edge where the little tent now stands. A shallow grave in the woods? Or rather, not that shallow—someone took the time to dig down four feet. That's not a five-minute job, in fear and haste. Were they trying to do the thing properly? With care and dignity? Or was it simply professional thoroughness?

Beyond the chicken-wire fence is a belt of well-established woodland—field maple, beech, and hazel—that then gives way to farmland, rising away from the river, thus safer from flooding, presumably less of a bargain for land-hungry developers. Here, by the water, standing still for even a minute means that midges and mosquitoes form a cloud around me. This isn't somewhere I would have chosen to build a house, but then, the businessmen who chose it and the builders who build it aren't going to live here.

I imagine stopping here in a trailer, in the old days, what it would have been like. It would have been a lot smaller, largely hidden from the road by trees. It is, in any case, a quiet road, not a direct route to anywhere. There are no buildings in sight, within earshot. As long as other Travelers weren't stopping here, it could have been a good place to dispose of someone. Of course, I can't prove that they ever came here. Or rather, the only proof I have is that Tene made a mistake. He said "the Black Patch," and then tried to divert me by claiming it was somewhere else. Why would he do that? Why would the words come tripping out of his mouth if he wasn't haunted by them?

I stare back at the tent. One of the tiny creatures flies into my eye; another brushes my nose. I take out another cigarette and light it, just to try to fend off the wildlife.

The rain begins to patter down harder, slapping the smooth surface of the water, extinguishing the cigarette in my hand. I throw the stub into the water, where some hidden current bears it swiftly away. It looks uncanny and purposeful, like a magnet moving under a table. Whatever happened to Rose, I have to find out. Whatever hidden current took her, it must be under the surface still.

"Are you Rose?" I say softly but out loud. "If you are here, tell me. Give me a sign. I know you've been waiting."

I ask the woods, the water, the accommodating earth: "Is she here?"

35.

JJ

It has started raining again. I like the sound of water falling onto the roof here—it's quieter than it was in the trailer. But at least here you can still hear outside noises. Like the rain and the fox that barks in the night. I've always liked the sound of foxes. They sound so desolate.

By the time it gets dark, my arm is on fire. Katie brings me some antiseptic and a bandage, and we put it on. She stays with me and wants to fool around a bit, and although in theory I want to, I feel really sick and I'm not that into it. I'm scared I'm actually going to be sick. I think she's a bit pissed off. After a while she goes away. Maybe the antiseptic was too late; it doesn't seem to have helped. Sometime later, I wake up and I'm alone. It's completely dark. There was a cry, like someone screaming for help; that's what woke me up. Maybe it was the old fox, or maybe it was a dream.

Maybe it was me.

My arm is pumping out heat like a stove. I lift it up, but it's too dark to see anything. It feels like it's made of lead. Pulsating with a dark red pain. I'm scared. Perhaps for the first time in all this, truly scared. My deepest fear rises to the surface and looks me in the face. It's always the blood with us—what's inside—that lets us down. I wonder—a dark fear I haven't felt for a long time—whether I, too, have the disease. Perhaps this is it. Perhaps it's been lying in wait all this time, choosing its moment to jump out and attack me. I feel weak, floppy, useless. What if I die here, in this stable? What will people say?

I've slid off the straw stack, and I'm on the floor again. No matter where or what I come from, I don't want to die in a stable, with only a horse for company. Subadar looks around, mildly interested, recognizing my time in his stable has come to an end. I push myself upright— I feel really peculiar, like my arms are very long and my hands are very heavy—and wander over to the door. Luckily, the lock is just a Yale: I walk outside into the rain. I have to walk all the way around the stables to get to the house. It seems to take forever. The house is in front of me, but it doesn't get any nearer. At some point I realize that I'm crying, sniveling like a baby. It's disgusting, but I don't seem to be able to stop. I seem to be walking sideways, like there's a force field around the house to keep dirty Gypsies from coming any closer. In this way I stagger around to the front. Katie's bedroom is at the front, but I can't work out which of the many windows is hers. No lights are on. Then I wonder whether Katie is the best person to wake. I have a feeling she wouldn't want her parents to know, however ill I got, so that she can keep me in the stables like she keeps her horse. Like her pet. And right now I need an adult.

I fight the force field for miles—all the way up to the front door. When I get there I'm panting. It's taken hours. I lean my face against the deliciously cool glass panel with a silvery floral pattern and press the doorbell. I don't care what they do to me, because it can't be anywhere near as bad as what my blood is doing to me already. I don't know how long I press it for, I don't hear anything, but, eventually, a light comes on inside. I slump against the door, thinking that soon someone else will decide what to do. I don't care who or what it is, but it won't be me. There's a voice yelling, but I can't hear what they're saying. It's too much effort to stand up straight again, especially when there's a lovely cool door to lean against. When the door opens, I slide gracefully to the floor at the feet of the council leader. This time, I don't have to pretend.

36.

Ray

Lulu sounds tired.

"How is Christo?"

A sigh.

"All right, I think. Kath's with him now. I've just got home."

"You heard about Ivo, then?"

"Yeah. Look, you should know, I'm . . . we're all very grateful for what you've done for Christo. The specialist and so on, and all you did yesterday. And I'm sorry about Ivo and everything. Messing you around like that."

"It doesn't matter. As long as Christo's all right, that's the main thing."

"Well, thank you. I daresay he has his reasons, although I must say I don't know what they are. I expect my brother gave you all that last night. 'Poor old Ivo' stuff."

"Something like that. I felt sorry for him."

"Don't bother. He's had it no worse than the rest of us."

"I mean your brother. So much bad luck; it's . . . almost unbelievable."

There is an uncomfortable pause. I could kick myself: I keep forgetting that she, as his sister, has shared most of those griefs.

"Yeah, well . . . You seem to have made a hit with him."

I experience a powerful and treacherous urge to tell her about the bones at the Black Patch. What would she say? I rein it in, with an effort.

"Well, if there's anything I can do . . ."

Silence.

She sounds like she's wishing she hadn't said that.

"Have dinner with me. Just as friends."

Another long pause.

For God's sake, Ray, when will you learn?

And then she says yes.

Things are looking up. Things are definitely looking up. Not only do I have a lead in my case, albeit a slender, tenuous thread of a lead, but Lulu has agreed to meet me for dinner. For a date. A Saturday-night date. As friends, admittedly, but it's a step in the right direction. Not only that, but at half past five, it finally stops raining.

I walk down London Road, showered, shaved, in a new shirt I found in the wardrobe, as a jet climbs joyously overhead and a tentative sun shows itself through melting clouds, pale and uncertain, like a fever patient on the first day outside. At long last, it's even warm.

And then there is one of those moments. You know what I mean—when there is an inaudible click, and the universe holds its breath. When beauty descends unheralded, a moment of grace. For no reason that I can see, Staines is suddenly empty of traffic and I am quite alone. In the low sunlight the raindrops clinging to leaves and lampposts glow with a million tiny flames; iridescence blooms on the oily tarmac. I am surrounded by crystal and mother-of-pearl. The plane has soared out of sight. There's no sound at all—no hum of traffic, no chirping of summer birds. No one shares the pavement to see this. The street is mine.

I take a long, deep breath—the air is soft and sweet, as though a perfumed battalion has just marched across the traffic lights. I want to shout, I want to stop, say hold it, wait, hold it . . .

That's when I see her. Walking up the road toward me in her black, shiny coat, unmistakable as always, even a street's length away. Sharper somehow and more definite than other people, as she always was. And now there are other people around—cars, too, released from their spell. Sounds return to normal levels. She's on her own. I want to run, I want her to run, but neither of us do. She sees me and doesn't break stride or falter or betray any shock whatsoever. I stand there by the lights as though I've grown roots.

She smiles a slightly weird smile.

"Hello, Ray."

"Hello."

It's so annoying. It's so unfair. I'm not even stalking her. I haven't thought about her since the phone call to Lulu. For three whole hours. And now my heart has turned over and is cowering in my chest, because of some straight black hair, some purple eyeshadow; because she is Jen, my wife, and there never was anyone else.

"How are you?"

"All right. Yeah. Just . . . going to meet someone."

I hadn't meant to say anything, but I don't seem to have control over my words.

"O-oh?"

She opens her eyes wide and weights the word, which makes her sound artificially interested and bright. Maybe she is jealous, after all. Maybe . . .

"I've been meaning to ring you, actually. My lawyer keeps calling me. Will you sign the papers?"

"Oh, God, yes . . . I'd . . ."

The divorce papers, of course. Jealous? What was I thinking?

"It's been such a long time, Ray."

I nod. Of course. I know it's been a long time. I've felt every minute of it.

"Yeah. Sure, I'll do it."

I smile, or something like it. Really I want to throw up.

"Okay, well . . . Good to see you. You look . . . good."

"Thanks. You, too . . ."

She walks on, her coat flashing in the sun, and turns the corner by Boots. Then she crosses the road and disappears into the post-shopping crowds. She doesn't look back once. Not once.

How do I know? How do you think? Because I follow her. It takes me almost a minute to regain my balance when I finally come to my senses and stop, walking into a shop to lose myself.

I am dull and awkward all through dinner. If Lulu finds this puzzling after my earlier persistence, she doesn't say so. I apologize, once before we order, once during the starter, and a third time over the steak, for being tired—I say I haven't slept much in the last three days.

She says, "Makes two of us."

There is a prawn cocktail in a pink sauce, and steak with another type of sauce, and white wine with the prawns and red wine with the steak, but I don't taste much of anything. I do a terrible thing, the thing you should never do: I look at the woman sitting opposite me—the complicated, patient, generous, secretive woman on the other side of the table—and compare her to my soon-to-be-ex-wife. And these are the wretched, mean-minded things I think: she's not as fashionable as Jen, not as well educated, not as tall. Undoubtedly, as a carer, she doesn't earn as much. She's not as forthright. She's not as good-looking, if I'm objective. Of course she isn't; she is herself. I should be ashamed. I am.

She seems to have made an effort. There is a subtle blackberry glint in her hair. She is wearing the shiny black boots with high heels. A pencil skirt that shows off her slim waist. Is this friendship dressing? I wonder if she considered the red shoes—rejected them because they are for him?

There is so much I don't know about her; I don't understand the first thing. So I try. I ask about her childhood, but she is reticent, as if sensing a certain forced note. I try to recapture the feeling I had earlier: I was so excited about meeting her. I was happy. This is what I wanted. What I want. I take a deep breath; try to remember the perfume, the mother-of-pearl.

"So how long have you been working for this guy in Richmond?"

"David? Oh, about two years."

"You like it?"

"Yeah. It's a good job, for what it is. After an old people's home, you know . . . Sometimes I get a bit hacked off with his mother. She's quite posh and, you know, used to bossing people about. But she's wonderful with him, really. She gave up her job and everything . . ."

Her voice trails off, distracted. I was hoping she hadn't noticed. Someone's fork scrapes loudly against a plate: it's mine.

"I don't think I told you where I work."

I don't dare look up. I stall, chewing. I could lie. It would be fifty-fifty. Maybe I could pull it off. But after what I have concluded, how could I be a person who lies? If I have regard for this woman, if I want to have any future with her—or with anyone— surely I have to tell the truth. Liars always get found out in the end.

"None of my family know where I work. Who I work for."

She is frowning, the double crease appearing in her forehead. "Is this what you do? Find out all about the people you question? Is this part of your . . . investigations?"

She doesn't actually seem that angry about it. But if I agreed now, that would be a lie, too.

"No. Um. Well, sometimes it is. But not in your case. You're not a suspect or anything. I wanted to know more about you because I like you, and I . . . I followed you once, to Richmond."

I've drunk only a glass and a half of wine. Tonight, it acts as a truth serum.

Lulu looks astonished, as well she might, as if she's trying to make up her mind whether to be outraged or . . . or what? Flattered? Hardly.

"You followed me to Richmond? When?"

"Er, a couple of weeks ago."

She swallows with a jerk of her head, as though her throat has closed up with disgust.

"Why didn't you just ask me where I worked?"

I'm taken aback. Why did that never occur to me?

"I don't know. Because . . . because it's what I do, I suppose. I'm used to it."

A shadow crosses her face.

"And what did you do when you got there?"

I could lie. I could lie. But then I'd be a liar.

"I . . . saw you go into the house."

There's still time to back out. Still time to salvage something from the evening—my reputation, perhaps. Her dignity. A future.

"I got out of the car, went round into the back garden, and watched you for a while."

Her face is, if that's possible, whiter than ever. Her tongue flickers over her lips as if she's desperate for water.

"And what did you see?"

My throat is strangely tense and hard. Perhaps my voice won't come out, and I'll have an excuse.

I could say nothing.

I could say, "Nothing."

"I saw . . . you and a man in a wheelchair in a sitting room. With a fire going. An older woman—I assumed his mother—coming in and going out. You were wearing red high-heeled shoes. I noticed you'd had them mended. The soles, I mean. And . . . I saw you on the chair—with him."

She looks past me, frozen.

"And then I left."

She leans back in her chair—away from me—her face closing up, eyes like needles. Her cheekbones sharpen. Everything becomes pinched. I think she's trying not to cry. Oh, please, God, I think. I will be destroyed if she cries.

Her voice comes out like the rasp of a saw.

"Why did you ask me here tonight? Why are you telling me this? If you're such a fucking pervert, why tell me about it? Does that give you a kick, too?"

I shake my head. One of the things about telling the truth—you are desperate to be believed.

"No, it doesn't. I was curious about what you do. I wasn't expecting . . . I like you. I really like you. It was because of that, and I . . . I'm really sorry; it was stupid and wrong. I don't want to lie to you. I will never lie to you."

She gets up, scraping back her chair, pressing her lips firmly down on her horror or her disgust, whatever it is she is feeling. I am despondent, but no more so than earlier. In fact, if anything, less.

"You're so full of shit! What gives you the right to spy on me? You're the big detective, so you can do whatever you like? You think you're God, poking your nose in where you have no business? You think you have the fucking right?"

She spits the words out. I have never heard her enunciate so clearly.

I open my mouth, meaning to say no, but I can't in all honesty deny it. Instead, I say, "It was my birthday."

Her mouth stops open in the act of drawing breath. She laughs a little, a jerky, graceless explosion of disbelief.

"You need help."

"Yes. I expect so."

A waiter hovers in the background, frozen with horrified curiosity. Neither of us says anything for I don't know how long.

Incredibly, she doesn't continue to go. Incredibly, she sits down again. And with that, she wins.

She picks up her glass and takes a big swallow of wine. Then she picks up her bag and takes out cigarettes and a lighter. I watch, not daring to say anything else, wondering what's coming next. The waiter collects our plates, eyes firmly on the table.

"So . . . what did you think, when you saw us?"

"I don't know. No, I do. I was disappointed . . . No, yes, hurt."

She stares at me through the smoke.

"You thought it was a service he pays for?"

"No! No. I was jealous. And ashamed. Mainly jealous."

She seems to think about this for a minute.

"Not surprised?"

"Yes. Although . . . I'd never thought about it before. He's . . . still a handsome guy."

" 'Still a handsome guy'? Yeah. A rich one, too. Rich . . . helpless, isn't that what you mean?"

"I don't . . . I didn't . . ."

Not lying is hard. I'm not sure what was in my mind that night.

"Nothing about you is what I expected."

She rolls her eyes at that, shakes her head. She smokes in silence for a minute, and then she grinds the cigarette out in the cut-glass ashtray. A waiter brings our dessert.

"I'd like to tell you something else. About the investigation. About Rose. Something has come up, partly due to your help. We may have found something. Nothing definite at the moment, but . . ."

"Really? Is she all right?"

"Where she disappeared . . . human remains have been found."

Lulu's eyes grow enormous. Her hand goes to her throat.

"And they're hers?"

"We don't know yet. It's possible. It's . . . We'll find out soon enough."

She is obviously deeply shocked. She shakes her head slightly and shifts in her chair. Miserably, she says, "Why are you telling me?"

"I don't know, really. I feel I owe you something. That's all I have to give, at the moment."

"I don't believe it. I don't." She means Rose. She means her family, killing her. And then, "You mean at the Black Patch? It was there?"

We sit in silence for a couple minutes. Neither of us touches our dessert, even though it's included. I'm exhausted. I want to crawl into a corner under a table and lie down. I shouldn't have told her anything, but I couldn't stop myself.

"Why tell me? Am I supposed to tell my nephew about this now? Tell Tene? God . . ."

I shake my head.

"I'm not trying to put you in a difficult position. I can see that I have. I'm sorry. I'm not thinking very clearly at the moment."

"But you don't know that it is her, do you? You don't know anything yet."

"No."

"It could be anyone. Someone . . . else."

"Yes."

"When will you know?"

"They can't say."

"Oh."

She pulls herself together and glares at me.

"You can't leave me with this. I don't know what to do. You have to go and tell them as soon as possible. I can't have this on my mind. I can't."

"All right. I'll go tomorrow. I'll tell them."

"First thing. Promise?"

"Yes. I promise."

It's not what I planned, but then, why not? After all, what else can I do, other than wait?

"As I said, we don't know anything for sure. The . . . remains could have been there twenty years, not six. It could be anyone."

"But it could be her. That's what you think."

The sadness I feel now is as acute as the happiness I felt on the London Road a few hours earlier. All around us, the other diners seem to feel it and bow their heads, crushed under the weight of my fumbling, stupid melancholy. The waiters are hushed and mournful, gliding about with downcast eyes. The crêpe suzette wilts on our plates. It knows it wasn't wanted. As we're waiting for the bill, I gather the nerve for one more outrage. After all, I probably won't get another chance. I don't think I have anything left to lose.

"Can I ask you something?"

She squints at me over the cigarette she is in the process of lighting.

"Isn't that always a stupid question?"

"Yes. You don't have to answer. Are you happy with him?"

She sucks in some smoke, waits for a minute, then it reappears slowly, transformed, like magic, like smoke from her fiery core. How I envy smokers; they have built-in excuses for stalling. Her eyes are far, far away—in the past? In the future? With him? Then they snap back to me.

"You've got a fucking nerve."

Outside the restaurant, she says, apparently genuinely curious, "What brought on this . . . honesty? I don't remember what I said."

"Lying hurts people."

"The truth hurts people, too, I assure you."

I asked for that.

"Okay, yes . . . but . . . only when it follows lies. Lying does the damage. At least . . . it did to me."

"Oh. Hence the divorce?"

"I suppose so. My ex-wife lied to me. She had her reasons, I know, but . . . it nearly killed me."

"Really?"

She peers at me with a wary, sardonic interest, as if I am a new, pathetic species of creature, unfit for this harsh world.

"My ex-husband lied to me. I nearly killed him."

37.

J J

I've never spent even one night locked up in bricks and mortar like this. It's horrible. It makes me want to scream. Okay, so there was the stable, but it wasn't like a proper building. It still felt thin; noises and air and the smells of rain and earth passed in and out. Not like a house. Not like this hospital, with its endless corridors and double-glazed windows that look like they never open—like being sealed inside a giant vacuum that's running out of air.

It's as hot as buggery: a stinking, stifling heat that's like death breathing in your face. That awful smell of sickness and bog cleaner that I smelled the night we took Christo to casualty. Now I'm stuck in it, surrounded by it. I probably smell of it. The air's so dry and artificial I can't breathe properly. And there's a constant buzzing noise, coming from God knows where. If it was up to me I'd walk out now, but since last night it's not up to me.

There's a tube with a needle on the end going right into my arm, Sellotaped on so it can't fall out. They could put anything inside you and you wouldn't even know. That's my right arm. The left one is all bandaged up, so I can't see how swollen it is, or how red it is, but I know it's both—it's a blast furnace of heat and throbbing like an engine. My fingers—the only bit poking out that I can see—are swollen and stiff like sausages and strangely red. I woke up earlier, feeling awful: ill and hot and stupid, but like I didn't much care about anything. I had vague memories of the council leader and Mrs. Williams bringing me to the hospital—she was lovely, not cross at all but kind and concerned. She kept stroking my hair. I think she was really worried how I was. She kept saying, "John, how could they?"; "John" being, I suppose, the name of the council leader. Obviously, he didn't know how they could.

But can that be right? Surely she wouldn't have left Katie on her own. Maybe she did the stroking at the house and then he brought me here on his own. I really can't remember. I wonder if Katie got into trouble for hiding me in her stable. I wonder if she lied and said she didn't know. I wonder what she's doing right now. Actually, truth is, I don't care.

I'm wearing a sort of paper smock. I don't know where my clothes are or anything. I wonder if any of my family know I'm even here. I suppose it's only a matter of time. I mean, Katie will tell them what she knows, she won't dare not now, and the council leader dropped me off near the site that time, so it won't take them that long to find Mum and tell her. I haven't told them anything, though. I'm not going to make it too easy. She'll only be cross. Actually, I wonder whether she'll even come and see me. Maybe she'll be too angry after our fight the other night—I can't remember exactly what I said now, but I remember feeling vaguely ashamed of myself. What did she say to me? I can't remember that either.

I wish she would come. I really do.

"Cheer up, James."

This is the nurse. I remember her from last night, I think. She's nice. She's quite pretty, too. And quite young. She bends over and smiles at me, putting her hand on my forehead. It feels nice when someone does that—as long as the hand's not sweaty, of course. Hers is warm but dry.

"Ooh, I think your temperature's gone down already. Let's see, shall we?"

She takes a thermometer from somewhere near my head and shakes it. I open my mouth obediently—funny how you do that automatically. Being in the hospital makes you feel like a baby.

"Do you want the bedpan?"

I shake my head, mortified. I hope I'm not blushing, but I suspect I am. Actually, I do need to go, but I'm not going to tell her that. There are limits. It means I'll have to wait till one of the scary old nurses is around. Or the male one with ginger hair and moles and the pale blue overalls.

"Okay . . . Yes, you're down a bit. Excellent. Great to be young, isn't it? Last night you were delirious. And now look at you."

She smiles again. It's nice having someone like her around. It's . . . restful. Although I don't want to get carried away. I got a bit carried away with Katie, I think, and look what happened. There is one advantage to feeling so ill: I can think about how nice this nurse is, about her smooth blond hair that looks like it would be slippery and silky to touch, pulled back in a ponytail—all that kind of thing—while lying here in nothing but a paper smock, with a thin sheet over me, and I don't even get an erection. Miracle.

At nine o'clock in the evening, Mum turns up. Visiting hours are nearly over—I already know about visiting hours—but they've obviously given her special permission, seeing as she's my mum and I've been on my own here for nearly twenty-four hours. Her face is blotchy with crying; all red around the eyes and nose. But she doesn't look like a stranger—she looks like Mum again.

"Oh, JJ . . ."

She practically throws herself on me to give me a hug, knocking my arm painfully in the process, but I restrain myself from going "ow." I'm so happy to see her I think I'm going to cry myself, but I manage not to.

"Hi, Mum."

"Sweetheart. You stupid bugger . . ."

She strokes my face.

"Ohh."

She hugs me again, then pulls herself together before anyone sees her being too soppy.

"I should give you a right bollocking for what you did. Scaring me like that. What were you thinking?"

What was I thinking? Has she decided to forget all about our fight?

"I dunno."

"And going to those people? Who are they, anyway? This man came round to tell me about you, looking down his nose at everything. How do you know them, anyway?"

"I don't know him. Katie's in my class."

"Hm."

She can't be too disapproving; she's always been so keen on that school.

"He's on the council."

"Hm. Is he indeed?"

This is a rhetorical question. If Mum is asking rhetorical questions, then I reckon she can't be too cross with me.

"What on earth did you do to yourself? They said you've got blood poisoning!"

"Um . . . When I ran off, I tripped on the road in the dark . . . and there was some glass."

Mum tuts. She doesn't seem to find it unlikely that I would do such a spazzy thing.

"But that was on Friday. Where've you been since then?"

I sigh. I don't want to tell her everything. But I don't know how much she already knows.

"I . . . um . . . Katie's got a horse. I hid in its stable."

Mum shakes her head.

"What are you like? You know what they think of us now? That we're bloody barbarians letting you run off like that. And to run to *gorjios* . . ."

"I wasn't running to *gorjios*. I was just . . ."

Running away. But I can't explain to her exactly why I had to run away from our family. I shut my eyes, hoping she'll leave it.

"Oh, sweetheart, I'm sorry . . . How are they treating you in here?"

She has dropped her voice, as though I'm about to rat on them.

"All right. Fine."

"And the food? Is it awful? I'll bring something in for you tomorrow."

"It's okay. Really. You don't have to."

She will anyway. She has this deep distrust of *gorjio* catering. School lunches are bad enough.

She touches my bandaged arm.

"You herbert. I'm always telling you to look out for glass."

"I know."

She's smiling now. Maybe I could forget about the other night. Pretend it didn't happen. Because what do I do about it? What can I do?

"Sorry, Mum. I didn't mean to . . . make you worried. Just sometimes, you know?"

"I'm sorry, too, sweetheart. It's all forgotten, yeah?"

I smile a bit. I'd love to forget it all, I really would, but there are some things I can't forget, no matter how hard I try.

38.

Ray

I was hired by Georgia Millington's parents after the police had drawn a blank. They were a mild-mannered, bewildered couple. Every time I met them, Mrs. Millington was wearing a headscarf, as though she had been interrupted in the middle of scrubbing the floor. And their house was immaculately clean. They seemed pleasant, a bit dull, like decent parents everywhere. The disappearance of their daughter was the worst and most inexplicable thing that had ever happened to them. I really wanted to help.

When I found Georgia, in an enormous run-down squat in Torquay, I was on top of the world. I told myself I had won. I had beaten the police, and the forces of stupidity and chaos, and the silly girl who wanted to lose herself with her dope-addled boyfriend. It's not that I didn't ask her what she was running from. But I couldn't have asked in the right way. I didn't realize, then, that she was afraid of me. That she had spent her whole life learning how to be afraid. And what occurred to me was not the truth. I had thought about sexual abuse, of course. Mr. Millington was her stepfather, and you do hear of such things. When I asked Georgia about it, she laughed, scornfully.

When, months later, she was found beaten to death with a hammer, Mr. Millington was arrested. He didn't attempt to deny it, but it came out, eventually, due to anomalies in his statement, that it was his wife, the obsessive, anxious cleaner, who had killed Georgia. Her mother. A woman subject to violent rages, furiously possessive of her husband. She didn't want to share him with anyone, not even her daughter.

Why didn't I foresee it? How could I have prevented it?

I didn't understand anything after that. Not a thing.

I wonder if my marriage didn't begin to founder back then. This was after I met Hen, and he taught me how to drink. Drinking wasn't the most logical way to forget the extraordinary violence inflicted on Georgia, I realize, but to an extent it worked. Jen got sick of me going on about it, and when I drank I stopped. But when I didn't go on about it, the thoughts circled like sharks beneath the surface, consuming me.

When I reach the M25 the following morning, I turn right rather than left without pausing to think. I might have made a promise to Lulu last night to visit her family and tell them what has been found, but I made an earlier promise to Rose. The point is, I want Rose to know that even if no one listened when she was alive, I am doing my damnedest to listen to her now. I find myself muttering out loud as I drive—apologizing to her. I can't change the past—I made a terrible mistake with Georgia, and I should have done something—I was there. I can't save Rose, of course, and never could. The least I can do is find out what happened.

When I pull up near the gate, at first I don't understand what I'm seeing; it looks so different. Then I realize: overnight, the river has claimed her.

The Black Patch is improved by flooding. The scarred earth is hidden by a sheet of brown water. The trees, the steel reinforcing rods for the foundations, the poles planted by the police to mark the site of their operations, all poke out of it. All other evidence of the building site has gone, except for one of the diggers, which didn't get out in time—alone and stranded, its yellow jaws gape at the sky. The green tent is still there, too, sagging, looking like a lost hat in a puddle.

I get out of the car, pull on damp boots, and walk over to the young PC on duty. It's raining again, a steady drizzle, and he's shivering with cold even though it's the end of July and he's sheltering under a waterproof cape like something out of a Victorian detective serial. His name is Derek. He doesn't smoke, but he's still glad for someone to talk to, even a private detective. I tell him a couple of stories and drop hints that I might know something. Eventually, he laughs.

"I can't tell you anything, mate, no matter what. 'Cause I don't know anything!"

His accent is a soft Fenland burr.

I show him the pictures of Rose and tell him about her, and he stops laughing.

"They did say it might have been a child, or a young woman, 'cause of the size of the arm bones. Only might have been, mind. Now they have to wait till the water's gone down and they can find the rest. I didn't tell you that. There's no proof, is there? It could have been put here five years ago; it could have been twenty-five. They just don't know."

Unsurprisingly, from a few pieces of arm bone and rib, and some pieces of vertebrae, they have no inkling of cause of death. They were splintered fragments. The digger clawed right through the grave.

"When do you think the water might go down?"

He shrugs, making a noise with his lips, dismissive of those who ignore where the water goes, which is where it has always gone.

"Crazy, isn't it? Building here. Asking for trouble."

"Wouldn't you live here, Derek? In one of these nice new houses?"

He bursts out laughing again.

"Must be joking! Couldn't afford them, anyway. I'd have to save up for a hundred and fifty years before I could buy one of those. Or be promoted to chief superintendent. And you have to wait for them all to die off before you get promoted round here."

Then, before I leave, he leans toward me, made garrulous by cold and boredom.

"I don't like being here on my own. No one round here does. It used to be a burial ground, you know? Hundreds of years ago— during the Black Death. People died too fast to be buried in the churchyards, and anyhow, there weren't enough people left alive to bury them. They just brought them here in carts and tipped them into a pit. Set fire to it. God knows how many bodies are buried below that one."

He lowers his voice, deadly serious.

"The dead come back, you know. They really do. Have you ever seen a ghost?"

I don't think he's joking. A shiver goes down my spine, despite myself.

"No. I haven't."

"I have. My granddad came back after he died. I saw him. I can see you don't believe me, but I know what I saw; he was as clear as you standing here."

"Oh." I can't think of anything to say.

"That's why I don't like being here on my tod. All of them, down there. Would you want to live in a house on top of all that?"

As I drive away, a wary sun comes out. The river at the Black Patch must have risen three or four feet. How long will that take to drain away? And how long, then, before the mud is stable enough to resume work? I don't think I can wait that long.

I can't think of anything else to do, so I keep driving past my turnoff to fulfill my second promise. The route is familiar now. And, as if blessing me, sunlight pushes long fingers through the clouds. Steam rises off the damp, glistening meadows; the woods are a deep, secretive green. All the rain has held back the attrition of summer: it's the end of July, but everything looks fresh and new.

I am trying not to think about last night. I can't believe I told Lulu those things. And yet, in some way, I'm glad I did. I'm not sure what I feel for her. You can't call it love. You don't love someone you hardly know. But this violent tenderness deserves a more dignified name than "crush." I don't know whether she will ever speak to me again, but my confession unburdened me. You can't unsay such a thing. The jury cannot disregard it. You take your fragile secret out of the darkness and expose it to the light. You lay it on the ground, where anyone can tread on it.

I waited for her to tread on it.

After walking her around the corner to her car, I said good-bye. I didn't ask if I would see her again. She said good-bye without looking at me. She didn't walk away. Could have—should have, perhaps—but she didn't walk away.

When I pull off the side road a couple hours later, the site is basking in some rare sunshine. It seems deserted, the trailers quiet and shut up. I knock on the door of Ivo's trailer. No reply. It's locked. Total silence. All the cars are absent. Then I knock on Tene's door and wonder what I should do next, when there is a ragged shout from within.

"Who is it?"

"It's Ray. Ray Lovell."

"Come in! Come in. 'S open."

At first glance the trailer is empty. Then I see something moving—it's Tene's hand—raised in a wave from the floor beside his chair.

"I'm all right. All right. I've just fallen. Got stuck."

"Don't move. What happened?"

I kneel beside him.

"Was trying to get into my chair and—"

"Don't try and stand up. It's okay . . ."

He's tugging at the waistband of his trousers. I can't help seeing that the fly is undone. He was probably using the toilet when he fell but, too embarrassed to be found like that, somehow dragged himself into the living room before his strength gave out. I search my memory for fragments of the first-aid training that Eddie Arthur insisted I do as a junior investigator.

"Did you hit your head? Mr. Janko?"

"No. Just get me up again. Get me up. Be all right."

I examine his face for signs of a stroke, but as far as I can tell, he looks normal.

"Maybe I should call an ambulance . . ."

"No, no, no. I fell. Just get me up!"

"What day is it?"

"Bloody hell!"

I thread my arms under his shoulders, lock my hands together, and heave him upright, terrified I'm going to make something worse. Although not much could be worse than paraplegia, I tell myself. Despite the weight of him, I'm shocked by how sharp his bones feel, how small in their sack of flesh. I'm scared that if I squeeze too hard, something will snap. Then there is an embarrassing pantomime whereby, once I've got him upright, I have to pull him up into mid-air so that he can haul up his trousers and fasten them, but then, at last, he is restored to something like dignity, slumped in his wheelchair. His face is an unhealthy color, far paler than usual.

"How long were you on the floor?"

My voice sounds sharp, the way it used to with my dad when he wasn't looking after himself.

"Not long."

"How long, Mr. Janko?"

"They all went off . . . went out, and there was no one around . . ."

"When was this?"

"Oh, I don't know. Not long."

"Okay. Well, let me make you some tea."

"Now you're talking. Cup of tea. I wouldn't say no."

In the tiny kitchen at the far end, I put the kettle on, and open and shut doors, looking for mugs and plates. I find packets of biscuits and a whole cupboard stuffed with bags of crisps. There are tea bags and cartons of UHT milk. There is chocolate: an economy-size bag of Marathons and Mars bars. My dad was the same—addicted to salt, grease, and anything convenient and unhealthy.

When I bring over biscuits and mugs of tea, Tene looks a little better. He adds spoonfuls of sugar to the tea—I lose count—and blows on it.

"Not that easy, living in a trailer."

"Oh. Best way to live."

"But living in a house would be a lot easier, wouldn't it? A bungalow. You'd have a lot more space . . . and no steps. Be easier to get in and out."

Tene looks up at me from under lowered eyebrows.

"Ray, kid, look at me. I'm sixty years old. I've lived on the road all my life. I was born in a horse-drawn vardo. Our mare when I was little, Bryn, she was my best pal. We didn't get a motor trailer till I was thirty. Of course, we had to move on. That was what you did in them days, or you got laughed at. We kept Bryn with us till she died. She was a true friend."

I do sums in my head. Of course, there were still horse-drawn wagons on the roads in the forties and fifties—even later. Painted wagons were the norm. Bender tents. My dad saw that, when he was young.

"Can you imagine Tene Janko in a house? Little brick box in a row of brick boxes? It would be putting me in my coffin. It would be my death. They tried to make me give it up when I first had my accident; they kept saying, you can't live in a trailer no more—it's not possible. You can't do it! Well, I've proved them wrong, haven't I?"

I nod. "Yes, you have."

"You can't change what people are. This is what I was born, and this is what I'll be when I die. *Gorjios* don't understand that. I told them: you'd be killing me the same as sticking a knife in my heart. I might as well have died in the crash. It's in my blood. All of us. Even Christo. It's in our blood!"

His voice is fierce.

"'Assimilation,' they call it. Annihilation, more like."

He chews savagely on a digestive. His eyes are feverishly bright. At least anger has brought some color back to his face.

"How did it happen then—it was a car crash, I think you said?" His head goes down; he takes a long slurp of tea. "Was that after Rose left?" Silence. The silence of a storm cloud. "Or before? You said it was about six years ago, so I just wondered . . ."

"Wondered what?"

"Well . . . just, it must have been such a difficult time, what with Christo and all that."

He makes a noise that I can't interpret, followed by silence. I drink some more tea, chew on a stale biscuit, and wonder if he knows I am checking on him.

"She was long gone by then."

That was the phrase that Lulu had used: long gone. But it couldn't have been that long, with Christo still so young.

"I can't remember the crash. Just afterward. When they were telling me what I could and couldn't do. And I was in terrible pain. Terrible."

He looks at me accusingly.

"Of course. It must have been. But you've showed them, haven't you? That you can live the way you want."

"Yeah. Yeah."

"You're lucky you had your family around you."

"That's what families are for, isn't it?"

"Yes. Still . . . some families are closer than others."

"You're thinking of my sister Luella, I can see that. Well, despite everything she might say, she's still a Janko."

Outside, a car engine gets louder as it swings into the paddock and then cuts out.

Tene cranes his neck to see out the window.

"Look now. There's Ivo. And she's let him stay with her, of course, while the boy's in the hospital."

I nearly spit my tea out.

"He's been staying with Lulu?"

"Yeah. Course. She lives the nearest out of anyone. These are the times when you've got to be with family, no matter what."

I take another bite of digestive, to give myself time to think. Why didn't she say anything about Ivo staying with her? *Shit. Shit!* I'd never have said anything about the discovery at the Black Patch if I'd known . . . *Fuck.* No reason why she would have told him, though. She might not have seen him since . . .

There are footsteps outside, and Ivo knocks briefly on Tene's door, opening it without waiting for an answer. He stands half silhouetted in the doorway, shopping bags in one hand.

"Mr. Lovell . . . Dad . . . All right? I've brought you that stuff."

"Thank you, my kid. Just put it in the kitchen there."

Ivo brushes past me on the way to the kitchen and empties the plastic bags onto the counter. More bags of crisps, from the look of it. Instant meals in pots.

"Why don't you stay and have a tea with us?"

"In a bit, maybe."

I stand up.

"I don't want to keep you. I really should be . . ." I look at Tene. "You're sure you're all right now, Mr. Janko?" I turn to Ivo. "Your father had a bit of an accident—he fell getting into his chair. There was no one else here. Lucky I came by, with everyone away . . ."

"You what? You fell? How did you manage that?"

He sounds irritated.

"It's nothing, kid. You know, happens sometimes. I'm fine." Tene flaps his hand dismissively. "Mr. Lovell is making a mountain out of a molehill. He's been very kind, though. Very kind. Glad you stopped by, Mr. Lovell. Yes, indeed."

Ivo looks at me, his eyes steadier now, as if he's really seeing me for the first time. He steps aside to let me pass through the doorway but then speaks before I get there.

"Mr. Lovell, don't go yet. Stay and have a bite to eat with me. I wanted to say thank you for everything you've done for Christo . . . And sorry for . . . you know. Please?"

He smiles, if you can call it that. I think you can call it that.

"I don't want to put you to any trouble; there's really no need . . ."

"No trouble. Please—stay."

There's a look on his face I've never seen before. Almost . . . warm. I look from him to Tene.

Maybe this is the perfect opportunity. Maybe the barriers are finally coming down. Maybe this is the time to tell them my news.

"Tell you what," I say, "why don't I nip to the nearest offie and get some beers. What do you say?"

39.

JJ

This morning they took the tube out of my arm, so I'm free to get out of bed. My arm still hurts, but some of the heat has gone out of it. And I feel almost normal. When Emma, the nice young nurse, changed the dressing, she congratulated me on making such a fast recovery.

Then Gran came and brought loads of food, convinced I must be starving. She stuffed packets of crisps and bought sausage rolls into the cupboard by my bed "for later." I'm not really that hungry at the moment, but I didn't tell her. She also brought me a set of pajamas, striped, a dressing gown, and a pair of leather slippers—proper men's ones. They're too big (of course, so I can grow into them), but still, they're not too bad. The dressing gown's a sort of velvety tartan long thing with a belt like a rope with tassels on the ends. It's far too hot for this weather, but I like it; it makes me feel like Sherlock Holmes. I thought she'd just be angry with me, so I was touched.

I'm walking down one of the corridors on the upstairs floor, shuffling along in my too-big slippers, poking my nose into places, when I find him. I wouldn't say it's the very last thing I expected, but it's got to be pretty far down the list: the private detective, Mr. Lovell, is in this hospital, too! I peer into one of the little rooms where there are only one or two beds, and there he is, with my friend Emma bending over him. I stop and stare harder, just to be sure.

"Mr. Lovell!" I practically shout in my surprise. It's like seeing an old friend—I'm delighted. He's lying in bed but turns his head and stares. His face looks strange, sort of blank and slack. I'm not sure he remembers me.

"It's me, JJ!"

"Hello, JJ," says Emma. "Do you two know each other?"

I nod, suddenly unsure what to say about just how we know each other.

Emma puts down whatever she's fiddling with and comes toward me, talking over her shoulder to him.

"I'm just going to have a word with JJ. Back in a sec."

Outside in the corridor, she puts a hand on my shoulder.

"JJ, I'm afraid your friend Mr. Lovell is really quite poorly. He gets rather . . . confused. He might not recognize you."

"Oh! What's wrong with him?"

She pauses, and for a moment I think she isn't going to tell me.

"He's had a rare form of food poisoning."

I try to stare past her at the figure in the bed. She smiles, but she's blocking the door with her body.

"Oh! But he is getting better?"

"Oh, yes. We're sure he'll make a full recovery. But at the moment he's still quite poorly, so . . . maybe you should come back tomorrow. Okay?"

"He's going to be all right, though?"

"He'll be fine. It just takes a while to work itself out."

"Oh. I see."

Actually, I don't see at all, but sometimes you have to pretend you do understand just to make people feel comfortable. Just as (much more often, in my experience) you sometimes have to pretend that you don't understand what someone has said or what's going on, otherwise things can get awkward.

"What type of food poisoning causes that?"

I've heard of getting ill after eating a dodgy kebab—it makes you throw up and gives you the runs. But I've never heard of anyone eating something that makes them confused. What does that mean, exactly, anyway? Why would he not recognize me?

"It's very rare. Don't worry. It's not catching."

I shuffle off down the corridor feeling weird, but not in a way that's anything to do with having blood poisoning in my arm. More like someone's walked over my grave.

Mum comes a few hours later and brings Great-uncle with her. No one refers to the argument we'd had. I wonder if Mum has mentioned it to anyone. I think she probably hasn't. One thing I do discover, though, and this is really good news: Ivo has gone up to stay in London to be near Christo, and no one knows when he's coming back, so that's a relief.

"You'll never guess who I saw in here," I say to Great-uncle. "Remember that private detective, Mr. Lovell? He's in here!"

Great-uncle doesn't look at me for a moment. I think he hasn't heard.

"Mr. Lovell . . . You know? He's here!"

Mum says, "Oh, dear. What's he doing here?"

"He's got some weird form of food poisoning. He's quite ill, actually. They said it makes you confused. What sort of food poisoning does that?"

Great-uncle looks at his hands and sighs.

"I don't know, kid. I really don't know."

"I can talk to him tomorrow, they said."

Mum says, "Goodness, the poor man."

Great-uncle says, "Yup. There's a lot of it about. Jimmy's brother Bill was taken poorly the other week. Horrible, it was, he said."

Mum says, "I brought you some grapes, love. And some biscuits. Look . . . your favorites."

"Thanks, Mum . . ."

I offer them the bag of grapes.

"No, you keep them for yourself. Don't want you to fade away, do we?"

Grapes are a special treat. She must have bought them downstairs, from the hospital shop, where everything's really expensive. As far as I can remember, she has never bought grapes before; I've eaten them only once or twice, at school. In Katie's house there was a huge bunch of them, purple and foggy, spilling over a glass plate on the breakfast bar—or was it the tea table? They looked so perfect I didn't dare touch them. I thought maybe they weren't real.

Mum says, "Didn't he come back the other day? The day I came to see JJ. What was that for?"

Great-uncle shrugs. "I dunno. Something about Christo, I suppose. He wasn't there long."

"Making friends, apparently, him and Ivo! That's nice, isn't it?"

Mum winks at me. Great-uncle clears his throat.

"You mean Mr. Lovell went to see you again, at the site?" I ask.

Great-uncle looks at me sharply, then looks away again.

"Yeah. That's his job, isn't it?"

He seems uneasy, though. I have that sensation again, the one I felt outside Mr. Lovell's room, the prickly cold thing that walks up your spine.

"Sweetheart? Are you all right? You've gone all peaky."

The thing is, there's another word for *chovihano*.

Mum leans over and strokes my hair back from my forehead. "It's getting so long, you look a right hippie . . . Are you tired? Do you want to go to sleep?"

"*Mm.* Yeah."

She kisses me on the forehead and makes some cooing noises. I'm afraid I might cry, so I shut my eyes. I wish I could just enjoy it. I wish I was her baby again, just a kid who's too young to see things and too young to worry about anything, but I'm not, and never will be again.

I know too much, and I'm pretty sure it's only going to get worse.

The other name for a *chovihano* is *drabengro*, which means "man of poison."

40.

Ray

I went to get beers and ended up having to drive around to find a pub that did takeouts, so it was more than half an hour before I got back to the site to find Ivo cooking with a cigarette in one hand. I suppose after Rose left, he had to get used to fending for himself. But it still strikes me as odd—a Gypsy man in the kitchen is a rare sight. There are packets of crisps on the table, and he indicates that I get started on them.

"I'll go back up and see Christo tomorrow," he says.

"Oh, good . . . You're staying with your aunt?"

"Yeah. Handy that."

"Yeah. Do you see a lot of her?"

"No. Haven't seen Auntie Lulu for years."

She couldn't have said anything, I decide.

"He's a lovely boy, Christo," I say.

Ivo smiles at the pan. "Yeah, he's the best."

He stops smiling.

"You must miss him."

"Yeah."

Ivo scrapes something from a bowl into the pan. I can't see what it is. Then he throws in lots of salt. He stirs the pan's contents—some sort of stew. He leans his hip on the counter, keeping an eye on the pan, chain-smoking. The stew doesn't seem to need much attention, but he doesn't leave it. He needs something to do, and this way, he doesn't have to look at me . . . or be looked at. He doesn't have to talk.

"You never thought of giving him up to another family? Your cousin, say?"

Ivo gives me a brief shocked look, then shakes his head. I ask because Gypsy men don't often bring up small children on their own; it's not uncommon for a widower to pass his children to a female relative to look after.

"I never thought of that—no, never," he says quietly. "Christo's all I got. And I understand him, you know, knowing what it was like."

"Yes, of course. You must know more about it than anyone."

I'm fascinated by his survival. It's truly extraordinary, when you think about it.

"Can I ask . . . Was it painful?"

He sighs. "Sometimes. Not all the time."

"Were you just like him?"

"Not as bad."

"So how old were you when you started to get better?"

"Fifteen . . . sixteen. Lot older than Chris."

I sip my beer. Ivo washes potatoes in a steel bowl, then peels them, hunched over his work.

"Your father said you had uncles and brothers who died from the disease. You must have been incredibly lucky."

"Yeah."

"A medical marvel. The doctors will be interested to see why you got better."

Ivo drops a potato back into the bowl, splashing himself.

He grunts.

"Has anyone else recovered, like you?"

There is a silence for a moment.

"I think one of my uncles—Dad's uncles—got better. I didn't know him. It was ages ago."

"And it's just men who suffer from it, is that right?"

Another pause. "I'm not sure. I think so."

He's mumbling into the saucepan, reluctant to talk about it.

"Well, I know Gavin's very keen to get to the bottom of it."

Ivo cuts the potatoes into chunks and drops them into boiling water. He turns around for the first time.

"I'm glad that you got him to see Christo. We all are. Really grateful."

"Well, I'm sure once they know what it is, they'll be able to help."

He makes an attempt at a smile.

"I've just got to get something from Dad's, okay?"

"Sure."

I let out a deep breath when I'm alone. It's an uphill struggle getting him to talk. Being asked about the disease is clearly painful for him, and the overwhelming impression I get is of extreme shyness. I open another packet of crisps and a second beer—Ivo doesn't seem to be much of a drinker—and try to think how to work the conversation around to Rose.

Ivo comes back after a couple minutes and resumes his perch at the counter. We sip our beers in silence for a while.

"Nearly ready," he says.

"I'm just going to nip outside," I say.

In the clearing it's getting dark, but there is a soft golden light in the sky. It's still and humid. Under the trees a hush holds fast; there is no birdsong, no sounds from the other trailers. After a short wander, I find an earth toilet among the trees, sheltered by a green tarpaulin. It's more than I was expecting. And Ivo's left a metal churn of water outside his trailer for washing—he pointed this out as I left. My grandfather had the same arrangement. I pour the cold water over my hands, hoping that will do.

I am gone for about four minutes.

Is that when it happens?

When I go inside again, Ivo is already at the little table. He has poured two shots of dark rum, and two plates of food are laid out. I take my place. He lifts his glass in a toast.

"Well, here's health."

"Absolutely. Here's health."

I tap his glass and swallow the rum. Tears spring to my eyes—it's overproof, something cheap and naval. Ivo swallows his, screwing his eyes shut briefly as it hits.

We eat.

"It's good," I say, and really it isn't bad. Ivo has switched off the light in the kitchen, and we sit in semidarkness. I suppose they have to save the generator for when it's really necessary. He eats as if he is starving, head down. He dips a slice of bread into his stew, folds it into quarters, and stuffs it in his mouth. He's almost finished with his plate when he speaks again.

"Had a sister, you know. Christina. She gave her life for me."

I stare at him—presumably, what he intended.

"I thought she died in a road accident?"

Ivo shrugs. "If it wasn't that, it would've been something else." He sounds casual, as if he's discussing the weather.

"I don't understand."

Ivo chews a piece of gristle and takes it out of his mouth, inspecting it.

"Dad wanted a miracle. For me. But you have to pay for that, if you're a Gypsy. It's a life for a life, isn't it? That's what the Bible says."

"Um, not in that way, I don't think."

"'S true though. That's the way it turned out. Only one of us could live."

"I suppose you . . . could see it like that, maybe . . ."

Ivo puts down his spoon and takes out a cigarette, lights it without looking at me. I look away, irritated. I'm feeling slightly sick, I now realize.

"Dad knew he would lose another child. He knew it. And . . . Ivo Janko was the last one. The only one with the name. And I have to pass it on."

I register that this sounds a little odd. But I'm feeling a little odd. Not myself.

"Is this . . ."

I'm trying to think of the word Lulu used . . . what was it? *Pri—* something? I can't quite grasp it. It's annoying.

"What's that thing . . . like karma? *Pri . . . kada . . .* No . . ."

Why is my heart beating so fast?

"Prikaza?"

He looks at me. A direct, curious look. His gaze, when he wants, is perfectly steady.

"You know. If you've done wrong, you are punished. Christina was punished. It's not fair, is it? Sometimes, I think, would've been better if she'd . . . but the family . . . it's dying."

"You're young. You could always . . . marry again."

Is that a heartless thing to say? As though ashamed, I'm tremendously hot all of a sudden. I take a swig of beer to try to cool down. I have a nasty feeling some of it dribbles over my chin. Ivo looks down, so doesn't see. He gives a sort of sigh.

"You could have more children."

Ivo looks up then, his eyes wounded. His mouth opens, but he doesn't speak. My tongue feels thick, but I struggle on.

"You could . . . the odds . . ."

Why am I so hot? My heart is hammering. My face is burning— it must be red. I pass my right hand over my forehead. It feels heavy and uncontrollable.

"Ray? Ray?"

My hand slaps down on the table with a crash, as though it has a point to make. I stare at it in horror. I suddenly realize there is something crawling toward me, just visible in the corner of my eye.

"Could I . . . have some water?"

"Are you all right, Ray?"

Ivo is leaning toward me, looming over me. The last thing I remember is his look of concern. A look that is almost . . . tender.

41.

St. Luke's Hospital

Hen and Madeleine have come to see me. They bring grapes and flowers; both are her idea. I know it's nice of her, but I wish she hadn't bothered. Around Madeleine I need all my energy not to feel hopelessly oafish and inferior. Lying in bed in a paper smock, with a thick tongue and a dead arm, I haven't a chance.

"How are you, Ray?"

"Erm, not bad, really."

"It's so good to see you looking better. We've been so worried." She looks at Hen. "You gave us a real scare."

I have to resist the urge to apologize.

"Still, you're all right now, they said." Hen leans forward, shaking my good arm. "You seem so much better than the other day."

"Yeah. Have you been to the site?"

"The site?"

"The Janko site. You need to speak to Ivo."

Hen and Madeleine exchange glances.

"Don't worry about work. It's all under control."

He looks almost smug. He doesn't know. This is not his fault—I didn't tell him.

"There's something I have to tell you . . ." I look meaningfully at my partner. "I'm sorry, Madeleine, could you . . . ?"

"Oh." Madeleine gets up. "Of course. I'll go and get a coffee."

She smiles brightly on her way out. Hen sighs.

"She came all this way to see you, you know. Could you be a bit more . . . civilized?"

I'm startled. "Sorry. It's important."

"So important it can't wait fifteen minutes?"

He raises his eyebrows at me.

"Ivo poisoned me."

"What?"

"Did you talk to the doctors? Did they tell you? I have been poisoned with ergot and, um, and henbane. How do you think that happened?"

Hen looks at the floor.

"What do you think I was doing in a wood in the middle of nowhere?"

"Okay, tell me what happened."

I tell him what I remember. Or rather, I tell him what's relevant—not about seeing Lulu, and our conversation, or meeting Jen, for that matter.

He frowns when I tell him about the find at the Black Patch.

"When were you going to tell me about this?"

"It was Saturday. You know—weekend. I thought Monday would be soon enough. But on Sunday I went down to see the Jankos."

Hen looks more and more disapproving. I suppose I should have told him that, too. But then, he would only have stopped me.

"Then Ivo invited me for dinner. And here I am."

"You didn't tell him about the human remains?"

That was what I had gone there to do. But the thing is, I don't remember saying anything about it.

"Um . . . I don't know."

"So . . . why do you think he poisoned you?"

"I must have told him. To see what sort of reaction there would be."

Hen sighs.

"Leaving aside your judgment about all this . . . You're presuming that he already had the poisonous plants to hand . . . Or did he go off into the woods and collect them while you were there?"

"He could have. I went to buy beers . . ."

I stop, because I know I didn't say anything to him before I went to the pub. Unless my memory, in returning, is playing me false.

"The police said you had the plants in your car."

I stare at him, genuinely puzzled.

"There were traces of henbane in your car."

"How could that be? Unless Ivo put it there . . ."

Hen looks stern.

"I don't know, Ray. Maybe you put it there."

"Me? Why on earth would I do that?"

I still don't understand what he's getting at. He shrugs.

"I know things have been difficult, with Jen and the divorce . . ."

He won't meet my eyes.

I push myself upright.

"You think I was trying to top myself! For God's sake, Hen!"

He looks at me, his eyes wounded and unwilling.

"You have seemed odd recently. Jen told me about bumping into you on Saturday and asking you to sign the divorce papers. Said you looked . . . well, poleaxed was the word she used."

"Yeah, so? Things are better now than they have been for a long time. The case is cracking . . . and as for her, yes, I was finding it tough, but now it's okay . . . I think I've met someone else."

Hen nods, fidgets with his watch. He smiles again with that horrible, painful kindness.

"Is this Lulu Janko?"

I don't want to say yes, and I don't want to say no. I shrug.

"I spoke to her, too."

He says this flatly.

"What? And?"

"She rang the office. She told me about your dinner the night before . . . all this happened. I got the impression that you'd taken a bit of a knock."

He sounds embarrassed.

Really? I think. Fucking . . . really!

"Hen, for God's sake, I did not do this to myself. If we are going to continue this conversation, you have to believe that."

He looks at me and nods slowly.

"So if I didn't do it, and I didn't, the plants must have got into something at Ivo's—either deliberately or, possibly, by accident."

"But you don't know that you told him about the remains at the Black Patch. He may not know even now."

"Then you need to find out."

He nods.

"There's another thing. I went back to the Black Patch on Sunday, and it was underwater. All work suspended. But that was days ago."

"Okay. I'll go up there."

I feel relief flooding into me.

"I think we're finally getting somewhere."

Hen looks at me. He looks nervous.

"What?"

He shifts in the chair, which squeaks under him.

"A couple of days ago I got a phone call. In response to our ad."

"What ad?"

"The hooker—the ad about Rose."

"And?"

"A man who wouldn't give his name says he can give us information about where she is now."

I stare at him. I wonder for a wild moment if he's making it up, but he looks completely serious.

"A crank."

"Could be, and maybe not. He's not after a reward."

"He says. So what's he waiting for?"

"A face-to-face meeting."

"I'll be out tomorrow. We can . . ."

"No, you won't. Anyway, he said he wanted to think about it some more first—he asked lots of questions about who was looking for her, and why."

"He is after money."

"Anyway, I've got to wait for his phone call."

"Sounds like crap."

Hen shrugs, smiling.

When he finally gets up to go find Madeleine, Hen looks down at me with a small smile.

"Of course, Raymond, you know what your problem is?"

I can think of hundreds of problems that I lay claim to. I don't know which particular one he is talking about.

"You're a snob."

"What? Me?"

I start laughing.

"My father was a Gypsy postman!"

"You treat Madeleine differently because her background is different from yours. She didn't have to claw her way up from the gutter, so you think she's had it easy."

I gape at him.

"I don't know what you're talking about."

But I do. And he knows I know.

"She's married to me, remember. And she stuck with me, through all my crap. She had to struggle."

I blink several times.

"I put up with your offensive poshness."

Hen grins.

"I'll see you."

"Don't forget the Black Patch."

"I won't. It's one lead, that's all. Like the phone call. Might come to nothing."

I know it. I do. But at the same time, you get hunches about things. You get them, and they don't go away.

42.

JJ

Nurse Emma told me I could go and see him. I knock softly on the door, thinking maybe he didn't recognize me because he doesn't remember me—that would be embarrassing. But I'm here to find things out, so it doesn't really matter.

He smiles as soon as he turns around.

"Hello, JJ. I thought I saw you before. Then I thought, maybe I was hallucinating."

"Um, no. I was here. Nurse Emma said you were feeling better."

"Yes, I am, thanks. Come in."

He gestures to my left arm, which is still heavily bandaged.

"You've been in the wars. What happened to you?"

"Oh . . . I fell on a piece of glass. It got infected. Blood poisoning. 'S fine now, nearly."

"Oh. Good."

"How are you?"

"Getting better. I think they'll let me out in a couple of days. Can't wait. Drives you crazy being stuck in here, doesn't it?"

"Yeah. Can you go for a walk?"

"Sounds like an excellent idea."

We go outside, and I turn toward the lake on the edge of the gardens. It's the nicest thing around here, although that isn't saying that much. I have to slow my pace to match his.

"Funny us both being here, isn't it?"

"Yeah. Quite a coincidence."

"So . . . what happened to you?"

"Food poisoning."

"Oh. You don't normally end up in hospital with that, do you?"

"No. This was a . . . an unusual form of it."

"What did you eat?"

"That's the funny thing. I can't remember."

"So how long have you been here?"

"Oh, a few days."

This is harder than I thought.

"I came in on Saturday night. Were you here then?"

"Um . . . no. They tell me I was brought in on Monday."

"Monday?"

I stare at him. He looks back, a bit surprised at my tone of voice. Monday. The day after he was with Ivo. I look at the water, glittering between the trees. There seems to be something stuck in my throat.

"Do you live round here, then?"

"No. I went to see your relatives, actually, on the Sunday. Had something to eat with them, too. Maybe they nobbled me!"

He gives a short laugh, to show it's a joke. I try to laugh, too.

I can't think of anything else to say.

The lake is actually more of a pond than a lake, and it doesn't get prettier the nearer you get. It smells a bit, to tell the truth. The edges are hard and straight, bordered by a concrete path. Green-and-yellow scum is gathered at one end. It's not like the lake in France, which was fresh and clean. It occurs to me that I'm not like the JJ who was in France, either. That person seemed happy and young and unsuspecting—a bit of an idiot, really. We amble up the path to where the boats are moored. There is a little hut where a man leans on the bottom half of a stable door, a fag in his mouth, hatred in his eyes. Next to him is a sandwich board that says "Boats £1 an hour." He looks like he's guarding them against anyone who might dare hire one. But today, there are no takers. The boats are nice old ones, made of wood planks covered with thick glossy varnish the color of honey. They barely move in the soft lapping water. They don't seem to go with the straight-edged pond and the foamy scum. I wonder where they have come from; they belong somewhere more beautiful.

"They've all got girls' names," I say, stating the obvious.

"Ships always do," he says, "I think."

Here, at least, it's true; painted on each stern in white capitals is a name and capacity: AMY—TO CARRY TWO. CHRISSIE—TO CARRY THREE. VIOLET—TO CARRY SIX. ISOBEL—TO CARRY FOUR.

"They're nice, aren't they?" I say.

"Yeah."

The water gleams like dirty satin. It's as clear as coffee—it could be six inches deep, or six feet, you can't tell. I find a stick next to the path and poke it into the water. I don't feel the bottom, but it's not a very long stick. Strings of duckweed cling to it when I pull it out. I push the side of one of the boats (CHRISSIE—TO CARRY THREE) so that it rocks; the water slops and sucks underneath.

"Oy! You, there! You hiring?"

The man's voice is aggressive. Mr. Lovell turns around.

"No."

"Then don't interfere with the boats!"

"Sorry!"

Mr. Lovell lifts his left hand in a friendly wave. I imagine punching the man, then think that might be a bit over the top. I give him a hard stare instead but drop my stick. He flicks his cigarette in my direction.

"Don't think anyone's going to be hiring, with him around!"

"No."

"They're nice, though, aren't they?" I say again, and immediately feel like a spaz.

"Yeah. Why don't we go for a row, anyway?"

I look at Mr. Lovell, worried. I haven't got any money, and I've got only one arm that works.

"Er . . . I don't think . . ."

I wave my bandaged arm.

"Yeah, I suppose you're right. Some other time, then."

He gives an awkward little laugh, as though realizing that there isn't ever going to be another time. Why would there be? Why would he ever want to see this stupid, spazzy kid again?

We start to walk around the water's edge.

"How's Christo? Is he back with you yet?"

"No. My uncle's gone up to London to be with him. Maybe he'll stay up there." I clear my throat. It sounds really loud. "He went up there on Monday, actually."

"Oh?"

"Yeah. The day after you saw him."

He stops and stares hard at me. I seem to have caught his attention at last.

"So what's the news on Christo? Do they know what's wrong with him yet?"

"I don't think so. Apparently, they're doing lots of tests. It takes a long time to get results."

"I'm sure. You know, your uncle ran off when we were at the specialist's. Just vanished—all because they asked him for a blood sample."

"Oh."

The image of red on white flickers into my mind. I feel myself blushing.

"Did you know he has a needle phobia?"

"No."

"At least he's with him now. In London."

"Yeah."

"Where does he stay—is it with your great-aunt?"

I look at him blankly.

"Who?"

"Your Aunt Lulu—she must be your great-aunt—Lulu . . . Luella."

"Oh. I suppose, yeah. I don't know, really."

Mr. Lovell looks around—there's a kiosk on the other side of the pond that sells ice cream and cups of tea.

"Should've brought some money with me. We could have had an ice cream."

I've noticed that Mr. Lovell holds his right hand in a strange way—it just hangs at his side. I ask him about it.

"I couldn't move at all when they found me, so this is an improvement."

"That's awful."

"Not much fun. They say it will recover, like the rest of me. But it's taking its time."

This just gets worse. He might have died, from the sound of it.

"Mr. Lovell . . . Do you know what a *chovihano* is?"

"I've heard of them. Sort of a Gypsy healer, isn't it? Herbs and stuff."

"Yeah. Well . . . I saw him once, doing an . . . an exorcism thing. On Christo. Trying to make him better."

"Who did?"

"Uncle Ivo."

There is a pause. He continues to walk, not looking at me.

"You're saying Ivo is a . . . *chovihano*?"

"Yeah. Well, that's what he said. And it's all herbs and stuff. He knows about herbs and . . . poisonous plants and things."

My heart thunders as the word "poisonous" blurts out of my mouth. My cheeks feel hot.

I definitely have his attention. I know he's looking at me, although I don't want to look at him.

"What makes you say this, JJ? Do you think there's a reason why he would have wanted to hurt me?"

There must be loads of reasons—to do with Rose, and my mum, and secret women. Maybe . . . even—why didn't I think of this before?—Rose is the secret woman. Which would mean that it's not Mum . . . but I'm not sure this makes any kind of sense.

"I don't know."

"There must be something."

"I think he's . . . You won't tell anyone—my mum or anyone?" I look up now—he shakes his head.

"I think he has secrets . . ."

"What sort of secrets?"

"Maybe . . . I dunno. I think he's got a . . . a secret girlfriend."

"Oh. Really?"

He walks for a while, as if he's thinking.

"Do you know who it is?"

I shake my head. I feel really stupid now. I was going to tell him what I found in the cupboard in his trailer, but now I can't. I can't say the words. And how can I tell him it might be my mum? I scrape the toe of my shoe along the concrete path, dragging up moss.

"Do you think he had a secret girlfriend when he was married to Rose?"

Mr. Lovell doesn't seem to be laughing at me. I think he's serious. It's never occurred to me, that possibility, although, now that I think of it, why not?

"I don't know. Great-uncle's the only one who might know."

"Have you ever seen anyone like that visit him?"

"N . . . no."

I think of that night, looking into my own trailer. Him and her. I take a breath. Then let it out. I can't say it.

"Have you ever heard anyone in your family talk about a plant called henbane . . . or ergot?"

"No."

My voice comes out in a stupid squeak, like an eight-year-old's.

"Of course, they can't say for definite how it happened. It could be that someone gathering herbs just made a mistake. It happens."

"Yeah, course."

"Ivo wasn't ill on Monday? He went up to London?"

"That's what Mum said."

"And no one else in your family has been ill?"

"No. They're all fine. They've all been to see me. Except him."

We're almost back to where we started now, approaching the boat-hire hut from the other side. I want to ask him what he's thinking, but I don't know how to. All I can think is that Ivo poisoned him. He can't have made a mistake, because if he had, he would have made himself ill, too, wouldn't he? And if Ivo poisoned Mr. Lovell—if he could have done that, then maybe he killed Rose, too. Maybe that's why he poisoned him, because he was afraid of being found out . . .

We both speak at the same time:

"What are you going to do?"

"Maybe we should go back."

We stare at each other.

"I'll find out what happened. That's what I'm going to do. It may not be what it seems. Try not to worry about it."

My mind fills with millions of questions until it's a hopeless jam. I feel terror, a sort of dizziness, and a terrible feeling of guilt, all at once.

"I don't know . . ."

Mr. Lovell looks at me.

"You haven't told me anything I wouldn't have found out in the next day or two, anyway. I appreciate what you've said. It's not always easy."

"But what about Christo? What will happen to him if . . . ?"

I'm ashamed to say that tears spill down my face; hot salt water runs into my mouth before I can swipe it away.

"Don't start worrying yet. Let's just see what happens."

We walk in silence back to the hospital. I can feel his eyes on me most of the way. He seems like a nice man, decent; I think he's a good person, but even though he's an adult, I can tell that he doesn't know what to say any more than I do.

43.

Ray

Hen didn't find Ivo. Not at the site, where the family claimed he was up in London with Christo, and not at the hospital, where staff thought it strange that the boy's father hadn't been to see him since the beginning of the week. He went to see Lulu, suspecting that she might be sheltering him. After his visit, he was convinced she wasn't. He told the police his suspicions, knowing there was little chance of their taking an interest on the basis of so little evidence. After three days of fruitless inquiries, it seemed that Ivo Janko, just like his wife before him, had performed a remarkably successful vanishing act.

I wonder if the whole site will be empty, and the Jankos melted away, in his wake. I wonder whether, that being the case, I could prove they were ever there. But the paddock, when Hen drives me down the day after I am released from the hospital, looks much as it ever did. All the trailers are still here, parked at their old, odd angles, including Ivo's.

"Wouldn't you rather I waited?"

Hen agreed to be my chauffeur only after I threatened to drive myself, which, considering my right hand is still useless, is just as well.

"No, come back in an hour or so."

A few days ago, Tene told Hen that Ivo was up in London. Apparently, he was all innocence and charm. Since then, his confidence is gone.

"Mr. Janko?"

"Mr. Lovell. How are you?"

"I know you heard about my spell in hospital."

"I was sorry to hear that, Mr. Lovell. I hope you are fully recovered."

"Well, nearly. It was a nasty form of food poisoning. It seems I must have picked it up while I was here last Sunday gone. I wanted to check if anyone else had suffered as well. Particularly . . . if Ivo is okay."

"Ivo's up in London. We haven't seen him for a while. I think he's all right."

"And you were all right, then?"

"I didn't eat with you, Mr. Lovell."

He keeps looking just past my face—apparently, unwilling to meet my eyes.

"When was the last time you saw Ivo?"

"He went up on . . . Monday or Tuesday, I think. To be near the boy."

He sucks the last drop out of his cigarette and squashes it into the pile of butts in the ashtray. The whole place has a slightly grubby, unkempt air, the windows no longer as sparkling, the Crown Derby not quite as bright.

"But he hasn't. My partner checked with the hospital. They haven't seen him for days. Ivo hasn't been in to see Christo at all."

"That can't be. They're making a mistake."

Tene speaks to the table. His hands are clasped on his knees, but he keeps locking and interlocking his fingers.

"He would never leave the boy."

"Hen thought the same thing. So he kept going back. In the unit that Christo is in, you can't sneak in and out—someone on the staff is always there. There's only one entrance. They would've seen him. He hasn't been there."

"Then something must have happened. He'll be back."

"Bit odd, isn't it? I thought his world revolved around Christo."

Tene Janko looks at me now, his face drawn.

"I know my son. He would never leave him."

"But he has left him, Mr. Janko. For nearly a week."

His eyes search the corners of the ceiling, then the corners of the floor.

"Then something must have happened to him. Maybe something bad."

"Like with Rose?"

Tene sucks in a breath and glares. "You are taking my words and twisting them. I am talking about Ivo!"

"Bit of a coincidence, isn't it? First Rose disappears without a trace. Now Ivo."

"No! You're wrong. He never hurt Rose! One day you will realize that."

"I hope so, I really do. The thing is . . . at the Black Patch, at Watley . . ."

I say this very softly. He closes his eyes in pain—or is it just a slow blink?

"At the Black Patch, where you used to stop, they have found the remains of a young woman. They were buried over by the trees, to the right as you come from the road. About four feet down. It's the right age . . . the right period. Police forensics are doing tests at the moment, to find out what killed her."

This isn't strictly true, but given time, it will be.

"Well, it's not Rose! Mr. Lovell, what we told you was the truth . . . None of us hurt her. She ran away. And no one has stopped at Watley for more than ten years. She was never there, as far as I know, and she isn't there now."

He sounds sincere—and it just makes me angry.

"I was poisoned with henbane—on Sunday, while I ate with your son! How do you explain that? How, exactly, do you suggest that happened?"

Tene is shaking his head, his eyes sorrowful.

"I don't know, Mr. Lovell, I don't know. He must have made a mistake."

"I could have died!"

"Mr. Lovell. I am truly sorry, but if it happened here, it wasn't deliberate."

I stare at Tene in frustration. I have two problems—the first is that, almost against my will, I believe him. I was sure that I would see something in his face at the mention of the remains, but, although I'm sure that something about the Black Patch bothers him, I don't think it's anything to do with Rose. I have to think that if Ivo acted against me—or against Rose, all those years ago—then he did so alone. The second problem is that, despite myself, I like him. And I feel sorry for him. I know that can cloud your judgment.

"I know you're angry, Mr. Lovell, and I don't blame you, but that doesn't mean we are bad people. We aren't. We are the ones who get hurt, over and over again. Is it because we're Gypsies? I don't know. But we are cursed. What did we do to deserve this? You think I'm making myths? I have lost so many of mine I no longer care what anyone says. I lost my uncles, my brothers . . . my own little boys, my dear wife . . . I lost my only daughter, my daughter-in-law . . . And now, it seems, my last child, my one remaining child . . . is gone. What can I say? What can I care about now?"

His voice is low, but he could have been shouting. I feel disarmed. I grope around for my point, my argument, but it seems a blunt, cruel weapon.

"The Black Patch . . ."

"The Black Patch! People make mistakes, Mr. Lovell." There is a trace of spittle at the corner of his mouth. "I made a mistake! I am sorry to have misled you, if that is what you think."

"And Ivo disappears—when the remains of a young woman come to light, and I am poisoned? Are they all mistakes?"

"I don't say that I understand everything in the world. I doubt you do. Do you understand why my family is cursed with this affliction?"

His eyes are glittering with unshed tears.

"Do you know where your son is, Mr. Janko?"

Tene blinks again, and this time the tear runs down his cheek, into his mustache.

"No."

I feel like a murderer.

Outside, I turn my face up to the sun. I feel exhausted. With a nagging hunch that I have missed something important. I knock on the door of the trailer where JJ lives. Sandra answers, sheltering her eyes against the sunlight. She doesn't move from the doorway, but she smiles.

"Hello, Mr. Lovell. It's good to see you up and about again. JJ told us you were in hospital."

"Yes, thank you. I was just wondering how JJ is. How's his arm now?"

"He's fine. Right as rain, really. He's not here right now. Out with friends."

"Oh. Good. He's a bright boy, isn't he? Thoughtful."

"Got his head in the clouds, you mean."

"You must be proud of him."

She smiles but looks embarrassed. Praise draws the evil eye.

I study her face in sections: pale, grainy skin; dark brown eyes with slightly drooping eyelids; a way of tucking her fluffy, sandy hair impatiently behind one ear. I'm trying to trigger jolts of familiarity, memories of the other night . . . but I experience none. And she shows no signs of awkwardness or embarrassment at my presence.

"I don't suppose you know where I could find Ivo?"

"He's up in London; that's all I know." She doesn't look as though she's hiding anything. "You could try his aunt Lulu. I think he was going to stay with her again. I've got her address back here somewhere . . ."

I don't tell her I already have it. She steps back and gestures for me to come in. I stand in the doorway, looking around. Her trailer is tidy and clean, and pleasantly old-fashioned. Dark oak-veneer walls. The windows are spotless; the chair covers are a plain bright green.

"This is nice," I say, meaning it.

"Thank you . . . Here we are."

She opens an address book and copies down an address in careful capitals.

"He might be staying with her."

She passes me a piece of paper that appears to be torn from one of her son's exercise books.

"Thank you. Or maybe he's at his girlfriend's?"

I say it as casually as I can manage, but I don't think the way I say it makes any difference. Her pale lips blanch; her eyes shrink: black holes in ash. Her lips work soundlessly for a second.

"Ivo hasn't got a girlfriend."

"Oh? I thought . . . Someone said something . . ."

"No, I . . . No. We would have known. I would know."

She tries to smile but looks stricken.

Oh, I think. Oh . . .

"Oh, well . . . Must have got hold of the wrong end of the stick, I suppose."

I fold Lulu's address and tuck it in my breast pocket, careful not to crumple it.

"Are you close, then, you and Ivo? Do you think he'll be in touch?"

She gapes at me before deciding that I probably mean close in a cousinly sense.

"I expect so, yes."

But she looks down, miserable, her arms folded protectively over her body.

"Are you the only cousins?"

She frowns; I am pushing a little too hard now.

"We've got cousins in Ireland . . . Why?"

I shrug.

"I'm half Gypsy myself. There are usually a lot of cousins."

She stares at me; I could kick myself. Hen is right—I should go and sit quietly at home until my wits have returned to me.

"Not in our family, Mr. Lovell."

The sound of Hen's engine fills me with gratitude. I stumble outside, apologizing and thanking her. She shuts the door with a brief nod, without saying good-bye.

44.

JJ

I don't recognize her at all—the short, thin, done-up woman with a crappy car who's just hammered on our door.

She says, "You must be JJ."

"Yeah . . . ?"

She looks me up and down.

"What happened to your arm?"

"Cut it on some glass."

"You look like your great-grandfather. Does anyone ever tell you that? I'm Lulu, your great-aunt. You don't remember me."

A statement. But she smiles as she says it.

"Sort of . . ."

So this is my auntie Lulu. It's been years since I've seen her. Since I don't know when. She has black hair and pale skin and red lipstick; her clothes are smart and tight. She looks like she belongs in the town, with clean pavements to step on in those high, shiny heels, not out here, in the country mud.

"You don't have to pretend. I won't mind. I barely know you—but you must have been only about eight or so last time we met. I haven't changed as much—well, then, maybe I have."

She shrugs and smiles. When she smiles, it's hard not to smile, too. It's hard, too, to think that she is Gran and Great-uncle's

sister—she doesn't seem old the way they do. She's the youngest
sister, of course, but even so.

"Do you want to see Great-uncle? That's his trailer."

I point to the one with the ramp going up to the door.

She heaves a sigh.

"I want to see all of you. I don't suppose you know where your
uncle Ivo is?"

The name still sends a shiver through me.

"No. We thought he was in London."

"Yeah. We need to talk."

It turns out that the hospital keeps ringing her because they want
her to take Christo away again. Apparently, there's nothing more
they can do for him at the moment, and he's not ill enough to stay.
I suppose that's the good news. Of course, the hospital would rather
Ivo took Christo away, but they can't find him, either. The bad news
is that if the family doesn't go and get him, they'll put Christo into
care. So we have to decide who's going to do what.

Lulu looks around at all of us—at Mum and Gran, anyway, and
me, because I refused to be excluded, for once. Granddad is out somewhere (a pub, perhaps, possibly, maybe?), and Great-uncle isn't feeling too well.

It seems perfectly obvious to me what we should do.

"He should come and live with us, shouldn't he, Mum?"

I stare at her, willing her to agree. I read somewhere that this
works, if you will hard enough.

"I don't know, JJ . . ."

Mum looks tired. Somehow she looks colorless next to Auntie
Lulu, like she's been washed too many times.

"We've got to take him!"

It seems to me that it's the only thing that makes sense, because
Gran is really too old, and Great-uncle can't, and Auntie Lulu

doesn't do children. I don't feel I should say all this out loud, but it's obvious.

"He's like my brother, anyway. And it's what he would want."

"I know, sweetheart, but . . . you don't know what you're saying . . . what it involves. He's a disabled child . . ."

"So?"

"Looking after him is a lot of work, and I've got my work, and you've got school, so who would be around during the day . . . And he'd have to go to the hospital, what, every week?"

She looks at Lulu.

"I think so. Yeah."

"And . . . I don't know. Ivo's bound to come back—he could come back at any minute. And what will he think?"

Gran says, "He hasn't got any right to think anything. Going off like that." She sniffs.

Lulu says, "I don't think Ivo will be coming back."

There's something so cold and definite about the way she says it that we all look at her. She inhales on her fag, so that little lines appear around her mouth. I wonder if she knows something. Because I don't think Ivo will be coming back, either.

Mum shakes her head. "I don't know. It just seems wrong. Ivo dotes on Christo . . ."

"So where is he?"

Gran and Lulu exchange looks. They seem to be in agreement about Ivo.

"Mum, I'll help! We'll all help. Like we always did."

"It's not just the work. It's . . . other things, isn't it?"

"Like what?"

Mum sighs and rubs her hand over her face.

"What your mum means," says Auntie Lulu, "is that they're probably going to assess any of us who offers to take him, since we're not his immediate family. And they're . . . well, they're unlikely to approve anyone who lives in a trailer."

"But he's lived in one all his life!"

"Yeah, but . . . he's on their radar now, JJ. They've started asking questions. And since . . . Like San says, he's disabled, so they're being extra, well, nosy."

"Bloody *gorjios*. How do they have the right?"

Great-uncle would be proud of me.

"They don't think a trailer is a suitable environment," says Mum. "The social . . . you know."

Gran taps her ash off her fag.

"There won't be much we can do about it. But you know we'll help out as much as we can—money and that . . ."

She means her and Granddad. This is when I realize that this isn't the first time they've talked about the problem of what to do with Christo. Mum doesn't normally go around saying things like "suitable environment."

For the first time I get the feeling—a strong, scary feeling—that things are going to change a lot. I suppose they already started to change when Ivo went off, but now I realize that things cannot continue as they are. And suddenly I want them to. I don't want to have to move and go to a different school where I don't know anyone; I don't want us all to split up. We're the last of the Jankos—there's no one else. If we don't stick together, what will happen to us?

"But why is it up to them now? He's family. One of us!"

"Because Ivo's buggered off! And God knows what else . . . And he's left us in the shit, frankly."

Mum looks really upset.

I look at Auntie Lulu. She lives in the city; she must know how to cope with Them. She's not smiling now.

"Would you be prepared to live in bricks, JJ?"

My head starts buzzing with a nameless fear. I force myself to think about Christo, stuck in the hospital. On his own.

"Course, if that's what we'd have to do."

Even as I say it, the memory of the stifling hospital air seems to fill my lungs and throat like cotton wool.

"But I don't understand how they can say where we have to live. We are who we are. And Christo is who he is. How can it be up to people who don't know anything about us?"

"It just can, lovey."

This from Mum, sounding weary. Gran leans forward.

"Ivo got away with murder. Tene helped out more than you know, with money and the like—otherwise, he'd've got into trouble before now. And now we've got to pick up the pieces."

"Christo's not a 'piece,'" I say.

"You know what she means, JJ."

Lulu is the only one of us still sounding fairly calm. She turns to Gran, who's sucking on her Rothmans like a baby at the bottle.

"What do you think, Kath?"

Gran sends twin plumes of smoke out of her nostrils.

"I don't see why you can't take him, Lu. You're the one with the house."

Auntie Lulu is lighting up her own cigarette. Lucky Mum doesn't smoke, too, or we wouldn't be able to breathe. She speaks without looking up.

"I don't know if that would be the best thing for him, Kath. He doesn't know me like he does you. I mean . . ."

"Mum, we have to take him! I love him—and so do you. And he'd be happy with us. I'll live anywhere—we can always open the windows, and if we were on the edge of a town, it wouldn't be so bad . . . You have to say yes, Mum, don't you see that?"

Mum shrugs; she really does look tired. I suddenly see that she's been thinking this over night and day—for a while, probably.

I find myself jumping up and throwing my arms around her.

"Christo deserves a mum like you, Mum. He always did."

"Oh, sweetie pie." Mum buries her face in my shoulder. Her ribs jerk under my hands—she lets out a shuddery sob. I can't believe I ever shouted at her.

"I never thought I'd live in bricks again . . ."

"It really would be the best thing if you could, San," says Auntie Lulu, her voice all warm and enthusiastic. "I'll help any way I can. Housing and stuff."

What with all that, Mum seems to be on the verge of giving in. They discuss it some more—circling nearer and nearer the certainty that Christo will come to us. Then Lulu offers to drive the three of them to the pub for a drink, "Because we deserve it."

I think Mum deserves it. I say I'll stay and keep an eye on Great-uncle. Mum smiles at me. Lulu kisses me on the cheek and says I'm a credit to her. It's only much later, when I glance in the mirror, that I see the stupid red smudge of lipstick on my cheek, and scrub it off.

45.

Ray

The forensics team is back—and in their white plastic suits and overshoes they look like bargain-basement astronauts crawling over a desolate moonscape. The receding waters have left their mark on the site in odd ways: some creaturelike current has left a twisting trail that slithers up to kiss the tent's wall before veering away; detritus has been carried here and dumped: a tractor tire, plastic feed sacks, a twisted pram, broken boughs. The soil is studded with featureless small mounds; the one nearest to us is covered in fur. And everything is rendered drab and dun by the enveloping mud.

This is Hen's first visit to the Black Patch. We're not going to find anything useful, but I can't stay away. As I said, in my defense, at least we'll know whether the police know more than they say they do—and they say that work has only just begun again, that after the flood it's like starting from scratch. Even finding the exact spot where the bones were located is proving difficult. Looking at it now, I believe it. No way to keep the floodwaters out of that makeshift grave.

Considine isn't here, and the mud-smeared forensics woman sent to talk to us doesn't want us setting foot inside the gate. We'll be informed, apparently.

Then a thought strikes her.

"Your missing person . . ."

We nod.

"Got a medical history?"

"We can ask. Have you got something?"

"One of the arm bones . . . seems to show a historical break—I mean a greenstick fracture, from early childhood. Not particularly well mended. Ask about childhood accidents."

"Which arm?"

"Right. Radius. About here." She places thumb and forefinger, calliperlike, on her own wrist. "That's all I can tell you."

When we get back to the office there is a message from Andrea—the mystery Rose caller has rung again. She told him to ring back, and at four o'clock he does so.

By then I have spoken to Leon. He told me he didn't think Rose had broken her arm. Then, half an hour after I called him, he rings back.

"Just spoke to her sister," he says gruffly, warily.

I didn't explain why I was asking, but he's not stupid.

"She said . . . She said Rose fell and hurt her right arm when she was about five. We didn't take her to hospital; thought it was just a sprain . . . I'd forgotten—"

His voice breaks off abruptly.

"Well, maybe it was," I say carefully, but with my heart knocking against my Adam's apple.

"You're asking 'cause you've found something, haven't you? You've found a . . ."

He can't bring himself to say the word "body."

"Mr. Wood, we don't know anything for sure yet. Some . . . remains have been found. But we don't know yet whether it's the right age . . . It may not be. There's not much to go on at the moment. But there is damage to the right forearm: a greenstick fracture, they called it . . ."

"Oh, God—" He breaks off. Squeaks and wheezes come down the telephone line.

"I'm sorry, but you have to remember that the search isn't over . . . They can't identify the remains yet. It may just be a coincidence. Please don't assume the worst."

I say the words I'm supposed to say, but my heart isn't in it, and I think he can tell.

"Oh, God," he says again. "At least . . . At least her mother isn't here to hear this."

I wish I had spoken to him face-to-face now, but he insisted I tell him over the phone. And really, as I tell him again, it's just a small piece of the jigsaw puzzle, not enough to assume the worst, not nearly enough to tell for sure.

Hen is talking to the anonymous caller now. I told him Leon's news, and he is treating the caller to his politely bored voice.

"Wales?"

He rolls his eyes.

"I think we could come down tomorrow . . ."

He looks at me—a question. I shrug acquiescence—we can wait there as well as here, I reckon.

"Fine, then. All right . . . You'll be . . . ? Okay. We'll see you then."

"Might be worth the trip, from the sound of him."

I smile, feeling the butterflies jumping in my stomach. Case-end butterflies.

"Course, you don't have to come, too."

I just look at him in response.

46.

JJ

Mum was really quiet when they came back from the pub. She barely spoke all evening. Later that night, I woke up, and I was pretty sure she was crying, very quietly. I didn't know what to say, or whether to say anything at all. The next day, I try my hardest to cheer her up, but she almost seems not to see me, like she's in a trance. I know she doesn't hate Christo, so I'm pretty sure it's not that. Eventually, I go over to Gran's.

"I know your mum's upset, love. It's not fair on her, all this. She was really fond of Ivo, too, probably more than any of us."

I let that one pass.

"She seems so . . . depressed."

"We all are. We've all been thinking about it."

There's something odd about this, and Gran sort of stops what she's doing, and then starts again, tutting to herself.

"Gran . . . thinking about what?"

She pretends there isn't anything at first, but eventually she tells me. I can tell she wants to, really. She tells me that in the pub, Lulu told her and Mum something awful—she told them about the skeleton the police have found in the Fens, a skeleton they think is Rose.

. . .

I haven't been near his trailer since that night. I haven't wanted to go near it. The window I broke has only been patched up with a bit of board tacked to the door. Strange that no one ever said anything about it. I force it out and open the door, only breaking off one more bit of glass in the process.

The trailer's been empty for well over a week. It smells inside— stuffy and airless, with a faint whiff of something bitter. I have a sudden fear—what if he has booby-trapped the place? . . . Herbs that can kill if you only smell them . . . Is there such a thing? I open the door wide, just in case.

To be honest, it doesn't look that different from the way it did the last time I was in here. In the kitchenette, everything has been cleaned and put away. The fridge is empty, and only a packet of biscuits and some instant mash remain in the cupboard. I force myself to check the back of the cupboards, but there's nothing strange there this time—the poly bag behind the cleaning stuff is gone—he didn't put it outside with the rest of our rubbish, so he must've taken it straight to the dump. I can't see anything suspicious.

I pull out drawers and open the cupboards. The only things that seem to be gone are clothes. I can't remember exactly what was here before, but all the pictures, the knickknacks, even some of Christo's toys and kids' books, they're all still here. It's like when someone has gone away for a few days and could walk back in at any minute. The thought gives me the shivers. All in all, I can't find anything out of the ordinary. The women's things have gone. And despite the strange smell—which I can't smell anymore, so maybe it's been blown away; either that or I'm used to it—I can't find any traces of plants or twigs. Nothing funny like that. None of the stuff I saw during the casting out, not even candles. Nothing that obviously belongs to a murderer.

But in a locker under one of the seats, I do find a plastic jerry can. It clearly hasn't been touched for months. It's one of the ones I filled with holy water at Lourdes, but it's still almost full, still with my homemade label on it, and the pencil drawing of Mary (or was it meant to be Bernadette?—I can't remember), complete with halo and childish exclamation marks. I didn't see it last time, or maybe I just didn't notice. I feel hot just looking at it. Ivo must have stuffed it in here soon after we came back, and left it to gather dust.

He must have laughed at me.

When I pick it up, there seems to be some dirt swirling at the bottom of the can, clouding the holy water. I rip the embarrassing label off, shame and anger rising up in me like a tide, like a volcano. Then I unscrew the cap and upend it, emptying the water over the seats and cushions, over the carpet, and then back over the seat cushions, so that they are good and wet. After a few days they'll start to stink and go moldy. When all the water has gone and I don't feel any better, I just lift the can and hurl it to the floor as hard as I can. It bounces. I feel like a child. An idiot. A four-year-old idiot child. Ivo made a fool of me. He made fools of all of us. We don't even know what he did—lies and secrets, certainly, and now, it seems, worse—hurting Mr. Lovell, carrying on in secret like that, killing Rose, even . . . maybe. And we all were nice to him and pitied him and jumped about like puppets for him and went to Lourdes and pretended to believe.

I feel like ripping this place apart with my hands. I kick the drawers, which don't even dent—I just hurt my foot. I grind my teeth with rage, but that isn't going to help. I tipped holy water over everything! I have baptized this place rather than vandalized it. I am worse than useless.

I go back outside, slamming the door. I don't care who hears me now. Another little piece of glass falls out of the broken window. Fuck it. Fuck him. Fuck fuck fuck.

I rub my face with the back of my hand. Like the carpet, and the upholstery, it's wet.

47.

Ray

The chapel of the Welsh seaside town we come to is a plain brick box. It stands at the end of a street of identical Monopoly houses. The only concession to its purpose is a narrow cruciform stained-glass window in acid turquoise and orange, which, from the outside, suggests a gun slit more than a source of divine inspiration.

I look at Hen doubtfully.

I can see he's thinking the same thing. The man refused to give us a telephone number. The only thing we know about him is the name he gave us—Peter. The Rock.

As it's a Wednesday afternoon, it's quiet. But the door to the church is open, so we walk through a vestibule into a large, cold room where a few rows of padded chairs face a blond wood lectern, and a green nylon carpet crackles with static. The windows—apart from the stained-glass cross—are steel-meshed, for some reason. But there is someone waiting for us. He's standing at the front, by the lectern, hands clasped in front of his genitals, and he's wearing a clerical dog collar.

"Peter?"

The man smiles. He's young: no more than thirty, with fair hair and a square jaw, very clean-shaven and ruddy, but with such an air of calm and authority that I don't doubt he is the pastor of this church, and that the ladies of the congregation find him both an inspiration and a comfort.

"Thank you for coming all this way. We appreciate it."

He inclines his head in a slight bow. I look around for the someone else he refers to, but we are alone. Perhaps he is referring to God.

"I apologize for not being more forthcoming on the phone. Why don't you sit down."

He speaks fast—his voice is brisk and very Welsh. He gestures to the rows of seats. I don't want to sit down with him standing there, as if I am one of his flock, his sheep, but he picks up a chair and turns it to face the front row, and sits down with us.

"You wouldn't think it was August, would you? We don't put the heating on during the week—saves money."

He smiles again, ruefully.

"Er, before we start, could I please see your identification?"

We hand over our licenses. He studies them carefully before handing them back.

"Thank you. I'm sorry if all this seems unnecessarily . . . cagey, but, well, I expect you want to know what I have to tell you. As you know, I saw your advertisement in the newspaper, asking for information about Rose Wood—Rose Janko, as she was once. Before I tell you, can you tell me who wants to find out, and why?"

"As I said on the phone, I'm afraid we can't breach client confidentiality."

Peter the pastor frowns slightly.

"Not even their name? You're asking for a breach of . . . our confidentiality. It could be a matter of personal safety."

"We can assure you that your name needn't come into it. We'll treat any information as strictly confidential; our client just wants to know if . . . Rose is all right. You needn't be brought into it at all."

He looks puzzled.

"It's not myself I'm thinking about."

If not himself, then . . . who?

"Look, I can assure you"—I'm thinking of Georgia Millington now— "no one will be forced to do anything they don't want to do. If it's a question of contacting the parties concerned, that will be entirely up to you."

Admittedly, at the back of my mind I'm thinking: How much discretion does a skeleton need?

Peter leans back in his chair. He looks as though nothing could ruffle him, although there is, perhaps, a touch more blood in the rosy cheeks.

"I'm sorry, gentlemen, if you don't tell me who's looking for Rose Wood, then I won't be able to help you."

I look at Hen. He gives a slight shrug.

"I was approached by Leon Wood."

He nods, as if it was what he expected.

"When?"

"Several weeks ago."

"Why now?"

"I understand that Mrs. Wood recently passed away, quite unexpectedly. I think Mr. Wood is aware that he is not going to live forever."

Peter looks concerned.

"Is he ill?"

"I don't know, Mr. . . . ?"

"Reverend. Reverend Hart. And is it only her father who wants to find her?"

"Mr. Wood is our only client."

He nods, clasping his hands together and leaning his elbows on his knees. His hands, with their broad, pale nails, are extremely clean and pink, as though he has just spent five minutes scrubbing them.

"I ask because, as I am sure you know, Rose made an unfortunate early marriage, although it was a marriage only in the eyes of the Gypsy community, not in the eyes of the Church."

For the first time, I feel a sense of urgency awaken inside me. He seems to know a surprising amount about her . . . Surprising, that is, unless . . .

"It was an episode in her life that she wished to put behind her forever. Some things are so painful that no one should be forced to relive them."

"All I have to do," I say, a sense of light-headedness coming over me, as though I am at one remove from all this, "is pass the details of Mr. Wood on to . . . whoever. No one has to see anyone, or even talk to anyone, unless that is what they want."

I can't bring myself to say "her" or "she." Because how can it be?

"You sound as though you knew Rose rather well," says Hen.

Peter smiles.

"Oh, yes."

A trace of impatience creeps into Hen's voice, though it's apparent only to me, because I know him. "So do you know where Rose is now?"

"Excuse me a moment."

Instead of answering, he stands up and walks to a door at the side of the church, opens it, and disappears.

I meet Hen's eyes.

"What is he playing at?"

He shrugs—give it a chance.

A minute passes. Then another. We sit in silence, with just an occasional car passing to break the monotony. It really is remarkably cold in here—it reminds me of sporadic trips to church when I was a child. Church was always cold then, too. Dimly lit, cold, with murderously uncomfortable seats. No wonder numbers have dwindled.

Fully five minutes pass, by my watch. Then the door reopens and Peter comes back in. With him is a woman. He leads her by the elbow, unsmiling and solicitous, as though she is a delicate creature with porcelain bones. She has her eyes cast down. Yeah, all right, I think, so she does look a bit like Rose, I'll give him that.

"Please, gentlemen, this is my wife—Rena Hart, but in a former life, she was Rose Wood."

The woman stands in front of us in silence, looking into space. In silence, Hen and I stare at her. She has ash-blond highlighted hair sprayed back into flicks that form a halo around her face, pale blue eyeshadow, matching pink fingernails and lipstick. She wears a loose, long skirt suit with a high-necked blouse that ties at the throat in a bow, Princess Diana–style. The suit seems too big for her; it comes nearly to her ankles. But despite the demurely high neck, I can see one thing quite clearly: a port-wine birthmark that spreads up her neck toward her chin, looking for all the world like a dark hand reaching around her throat.

"Rena Hart?" I say at last, unable to think of anything else.

She looks at her husband, as if he has all the answers. The pastor holds her hand in both of his.

"When we married, Rena decided she wanted a complete break with the past, so she chose the name Rena—it means reborn, and also, in Hebrew, joy. In our church we are baptized and, in a very real sense, are reborn in the light of the Lord, so it seemed most appropriate."

He smiles at her and pats her captive hand. I clear my throat and attempt a smile. Awkwardly, I put out my limp hand—awkwardly, that is, until Peter Hart releases her hand again, and she shakes mine briefly, avoiding eye contact.

"I'm very happy to meet you, Mrs. Hart. My name is Ray Lovell, and this is my partner, Henry Price."

We are all standing up now. There is a pause. No one seems much inclined to sit down again.

"I must say, I wouldn't have recognized you . . . Do you mind? . . . I brought these."

I fish out the photographs of Rose at age sixteen and eighteen. The second, in particular, is poignant; the girl in the wedding dress appears to stare beseechingly out of the picture, asking to be rescued.

But comparing the pictures and the woman in front of us, it is hard not to conclude that this is, no matter how changed, the girl who was once Rose Wood and, briefly, Rose Janko.

"This is a bit of a giveaway, though, isn't it?" She fingers the dark skin on her neck. "I used to cover it up completely . . . until Peter persuaded me not to."

She blushes slightly and looks at him; the sight of his face seems to reassure her. She has developed the trace of a Welsh accent, and a slightly clipped delivery, like the Reverend Hart.

"This is . . . amazing. Your father was . . . well, he was afraid that you were dead."

She lifts her chin, a stubborn movement, emphasized by the heavy jaw.

"Ha. Well, I'm not. Not that anyone made an effort to find me all these years. Where was he when I needed help?"

"Did you ask him for help?"

She doesn't answer this.

"I would like very much to tell him that you are—evidently—very well."

She looks at her husband again and nods slightly.

"Yeah. Okay."

"Would you mind if he contacted you?"

She looks up at her husband, checking.

"I'd like to think about that."

"Yes, of course. I can leave his details with you. And your sister, Kizzy, she seemed very sad to have lost touch with you. Margaret, too."

Rose—Rena, I suppose I have to say now—shrugs, with a twist of the mouth.

"And, of course, there's your son . . . although I know it's been a long time . . . He's six years old now."

The temperature inside the church suddenly changes. From cold to icy. Both the pastor and Rose stare at me, eyes wide and hard. They both speak at once:

"I think you've made a mistake . . ."

"My what?"

"Your son; your and Ivo's son—Christo."

Rose and her husband exchange glances. His—doubtful? She shakes her head, a scornful smile on her face.

"I don't know who you've been talking to. I don't have a son. I don't have kids. I can't."

I think back to Ivo, his claim that she was depressed, delusional, in denial. Maybe he was right. But she doesn't seem delusional. Just very, very angry.

Peter Hart holds her hand again and takes a step closer to her.

"My wife is sadly . . . unable to have children."

"Who told you about this boy?" Rose is demanding. "Not Dad? . . . Not Ivo, surely?"

"Why not Ivo?"

She lets out a sharp exhalation. Shakes her head again and again, a hard, bright light in her eyes.

"Christ!" bursts from her at last.

Her husband looks shocked; his mouth thins.

"Sorry . . . but I've never heard such rubbish! If Ivo has a kid, it certainly wasn't with me . . . That was never going to happen."

She gives a short, mirthless laugh. Peter looks at her pleadingly; clearly, he thinks this is going too far.

"Perhaps we could leave it at that, gentlemen. You have found out what you wanted to know . . . It's . . . You appreciate that these are distressing memories . . ."

But Rose looks at him, no longer his porcelain damsel, now iron-tipped.

"I don't want these gentlemen believing someone's lies about me."

She turns toward us, away from him.

"Perhaps we should go somewhere and talk. Somewhere . . . else."

We arrange to go to a coffee shop on the high street. While Rose goes off to get her coat, Peter gives us a slightly strangled, disapproving smile.

"Please, I would ask you not to push her too hard. I hope you appreciate that my wife is a . . . rather fragile person."

His tone remains standoffish, as though he is delivering a sermon, but his eyes plead. Perhaps he can't help sounding like that.

"She has been through a great deal, and—" He breaks off as Rose comes back, now wearing a pea-green jacket with padded shoulders and carrying a handbag. "Fragile" is not the first word that comes to mind.

"Well . . . I'll leave you to it. See you later, darling."

He gives her a peck on the cheek, and she smiles at him. He still looks miserable.

"How long have you known your husband, Mrs. Hart?"

We are sitting in back of the local bakery, its slightly unsettling atmosphere courtesy of fluorescent strip lighting and an insect zapper that buzzes every few seconds as it claims another victim.

Rose—I still can't think of her as anything else—stirs a cup of tea. She has ordered a plate of little iced cakes, which sit, glowing like radioactive waste, in the middle of the table.

Instead of answering the question, she sips her tea and looks around with a smile.

"It's nice here, isn't it?"

"Yes. Very nice."

Hen nods in agreement.

"Peter. I met him when I was trying to run away from my first marriage. Getting married to Ivo Janko was all a horrible, awful mistake. You're Romany, aren't you, Mr. Lovell?"

"Half. My father was; my mother was *gorjio*."

"Maybe you have some idea what it's like. It was difficult for me . . . You know, from a family like mine . . . They wouldn't have wanted me back after I got married. The disgrace, you know? Peter helped me. I don't know what I would have done without him."

"Did you know Ivo well before you married?"

"No. Barely at all. I think we'd met twice, and never alone, you know? Just sort of, see if we could stand the sight of each other."

"So it was arranged by your families?"

She nods.

"Dad was keen—'cause they're a real Romany family. Mum wasn't so sure, but he always got his way."

She swallows, staring at her plate. I suppose her husband has just told her about her mother's death. She's doing remarkably well, considering.

"It was all arranged by Dad and Mr. Janko. I wasn't much of a catch . . . what with this." Her hand gestures toward her neck, a bitter smile. "People saw it as bad luck."

"Ah," I murmur.

"And him . . . he was good-looking enough, certainly—but there were these rumors. They tried to keep it quiet, but there was some family disease—I don't know what. They weren't popular. I think they thought neither of us would find anyone better."

She picks up her teacup and sips, gathering herself again. Then she tosses back her hair—which barely moves—picks up a lurid pink cube, and smiles at me. The sudden change in her expression is disconcerting. She pushes the plate toward me.

"Aren't you going to have one? They're lovely. Homemade."

This seems unlikely, but, obedient, I pick up the nearest one—a yolk-yellow blob that reminds me of a giant pustule—and put it on my plate.

"And the wedding took place in . . . October of '78?"

She nods.

"So how long did you live together?"

"Oh . . . A few months? Not much more than that . . . We got married in October; then I went on the road with him and his father—went to Lincolnshire and the Fens, I think, somewhere like that."

She trails off.

"And what happened?"

She sighs. Her head is bent over, eyes glued to the flowered tablecloth.

"I know it must be difficult to talk about, Mrs. Hart. Take your time."

There is a longish silence.

"He didn't want anything to do with me."

"You mean Ivo . . . ?"

"It was like, the day after the wedding, as soon as we were alone, he couldn't stand the sight of me. He wouldn't barely say anything. I didn't know what I'd done wrong."

Her voice is so low we both have to lean forward to catch it.

"We had one trailer, and Mr. Janko had another, but he spent most of the time in his dad's trailer. When I did see him, he was really cold."

"Cold in what way?"

"Cold! You know. Unfriendly. In a bad mood the whole time. I'd just be sitting there, wondering what on earth I'd done."

"Was he . . . violent toward you?"

"I heard him shouting at his dad sometimes."

"Did he shout at you, too?"

Rose looks down at the crumbs of pink sugar on her plate and presses her fingertip to one. Lifts her skinny shoulders in a way that reminds me she is only twenty-five, a young woman, despite the middle-aged clothes and hairdo.

"Mrs. Hart?"

"Well, he . . . I didn't understand. I thought we had got married, you know? That we were man and wife, but if I . . . if I tried to . . . he acted like I was completely stupid and ugly. Wouldn't touch me. Wouldn't let me touch him. Wouldn't . . . undress in front of me."

She is speaking to the plate in front of her.

"Did he ever hit you?"

She traces the outline of a flower on the tablecloth but shakes her head vigorously.

"No. Just . . . said things."

She takes out a tissue and carefully wipes the corners of her eyes, so as not to smear the blue shadow.

"So, forgive me, are you saying that . . . there was never any . . ."

I search for the polite term.

She smiles up at the fluorescent tube above us, blinking back tears.

"What do they call it? Unconsummated? That was it. So if he's had a kid, it was . . . with someone else."

She says this with a tight little smile.

"It might have been after you left. Christo was born in October of '79. The twenty-fifth, I think."

She thinks back, counting.

"I left during the winter—February, I think. End of February, yeah . . . Bloody hell—he must have been off with some slut while I was still there!"

Her voice quavers. I give her a bit of time to digest this. It seems to leave a bad taste in her mouth.

"I think I'd like some more tea, please."

"Of course . . ."

Hen is on his feet in an instant. It's strange—the girl opposite me seems to have shed years, and with them, her brittle confidence. She curls into herself like a hedgehog; underneath the suit, I realize, she is brutally thin. Hen sits down again, and three more teas are placed on the table, along with some more of the neon cakes.

"Did you suspect your husband of having a girlfriend on the side, Mrs. Hart?"

She grimaces.

"Well, now that you ask . . . I think I did wonder. But not a girl-friend, no—if you know what I mean . . ."

She looks at me significantly.

"I didn't know anything then, did I? I thought maybe he didn't like girls, you know?" A quick and brittle smile. "But he just didn't like me."

"So after—what?—four months of this . . . what was it that made you finally leave?"

"I'd have gone sooner, if I'd had anywhere to go. I started going to tent church meetings somewhere outside Lincoln—it was a place to escape, you know, once a week at least. Peter was one of the preachers there. An assistant. But . . . it was funny. I couldn't have gone at all if old Mr. Janko hadn't lent me his car. He could be nice, sometimes. Then I found out that the church was moving on, and I was really upset. It was the only good thing I had. I didn't know what I would do without it. And I told old Mr. Janko one day . . . I couldn't help it: I started crying and crying, and he said I should tell someone—at the church, I mean—how much it meant to me. It was funny, because it was almost like . . . he was telling me to ask them to help me . . . Get away, I mean. You know? D' you see what I mean? Like he felt sorry for me, in a way. So . . . that's what I did."

She shrugs again.

"I told Peter I was trapped in this awful marriage . . . and going off my head. And right away he offered me a job with the church. So I could go with them. I mean, there was nothing"—she blushes deeply—"funny going on. Nothing like that. He's a reverend. He just wanted to help me. I worked for the church. That's all it was—to start with."

"You didn't feel you could go back to your own family then?"

She shakes her head vehemently, clicks her tongue on her teeth.

"Not after what they spent on the wedding. I mean, I've got two sisters, and we all had to be got rid of—Dad never stopped moaning about it. No. They were only too glad to get rid of me."

"I know that's not the case," I say softly, but she just shakes her head again and tuts.

I glance at Hen. He seems to be concentrating on the virulent green thing on his plate, his face registering polite horror.

"So Ivo and you—it wasn't a real marriage at all?"

She shakes her head, her eyes briefly wide. I find it almost inconceivable that she isn't telling the truth.

"The thing I thought was that he was, you know . . . queer."

She lowers her voice until the last word comes out less than a whisper. She mouths it.

"I thought maybe I was like a smoke screen or something. But maybe he did have someone else, a woman he wasn't allowed to marry or something . . . I don't know." She shrugs again. "If he has got a kid, I pity the poor bastard."

We all sit in silence for a minute.

"Did you have any idea what Ivo and his father were arguing about?"

"No. It was never in front of me. I didn't understand anything. I had no one to talk to—until Peter. It was the loneliest time of my life."

She says it matter-of-factly. But I feel the first real sympathy I've felt for her.

"Thank you for telling us all this, Mrs. Hart. It's . . . very helpful."

Hen has reduced the green cake to a small pile of crumbs. Good work, I think. Now he looks up.

"Did you ever meet Ivo's cousin, Sandra Smith?"

"Sandra . . ."

She wrinkles her forehead in concentration.

"I might have met her at the wedding. I only met anyone at the wedding. They kept themselves to themselves after that. Why . . . Was it her?"

A feral look sweeps across her face but is gone as quickly as it came.

"I can't believe he cheated on me! I should've realized, shouldn't I? I'm so stupid!"

I shake my head.

"No, you're not. You're a better person for not realizing."

That's what I say to my clients. Hen looks at the table.

Our cups are empty, and our plates—except for mine, that is. Rena Hart, composure regained, looks disappointed.

"Didn't you like yours?"

"Oh, I'm not much of a cake . . . person."

"Mr. Lovell is sweet enough," says Hen gravely.

Rena looks at him, then lets out a high, girlish laugh. It sounds rather strained.

We walk down the street with her, back to the church and the car. She tells us not to bother coming in to say good-bye to her husband, and disappears into the concrete bunker. From behind, she gives the disconcerting impression of a middle-aged woman.

"Well, congratulations to us."

I look at Hen incredulously.

"Come on, Ray. We've just successfully concluded a case. We should be celebrating."

I shrug. The photos of the young Rose are in my breast pocket. We may have found Rose . . . No, we found Rena. I think Rose is gone for good.

Hen fiddles with the radio before switching it off.

"You're disappointed, aren't you? You can't feel sorry for her anymore."

"No, no!"

But it's true. My character flaw—one of many, I realize—is that I tend to like people more when I haven't met them.

"We haven't finished, though, have we?"

I feel an overwhelming tiredness drop over me like a cloak. I mutter, almost to myself, "Do we believe her?"

"About the marriage—and the child? We'll have to check. But for what it's worth, yes, I did believe her."

"So why do the Jankos tell people that Rose is Christo's mother?"

"To hide the fact that someone else is his mother."

We both think about that, as we drive past the sprawl of Monopoly houses and head for the bypass. Hen glances at me.

"But it may not matter much who Christo's real mother is. Some local girl who didn't want to know . . . It may be as simple as that."

"Then again, it may not."

"The important thing is to find out who is in the Black Patch. And then, hopefully, we'll know if they have any relation to Ivo Janko—or not."

Hen falls silent, but I know he's thinking what I'm thinking. We have to resist the temptation to assume that the answers to those two questions are one and the same. But my investigator's instinct tells me that they are the same. Christo's mother is in the Black Patch. It all fits. I let my head loll back against the headrest, the drone of tires sending me to sleep. We're getting nearer: all we need is a name.

48.

Ray

It's not that I wanted her to be dead. I can't explain it. Well, that's not strictly true; I don't like being wrong, any more than anyone else. I'm not disappointed that she's alive and well and happily married (we must suppose) to the scrubbed Welsh pastor. That she paints her nails frosted pink and has a laugh as unconvincing as her highlights.

Leon Wood sounds shocked, almost speechless.

"Alive? Are you sure?"

I wait for the sobs to subside, embarrassed but also strangely happy. It's not often I get to deliver such good news.

"I'm sorry, Mr. Lovell. 'Scuse me."

"No, no, quite all right. But you have to understand—it was a shock for her as well. Finding out her mother has passed away. She'll need some time to adjust."

"So when can I see her?"

"That has to be up to her."

"But where is she?"

"She has asked me not to pass on any details for the time being, while she gets used to the idea. She will get in touch with you when she's ready."

"Why?" he says, growing aggrieved. "I just want to know where she is. What's she got to get used to?"

"Please don't worry . . ."

"I'm not worried, Mr. Lovell. I'm not worried! I just want to see my dear daughter after seven years, and you are hindering me!"

There is much more of this sort of thing. I have to grit my teeth to keep my voice from rising, and, when tempted just to pass over name and address—what is the matter with people, for God's sake?—and let them sort it out between them, remember Georgia.

Hen raises his eyebrows in sympathy when I finally put the phone down.

"He will be delighted. Now, Andrea and I haven't been entirely idle in your absence: we've got some new cases. Want to take a look?"

I stare at him.

"What about the case of who poisoned your partner—and why?"

"Remind me who's paying for that one."

"What I want to know is, who is Christo's mother? And what happened to the sister?"

Hen leans back; his chair gives a protesting squeak.

"So you think the sister gave birth to Christo, and they killed her . . . incest or something . . . and she's in the Black Patch?"

"Well, it's a possibility."

"A lot easier to just fake a father, surely?"

"Well . . . what about the Janko name? And why did Ivo take off? It's something to do with the Black Patch. I . . . know."

He peers at me over his glasses. This is an affectation—he can't see a thing without them.

"You don't know that—because you still don't know that he knows anything about the body. And there may be a simple explanation."

"Well, when we have the simple explanation I will . . . leave it. Until then . . ."

I have kept the piece of paper with Lulu's address written in Sandra's childlike handwriting—I couldn't bring myself to throw it away. I look at it often. I thought—I hoped—she might ring once I got out of the hospital. Then I think of what Hen told me. How they'd discussed me. Perhaps I should have more pride than to pin my hopes on her. Then again, perhaps I should have less pride. She held my hand, after all. But I find reasons to wait until I am home before I ring her. I have plenty of other phone calls to make, and one fax I want to receive—to be sure.

To my surprise, she answers almost immediately. Somehow I thought she would be at work, and I was preparing to leave a message.

"You're not at work?"

"No. How are you?"

"Good. Yeah. I wondered if we could meet?"

A pause.

"For what?"

"For what? Well, I, um, there are some more questions I'd like to ask you."

"Oh."

Is she disappointed? She doesn't say anything else.

"I don't suppose you've heard from Ivo?"

"No."

"And Christo? Any news about him?"

She sighs, unmistakably this time.

"It's complicated. I mean, he's all right . . . He's fine. Just, well. I can tell you when we meet."

"Okay."

My heart, afterward, is beating like a sprinter's. I have to make an effort not to pour myself a drink. Don't fall apart, I admonish myself. Not now.

Those boats, the rowing boats at the lake, they've stuck in my mind ever since. I so wanted to get in one and row away. The color

of the varnish, the sound and suck of water. And the names: AMY—
TO CARRY TWO. ISOBEL—TO CARRY FOUR. So capable. So generous.

Ray—to carry one. And barely, at that.

Since I still can't drive, she comes to the pub at the end of my road.
From the window—I am early, of course—you can see the trains
trundling over the bridge with their work-worn cargo. The light has
started to fail again; even as summer has finally, tardily, arrived, the
light is fading.

Lulu arrives silently and slips into the chair beside me.

"I have some news for you," I say.

Her eyes widen in alarm.

"It's good news. We've found Rose."

"Oh my God . . . ! And she's—all right . . . ? Really?"

"Right as rain."

"Oh!" Lulu digests this. "So the body, at the Black Patch . . .
That was nothing to do with Ivo?"

There is a great ebbing of tension from her body.

"Well, whoever it is, it isn't Rose Wood."

"A happy ending . . ." She raises her glass with a smile. "Shouldn't
we be drinking a toast?"

"Not yet."

Her face falters. "No. It's not the end, is it? Because of what happened to you—and Ivo's still gone."

"Yes. There's that."

"Do you still think he hurt you on purpose? Why—if he had
nothing to cover up? If he didn't have anything to do with Rose?"

She lights a cigarette and takes a sip of her Bacardi and Coke.
She seems nervous again; she knocks the glass against her teeth,
spills a little, dabs her fingers to her lips while looking at the table.

"But it could be anybody. Someone completely unrelated. Don't
they know who?"

"Not yet. Ivo was scared. If it was unrelated, why poison me?"

"You're . . . assuming he did it on purpose."

"If he didn't, why disappear? Why abandon Christo?"

She stares out the window and shakes her head; she looks worried.

"What did you want to ask me?"

Her voice is very low.

"Ivo stayed with you the night we had dinner, didn't he?"

Lulu looks down but says nothing.

"I just wondered . . ."

"But you told him, anyway, didn't you? You promised you would. That's what you said . . . ?"

So she did tell him.

She goes on without looking up. "I was so angry. With him—and with you. It just came out. I'm sorry. I knew I shouldn't have told him. I was so worried. I thought it was my fault—your being ill . . ."

The hand that holds her glass is shaking. I want to put my arms around her. I imagine putting my arms around her.

"None of it was your fault. I shouldn't have put you in that position."

Ivo knew. I have proof.

"How did he react when you told him?"

"Oh, well, he . . ." She lets out a deep breath. "Didn't really. Didn't look at me. I had to say, 'Did you hear me?' and he just went 'Yeah, so?' In that tone of voice he has. You know. But . . . why does it matter? She's all right."

"The body at the Black Patch belongs to somebody."

"Yes, but . . ."

"Could it be Christina?"

"Christina?" She almost smiles, looking at me in disbelief. "She died years ago. You're not suggesting it's her! That's ridiculous."

"No one has told me when she died, exactly."

Lulu sighs and purses her lips. The frown is back between her eyebrows.

"It was years ago. She was seventeen, so . . . twelve years ago. Twelve years! Besides, she died in France. It couldn't possibly be her in the Black Patch."

"Where in France?"

"I don't know exactly. It was when they went to Lourdes."

"Did you go to the funeral?"

"There wasn't one."

"There wasn't one? That's a bit . . . odd, isn't it?"

"It was . . . abroad, wasn't it?"

She swallows. Shifts uneasily in her seat.

"You know. They couldn't bring her home themselves. And arranging for something like that . . . Maybe the expense . . . I don't know. It didn't seem odd. It wasn't odd."

"So she died twelve years ago."

"Yes!"

"When did you last see her?"

"God . . ." She looks down. "A couple of years before it happened."

"It must have been terrible when she died—on top of everything else."

"Yeah."

"Do you know who was there when she died?"

"Tene, I suppose. And Ivo must have been there. That was after Marta died. Are you accusing them of killing her, now?"

"No. Just . . . trying to get things clear."

I sip my beer, left-handed. Lulu falls silent; she lights another cigarette, angry. A train rattles over the bridge, half empty now: diehards who have stayed late at work.

Tene and Ivo. Ivo and Tene. The two of them, the only witnesses to a number of strange and tragic events. Any number of deaths, the specter trailing after them like a black dog, a wolf in the shadows. But Ivo was just a sickly boy . . . Cursed, perhaps, as Tene said.

"How's your hand now?"

Lulu is looking at my—still—nearly useless right hand, tucked beside me. I lift it and waggle it in front of her.

"It's okay. It's getting better."

I flex the fingers with difficulty. They move slowly, like the limbs of some languid underwater creature.

"Can you feel anything with it?"

"Not very much."

"You have to be careful not to burn it."

"Yeah. They kept on about that at the hospital."

"That's because it's easy to forget."

Of course, she's a pro at this. I think of David. How much can he feel? She's the one who has to be careful of him. She looks at my hand but doesn't touch it. I wonder if she's thinking of him, too.

I find myself telling her about my former ward mate, Mike, and his gangrenous feet. Wondering how he's getting on now. Almost as though we'd finished with the messy family business of the Jankos, and could talk about normal things, like normal people. Except, as she said herself, it isn't the end.

"There's something else I have to tell you." I clear my throat, awkward. "When we talked to Rose, it . . . um, it turns out that Rose isn't Christo's mother."

Lulu stares at me.

"What?"

"She isn't his mother."

"Of course she is!"

Lulu smiles, trying to see the joke. Then she stops smiling.

"What do you mean? That's crazy."

"Rose said her marriage to Ivo was unconsummated. Rose had no child, either then or later."

Lulu stares at me accusingly. For holding this back. For making her feel sympathy for me first.

"Is that what she told you?"

"Yes."

"She's lying!"

I shake my head.

"How do you know she's not?"

I take a deep breath.

"We didn't. So we checked. Rose remarried less than a year after her marriage to Ivo. She left him in February of '79."

"No! It was 1980. In the winter . . ."

"She married her current husband on August the thirtieth of the same year—1979. Christo was born seven weeks later."

Lulu's eyes are huge; the skin seems to be cracking around them. Her lips are dry.

"That can't be right! No."

"That's what I thought, so I checked and double-checked. It is right. Christo was born in October of '79, right?"

Unwillingly, she nods.

"I've spoken to people who were at the wedding, in August '79. I've seen wedding photos. There is no doubt. She can't be Christo's mother."

She looks so lost that I wish I was wrong. I wish I could take it back. But I can't.

"I'm sorry, but I have to ask: do you know who is Christo's mother?"

She turns her eyes to me. Anger, disbelief, betrayal.

"I'm so sorry about all this, Lulu. I wish . . ."

Her head shakes slightly, more a tremor than an act of negation. An explosion of air escapes her throat. She puts her drink carefully down and puts her face in her hands.

"I'll get you another drink."

"No! I have to go."

The savagery in her voice makes me look away. When I look back, she is looking out over her fingers. She pulls her spine straight again with an effort.

"When Tene had his accident, and I saw them again, in December '79, Ivo said she was long gone—I thought he meant weeks."

"It didn't occur to me, either. It should have—that there was a whole year missing."

"So who was it, then? You think whoever it is . . . is in the Black Patch?" She whispers it.

"I don't know."

Lulu excuses herself to go to the ladies' room, taking her sack of secrets with her. I stare at the low table in front of us, the ashtray half full of lipstick-stained fag ends, the ring-marked beer mats. Her black jacket is still crumpled over the back of her chair, its cheap satin lining creased and warm from her body. I can't bear it. Every time I see her, we are hijacked by the drama of the Jankos. I have to tell her things that cause her pain. But there is something, some thing—thin, delicate, stretched almost to the breaking point—between us. I am almost sure of it. But what can I do?

On impulse, before she comes back, I pick up her glass, with its delicate red wax print, and drain it of the sweet ice melt. The scent of rum vanishingly faint. Just so that I can press my mouth to the ghost of hers.

49.

R a y

Tene Janko is greatly changed. He seems small, his skin grayer, thinner, as though he hasn't seen the sun since my last visit. I can't believe my first impression was of a large man.

"I have come because I owe you an apology," I start.

Tene looks up at me and waves for me to sit down.

"How are you? Are you all right, Mr. Janko?"

He shrugs. "I'm well enough."

"I have to tell you something. I would like to tell your son as well, but, well . . . We have found Rose Wood."

"I told you," he says, quietly.

"Yes . . . you did. And so my—implying that Ivo had something to do with her disappearance was wrong. I apologize, to you and to him. I'm very sorry for the distress I've caused you."

Tene seems to be staring down at the table. I wonder if he has taken in what I said. Why there isn't more of a reaction—more self-righteousness, more anger . . . more something. Then he says, "Have you seen her?"

"Yes. We saw her and talked to her. She told us how she had run away from . . . her marriage to Ivo. She said that you helped her. She was grateful for that."

I watch him. His face reveals nothing, staring down at the floor.

"Well, then. It's over."

"Not quite. Finding her poses more questions than it answers, as you must know."

"What do you mean?"

His voice is neutral.

"She said that she never had a child."

Tene nods eventually—a minute movement, slow.

"It's as I thought. She could not accept what had happened. It was too much for her."

"No. She can't have children. Never could. She is not Christo's mother."

I tell him about the dates. The wedding photograph. The witnesses. His eyes are downcast—I can't see his expression.

"Your accident took place in December 1979. Rose didn't leave Ivo weeks after Christo was born but many months before. A whole year had passed. She is not his mother."

He makes no movement. There is no sign, even of comprehension.

"So who is?"

No reply.

"Why did you and Ivo tell people that it was Rose?"

"Because she is his mother. I do not understand why you say these things."

I ride a surge of impatience.

"Mr. Janko, I know that that is impossible! Are you listening to me? What happened in that year? Did Ivo have a girlfriend? What happened to her? Where is she now?"

I am failing to keep my voice calm. I am leaning toward him, my face aggressively close to his.

"Why are you keeping his secrets?"

Tene lifts his head a little, but his gaze travels past mine, out through the window and beyond.

"She is the boy's mother."

I count to ten. My fist is balled on my thigh.

"Mr. Janko, I know you know! And in case you've forgotten, the police are investigating the body that they have found at the Black Patch. They will identify it. They know that Ivo has disappeared, and they know what happened to me. If you are hiding something . . . If you are protecting him—"

"Mr. Lovell, I am not protecting my son. He's beyond my protection. I can only tell you what I remember . . ."

He drifts off; his eyes stare at atoms of air in front of him. My leg flickers with irritation.

"I can't force you to talk, but the police may not be so accommodating."

He never says what he remembers. Not only does he not speak, he does not move. Even his breathing is imperceptible. He seems to have receded from here, to far within himself. The hyperactive ticktock of the gilt clock fills the trailer. It's maddening, hastening to remind me of all the time that is wasted, gone. That we are hurtling toward the end. I begin to get alarmed.

"Mr. Janko . . . Mr. Janko? Are you all right? Mr. Janko . . ."

Tentatively, my anger draining away, I put my hand on his shoulder. I shake him.

"Tene . . . Can you hear me? Tene! Please . . . Can you hear me!"

I don't know that he's not using some desperate ploy to avoid answering, but he is like a statue.

I am on my feet, rush outside and hammer on the doors of the other trailers. And soon Sandra, JJ, and Kath are in Tene's trailer with him, and I am squeezed out, like toothpaste from a tube, out into the sunshine. I stride from one end of the site to the other. I don't know whether to be angrier with Tene or with myself. That he is a good actor I don't doubt, but I was clumsy. Bad timing. Not a mistake, in this profession, that you can go back and rectify. Or am I guilty of worse than that?

The voices inside are raised, anxious, argumentative.

I begin to feel a cold dread. There is nothing I can do except stand and wait, since Hen has, at my insistence, discreetly left me alone, and is not due back for some time.

Please, God, don't let him die.

After a few minutes, the door opens and JJ comes out, alone. He comes over to me. His face is worried and wary.

"He's all right now. Just a bit groggy. He hasn't been all that well recently."

"Oh. Thank God. I'm sorry to hear he's not well. He's recovering, though, now?"

"Yeah . . . He's talking."

JJ shrugs, uncomfortable. Now Kath Smith bursts through the door and strides over to us. Her cheeks are mottled with blood, mercury-bead eyes vindictive.

"What the bloody hell were you saying to him?"

"I came to tell him that we have found Ivo's wife . . ."

Kath stares at me, her eyes nearly popping out of her head. I hear JJ's sudden intake of breath.

"Well! For fuck's sake. And are you happy now? You've only gone and given him a stroke!"

My blood stops in my veins. Please, no.

"I'm terribly sorry that it was a shock, but he had to be told."

"Well, now you've told him and nearly killed him, so I think it's about time you fucked off, don't you?"

Her hand, loaded with a lit cigarette, darts toward my face. I take a small step backward.

She looks around for my car, is affronted that there isn't one.

"I'll have to wait for my colleague to pick me up. He'll be here soon. We could drive him to hospital if that would help . . ."

"If he needs to go to hospital, we'll take him, thank you very much. I think you've done enough damage."

"Gran, he's been—"

Kath swats him aside like a gnat.

"And you—get inside."

"But we've—"

She points her finger in his face.

"Inside! Now! And wait till your granddad gets back . . ."

JJ gives me a despairing look, filled with questions, then slinks off toward his trailer.

Kath mutters something inaudible to me and slams back into Tene's trailer. JJ turns to me, looking miserable.

"Sorry about Gran. She's upset."

"I don't blame her."

"No, but it's . . . He hasn't been well lately. Listen, do you want to come inside?"

"I'm fine, honestly."

"Please . . ."

Inside the trailer, we stand facing each other, a little awkward. He seems unsure what to do next. He fiddles with the dirty bandage on his arm.

"When you said—you'd found Rose . . . Is she . . . ?"

I suddenly realize I hadn't finished the sentence.

"Oh, no, no. Rose is alive. She's fine!"

His mouth falls open, his face works.

"You mean . . . she's all right?"

"Yes."

A smile spreads over his face, and keeps spreading.

"But that's fantastic! That's great . . . I thought it was bad news!"

I smile, too; it's infectious.

"Yes, it is good news. I must say it's . . ." For the first time, it seems that this part, at least, really is great. "It's such a relief to know that she's well, after all this time."

"Where is she? Where has she been?"

"Um . . . she's in this country. She's remarried . . ."

"So, then, Uncle Ivo didn't . . . do anything."

"No one else was responsible for her disappearance. It's usually the case, you know; when people disappear, it's usually because they want to."

JJ looks at me shyly.

"Would you like some tea, Mr. Lovell?"

"Oh, no, thanks, I'm fine."

"I'm going to make some, anyway . . ."

"Oh, well, if you're making it . . . Thanks."

Relieved, he goes to the kitchen. I look outside and see a car driving away.

"They must be taking him to the hospital. That's good."

JJ drops tea bags into mugs.

"How's your arm getting on?" I ask.

"All right. Itches like crazy."

"Good. Good sign."

Then, as he's pouring in the milk, his face falls. He doesn't speak for a minute, then turns to me, his face stricken.

"Will she want Christo now?"

"Want Christo?"

"She'll want him back, won't she? I mean, she's his mum . . . He was going to come to us, and we were going to get a house and everything, so we can look after him, me and Mum . . ."

Momentarily, I am nonplussed, until I realize he's talking about Rose.

"No. No. She won't. Not at all."

"But she's his mum."

"Well, that's the thing . . ."

I hesitate. I suppose they'll all know before too long. And so I tell him.

50.

JJ

They sent Great-uncle home from the hospital yesterday after a few hours. They said there wasn't anything badly wrong with him; apparently, he hadn't had a stroke at all, but they gave him some pills, anyway, and told him to cut down on smoking—like that's ever going to happen.

Gran and Granddad drove off this morning in the lorry. They are being quite mysterious at the moment. And Mum has gone to work. She's got a job delivering pizzas. I think she really hates it, but there's nothing else around. She got the sack from delivering flowers, although she hadn't done anything wrong. They said there wasn't enough work to go around, although they didn't sack anyone else. Normally I like it when there's no one else about, but today I feel hollow, like there's not enough of me to fill the trailer on my own. Anyway, Mum made me promise to go and check that Great-uncle is taking his pills and to cheer him up.

When I go over, he is asleep in his chair. I tiptoe around and do a bit of silent washing up (Very good, JJ!), but although I'm really careful and make hardly any noise at all, when I've finished clearing and tidying the kitchen, I turn around to see that he's looking at me. I nearly have a heart attack—it gives me quite a shock that he's looking at me and he didn't say anything. He smiles.

"Didn't mean to startle you."

"Hello, Great-uncle!" I say. My voice sounds loud and a bit hysterical.

"JJ, my darling. Make yourself some tea."

"How are you feeling? You've got to take your pills about now, Mum said to say. Are these them?"

I hold up a plastic bottle. He nods and takes it but doesn't open it yet.

"How are you, kid?"

I smile at him, because it's such a weird question. I literally don't think he's ever said that to me before—like he doesn't really know me. Or I'm an adult. Or he really wants to know the answer.

"Um . . ."

I feel like saying, I'm JJ—you know how I am.

"I'm fine."

"You're a good boy, JJ."

I bury my face in the fridge so that I don't have to look at him. Then I bring him his cup of tea, nice and stewed, with lots of sugar. I find the remains of a loaf of white sliced and make bread and butter as well.

"Shall I put some music on?"

"If you like, yes. Why don't you do that."

I flip through his records—grateful to have something to do, to be honest—and pull out a Sammy Davis Jr. double album. It's got some of my favorites on it. I put it on but turn the volume down low, since he hasn't been well.

"Look." He pops a pill into his mouth and washes it down with the tea. "You can tell your mum."

I sit down with my tea, cradling the mug in both hands, even though it's a bit too hot. I can't think of anything to say. All I can think about is Rose. Then I wonder if maybe Great-uncle didn't know about it, either. What if, say, Ivo had a secret girlfriend and she had a baby and didn't want him, so Ivo brought him home and that was that. It doesn't need to be so sinister. Maybe Great-uncle had never met her—after all, it was while Ivo was married to Rose. I mean, it may not be very nice, but it happens. Look at my so-called dad.

I want to ask him, but I'm scared he'll have another funny turn.

Great-uncle clears his throat. It takes a while.

"How's school, kid?" he says.

I look at him, really worried. Maybe he's losing his mind.

"It's the holidays. We broke up on—"

"I know, kid. I know. But I mean in general. How is it? Are you going back to do your exams?"

"*Um* . . . yes. I think so."

"That's good. You should. You really seem to be learning something. We need that."

"Yeah."

I don't know what to say. Although he does ask me about school now and again, he's never seemed that interested.

"Just don't let them *gorjify* you too much."

"Course not."

"I'm glad Christo is coming to you and Sandra. You'll be fine."

"Well, unless Uncle Ivo comes back."

At this, Great-uncle just grunts and blows on his tea.

"You don't think he'll come back?"

He sighs. I hold my breath.

"Why're you asking me?"

"You're his dad. You know him better than anyone."

Great-uncle shakes his head slowly.

"Ivo's not coming back. I should never have tried to make him stay."

I didn't know he tried to make him stay. I suppose that means they talked about it.

"Do you know where he's gone, then?"

"No," he whispers.

Great-uncle hangs his head, as though it's a great heavy weight and his neck might break.

Something, or someone, walks over my grave.

"I love this song," I say loudly, to change the subject. I do. It's a true story. The man who wrote it was in jail in New Orleans when all the down-and-outs were arrested after some murder. He got talking to one old guy who told him stories of dancing for food, and how his dog got run over, and that made him so sad he became an alcoholic. All the down-and-outs had nicknames so the police couldn't identify them, and his was Mr. Bojangles.

I would rather think about this than why Great-uncle is talking to me in this odd way. When I look up again, Great-uncle is looking at me in a way that makes me squirm.

"We never paid you enough attention, did we?" he says. "We should have."

I mumble, because I don't know what he means. "Course you did." I smile, to make things normal.

"You were there all along."

"What? What do you mean?"

But Great-uncle shakes his head again.

Sammy gets to the bit where he lets rip, and all the brass and violins swoop together into a beautiful climax. And I watch in horror as a drop of water slithers down Great-uncle's cheek, leaving a gleaming trail.

"What's the matter, Great-uncle? Are you feeling ill again?"

He shakes his head.

"No, I'm all right."

"Are you sure?"

He attempts to smile at me, though his eyes are wet.

"Yes. I'm all right, my kid."

"What can I get for you? More tea?"

"No . . . Nothing."

"You're probably tired, yeah? Do you want me to go?"

My chair seems to be pushing me out. It's excruciating. I've never seen him like this before, and I don't know what to do.

"I'm all right." He looks up at me, jigging around. "Well, yeah, I am a bit tired, kid. Maybe I'll have a bit of a kip."

"Okay, then. Are you sure?"

I'm standing up, smiling, with no intention of staying. Because if I smile, then it will all be all right.

I go back to our empty trailer and turn all the lights on, but I can't sit still there, either. I look through the videos but can't find anything I want to watch. I put some music on and immediately turn it off, because it makes me feel guilty. I hate myself. I am useless and pathetic, and, what's worse, unkind. Great-uncle is ill and sad, and I can't even bring myself to sit with him. I'm too much of a coward, is the truth.

I go back outside and pace around the site, torturing myself with what might be happening inside his trailer (but doing nothing!), glancing up at his unlit windows, on the verge of tears, until the day has faded so much that I am shivering in my T-shirt, and the birds have stopped singing, and I can't tell the color of anything.

51.

Ray

Last night I signed the divorce papers and put them in an envelope ready for posting. I signed them without emotion. Now, at last, I thought, I am getting on with my life. I am moving on.

This morning I have one of those dreams that seems more real than anything in your waking life. I dreamed that I was still with Jen, in our house. She came in and casually introduced me to her lover, who was Hen. There is nothing more of the dream that I remember, just the shock of finding out: a sensation like that of having a chest wound ripped open. There was never anything between Jen and my business partner—he has never been unfaithful to Madeleine, nor, I think, has he ever wanted to be—this is pure masochism on my part.

I switch on the bedside light, which makes the grayness outside turn back to black. It is not yet dawn. I blink, sticky-eyed; my mouth is dry; my teeth feel rough and taste of monosodium glutamate. At this hour there is never anyone to turn to. Never was. I go to the bathroom, drink noisily from the tap, and splash water on my face. And on the way back to bed I am stopped in the doorway by the reflection in the window.

Yesterday, I had a strange impulse. I was walking back from the Chinese takeaway when I passed the late-night newsagent's. My eye was caught by a patch of red among the buckets of flowers. I didn't know their name, but their color, their waxiness, reminded me of Lulu. I bought all the red ones, took them home, and put them in the biggest jug I could find. I put them on my chest of drawers, where I could see them from the bed. Rows of little red bells with pale, freckled throats, a sweet, cloying perfume. I went to sleep thinking of her. I was happy. So how could I have been ambushed like this? Brought down by memories that still have the power to draw blood?

The reflected room bears little relation to this one. A warm glow of light falls on the mass of red flowers, which pulse with a horrible vitality. Beyond them, a figure of a man is a shadowy, sinister presence. When Jen finally told me of her affair—I have forgotten the exact words she used—she started to cry. As if my reaction genuinely surprised her. As if she had convinced herself I wouldn't mind. I was insulted, furious at her stupidity: how could you not know how much this hurt? How could she be that dumb? I wanted to howl like a wounded animal. I wanted to set fire to her car. Beat whoever the fucking cunt was to death with a shovel, and carve patterns on his tawdry, self-justifying face. Perhaps out there, in the other room, is the man who did that.

There is a dark glamour to the room out there that beckons and appalls me; it is the glamour of the cliff edge, the waterfall, of the pain that creeps out to snare me when I think I am past the worst. To be honest, I wonder, sometimes, if I have the will to escape it, or if this coruscating grief will always be the deepest, the brightest, thing of my life.

I know I am not going to sleep again, so I pad to the kitchen to make coffee. As the kettle boils, something comes to mind that I haven't thought of in years: early in our marriage, Jen and I went for a walk on a lakeshore in Scotland. The water was flat and still; barely a wrinkle disturbed its brittle calm. We searched for flat pebbles on the shore and tried to make them skip over the surface—something

I have always been good at. Jen, to her annoyance, was hopeless; her stones plunged into the water a few feet from the edge, or sailed into the air. I wandered along the water's edge, improving my total—six, seven, nine . . . when something hit me extremely hard between the shoulder blades. I shot around, flaring with anger, to see Jen, face in hands in horror.

"Sorry, darling, sorry!" she cried. "It went wrong! It was an accident!"

Clearly she was trying not to laugh as well. I smiled, although it hurt and developed into a small deep bruise that we joked about.

She never managed one skip out of those stones. Couldn't hit a wastepaper bin from three feet ("Not fair—it moved!"). But when it came to a direct hit on me, her aim was unerring.

At long last it's a beautiful day. The sun has come out, burning off an early mist. From the train, I watch its light winking off ditches and little temporary lakelets that have formed in hollows. I get to Ely at half past ten.

Considine maintains his veneer of gruffness, but I think he's actually thankful for a bit of novelty.

"What's the matter with your arm?" he asks, having poured me a cup of stewed coffee and noted my right hand's lack of response.

I explain, briefly. It is, after all, relevant to why I'm here.

"Come with me," he says, when we've swallowed our coffees, before ushering me out and driving me to a building on the outskirts of Huntingdon.

It's the forensics laboratory. He sweeps me inside and up to an office on the third floor. Inside a small, cluttered room, a woman looks up over her glasses, gray hair coiled back into a smooth knot, dressed in an expensive-looking trouser suit. She's barely recognizable as the woman from the Black Patch; when I last saw her, she was in slime-spattered plastic overalls, with boots and gauntlets of mud.

"Dr. Alison Hutchins, this is Ray Lovell."

"We met. I haven't anything new to tell you, Considine."

The meek way he accepts her casual authority is interesting.

"I'd invite you both to sit down, but . . ." She sweeps her hand over the ragged stacks of files piled on her desk, on a couple chairs, even on the floor.

We both insist that we like standing.

"It's about the possible ID he brought us. She's turned up, alive, so that's that."

"Oh . . ."

She peers at me over the specs.

"Bugger."

"But he's got something else to tell us."

Hutchins raises her eyebrows.

"I can't give you a name, but I've still got a missing person. She was the mother of a young child. She gave birth nearly seven years ago, and then seems to have completely disappeared. There's a definite connection with the site. I thought the woman I was looking for was the mother of this boy, but it turns out she isn't."

"Can you give me any details—age she went missing? Anything?"

"No. I've got nothing. I just have a"—I lift my shoulders. How do I describe it?—"a blank hole in this family."

She looks at Considine.

"And what makes you think that our body might fit your . . . hole?"

"Well, the family has always claimed that the child's mother was Rose Wood, who had been missing for some years. But when we found her, it turns out that she has never had a child—and that stands up. She can't be the mother. So they lied. Clearly, the child has a mother, but there's no sign of her. The child's father found out about the body here, and, er . . . well, after eating a meal cooked by him, I suffered a severe case of poisoning."

I lift my right arm.

"My right hand is still mostly paralyzed. And now he has disappeared."

"Ergot poisoning," says Considine.

Dr. Hutchins looks impressed, despite herself.

"Ergot and henbane. I find it hard to believe that two poisonous plants got into my food—and only my food—by accident. I'm convinced he knows something about the body in the Black Patch. His behavior is suspicious, to say the least."

Dr. Hutchins leans back in her chair.

"What an eventful life you lead, Mr. Lovell. Well, well. Can we get DNA from the child?"

"I don't know. He's in hospital at the moment."

"Oh? What for?"

"He suffers from a chronic disease that they haven't identified yet. It seems to be hereditary. Many members of his family have suffered from it, and several of them died young—mostly males, as far as I can tell. His father was ill when he was younger but recovered."

"Curiouser and curiouser. Like the Romanovs."

Apparently, I look blank.

"The last Russian Tsars. Only their problem was hemophilia. And you wouldn't recover from that."

She pulls a face. I can't guess what it means.

"So you think our unidentified body could be this child's mother—and that she was put there by the father?"

I shrug again.

"It's at least a possibility, wouldn't you say?"

Dr. Hutchins taps her pen on the edge of her desk. She seems to be lost in thought. She takes her glasses off and pinches the bridge of her nose.

"That's interesting."

She pulls out some papers covered in tiny writing and studies them for a couple minutes. For long enough that I wonder whether she's going to say anything else. Without looking up, she says, "How much do you know about forensic osteology?"

"Very little. I've read a couple of books . . ."

She waves her hand, dismissive.

"People tend to think it's very obvious. Sex, age—everything's clear-cut. But it isn't. Some skeletons are easy, of course—if they're whole, or if there are corroborative features. But it's rare that you can be a hundred percent sure of an identification from hard tissue alone. Even if you've got a perfectly preserved sexually dimorphic bone—the pubic bone, say: you think if it's square it's from a female, if it's triangular, from a male. But what if it's halfway between the two?"

She's watching me as she says this. Partly to read my reaction, and partly, I suspect, because she enjoys the sound of her own voice. I don't blame her for making us wait; I suspect she's had to earn it.

"And the younger the skeleton, the harder it is. But few skeletons I've come across have been quite as frustrating as this one. Of course, there are only a few bones—so far. And almost all of those have been broken. But there are other features about them that make it especially difficult. The size, for one thing—they're very small, in some ways I would have said from a juvenile, but other features, and the epiphyses, suggest a higher age at death."

She pauses for us to wonder what that means.

"So what age do you think she was?"

"Well, adolescent. Anywhere between thirteen and eighteen; I can't be more precise at this stage."

"Okay . . . But it is a girl?"

"From the size and form of the bones we have found, I would say they are more likely to belong to a female—but I can't be definite until we find a dimorphic bone."

She cocks her head at Considine.

"Did you tell him what we found yesterday?"

He shakes his head.

"You found something? What?"

Considine says, "We found a length of narrow gold chain. Not particularly expensive. It's broken, but it was near some rib fragments, so that suggests it could have been worn at the time of burial."

"So it's unlikely robbery was a motive."

"And there was something else. Something much . . . odder . . ."

Hutchins takes over, unwilling to let him take the limelight. Surprisingly, Considine doesn't seem to mind.

"We've found plenty of plant matter near the body, as you might expect, but this one was different. About four feet down, at the same soil depth as the body, there were a number of stems tied together with a piece of yarn. What does that sound like to you?"

Feeling as though I am taking an exam in primary school, I say, "A bunch of flowers?"

Hutchins smiles, waiting for me to go on.

"But . . . how could it be? Plants wouldn't survive that long in the soil, would they? I mean, they'd rot very quickly."

Her smile broadens.

"Usually. But these were wooden flowers—wooden chrysanthemums, you know?"

There is a loud silence in the office.

"Were they . . . Can you tell what they were like?"

"Well, they are rather the worse for wear."

"Did they appear to be handmade?"

Hutchins and Considine exchange glances.

"I would say they were handmade but quite well done. Not something a child would make."

My heart has speeded up, but the significance I feel is not quite—yet—tangible. I search for the right questions.

"Can you tell from the bones whether someone has given birth?"

"There's no way to be absolutely sure. But finding some pelvic bones would be a start; sometimes there are traces there. We live in hope, don't we, Considine?"

"You're thinking: who make wooden flowers? Gypsies do."

Considine is looking at me.

"Well . . ." I lift my shoulders. "It's a traditional craft . . ."

I comb my memory for images of wooden flowers in any of the Janko trailers. I don't come up with any.

"In itself, of course, it doesn't prove anything."

"No, of course."

We all stand—or sit—in silence.

Maybe it's not proof. Not evidence. But it is a fact. It means something. It means, perhaps, that rather than simply being concealed, the girl at the Black Patch was mourned.

52.

JJ

I seem to have a new hobby: it's called Expecting the Worst. I don't know what the worst is, but the last few weeks of my life seem to have worn me out. Whatever the worst is, I feel its closeness. Awful things keep happening—it's not my imagination. There's Christo and Ivo, of course, and Great-uncle being unwell, and Mr. Lovell and me in the hospital. Some poor person being found dead at the Black Patch. The radioactive rain that's poisoned all the sheep. The giant hailstones that fell out of the sky and killed people—in India, of all places. Everything's gone mad. I can hardly get up in the mornings. Of course, it's the school holidays, so there's not much to get up for, but still. Mum usually goes out at about nine, while I'm still lying in bed behind the curtains, drifting in and out of sleep. She's given up shouting at me. Then I get up and eat some cold breakfast that Mum's left out for me. Then I usually go back to bed. I've tried reading and wanking and listening to music and watching videos, but nothing grips my attention like worrying about all the awful things that have happened to us, or are just about to.

I've been Expecting the Worst since we arrived at the children's hospital up in London—in fact, since we set off in the car early this morning. Christo's doctor is Indian and young; he has very dark skin, very thick hair that grows straight up off his forehead like a dense fur, and round gold-rimmed glasses. He speaks very precisely. He seems fond of Christo, and for that, I'm prepared to like him. Mum and me are sitting at the edge of a waiting area, in front of a sort of indoor playground for young kids. It's full of brightly colored toys and has brightly painted walls. Even a small, colorful climbing frame. I think it's meant for the brothers and sisters of children who are patients here. But there are also a couple kids playing here who don't have any hair, so I suppose they are patients. There are a lot of bald kids in the hospital. It gave me the shivers when I first saw them; they look like little aliens. Then I remembered that having treatment for cancer makes your hair fall out, and now I smile at them if one of them happens to look at me. It makes me feel bad about having so much hair myself.

Now the doctor is about to tell us something, and I wish he would hurry up.

"You are Christopher's half brother?"

The doctor, whose very long name I am never going to remember, looks at me.

Mum and me both nod. I was warned about this. I don't know what they've said to the hospital to bring them around, but it probably helps if they think that. Ironically (I try not to dwell on this), it might actually be true.

"We think we are making progress toward a diagnosis of Christopher's condition. But before we'll know for sure, we have to send his test results to a hospital in the Netherlands. They are more experienced in this field. We think that it is an X-linked recessive genetic disorder, so the more information you can give us about the health of your family, the more we can narrow it down."

Mum looks puzzled and worried. I imagine I look puzzled and worried, too.

"A what? What's that?"

"It means that it is a type of hereditary disease. Females can carry the disease, and they can pass it on to their sons. Only males are actually affected by it."

"Pass it on, like . . . ?"

Mum stares at me, horrified.

"There is no need for you to be alarmed."

He looks from her to me.

"It is most likely that the onset of the disease would be seen very early, in infancy. So your son is not at all likely to be affected. However, it would be best to take blood samples from you both—in fact, from as many family members as we can, so that we can build up as full a picture as possible."

"Blood . . . from us?"

Mum's voice is a squeak.

"It is a very quick procedure. It doesn't hurt at all. It will be very helpful for Christopher. And for you, too."

"Well . . . we want to help, of course."

She sounds doubtful.

"You can go to your own GP, or you can do it here."

He seems to have finished, without getting to the main point at all, as I see it.

"But can you cure him?"

The doctor looks at me and smiles. It's not a hopeful smile, and I wish he hadn't bothered.

"With genetic disorders it is very difficult or impossible to actually effect a cure. It would be like curing the color of your eyes. But we may be able to alleviate some, even many, of Christopher's symptoms. It is to be hoped we can give him a good quality of life, certainly better than he has now. But until we know what it is, we cannot say for certain."

"So then . . . maybe you could cure him? If you don't know yet, maybe when you do . . ."

The doctor glances from Mum to me, and back to Mum.

"Well, this is true, what you say. But . . . I would not get your hopes up too high about a complete cure."

. . .

When we go back to Christo's ward, there is someone sitting beside his bed. Aunt Lulu has arrived. When she sees us, she jumps to her feet, her face changes, and she holds up a piece of paper in front of us.

"A nurse just brought this," she says in a hiss-whisper. I realize that she's talking like this because she's furious.

"You won't bloody believe it—it's a letter from bloody Ivo!"

This is what the letter says:

MY DARLING CHRISTO

IM SO SORRY I HAD TO GO AWAY I
DIDNT WANT TO I HAD TO I KNOW SANDRA
AND YOUR CUZIN JJ WILL LOOK AFTER
YOU RITE AS YOU DISERVE BETER
THAN ME SO DONT WORRY I LOVE
YOU ALWAYS WITH ALL MY HART DEAREST
BOY YOUR EVER LOVING PAIRENT

XOXO

PS SORRY

What do you say to that? That's all there is. Ivo's farewell letter to Christo. Lulu pushes it into Mum's hand, and she reads it, me looking over Mum's shoulder. I recognize Ivo's writing—the way he prints the letters, and his spelling and so on.

"Is it really from him?"

We both nod. The envelope is addressed to Christo at the hospital. It was posted in Southeast London three days ago.

"Are we supposed to read this to him? It's . . . cruel. It's . . ."

Mum sounds horrified. Lulu sighs.

"But it's what we suspected, isn't it? At least now we know. And you have his blessing."

She adds a frosty smile to this, because, as we all know, Ivo's blessing isn't really what matters anymore.

"The fucking nerve. Oh . . ."

Mum is shaking with anger. We're all still jammed into the doorway of Christo's room, so that supposedly he can't hear us. We look at him. He looks back at us with a calm, watchful air. I wonder if he already knows what's in the letter. He was the last person to see Ivo—he must have been. I wonder what Ivo said to him when he went away—maybe he told him the whole truth, and Christo knows more than any of us.

I go over to his bed and take his hand, the ends of my fingers interlocking with his little fingers, and say, "All right?"

And he says, almost totally recognizably, "All right."

53.

Ray

For the next couple days I stick to my desk, the phone glued to my ear, checking records, making inquiries, begging for favors. We have offered a reward for information—without much hope that it will lead to anything. I talk to all sorts of people in the Traveling community—relatives of mine I haven't seen for years; distant members of Rose's family; even, awkwardly, my brother. People promise to think about it. Ask around. Some of them even call me back. My brother mentions a possible visit, when the selling of vacuum cleaners permits. But at the end of it all, I have not found one suitable candidate for Christo's mother. No girl in the Traveler community mysteriously vanished. No girl of the right age went missing from that part of the country. Realistically, Christo's mother could be anyone—a local *gorjio* who didn't want to or couldn't take care of a child. There are too many possibilities—too many puzzles jostling for space: the identity of Christo's mother, the body of the Gypsy girl . . . or, at least, the girl mourned by Gypsies. And there is one more mysterious woman, very much alive, who, until now, I have pushed to the back of my mind.

When I ask Hen if I am missing something obvious, he shakes his head.

"When it comes to the boy's mother, I'd be inclined to look closer to home. The cousin who lives there . . . What's her name?"

"Sandra Smith. I did consider her, but . . . I really don't think so."

"Assume for a minute that the person at the Black Patch is totally unconnected. Sandra really seems to be the strongest candidate. She's the right sort of age, they definitely know each other, she may well carry this family disease . . . You even said she might have some, I don't know, feeling for him, didn't you? That could be based on their history."

"Yes. Yes, but . . ."

I shake my head. But what?

"I know I got that impression, I know, but somehow it just doesn't ring true."

"Why not?"

"Because . . . it wasn't her."

"But you don't know that."

"I don't mean about Christo. I mean it wasn't her that . . ."

I sigh.

"There was something else, something I didn't tell you about that night. When I was poisoned. It was all so confused, and it doesn't make sense . . ."

I stop. Because I don't know how to go on.

"And you were tripping out of your tree."

"Yes. But despite that, I am pretty sure that . . . I had sex that night."

Hen raises his eyebrows.

"You didn't say that before."

"I know. Well, you know. It all sounds so . . . crazy."

"What makes you so sure that it wasn't another of your hallucinations?"

"I've thought about this a lot, believe me. It was a very different feeling from any of the visions. I know I saw some crazy things, but I always knew, on some level, that they weren't real. And this was . . .

It was different—totally different from the monsters and the flames and . . . so on."

Hen looks worried.

"I know that doesn't make a lot of sense," I say, and attempt a laugh. "I mean, who could it have been?"

"I don't know, Ray. Maybe you should be talking to a doctor about this stuff. Maybe they could help you sort it out."

"So you don't think there's anything in it?"

"I don't know. I really can't say. Do you remember what she looked like?"

"No. I think . . . she may have covered my face."

"Covered your face?"

He stares at me; he looks like he's about to laugh, then thinks better of it.

"Why on earth?"

I shrug.

"But despite being off your face, and not being able to see a thing, you somehow know that it wasn't Sandra Smith?"

"Yes."

"Ray, you can't possibly know that."

"She gave no sign of it. We've talked since, and . . . I'm just sure."

"That holds no water at all. As you know. And after what Rose said, well . . . couldn't it have been Ivo?"

I have thought of this. I have. I have scraped away at my memory of that night, the peculiar details, the sensations.

"I've considered it. And no, I think I would have noticed."

Hen studies me. I try not to look away. At length he throws his hands in the air in exasperation.

"Either way; I mean, whether it was a . . . real person or not, whatever . . . it doesn't help us with the things we're concerned with, does it? It's not . . . evidence of anything."

We look at each other in silence, then I find I have to look out the

window. There is a thick, cloying feeling in the room. I wish I hadn't
mentioned it.

At home, after work, staring at planes climbing into the gilded sky,
listening to trains rumbling past—how is it that other people are
constantly in motion?—I tell myself that it must have been a hallucination. I should never have told anyone. Why do I have the conviction that it is relevant?

The thing is, I don't believe it. That tumble of sensations, the
smell of smoke, the ashy taste . . . God, surely it wasn't a man!—no,
the slippery hot cleft of her, the thrust of her hips, it had to be a
woman, had to be . . . Despite myself, the memory arouses me. It
was real. And it is then, for the first time, that I think of Lulu. Why
didn't I think of this before? Surely that is what kissing her would
taste like? And she likes men helpless, immobile—I saw that for
myself. I confessed to spying on her—a terrible thing to do. Ivo was
staying with her that night; she kept that quiet. Were they in cahoots
from the beginning? Was this her peculiar, twisted revenge?

At home, after work, putting a steak pie in the oven with shaking
hands, I tell myself that I am going mad.

I am in limbo—have been for the last few months. I have run
aground. I don't seem to be functioning well, or even normally. It's
obvious to Hen, who tries teasing me. He tries discussion; he asks
me what the problem is—after all, we have solved the case of Rose
Wood, aka Rena Hart. And we've been paid. Leon Wood rings and
apologizes for his former truculence; his newfound daughter has
rung him, and he is hopeful for a meeting in the not-too-distant
future. He calls her Rose, then corrects himself and says "Rena." A
happy customer.

Hen takes to scolding: I am being self-indulgent, morbid, and weird.

My partner is right—we have achieved what counts as a success in our book. But between the lines, I have made a hopeless cock-up of things. I have never, professionally, been so convinced of something that was wrong, and that shakes me. Never gone so far down a dead end. Even now, I wake up in the night wondering if the guests at Rose's wedding were lying, if the date on the license was faked. Actually, it's not quite true that I've got nowhere this summer—I am now divorced, and I have lost most of the feeling in my right hand.

One of the new cases—a suspicious wife—turns out to be more interesting than it at first appeared, involving both of us uncovering a positive harem of other women and a web of financial wrongdoing. Andrea petitions for a raise, which Hen and I agree to—knowing we should have offered one, unprompted, months ago. She brings in a homemade cake to thank us, about which neither of us tells the truth.

Then Lulu rings me.

"I suppose I should tell you," she begins, without waiting for any awkward pleasantries. "There's been a letter from Ivo. It came to the hospital. It says he isn't coming back."

Andrea is working in the front office. She has a vase of yellow flowers on her desk, which catch the last of what sun can penetrate two layers of dusty windows. Hen is out. I clutch the phone to my ear, in that state of heightened sensory awareness that fear and love hurtle you into, indistinguishable.

"What else does he say? Does he give a reason?"

"No reason. He just says he had to go. It's a letter for Christo, saying that he's sorry and he'll always love him. It was posted in Plumstead on the fourteenth." Her voice is terse. "Can you beat that?"

"Can you tell it's definitely from Ivo?"

"I couldn't, but Sandra and JJ say that it's his writing. So, yeah. And he said he wants Sandra to take care of Christo, so obviously he's not coming back."

"Right . . . Well . . . thanks for telling me. I don't suppose . . . Could I see it? Do you still have it?"

"Sandra has it."

"Right. Of course. Did you get any impression from the letter— about why he was doing this?"

"No. He didn't say."

"Did it . . . seem like a suicide note?"

I hear her intake of breath.

"Suicide? I don't know . . . He didn't say anything like that. I suppose it could be . . . He said he was very sorry but he had to go away—he didn't want to, but he had to. Is that a suicide note? That's not what any of us thought."

"I don't know. I just wondered if you got a particular feeling about it."

"It just makes me angry. That he could dump on everyone like this and not explain himself—that was the only feeling I got. But then, I don't really know him."

It wasn't her, I think. All this elaborate charade cannot be her doing.

I say, "And Sandra—how did she react? She does know him well, doesn't she?"

"I suppose. She was angry. And upset. On account of Christo."

"What about your brother?"

"I haven't seen him. He's not been well."

"No. All this must have hit him pretty hard."

"I suppose."

"Can you remember how the letter was signed?"

"I can remember all of it. It was signed 'Your ever loving parent.' And underneath was the word 'sorry,' again, on its own."

"Thanks very much. I appreciate you telling me about this."

"Yeah, well. Have you found out any more?"

"No. No news."

"Oh."

She sighs.

"Thanks for answering my questions, Lulu."

"That's all right."

There is a pause.

"Are you going to keep looking for him?"

"For Ivo? Yes. I will."

"Okay, then."

She rings off before I say anything else.

Just then Andrea looks around and, seeing me turned toward her, smiles. She has seemed so cheerful recently—more, surely, than can be accounted for by the paltry raise. Perhaps she's in love. Perhaps someone is in love with her. I've never asked.

Perhaps I have always been too reticent.

54.

JJ

Today the hospital lets us take Christo out for a trip to the zoo. He seems really well now. They still don't know what's wrong with him, but they have started giving him exercises to make him stronger. He practices walking in a special gym for children with lots of special equipment. He has a nurse from Israel called Rahel who gives him his exercises. Christo loves her because he gets a lollipop after he's done them. But she's nice, anyway. She thinks we're brothers. I suppose she thinks Mum is his mum. We've stopped talking about it.

The hospital arranges a taxi to take us, even though it's not very far away—it's right in the middle of London. But when you get there, there are trees everywhere, and a hill, and there's a canal that goes around it like a moat goes around a castle. I suppose they did that to stop the animals from escaping. The sun shines down on us. Christo is in a really good mood; he laughs at the giraffes and the penguins, and is fascinated by the snakes, but his favorites are the monkeys. I like them, too. Even Mum, although she was moaning beforehand and worrying about him getting germs from the animals, seems to be enjoying herself. The hospital gave us a wheelchair for him, although they said it would be good for him to try to walk a bit, to get used to it. He's still too weak to walk, really, but they say he'll get better with practice. That's so good to hear. He'll get better! They actually said that. But for now, having the chair makes life a lot easier. We eat ice cream and get cups of tea and sit outside in the sun with the other families. There are lots of other kids running around and enjoying themselves, and several of the parents smile at us, or at Christo when they see he's not very well. It's nice. I barely think about Ivo at all.

The zoo's much more interesting than I thought it was going to be. We spend the whole day there, and leave only because we have to take Christo back to the hospital by four. And we've still got to drive home afterward. It's weird to think we won't be there much longer. Lulu has been helping to sort out a house for us. Apparently, she's found one to rent that's quite near her, just inside the M25—so that we aren't too far from the hospital up in London. And there is a school I can go to that's nearby. I thought all of this would be so difficult, but it seems quite easy. I can even think about living in a house without getting in a panic. I wonder whether anyone from school will miss me—like Stella or Katie. I bet they won't. Maybe Stella, a little bit. I don't know, though.

We've been driving down the A3, with the sun low and piercing through the windscreen, broken by trees, lighting up the squashed insects and other debris that smear the glass so that you can hardly see through it. The journey takes hours—and I'm really hungry, which makes it seem even longer. I'm trying to remember what's in the fridge, and wondering if Mum is in a good enough mood to splash out on a takeaway. There's a Chinese on the edge of the village and it's barely out of our way. I point out the benefits to her— no cooking, no washing up—and, amazingly, she agrees. So when we get there, we order our Chinese—chicken and cashews for me with egg fried rice, and she has sweet-and-sour wings and rice. We get a portion of chips, too, with curry sauce, to share.

"What the hell," says Mum.

Fragrant steam from the bag of food fills the car and mists up the windows, driving me almost dizzy with hunger. Suddenly I feel a reckless happiness sweep over me, quite different from my recent gloom. Christo is going to get better—he's on drugs to help his immune system; they'll find out exactly what it is, and then they can treat it. We'll go to the zoo again—and other places: like the seaside, and films. School starts again soon, and I find I'm looking forward to it, to thinking about something different, not just the family. Right now, anything seems possible. I grin at Mum, and she smiles back; she's probably thinking it's just because of the Chinese, but I don't care.

It's only a few minutes to home, when suddenly Mum says, "What's that?"

"What?"

"That! Oh, God . . . Oh, Jesus Holy Christ . . ."

I look out, through the steamed-up window, through the mist hiding most of the view, but not all, no; there's not enough of it to hide the thick black smoke that pours out above the trees. Our trees. Our site. Where we live. I swipe the windscreen clear. It can't hide the writhing black smoke or, as we get nearer, the flicker of blue lights.

As soon as we start bumping down our own little lane, I can see blue and red and black and orange—like a film, but one that jumps and jerks like something's gone wrong with the projector. Two red fire engines are parked as far as possible from the fire—which is Ivo's trailer, outlined in the middle of its own blazing light. White foam is already pouring from one of the engines onto the blaze, which fights back with more and blacker smoke.

A wave of relief clashes with a wave of horror at myself. Gran and Granddad's cars aren't there, and I can't see anyone other than the firemen. At least it's only Ivo's trailer, I think. And then: Has Ivo come back to do himself in? And then: Good.

A fireman—a bulky black figure whose helmet seems enormous, far too big for his head—sees our van and runs over.

"Do you live here?"

"Yes!"

"Who lives in that trailer?"

Mum shakes her head.

"It's my cousin's—but he's left. It's empty. Mum and Dad . . . ?"

She gestures toward their trailers, their chrome trim winking with reflected flames.

"There wasn't anyone here when we arrived," says the fireman. "We checked inside the other trailers, and they were all empty. I'm afraid we had to force the doors. To be sure."

"Oh . . ."

Mum is too relieved to be angry.

"So there's no one in there?"

I'd already seen that all the cars are gone. Presumably, Gran and Granddad took Great-uncle out somewhere—to the pub, possibly, maybe?

"What about the other trailers—are they safe?"

"It's coming under control. But I wouldn't go inside until we've got this out. Was there any flammable material in that trailer, do you know?"

I think back to my last, fruitless search. The holy water didn't do much good then . . . unless by a perverted miracle it turned into petrol.

Mum shakes her head.

"A gas bottle for the cooker, I suppose."

"It was burning so fiercely when we got here that we thought it might be a fuel fire. You didn't keep spare petrol or diesel stored in there?"

Mum shakes her head.

"No."

"Well, if you'll just stay back until it's under control . . ."

So we sit in the car and watch. It's incredibly weird, like being at a drive-in movie—or what I imagine that would be like. Only instead of a film, we're watching my uncle's trailer burn itself to a skeleton.

I eat my takeaway, but Mum says she can't eat a thing. So I eat
hers as well. Then all the chips we were supposed to share. In about
an hour the flames are out, and there's only a dark, evil-looking
smoke rising from the blackened metal. All the paint has burned away,
and the frame has buckled and twisted so that it's almost unrecognizable. The whole thing is covered with lumps of whitish stuff from
the foam.

Our fireman comes over to the car.

"It should be okay now. We'll keep an eye on it for a bit longer.
So if you want to go inside your trailer now, that's fine."

Mum nods; she still seems shell-shocked.

"But how could it have caught fire?"

The fireman shrugs.

"We won't know that until someone can go in and have a look,
and that won't be today. It'll take a while to cool down. Don't go
anywhere near it. We heard one explosion, but if there's more than
one gas bottle in there, it could still go off."

He looks from Mum to me, with a look of significance.

"Thank you," says Mum. "I . . . Would you all like a cup of tea?"

"Wouldn't say no."

"Right, then."

The fireman winks at me. I'm surprised to find that I don't mind.
When Mum goes inside to put the kettle on, I wander around
outside, looking at the damage on the doors. They don't look too
bad. Another of the firemen comes over and explains how they'll fix
the locks so that we can still use them. He's nice, very polite and
respectful. I wonder what it might be like to be a fireman; you
wouldn't get bored, presumably, unless there just weren't any fires. I
start to feel sort of important, like this is an exciting adventure that
has happened to us. Now that the danger is over, it becomes a story
I can tell people. I have to get it right, though; arrange it properly so
that it's really thrilling.

I walk through the trees and around the site, trying to notice all the details, all while keeping a wide gap between the burned, smoking wreck and me.

Because of the way he parked it—at an angle with the door and awning toward the trees and away from the entrance—I suppose that's why none of us noticed it before, and for a couple of seconds I can't make any sense of what I see, even though I'm staring straight at it.

It's leaning drunkenly against the steps, rendered strange and unfamiliar by fire and foam, but a dark murmur of dread stirs deep inside me.

I run to Great-uncle's trailer; it's empty, empty, empty.

Then I run to Mum, who's handing around a plate of biscuits. I grip her elbow and hiss in her ear.

"Mum . . . Great-uncle's chair is by Ivo's trailer. Why would he leave it there?"

We both know the answer to that.

Mum puts the plate on the ground; her eyes never leave mine.

"His chair? You're sure?"

"What's this?"

"My uncle's wheelchair—it's over there . . ."

She starts to run toward it.

"Does he have a spare?"

The firemen put down their cups of tea, all consternation, and two of them pick up their helmets and run to the trailer.

Mum's face is ash white. One of the firemen is in front of her, holding his hands out so she can't get past him. I'm trying to get closer, but someone is holding me by the arms.

"Please, you have to stay back. Please. It's not safe."

"Oh my God! Get him out!" Mum cries, her voice a shriek.

"Maybe they took him out without it," I say, trying to imagine such a thing, and failing. "Maybe they just went for a drive, and so, or . . . or . . ."

But the firemen go inside, and they call the police, and we know

the truth long before Gran and Granddad return from the pub on
their own, and before Gran starts screaming and wailing, and rant-
ing at the men in uniform, who ignore her and string yellow tape
around the whole site with us in it, as though we are bits of evidence, and whose cars sit beside us, with their doors wide open,
silently flashing their blue lights until daybreak.

55.

Ray

There is always the possibility that there will be no answer. That the broken pieces of bone will be filed away in a drawer unidentified, that no connection will ever be established. But, ignoring that possibility, I have come back to the Black Patch, because I don't know where else to go. I know most of the faces now. They've seen me with Considine, or Hutchins, and I am tolerated. Behind the wire fence and the poster advertising the future, there is little sign of building works; all the machinery has gone. The ground around the find is pegged out in a grid like an archaeological site; necessary because the digger and the flood between them did such a thorough job of spreading the remains. The surface of the mud is drying out and cracking. It has turned light brown, and smells. Eventually it will shrink; the forensics team will pack up their things. And then the diggers will be back.

In Huntingdon, Hutchins is in the laboratory, assembling pieces on a table like a large jigsaw puzzle. Although the dead girl's official name is Unknown #34, I am pleased to hear that the staff call her the Gypsy Girl.

"Still sniffing around? Any progress on your missing mother?"

"No. Nothing. You? Any more candidates?"

"If there are, they haven't told me."

"You're doing well here."

There seem to be hundreds of pieces of bone on the table, though most of them are unrecognizable as human—or even as bones.

"Well . . . yeah. We've got some skull fragments now."

She points with her pen. The largest piece is no bigger than my palm.

"Any sign of cause of death?"

"Nothing. No. But the same developmental abnormalities. What about the kid—got a diagnosis yet?"

"I don't think so."

She gives me the over-the-glasses look.

"You don't know? Have they stopped talking to you?"

"Well, now that Rose is found, we're not investigating anything officially. They haven't asked us to find the boy's father; he seems to have cleared out. So . . . it's not really my case anymore."

I must have sounded pathetic. She laughs.

"Sounds like a good time to go on holiday."

I haven't been on holiday since Jen left. "Yeah, I should think about it."

Hutchins goes to a drawer and takes out a plastic bag—it contains one of the wooden flowers they found in the grave. It's squashed and blackened but recognizable, and it instantly reminds me of my grandfather. When I was about eight he gave me a knife—against my mother's wishes—and tried to teach me how to carve a chrysanthemum out of a piece of elder wood, cutting strips of the white heart and curling them back. Sometimes they were dyed bright colors, but he liked them left raw. It's quite a skill. At eight, I didn't have the patience, and what patience I did have was devoted to model aircraft. Now I wish I'd paid more attention.

"I don't suppose . . ."

"Definitely not."

"Could I take a photograph of it? It might be useful."

"I've probably got one you can have . . ."

She rummages through her files—there seem to be several copies of everything. She also gives me a photograph of the gold chain they found entangled in the vertebrae. I feel new energy flood through me. I wonder how soon I can get down to the site.

"One more thing—could the remains have been there as long as twelve years?"

"Twelve? Yes. I would say so. It's possible. But then it wouldn't be your kid's mother, would it?"

"No."

"Why twelve?"

"The husband had a sister—a seventeen-year-old who died about twelve years ago."

"Did she suffer from the same disease?"

"Well . . . I don't know. Not according to the official story. But I don't have much faith in official stories anymore. She supposedly died in France, in a car crash, but there was no funeral. There is no record of death, in fact. It could all be a red herring."

She's polite, but I can tell she's not that interested in more of my wild theories. Conversation moves on to her forthcoming holiday in Switzerland. She tells me she goes there every year and climbs mountains with her husband and daughter. All three of them are doctors, although the rest of her family deal with the ears, noses, and throats of the living; she is the only one who picks up pieces of the dead.

56.

JJ

They interviewed us all, without, I think, ever believing that we were responsible for the fire. They asked a lot of questions about Ivo, which, of course, we couldn't answer, not knowing where he was or why he'd gone there.

I didn't say anything about what he might have done to Mr. Lovell, either. I thought about it, and it might sound weird, but I just couldn't do it, despite what I thought of him. I must admit, I clung to the idea that it was Ivo's burned remains in the trailer, even after they told us it was the body of an elderly man and it was wearing Great-uncle's rings.

The police told us what they thought had happened. That morning, Mum and I had driven off to London early to take Christo to the zoo. At lunchtime, Gran and Granddad decided to go and visit some friends. They said they wanted to take Great-uncle along, but he refused and insisted they go without him, so they left him all on his own, even though he hadn't been well. I didn't say anything about that, although I was angry at them, because who am I to talk? Once on his own, he went over to Ivo's trailer, left his chair outside, and pulled himself up the steps. Then he poured petrol over the soft furnishings, turned on the gas, and lit a match. They found him on the floor near the cooker. They said he would have been killed by smoke before he was burned.

They said it wouldn't have hurt.

I don't know if they can really know that, or if they just say it because it makes it less horrible to think about. One thing no one could tell us is why he dragged himself into Ivo's trailer to do it, rather than staying in his own. I wondered if he was so angry with Ivo for leaving that he wanted to burn the last traces of him away, or if he was destroying some sign of Ivo's crimes—something I had obviously missed. We all searched through Great-uncle's stuff for clues, or reasons, or anything, really. But there weren't any. None.

So they were saying that he did it on purpose. That he wanted to kill himself. Gran wouldn't have it. She told me I wasn't to repeat what the police said to anyone.

"After all," she said, "we don't know that it wasn't just a terrible, terrible accident. It's wicked, them saying he meant it. They don't know. They didn't know him."

I looked at Mum when she said this. I could tell that Mum couldn't, any more than me, think of any accident that could happen like that. But we didn't say anything.

I don't know for certain that it's true, but I remembered how odd he was that time in his trailer. Some of the things he said, now it seems like he was saying good-bye. I'd never seen him cry before. And while I think Ivo is a coward and despise him for running away and leaving us to clear up his mess, I can't feel the same about Great-uncle. He didn't have anyone depending on him. He was old. He was in a wheelchair. He had suffered in almost every way you can think of, and then, recently, had got a new illness to put up with. I cried. If I had gone back into his trailer that time, would that have made a difference? No one answered this question, because I didn't say it out loud.

· · ·

Word gets around. And with Gypsies, it gets around really fast. We had to get on and lay him out, because people started asking about coming to pay their respects, and it wasn't as simple as all that, because the police took away his remains and kept them. There was to be an inquest. And then there was a massive row about the trailer.

Great-uncle's trailer, even though he didn't die in it, was *mokady* now that he was dead. Auntie Lulu came down—this was two days after—and said that old Westmorlands like his were worth a lot of money and we should sell it, and keep the money for Christo, who needs everything he can get, and is Great-uncle's only descendant now (not counting Ivo, that is, because he is gone). Gran got really angry and said that it would have to be burned, that it should have been burned years ago when Great-aunt Marta died. In fact, it should have been burned when their first two sons died. And since it was still around after that, it should have been burned when Christina died. According to Gran, his trailer should have been burned four times, and it is four times *mokady* because it's still here. Basically, it's so *mokady* that if we don't burn it this time, we're all going to die. I've seen Gran angry before, but I've never seen her quite as angry as this. Lulu was furious, too. She said that if Great-uncle (they call him "our brother" now, instead of saying his name) wanted to keep it on after Marta's death, that was up to him, because he was hoping she would come back and see him, and Christo was going to need all sorts of equipment and special help, and that costs money. She said the trailer and the things in it were worth at least two thousand pounds. She said lots of people buy a cheap trailer for the laying out, and then get rid of that, and he didn't die in his trailer, anyway. She looked at Mum when she said this, as if she thought she would back her up, but Mum was never going to stand against Gran in this. No one asked me what I thought, but I agreed with Gran. I think we've had enough bad luck, and money's only money. Christo, who hasn't done anything to deserve all that's happened, deserves for it to stop. Mum said she was in favor of burning the trailer, and I was glad.

It's been horrible and weird waking up every day and suddenly remembering that he isn't here anymore, but his trailer still is, empty and kind of spooky. As soon as we could, we got someone to come and take the burned remains of Ivo's trailer away, thank God. It was terrible seeing that. Even now, there is a big black burned patch on the ground where it stood.

When the police eventually released the body, it was nearly two weeks later. Mum and Gran went in and hung sheets on the walls of his trailer, ready for the coffin. I couldn't help wondering what was actually in the coffin when it came from the undertaker's. That's an awful thing to think, but I couldn't help it. You're supposed to dress the dead in their best clothes, inside out—but who was going to do that? The closed coffin was put in his trailer, and the next day all sorts of people—loads from the site on the edge of town, as well as others—came by to pay their respects. Mum and Gran had to make tea all day. Granddad and I lit two fires in the clearing—one for men and one for women—and people came and sat around and chatted. I think Granddad enjoyed it; it's the most sociable we've been since we moved here. Lulu was here most of the time. Once the fight over Great-uncle's trailer was over, she helped out, fetching takeaways and making tea and things. I began to wonder what had kept her away for so long.

But in the middle of all this, something nice happened: a few days before the laying out, Stella came to see me. She got her mum to give her a lift. Somehow, everybody knows about the fire and that Great-uncle is dead, even people at school. I was so surprised to see her I didn't know what to say at first. Gran thought we should send her away, that it wasn't right for her to be here at such a time. And

I was terribly aware that there was this great black patch of ground right there, where it had happened. Stella kept looking at it, even though Ivo's trailer was gone by then. Luckily, Lulu was there, too, and she gave me ten pounds and told us to get out of there and go into town. So Stella's mum drove us and dropped us at the shopping center, and we went to see *Ferris Bueller's Day Off*.

Afterward we sat in the café opposite the cinema, drinking Coke floats and holding hands. I don't know quite how the holding hands started, but it was during the film sometime, and once it had started, it didn't stop. That sounds callous, only a week after Great-uncle died, I know. It wasn't as though I completely forgot about him. Even during the funny bits in the film, I sometimes thought about him, and I could tell Stella was thinking about him, too, even though she'd met him only once and it was embarrassing. I think that's why she held my hand.

I told her about Christo, and about having to move to a house and that I would have to go to a different school. Stella took her hand back and stared into her scummy glass.

"I'll write to you—if you want," I say.

She sighed. I didn't know what I'd done wrong.

"Stella?"

"You know, when you . . . went to Katie's?"

"Yeah."

I had been dreading this question, really, ever since that moment when she saw me in the stable and looked so angry.

"Were you . . . you know, going out?"

"Um, no. We weren't going out. I went to her house once—she took me back to her house for tea, when it was raining. She showed me her horse; that's how I knew where to go. I just couldn't think of anywhere else."

Stella raised her eyebrows in a way that made it look like she didn't really believe me.

"And . . . ?"

"And, um, we kissed. Once. And that's it. You know what she's like at school. She never even talked to me afterward."

"So you fancy her."

I wanted to say no, but I thought she would know that was a lie.

"I kind of liked her, yeah . . . but it was just that once. And we've never been friends. You know . . . I've always liked you more than anyone. I just thought there wasn't any, you know . . . hope."

"Oh."

Stella looked out the window and sucked on her straw. Her glass was nearly empty, and it made a gurgling noise. I sucked on my straw, which made a louder gurgling noise. Then she started laughing, so it was okay for me to laugh, too.

Looking into her glass, she said, "There's always hope."

For the funeral I'm wearing a new black suit, white shirt, and black tie, which feels very odd. But then everyone is dressed up in black and looks smart—all my family, and dozens of other people I either barely know or don't know at all, who have come to the church to pay their respects. They all shake hands with Gran and Aunt Lulu, who are the chief mourners. Great-uncle's other sister, Sibby, hasn't come over from Ireland because of her arthritis, but she and her husband sent a wreath in the shape of a chair, made out of red and white flowers. There are quite a few wreaths. There's even a wheel-chair wreath. I'm surprised. It never seemed like Great-uncle had that many friends, but these people must have liked him a bit. It's not like one of those funerals you hear about, where they have to stop the traffic for hours because of all the hundreds of people following, but there are quite a few.

Some of them shake hands with me as well, and murmur things about what a shame it is, or that it's a blessing and he's at peace now. Several refer to the bad luck he's had. None of them know that he killed himself. Some of the older people say that I look like him.

One elderly woman grabs my hair in both her hands—I'm not kidding; I don't even know who she is—and calls me the very spit. I complain to Mum after, and she says of course I am not the very spit; I just have the same coloring. She says it is just the sort of thing people say—and if I had more cousins, they would probably all get it, but I am the only one. Christo is not here, as he is still in hospital—and even if he wasn't, we probably wouldn't have brought him. It really brings it home to me: for a Gypsy funeral, there are not many young people or children. Normally, there are loads of kids running around, masses of cousins and stuff. Not in our family. Now it's me who is like the Last of the Mohicans. Me and Christo.

I am wondering—I suppose we all are—if Ivo will come, in disguise or otherwise, and I keep turning around in the procession, and staring hard at people I don't know, just in case. But I don't see him, or anyone who could be him, not remotely.

I wonder if he even knows his father is dead.

57.

Ray

In the end, it is the prospect of seeing Lulu that decides me. She did, after all, telephone to let me know the time and place of Tene's funeral. When she told me the manner of his death, we were both silent. I couldn't tell how upset she was. I wondered if she had seen him again before he died but didn't want to ask.

I drive down to Andover and find the red-brick Catholic church in the middle of a postwar housing estate. I am wearing an old dark blue suit that I last wore for Eddie's funeral. I found, when I put it on, that I have lost weight since then. This very slightly cheers me. I am glad, on the whole, that he isn't here to see the cock-up I have made of things.

I wait in my car until almost everyone has gone into the church, and then creep in to stand at the back. I can see the family up at the front, Lulu among them. She doesn't turn around. The back is a rather crowded place, and I find myself in a gaggle of men wearing rusty black, all of whom seem to prefer standing than taking one of the empty seats. More than one sneak out for a smoke and a chat during the short service. Several don't bother to go inside at all.

Afterward, I wait on the fringes until the Jankos are done with the followers. But as I am loitering, trying not to look conspicuous,

JJ appears beside me, looking stiff in a black suit, his hair pulled back into a ponytail. It makes him look different—more grown-up.

"Hello, Mr. Lovell."

"Hello, JJ."

I shake his hand.

"Thanks for coming."

He sounds like he means it.

"Thanks. You look very smart. I'm really sorry about your uncle."

"My . . . Oh, you mean Great-uncle. Thanks."

He looks all right—more confident than before. Maybe he is taller, or perhaps it is just the suit and the hair; you can see the man he is becoming. He tells me that they are about to move into a house with Christo. That he is making good progress.

"You're not going right away, are you?" he says. "Auntie Lulu will want to talk to you."

The blood thuds in my ears when he says this.

She has spoken about me to them. What has she said? He leaves me standing in the churchyard as the crowd starts to drift off and break apart, climbing into cars and vans, heading off to a pub.

I stand, feeling self-conscious and worried that she is going to walk off without seeing me, or worse: after seeing me. But at last she breaks away from the knot by the church door and comes toward me. She doesn't smile, but I smile at her; I can't help myself.

"Let's walk down here," she says, and steers me to an avenue between rows of gravestones.

"How are you?"

"I'm all right. Thanks for coming."

"Thank you for inviting me. I'm so sorry about your brother. It's a terrible tragedy."

A trailer fire. It happens. I've heard of it now and again. And worse—my grandmother's young cousin was playing beside the fire when her dress caught alight, and she died of her burns. But the timing of Tene's death—so soon after hearing the news about Ivo and Rose—is it really coincidence? Again, this is not something I can ask. Not here.

Lulu takes her cigarettes out of her bag—a black leather bag, in keeping with the occasion, but still almost as vast as her other one—and, after some rummaging, finds her lighter.

"He couldn't have gone on much longer living like that. Maybe this is better, even if it was . . ."

She shrugs and sucks on the cigarette with relief.

Some people make smoking look good. Lulu is one of them. Today she wears black, chunky-heeled shoes. A black skirt suit with a vaguely forties air. Her lipstick looks fresh, and her hair seems different, maybe lighter, perhaps a new color, with strands of bronze lifting the black.

She looks unattainable, perfect, beautiful.

"I've always wondered, what do you keep in that bag?"

She glances at me.

"You know. Stuff. Just in case."

"Ready for emergencies?" (What on earth am I talking about?)

"That sort of thing."

Her shoes tap-scrape on the concrete path. I could listen to that sound forever.

"I should apologize to you properly."

She speaks while looking over the gravestones.

"No . . . Why?"

She throws the spent butt behind a gravestone—Ann Mendoza, d. 1923—and digs another cigarette out of her bag.

"I've been feeling so awful. About telling Ivo—you know. It was stupid of me. I wanted to . . . I can't believe he'd do such a thing. Well, I can now—I can believe anything. But that he'd hurt you like that . . ."

"I was the one who behaved awfully. You have nothing to feel bad about. I told him anyway, so it didn't make any difference."

Sometimes, it is better to lie.

"I was so worried. I thought you were going to die."

I close my eyes to savor it. The sweetest sentence I have ever heard. The tapping stops. When I open my eyes, she is looking at me.

"Well, I didn't die."

She sighs, the small frown lodged between her brows.

"No."

"Lulu!"

The sound of footsteps hurrying nearer.

It's Sandra, cruelly walking toward us in her tight black suit, her eyes red with crying. She stops about twenty yards away and keeps her eyes averted from my face.

"Hello, Mr. Lovell. Mum's on at me, Lu. Are you coming with us or what? Everyone's gone."

"Yeah. I'm coming."

She turns to me, at the same time backing away. I feel I've taken the wrong step yet again, the distance between us increasing.

She smiles, a bland, public smile.

"Bye. Thanks for coming."

"Yeah . . . Good to see you."

I start to follow her back toward the main gate until I realize from her nervous pace that she wants to appear before her family alone.

"I'll ring . . . Shall I?"

I don't say it very loud, more to myself than anything. I don't know if she hears. Her head dips; I hope it's a nod, but I'm not sure, and in another second she has turned a corner and disappeared. I come to a desultory halt among the gravestones. The laconic chatter of the mourners has died away. I am the only living person left.

58.

J J

Now everyone has gone. We are all packed up, ready to pull out. Gran and Granddad are going to a site in Kent, where some of his relatives live. For the time being, anyway. Mum and I are going to camp at Auntie Lulu's until our house is ready—it's going to be only a couple weeks. Mum has found a buyer for the trailer. Christo is going to stay in the hospital until then. Next week I go to my new school, up in London. I can't imagine what my life is going to be like from now on.

We cleared out Great-uncle's trailer. The Crown Derby and a few things, like the fancy silver photograph frames, went to an antiques shop. I helped Granddad load some of the other stuff into his lorry—everyday crockery, the metal cans, knives and forks, all the heavy things, stuff that won't burn, all that . . . and late that night we drove to a bridge over the Itchen, and threw the stuff in. No one was around. You just throw it in and it sinks, and then it's gone.

There's only one thing left to do here, and we've left it till the last minute, because the farmer who owns the site can't know about it.

Everything left that belonged to Great-uncle—his clothes, records, radio, bedding, all those things . . . even photographs, although Mum picked out a few to keep in a drawer—everything else of his is in the trailer, just as when he was there. Granddad goes inside and pours petrol over everything. Then he comes out and shuts the door. I can hardly breathe, in case something goes wrong. I think I'm going to be sick.

He gets in the lorry and pulls out, pulling their number-one trailer. Gran drives the Land Rover pulling number two. And Mum and me are in her van with our trailer hooked up. The first time it's moved for months. We drive slowly down the lane, and there's no sign of anything. My heart's racing like a mad thing. I wonder if I'm going to have a heart attack.

When we're a mile down the road, Granddad slows to a halt. It's dark, so you can't see much, but I gradually notice that there is smoke rising above the trees—thin and pale against the dark blue sky at first but growing thicker and blacker. Like the last time.

With a roar, Granddad drives off. We follow.

III.

Civil Twilight

Morning

59.

Ray

She said, "Shhh."

She said nothing else.

I didn't see anything. I couldn't see. Because she covered my eyes, to be sure.

But I could smell; I could taste.

Smoke in my nostrils.

Ash in my mouth.

She must have kissed me.

Ridiculous, helpless desire swirled through me. Euphoric blurring; scopolamine fireworks—I assume that's what they were. But I know she was real. It is a memory, not a delusion. She elicited my stuttering confession. But this is where it falls apart, this memory: in fog and fear. A sudden picture in my head, and the sound of Tene Janko's voice: the ninth child, Poreskoro, dog and cat, male and female, neither one thing nor the other. And that is not a memory, of course, because how could it be?

So this is all I have left. Like a stupid, loyal dog, I persist in this one thing: I go to the children's hospital every week, when Christo has his physiotherapy. Sometimes I sit in my car, if I can park opposite the entrance, or I go inside, sit in reception where I can keep an eye on the door, and wonder whether the birds in the mural opposite are meant to be parrots or swallows. Fortunately, there is only the one public entrance: double doors with reinforced glass, they glide open automatically, to make it easier for wheelchairs to enter. Sometimes I chat to parents. All the time keeping an eye on the one door that he'd have to come in by. Only patience will do it, because there's no one else left to ask.

I will do this every week for as long as it takes. The next ten years, if I have to, because of what he has taken from his family. From all of us, including me. For assaulting me and leaving me in the dark. For my right arm, still suffering pins and needles, which occasionally, still, altogether fails to function. As long as it takes, Ivo.

Today, Sandra sees me as she brings Christo in. She nods to me. Normally, that is all the interaction we have—she disappears into the physiotherapy unit and I don't see either of them again until it's time to leave. But today, to my surprise, she comes back into the main reception area and sits down beside me.

"You really think he's going to come back?"

"Sometime. Yes."

"You're very, um . . ."

"Stubborn?"

"You could say that."

"How is Christo getting on?"

"They think they know what's wrong with him now."

"Oh?"

"It's called Barth syndrome."

"I don't think I've heard of it."

"It's very rare. They don't know much about it."

"Can they do anything?"

"They can't cure it. Not yet. But they can make him healthier. They said, on the whole, it's good news."

"Well, that's the first step. So . . . that's what's been affecting your family?"

"It's inherited, yeah."

She makes a face. I wonder if she's been tested for it, or if that's even possible.

"How are you getting on, all of you? You're settling down now, aren't you?"

"Yeah. We've got our house—we've moved out from Lulu's, finally."

"Oh. Right . . . How is she?"

Sandra looks sidelong at me, a little sly. I wonder how much she knows.

"She's all right. She's got a new job."

I feel my heart knock against my ribs.

"She rather liked . . . that other one, didn't she?"

Sandra doesn't react, so I assume she wasn't privy to the ins and outs of the job in Richmond.

"Where's she working now?"

"In an old people's home in Sutton."

"Ah."

We stare ahead in silence for a few moments.

"Could I get you a coffee, Mrs. . . . er, Mrs. Smith?"

I get drinks from the machine in the lobby and go back to my post. Sandra smiles as she takes the cup.

"My son's very interested in what you do."

"Oh? Well, he's a bright kid. I'm sure he could do all sorts of things."

"He keeps talking about you. It would be really nice if you could talk to him one day. Tell him about your schooling and stuff, you know. He's got to make all these decisions about exams and things. I don't know what to say to him."

"Of course. Happy to."

"I didn't have much schooling myself."

She sips her chocolate.

"Ow. They're always too hot, aren't they?"

"Yeah, they are . . . Would you tell me about Christina?"

"Christina? My cousin? God, why?"

"Because she . . . seems such a mystery. There wasn't a funeral, is that right?"

"It's not a mystery. She died abroad. And Tene was on his own with Ivo. You know . . ."

She shrugs: What can you do? These things happen.

"When was the last time you saw her?"

"Must have been before I had JJ. We were good pals, when we were little. Even though she was younger than me, she was braver. Fearless, you know. But then Tene took them all off on the road—we didn't see much of them after that."

"How old were you then?"

"When we were friends? Oh, about eight."

"What happened?"

She shrugs.

"Were you friends with Ivo, too, when you were little?"

"Yeah, but he was younger, and poorly, and he always had to stay at home. And when Christina passed . . . Tene and Ivo just vanished. He couldn't bear to see anyone, I think. I didn't see them again until the wedding . . . I mean, it was years."

"Years since you'd seen Tene and Ivo?"

"Since anyone had."

"Even Kath—even your mum? She didn't see them, either?"

"No. I don't know if they fell out or something . . ."

"What year did Christina die?"

"In 1974. JJ was nearly two. It was then Mum and Dad got in touch with me again. I think it gave them a shock—you know, we were all sort of used to the disease, but it made them see that people die of other things, too."

"So . . . you and Ivo became close friends, when you lived together?"

"We were cousins."

She sounds defensive.

"Were you surprised he didn't marry again?"

I know I'm getting near the knuckle. She won't look at me.

"Why are you asking all these questions?"

"I suppose I want to understand him."

She lets out a snort of contempt.

"Forget it! No one understood Ivo when he was here!"

"Not even you?"

"'Specially not me."

Her voice has dropped to nothing. She's picking at her empty cup, tearing the edge and bending the strips into tiny battlements.

"You were fond of him."

I try to say it as gently as possible. Still, I think I've gone too far, and she isn't going to reply.

Then, at length, she says, very quietly, "He wasn't interested. When you said he had a girlfriend, I thought . . . maybe that's why."

"Do you think he could have kept that a secret from you all?"

She sighs and leans back in her chair.

"Why not? That's what he was like, you know . . ." She holds up her hand, palm outward. "Wouldn't let you in."

She glances at me, her face weary. The look of one dupe to another. It sounds like Rose, all over again. Ivo and his secrets.

"Anyway, he's gone now. End of story."

She gets up, rather heavily, and throws her empty cup into the bin.

60.

R a y

Autumn is starting to bite. The belated, short-lived warmth has fled; the trees have begun to turn in the park outside the hospital. I cross the road and notice the first fallen leaves, pressed into the tarmac under my feet.

As usual, it's early in the morning when I arrive. I don't want there to be any chance of missing him—although it's a while before appointments begin. Today, for the first time, it's Lulu who brings Christo to the hospital. I haven't seen her since the funeral, not because I didn't want to but because my lack of answers demonstrates an unbearable—to me—incompetence. She looks just the same . . . No, she looks better. She doesn't seem surprised to see me. I imagine that Sandra told her about my being here. I allow myself, just briefly, to wonder if that's why she's come.

After leaving Christo with the therapist, she walks back into the reception area. She seems tense, I think. But then so must I.

"Hello, Ray," she says.

"Hello. How are you?"

"All right, yeah . . . You?"

"Can't complain. How's Christo?"

"Good. They seem pleased with him. He says things now and again, you know."

"Oh, yeah? That's good. And they've made a diagnosis, Sandra told me."

"Yeah. Although it's not too bright."

"At least you know what it is. It's always better to know what you're dealing with, isn't it?"

Lulu thinks for a minute, and then says, "I suppose so."

She's sitting beside me, so I can't get a proper look at her. She keeps her eyes on the middle distance, watching two kids eye each other up across the climbing frame.

"How's your work—you busy?" she says.

"Yes . . . You?"

"Very. Actually . . . I've left the job in Richmond. I'm working in a home again."

Her voice changes, takes on a slightly higher note.

"Oh . . . How's that going?"

"It's okay."

I wait for her to say something else about it.

"How's your hand?"

"All right. Still a bit numb. But I can do most things." I waggle it about, to demonstrate that I can waggle it.

"Must be a relief."

"Yeah, being able to drive, especially. And type . . . dial phone numbers—amazing what you take for granted . . ."

"Yeah."

She gives me a brief smile. The blood is beating in my ears. I wonder whether to take the smile as encouragement.

"So . . . are you . . . ? Your job, I mean . . . Are you, um, what sort of home is it?"

"Old people. They're not too bad, most of them. Not senile or anything, I mean. It's quite a nice place. Not too far away."

"Good. Makes a change, anyway."

"Yeah."

We sit in silence for a minute. I'm going to shoot myself if I don't ask, I think.

"Do you still see him?"

She goes still, and instantly I regret it.

"Sorry, it's none of my business. Forget I . . ."

"No, it isn't. No."

She takes a deep breath and looks at the mural on the wall opposite. At the top is a bright yellow sun. The unlikely birds fly in a circle around it. She smiles a little.

"It's quite funny, really. He met someone. Someone more like him."

"In a wheelchair?"

It pops out before I think about what I'm saying.

"No! Some posh *gorjio* woman."

"Oh. I see . . . Right. Yes, I suppose . . . Are you okay?"

"Yeah. Got to be, haven't I? Least I've got another job."

Her voice sounds strained. Maybe she really did care for him. I wonder what to say next. It feels vital that I get it right. She checks her watch.

"I should probably go and see what he's up to."

Then she looks up, looks past me, and freezes.

I look at her face, then follow her eyes to the double doors. My first thought is: it must be David from Richmond. The doors have opened automatically, because a young woman is standing behind them, but instead of walking through, she shrinks back, her eyes darting over the room, wary.

I relax: at first I think she looks vaguely familiar, but she's not someone I know.

It's not until her eyes meet mine that I realize. It is the reaction I see there that convinces me I am not dreaming. The terror in the eyes. The guilt. In a second, or less than a second, the doorway is empty.

Lulu has clutched my arm.

"Fucking hell!"

Her voice is a strangled rasp.

I jump up and run through the doors, Lulu beside me, and, maddeningly, we have to wait for the doors to slowly, gently, automatically, swing open again; we run down the corridor, out into the brightness outside. The staff car park. The pavement. Not there. Not there.

Lulu goes left; I go right.

Ivo—wearing a printed cotton dress and baggy sweater—could have come out only this way, but he's not there, and there's no crowd to hide among. An empty pavement. No cars pulling away.

I run down the street, checking doorways, turning my head— the park gates? No, it's open, no sign of him. He could have gone into a shop, I suppose, any shop, an office . . . A couple walking on the pavement opposite: I chase after them, ask them if they saw someone—a woman—a minute ago.

"He just came out a few seconds before me, black hair, blue cotton dress—I mean, she came out . . . You didn't see anyone like that . . . ?"

The couple—tourists, burdened with maps and rain jackets and cameras—stare at me dumbly, shaking their heads. They seem frightened of me.

I jog on, come to a crossroads. I can't see him. No reason to turn left rather than right. Take one course and you miss another. Get it wrong, you lose your chance. I turn right. I end up half jogging, half running, taking one random turn after another. My thighs burn, my lungs start to complain. I'm out of condition, since hospital. Kidding myself. When was I last in condition? I run back to the first turn and go the other way. I don't see Ivo anywhere.

At length, I find myself leaning, hands on my knees, pulling great tearing breaths into aching lungs, staring at a woman pushing a child on a little wooden horse with wheels. They stop at a zebra crossing. The child's blond head turns this way and that. I can't tell if it's a boy or a girl. The mother sees me watching and hurries them across the road with an alarmed, hostile look.

When I finally get back to the hospital's reception area, Lulu is already there, talking to a member of the staff. She rushes over to me, questioning.

I shake my head. I have walked back slowly, to let my breathing return to normal and the heat leave my face. And to think.

"You didn't see him at all?" She sounds anguished as well as furious. "I didn't see anything, but . . . the way I went, there were loads of shops, so . . ." She lifts her hands in frustration. "Oh . . . what the fuck?"

"Sorry, I didn't see anything. But there weren't that many places he could have gone. He must have had a car."

"I can't believe this. The fucking perverted little . . . fucker. How dare he . . . I'm going to fucking kill him!"

Her voice trembles with rage. Tears are threatening, glittering in her eyes.

I shake my head again. She isn't going to kill him. I am beginning to suspect that would be impossible.

61.

Ray

When I get home, I decide to have a stiff drink. I pour myself a vodka and tonic. I need it, even if I haven't earned it. I sit for a long time, not turning the light on, watching trains pass, their lights getting brighter as the day fades, hearing planes lumber overhead: monotonous, strident rhythms that I thought I would never get used to but now, when I spend any length of time elsewhere, I find I miss.

I switch on the answerphone. Andrea rings me on the days I spend at the hospital, to give me an update. Hen told me I should wait until morning, for all the good it's going to do anyone. But she still does it. Dear Andrea—on her message I can hear her pencil striking through the items as she says them.

"Hi, Ray. Nothing much to report today. Hen has been checking on the Porter money; nothing so far. Couple of inquiries on maritals. And a DI Considine called. Could you give him a ring when you've got a minute."

Thoughtfully, she has left a number. A home number.

When I say my name, I can tell from his voice that something has happened.

"You've got news."

"Yeah . . . of a sort."

"You've got an ID?"

"No. But Hutchins rang me today. Back from her holidays."

He sounds oddly hesitant.

"And?"

"Well, she's saying now that the body belongs to a young male, probably fifteen, sixteen years old but markedly underdeveloped."

"This is the Black Patch body?"

"Yeah."

"With the wooden flowers."

"That's the only one I know about."

"The body in the Black Patch is a boy?"

"Yeah. Bit of a turnup, isn't it? Apparently, it's pretty conclusive. Hutchins says there is about a three percent room for error."

I switch the phone from one ear to the other to give myself time, thinking, That's very precise, as well as very small.

The feeling that goes with this thought is, strangely, one of happiness.

"Ray? You there?"

"Yeah. But with young skeletons, I thought you couldn't be sure. I thought they were difficult."

"Well, she seems sure now. They found the pelvic bones and put them back together. Skull, too."

"Did she say what she meant by 'underdeveloped'?"

"She says he would have appeared younger than his age. Small and slight, you know. He might have been suffering from some sort of disease that retards development. And the other thing—there's no obvious cause of death."

"Right."

I wait. For what, I don't know.

"Sorry, mate."

I put the phone down. I drain the vodka in one go. My next call is to Gavin. It takes ages to get hold of him—the babysitter informs me he's out, so I have to wait until he comes back. He's not best pleased to hear from me at half past eleven, but, bless him, he is willing to talk.

When I hang up twenty minutes later, I know I'm not going to sleep.

She sounds suspicious and irritable.

"God, it's after midnight!"

"Were you asleep?"

"No."

"I thought you wouldn't be. I've been thinking about what happened today. And I've . . . Can I come over and see you? I've got something to tell you."

"Now? It's the middle of the night!"

"I know. Maybe there's somewhere that would be open—a caff or something? Anything like that near you?"

"I don't think so."

"Well, I suppose it can wait. Sorry to disturb you."

A sigh.

"It's okay. I can't sleep, anyway. My address is 24 Tennyson Way . . . Oh, you already know, don't you?"

Lulu has made a pot of tea and put it on a tray in the sitting room. The room is small but very neat. She is dressed as she was earlier. I have changed. I had a shower, too.

"So what's so important, then?"

I spent the journey over here trying to think of the best way to tell her. I still haven't reached a conclusion.

"This is going to sound crazy . . ."

She leans back in her armchair and lights a cigarette. She sends a stream of smoke in my direction. Already, she looks skeptical.

"Remember I told you about the human remains at the Black Patch?"

"The ones that aren't Rose."

"Yes. But there were wooden flowers in the grave, so it seemed likely that it was a Traveler Gypsy."

She stares at me.

"I was sure that Tene and Ivo had some connection with the . . . person there. I thought it could be Christo's mother, whoever that was. But tonight I found out—the remains are those of a boy, not a girl. A boy of about sixteen. He was small for his age, and weak. The pathologist said it was probably due to a developmental disease. That's what Christo has."

Lulu looks at me. Then she doesn't look at me.

"So?"

"I'm saying that . . ." I take a deep breath. "What if Ivo died at the Black Patch, twelve years ago. Ivo is dead; like his brothers, like his uncles. He had Barth syndrome. He didn't get better. There was no miracle."

She stares at me; she looks concerned, slightly pitying.

"We saw Ivo today!"

"The other thing I found out is that Barth syndrome can only be passed down through the mother. Christo had to have a carrier mother—he had to have a Janko mother, not a Janko father."

"But Ivo isn't dead! We saw him. You saw him."

Lulu stares. She is deciding, sadly, that I am out of my mind.

I take another deep breath.

"What if Christina didn't die?"

Her eyes bore into me. That's what it feels like: her eyes are hurting me. I wish I didn't have to do this. She shakes her head slightly, stares at the ground.

"That's insane."

"I know it seems incredible."

"Incredible! You're saying that . . . What are you saying?"

"Well, I'm saying that the person you know as Ivo has really been Christina, for the past twelve years."

Lulu is shaking her head.

A sharp exhalation, almost a laugh.

"You've been ill, Ray . . ."

"Think of what we actually saw today . . ."

"I saw Ivo!"

"What if . . . Just think, what if it wasn't Ivo disguised as a woman, but Christina, for the first time in years, not disguised as a man?"

She makes no answer to this. I plough on.

"The disease—Barth syndrome—it gives us the answer. Lulu . . . please listen, these are facts: Christo could not inherit it from his father. I spoke to Gavin, the doctor, and that can't happen. It's an x-linked recessive disorder. That means he could only inherit it from his mother. His mother, Christina."

"Christina died! She's dead!"

"The other fact we can know for sure, Barth syndrome is incurable. You can't get better. Ivo's recovery wasn't a miracle . . . It wasn't Ivo."

Lulu crushes her half-smoked cigarette in the ashtray. Her face looks hard and wooden.

"Christina's death was a . . . fiction. That's why there was no funeral. That's why no one knew how it happened, or where . . ."

I can't think of anything else to say. I dare to look at her again. She's lighting another cigarette. Her tea, like mine, is untouched. When she speaks, her voice grates.

"Why?"

The adrenaline, the certainty, that has been sustaining me suddenly decides to flag. I put my face in my hands. I think I know, but it is pure speculation. All so much smoke.

"Only Christina knows that for sure, and Tene . . ."

"My brother . . . ?"

"He had to know. He was there. Do you want me to tell you what I think? Lulu?"

Suddenly, tears are running down her face, although she doesn't make a sound. It would be more bearable if she collapsed in noisy sobs; if she broke down, I might be allowed to comfort her, but I am not to be given that chance. Her face is wet but perfectly rigid, like that of a mannequin left out in the rain. She shrugs minutely.

"Um, well . . . I think they were very close, Ivo and Christina. Ivo got worse and worse. Their mother had died—you know all that, of course. Tene took Ivo to Lourdes, in a last-ditch attempt to help him, but it didn't work. He died, perhaps at the Black Patch, I don't know . . . But whatever, they buried him there, in secret, so that no one would know. And between them, they decided that . . . that it would be Christina that had died. Ivo was the last Janko heir. The only boy—the one they had pinned their hopes on—and they couldn't bear to let him go."

She still doesn't speak. She doesn't look at me. Not knowing what else to do, I go on.

"They were very alike, weren't they? I've seen photographs. No one in your family saw Tene and . . . well, who they thought was Ivo, for years—until the wedding. And in that time the person you all thought was Ivo had gone from a sick child to a healthy adult—of course he had changed. I know it's tremendously shocking, but it's not impossible."

Lulu looks at me now, her face fierce. She spits the words out.

"Not impossible? Do you think we're stupid or something?"

"No! Of course not. I didn't know, either."

"Kath and Jimmy and Sandra saw him every day! For six years, every day! You think they wouldn't know?"

I swallow. I should have foreseen this.

"People accept what they see. When you all saw Tene again, what did you expect? You knew his daughter had died; you knew Ivo had recovered . . . If someone appears to be something, you accept it, don't you? And once it's accepted . . . I think he would have been more worried about seeing people like you—that he rarely saw—not the people he saw every day."

I can see that—however unwillingly—she is thinking about it.

"He married. Why would he get married? If you had to . . . keep that secret."

This is the most difficult bit. If my guess is right, it is dreadful. There doesn't seem to be enough oxygen left in the room.

"From what Rose told us, she never got near enough to Ivo to find out anything."

"So why do it? It's crazy!"

"Tene cared about the pure black blood, didn't he? The pure blood of the Jankos. I think they thought that if they found a really innocent, pureblooded girl, that he could . . ."

"Stop it! Stop it! Stop . . . saying those things."

Her voice—painfully sharp, like a broken knife. Her wet, white face is turned away from me.

I wait, hardly daring to breathe, staring at the side of her cheek, willing her to turn toward me, to say anything. Seconds crawl past. And then she speaks in a tiny voice, looking at the carpet.

"Maybe it's possible. I don't know. Maybe it's some clever answer that makes everything fit . . ."

She takes a deep, shuddering breath.

"But it's not true . . . and you can't accuse people like that."

"I'm not . . . maybe that's not . . . but—"

"I want you to go. Just go!"

"Okay. I'm sorry. I . . . Sorry."

She twists the little, mortal blade in my heart.

"I want you to leave us alone. I don't want to see you again."

After a moment I stand up. She doesn't look at me as I leave.

62.

Ray

A big dog fox runs across my path as I walk up to my front door. He's the only other creature who seems to be awake when I get home. There are no lights on in the houses. No trains, no planes. The road respects a deep and perfect silence. I pause with my keys in my hand, bathed in the yellow streetlight that banishes the wolf. No one knows I am here, because no one is watching. It is not yet dawn, but there is always enough light to see by, in the city—to see that a fox is a fox, that a dog is not a wolf, and that a private investigator has made a terrible error of judgment. But you have to be looking.

Lulu would have to find out sooner or later, I tell myself. They all will. Why should they be spared an unpalatable truth? There are some things they don't ever have to know, like the drugged seduction, and there are some things that can't be known, can be only guessed at. I guess at them, because that is my business. A business I have not conducted well in this instance. Mainly, I feel a fool. Stupid. Stupid dog, barking up the wrong tree for so long. I am sure Lulu feels a fool, too. Being lied to humiliates you. Belittles you. And the longer you are lied to, the worse it feels when you are faced with the truth.

I let myself in to the communal corridor, and stump up the stair to my flat, my footsteps sounding very loud and heavy, the key clattering in the lock. The truth hurts, too, that's what Lulu said; hurts maybe, but in the long run, surely it's better—isn't it?

The flat looks small and grubby in the overhead light. Because it's rented, I've never made much of an effort; I always thought there was a chance that Jen would take me back. I clung to that. Not anymore. It's long past time I moved. Got a proper place of my own. Something permanent. Somewhere I'm not staring at other people in transit.

Later I lie in bed, wakeful. The vase of dead flowers is still on the chest of drawers. I gaze at dim objects in the darkness; I've been told this cures insomnia, but I don't think anything is going to let me sleep tonight. Did I imagine it would impress her? Part of me did. But I hadn't thought enough about what it meant; what I assumed—implied—Tene and Christina had done out of desperation and grief, and a refusal to watch the family die.

They would have given anything to save Ivo, but there was nothing they could do. They begged for a miracle and were ignored. And when Ivo did die, in that lonely fen, shortly after they came back from Lourdes, I suppose it happened then. She gave her life for his, in the only way she could.

Crazy. Or perhaps that was the miracle.

I'm also assuming, I suppose, that she was willing to trade a life of structures and submission for a life of lies. What did Sandra say about Christina? That she was fearless. Yes. Maybe . . . Maybe it offered an escape she was already looking for.

Hadn't Tene, in his own roundabout way, told me all this? The ninth child, Poreskoro—neither male nor female but both. It explains many things about Ivo—the smooth skin I had thought a hangover from his illness, the heavy clothing, the fear of intimacy . . . And, of course, what happened to me that night.

Poreskoro, the most terrible child of all. It is extraordinary, I know. But some things are extraordinary.

I could be wrong. Perhaps Tene is not Christo's father. It's all conjecture. The only thing I really know is that the body in the Black Patch is that of a teenage Gypsy boy—and that Christo's mother was a Janko. Those are facts. That is evidence.

But everything else isn't even information; it's just so much smoke.

63.

JJ

Our new house is called 23 Sunningdale Lane. I liked the name as soon as I heard it. I thought it sounded like a country lane in summer, arched over with green branches. Quiet. Girls on ponies clopping down it.

Of course, it isn't—it's a red-brick box surrounded by other red-brick boxes on a long road the buses go down, so it's noisy from traffic. But my bedroom (God, that sounds weird) is at the back and looks over our garden(!), which is quite big and backs onto the playing fields of my new school, so it's quieter. I can leave the window open and hear tree branches moving and birds singing, even foxes barking—all that and we're practically in London, although not according to the postcode.

It's so weird being in a house. Mum has lived in a house before—when Gran and Granddad threw her out for having me (so I suppose I have, too, but of course I don't remember). Actually, it's more that sometimes it's really weird, and the rest of the time (most of the time, if I'm honest) it's not weird at all. When I first moved into my bedroom it felt enormous and lonely—I didn't want to shut the door—and I didn't feel I could ever fill it with my stuff or me. But now it's only a few weeks later and I seem to be getting more stuff—expanding, somehow. We've talked about getting a piano. I'm going to paint my room sky blue.

One thing I really like is going upstairs to bed. Or just upstairs. Looking down from the window. You feel different when you're higher up. It's not that high, so if there was a fire I could jump out onto the lawn and not hurt myself. I think about that quite a lot. I dream about fire—nightmares, really. Great-uncle isn't in them, but the fire is. I don't have them every night, just sometimes. I wake up sweating, and I'm glad we're in the town rather than in the woods, because there's always a bit of light from the streetlights. I don't want to wake up in the dark.

The other thing that's changed is that I can't stand Chinese food anymore.

Christo's room is downstairs. He's got to have wheelchair access, although he's getting stronger with the physiotherapy. And he talks more, although not that much yet. They think he might have this disease that they've discovered in Holland. It's a rare genetic disease, and they don't know much about it at the moment, but there's always hope. The good news is that I don't have it, and I'm not going to have it, because I wasn't born with it. I'm relieved about this, and I feel guilty about being relieved. I'm just going to make sure that Christo has a really nice time. He can live with me for the rest of my life. I don't mind—in fact, I'd like it. It's the least I can do.

Christo had his latest appointment yesterday. Lulu brought him back in a bit of a state—she was in a state, I mean, not Christo. She said something to Mum, and then Mum told me to take Christo and go outside into the garden until she said I could come back in. That's the first time she's ever said that. I can see how *gorjios* keep so many secrets. Then she slammed the sitting-room door, and although I could hear that they were talking, I couldn't tell what they were saying. Luckily, it was quite a warm evening, and the last swallows were squeaking and swooping around the telegraph wires. We dug up earthworms and searched for cheesy bugs under the toolshed and tried to make them have races. Christo can do that for hours, although after about forty minutes Mum came and said we had better come back in or Christo would catch his death.

She was in a funny mood all evening.

That was last night. Then, this morning, Lulu comes around again. It's before nine, but I'm still here because it's Saturday. In fact, to be perfectly honest, when the doorbell goes, I'm still in bed. Mum answers the door, and I hear Auntie Lulu's voice—raised and upset-sounding. Sensing something's up, I creep downstairs in my paja-mas. They're in the kitchen this time, with the door closed, but Mum obviously thinks I'm still asleep.

"What? . . . What?" She's practically shouting.

"That's what he said. That they switched all those years ago . . . And he said it explains everything, 'cause of the disease, and . . . God almighty, San, I've been nearly going out of my mind since then . . ."

Lulu sounds like she might be crying, something I can't imagine.

"But how could that be true? You know him better than me . . . I mean, it's insane, isn't it?"

Mum doesn't say anything that I can hear from the stairs. What on earth are they talking about? From her tone of voice, it must be something awful. I start to move softly up to the kitchen door, when, to my horror, I hear Mum crying, little fluttery sobs that go on and on. That's too much, so I stop creeping and open the door.

Lulu and Mum jerk around and stare at me. They both look very white and strange; Lulu is hugging herself tightly, her face different—less colorful and sort of tired-looking. Mum has been scrubbing her hands through her hair so that it stands up in all directions. She hates it like that. I wonder whether to get cross with Auntie Lulu for upsetting Mum like this, on a Saturday, when I realize that I was wrong about the noise I heard. Mum is leaning against the cooker, wild-eyed and shaking, but she isn't crying. She's laughing.

64.

Ray

Several times over the following days, I think about ringing her. I should apologize. I should qualify some of my guesses. But I don't know how to apologize for the truth. I wonder about talking to Sandra, and then think perhaps I should leave it until the next hospital appointment, when, I imagine, Lulu will not be coming.

I haven't done much work since that day; I can't seem to concentrate. And every time I've been on the verge of telling Hen what has happened, something stops me. I'll have to at some point, but I don't know what it is; maybe it's the questions he's undoubtedly going to ask, that I have no answers to, although I feel I should.

Then, out of the blue, my phone rings; unbelievably, it is her. I break into a sweat.

"I was going to ring you—I wanted to apologize for telling you like that. It was stupid of me," I start in a rush.

"Yeah. It was. I've been thinking about . . . everything you said. I told Sandra, you know, and do you know what? After a while she started laughing. She said she can believe it. She knew him better than anyone—I mean . . . you know what I mean."

"Yes. Oh. Well . . ."

"I was so angry . . . It was just so . . . such a shock."

"No, no, I should have . . ."

. . .

We arrange to meet in the same pub as before. It's quiet, still only mid-afternoon, desultory drinking time for serious drinkers. Two solitary men stand like statues at the bar, smoke rising from gnarled fists. Don't get overexcited, I tell myself. My capacity to screw things up is endless. But still, hope leaps and flutters within me, in my Pandora's box of a heart.

I get to the pub early and order a half of lager. I sip it slowly, making myself wait. I have showered. Cut my nails. My hand is shaking slightly. The first thing I do when I catch sight of her across the road is look down at her feet. She's wearing the red shoes.

She doesn't smile when she sees me, and it strikes me that she is nervous. She has let her hair down in soft waves. With a thrill, I wonder if she has had it done—specially. I can't imagine how I ever thought she was less beautiful than Jen, than anyone.

She sits down beside me. I pass her the rum and Coke I've bought in anticipation.

"I shouldn't really be drinking at this time of day."

"Well, it's an unusual day—unusual week."

"Yeah."

She picks up her bag and fishes for her cigarettes and lighter.

"So are you all right?" I say.

She shrugs.

"I'm getting used to the idea. It's not so hard for me—I mean, I only saw him half a dozen times over those twelve years."

She doesn't correct herself, and I don't say anything. It feels less wrong to go on referring to Christina as "he."

"What about Kath and Jimmy? Do they know?"

Lulu rolls her eyes.

"No. We haven't told anyone else. We thought we'd leave that one for a bit. Maybe if there could be more proof—that the body really was Ivo's, or something, and then it's not so . . . you know."

"Yeah. Maybe. But Sandra believes it?"

"She said it made sense of a lot of things she never understood."

"Was she angry?"

"That's what I expected, but she wasn't. They were quite close, you know, and even . . . I think she had a bit of a thing for him. I think she was sad about that, but now she says she understands—why he didn't want her."

She shrugs again.

"Like I said, it'll take some getting used to."

"Yes. Well . . . thank you."

"What for?"

"For coming."

I take a sip of lager. The fruit machine burbles behind us. A quiet racing commentary on the television over the bar comes to a desultory climax.

"How's your hand now?"

She sounds abrupt.

"It's okay."

I stretch my right hand out on the table between us, fingers spread.

"You going to do that trick with the knife?"

"No."

"You can feel things again?"

"Yeah. Mostly."

She puts her hand on mine. Her palm is warm and dry. I turn mine palm up, under it. The last time she touched me, I couldn't feel anything.

65.

JJ

Today it's Christo's birthday, and we go to the big park that's a bus ride away from our house. And Stella comes to visit, as it's a Saturday. We pick her up from the train station. In the park there's a lake, and they have pedalos, which aren't exactly like boats but sort of. It's a lovely day, although it's pretty cold. Tomorrow the clocks go back.

Stella and I exchange school gossip. My new school isn't too bad. If I haven't made any real friends yet, at least I haven't made any enemies, either. And there are so many different sorts of people there that I certainly don't stand out. One boy, who can be a bit annoying, asked me why we are called Romanies. I said because we come from Rome. He looked quite impressed. I think he actually believed me. I said that because I thought he was going to take the piss, but afterward, it occurred to me that he had actually wanted to know. I feel a bit bad about it now. I'll have to go and straighten him out this week.

"It sounds all right."

"Yeah."

Stella stares at the ground. We're walking around the lake, while Mum and Christo tactfully stay behind, talking to the ducks.

She says, "I miss you."

"Yeah? I mean, I miss you, too."

My heart races. Does she really mean that?

"Thanks!"

She grins at me, but she's blushing a little bit.

"No, I do!"

"Yeah, right. All those new girls . . ."

I push her gently, and she pretend staggers into the trees. I follow her, and there she kisses me, on the lips, where no one can see us, and her lips are cold and warm at the same time. I wasn't sure whether she really wanted to be my girlfriend, but that, I guess, is evidence.

We persuade Mum to let us take Christo out in a pedalo as a special birthday treat. It's the first time he's been on a boat since we came back from France. Same for me. Mum refuses to get into one of those things—and anyway, someone has to look after his chair, and all our stuff. We get into the pedalo and push off. You can pedal quite hard, but it goes only very slowly, and it's quite noisy, with lots of sloshing underneath. It's hard work to get it to go in a straight line; both people in front—that is, me and Stella—have to pedal at exactly the same rate, which, it turns out, is really hard to do. And I keep turning around to check that Christo is okay and hasn't fallen in, which doesn't help. It's a rubbish form of transport, when it comes down to it.

Being on the lake reminds me of the beautiful rowing boats that Mr. Lovell and I saw at the hospital lake, so elegant and inviting. The ones we didn't go in. I really liked their names: VIOLET—TO CARRY SIX. CHRISSIE—TO CARRY THREE . . .

We narrowly avoid a collision in mid-pond with a father and daughter. Christo and the man's daughter, who's about five, shriek with delight. Stella is grinning. I look at her, wondering how that happened. She doesn't look at me, but she looks happy, laughing and encouraging me to play chicken with the other boat, her cheeks faintly flushed with red.

I'm not paying attention.

"JJ . . . JJ! Stop! We're going to hit the side!"

Stella is yelling at me. We've turned in a curve somehow. I'm not sure what happened. And then we do, indeed, ram into the bank. Not very hard or anything, because, like I said, it's a rubbish form of transport. But with a bit of a jolt. "Sorry sorry sorry!" I yell, and look around at Christo, who is all right and laughing his head off, thinking, or choosing to think, we've done it on purpose.

"Again!" he shouts. It's not very clear, but I know what he means, because I've heard it before.

"Again. Again!"

And so, because it's his birthday, and he's seven, and he isn't dying—and because I feel like shouting—we do it again.

READERS GUIDE

Discussion Questions

1. The author chose to tell this story with two narrators, each of whom offers a different view into Romany culture. Would the story have been stronger or weaker with just one narrator? Do the narrators' positions affect your perspective on the culture?

2. Why do you think the author chose JJ to illustrate Romany culture? How would the story have been influenced by a different narrator—Tene or Sandra, for example? What effect does JJ's voice have on the story?

3. JJ reflects on a disastrous study date with a classmate at the end of chapter 16, saying that he and Stella are "like trains on tracks that run more or less parallel but will never meet. I can't go on her tracks, and she can't go on mine." In what ways is Romany culture different from the outside world? In what ways is it the same?

4. Romany face a significant amount of prejudice and stereotyping. What are some examples in the novel? What impact does this have on the characters? How are Romany themselves prejudiced against outsiders? How does Ray Lovell walk the line between his two cultures?

5, Ray Lovell's viewpoint moves between his past and his present. How does solving the mystery "alongside" him enhance your reading experience?

6. "Pure blood" is a significant concern through this novel. How does pure blood shape the "one of us" mentality? How has the desire for pure blood affected the Janko family? Are there other cultures or instances in history where "pure blood" has been a valuable trait?

7. The Jankos visit the healing bathhouses at Lourdes in an attempt to cure Christo's mysterious disease, through prayer and holy water. JJ says that his family is not religious, though we learn that their culture is rich in folklore. How does their belief in the healing power of Lourdes align with their folkloric traditions? Are there ways in which it conflicts?

8. Luck is a prevalent theme in the novel. Are the Jankos lucky or unlucky? Explain with specific instances that the Jankos attribute to luck.

9. *The Invisible Ones* is set in the 1980s. Why do you think the author chose this time period? In what ways does it affect your reading experience?

10. Sandra and Lulu have very different reactions to Ray's revelation about Ivo. Sandra is arguably much closer to Ivo, but she responds much more calmly to the news. Were you surprised by this? Why do you think the two reacted so differently?